Christmas by the Coast

Christmas by the Coast

Mandy Baggot

HEAD
of ZEUS

An Aria Book

This edition first published in the United Kingdom in 2021 by Aria,
an imprint of Head of Zeus Ltd

A CIP catalogue record for this book is available from the
British Library.

9 7 5 3 1 2 4 6 8

ISBN (PB): 9781800243125
ISBN (E): 9781800243101

Cover design © The Brewster Project

Typeset by Siliconchips Services Ltd UK

Printed and bound in Great Britain by
CPI Group (UK) Ltd, Croydon CR0 4YY

Aria
5–8 Hardwick Street
London EC1R 4RG

www.ariafiction.com

For Mick
'You've gotta live your life'

December 2012

Dear Corporal Javier Gonzales,

I hope this care package gets to you safely and in time for Christmas. I can't imagine what it must be like to be there, in the desert, away from your family, fighting mostly for people you don't know. The world really is a crazy place.

My grandfather served in the infantry too and I know from his stories that he missed some of the items I've included almost as much as he missed my grandmother – particularly the beef jerky. My grandmother once said that if she had refused his marriage proposal he would have set up home with someone who worked for Pemmican. And I believe her.

Anyway, I hope you and your fellow soldiers enjoy the goodies, the socks (no animal print or Disney characters) and the games. I went for Uno (universal appeal), Monopoly (something featuring the UK where I'm from) and Texas Hold 'Em (maybe play for Haribos if you can't play for money).

Please don't feel in any way obliged to write back, I just wanted to do something nice in honour of my grandfather. But I have put my address on the back of the envelope if you need more supplies or want to complain about my choice of sweets, oops, I mean 'candy'. Good luck with the stick of rock. It's not for everyone, but it will last longer than the Maltesers.

Best wishes for Christmas and the New Year,

Joanna

One

November

'Like always,' Iain began. 'Remember... it can *never* be worse than Middleton Avenue.'

Twenty-nine-year-old Harriet Cookson took a deep inhale of the freezing misty air and adjusted her red woollen hat, tucking her blonde hair inside it. She was standing, with her boyfriend, Iain, outside the door of a small, terraced house she hadn't seen in reality before. She recalled from the photos however that it was coated in terrible pebbledash. This house had been a *very* last-minute decision at the auction. The property was in a pleasant area – a tree-lined street that wasn't a rat run – a twenty-minute walk from the centre of town, with nearby schools Ofsted had rated 'good'. The only thing that needed attention here was the building's energy efficient rating. Harriet was hoping the storage heaters all still worked and the

3

windows wouldn't need to be replaced, otherwise that was a big chunk of profit gone from the get-go.

Harriet closed her eyes, as was tradition, then put her fingers out to the stonework and touched. Yes, it even *felt* hideous, but it didn't matter. This might be their new *house*, but it wasn't ever going to be their home.

'And… the door is now… open!' Iain announced like he might be cutting a ribbon at the beginning of a fete. He nudged the small of her back now and Harriet recoiled slightly. Iain was rushing this a little bit, and he knew this moment was one of her favourites – especially when she had never set foot over the threshold before. Whenever they bought somewhere new, she wanted to wallow a little in that overwhelming what-have-we-done-buying-this-pile-of-crap feeling, amalgamating with the rush of I-have-all-the-quick-fix-inspiration-and-will-trash-that-yellow-tiled-work-surface-with-the-very-first-hammer-blow. Anticipation filled her now as her winter boots met thin carpet. She definitely remembered *that* from the pictures. It was mainly burnt orange in colour, with enough psychedelic swirls to make your vision swim. It was probably a good thing she couldn't see it now. She was already feeling a little bit sick because she had skipped a proper lunch in favour of a mince pie and another browse on Rightmove. A little cottage had caught her eye, but it was a bit out of their usual price range and Harriet wasn't convinced the margin would be adequate enough to make Iain bite. But it had kept her mind busy thinking about the possible potential and she knew she would probably come back to it again another day. She did get a bit twitchy if she didn't have enough projects on her plate. 'An idle mind is the Devil's workshop', her Nana Lorna always said.

'Bathroom?' Iain asked, a fingertip at her elbow guiding her a little to the left.

Harriet nodded. 'Of course!'

It *had* to be the bathroom first. It was their new house ritual. Each time their investment property business completed on a house, they did the same thing. The bathroom was usually the very worst room of the house, so the first exploration began there. Harriet carefully began to climb the stairs, her eyes still closed, Iain behind her, feet tentatively making their way, hand on the rail.

This bathroom suite, she remembered, was avocado in all the worst ways. And, from zooming in on the particulars six weeks ago, an hour before the auction began, Harriet had discovered the green and purple blind hanging at half-mast was far more mould than it was material. It was as if the owner had tried to inject a little modern into the space at one time and then it had succumbed to neglect like everything else. That blind would be the first thing to go before the black started to spread to other places. But, one thing that had caught Harriet's eye in a good way were the bathroom tiles in this property. They seemed to be authentic stone, looking almost as if they might have been chiselled directly from one of the rocks at Stonehenge. The current trend wasn't for *totally* sleek and white minimalist, it was for splashes of colour, light-up signs declaring 'love' or 'home' and lots of fake plants and books people would never read. Harriet couldn't wait to see what the tiles would look like once they had been given a good clean.

Usually they invested in small apartments or maisonettes that would suit young professionals, but Harriet thought immediately, with this one, that it might be better destined for a young family just starting out, with its two bedrooms and small patch of grass at the back.

'Ready?' Iain asked. Somehow her mind's eye knew they were stopped outside the snug-but-adequate family bathroom. The anticipation was building inside her. She wanted to see what was there, knowing she was going to make it more liveable and lovable for someone else to enjoy and for their company to reap the monetary reward.

'And... open your eyes!'

Harriet flicked her eyelids up and immediately, instead of feeling that initial fear that they had bitten off more than they could chew, she was floored...

The avocado suite was gone, replaced with a bright white bath, sink and toilet, taps a sparkling chrome. The blind was gone too and instead there was a cheap metallic silver venetian alternative. And, as for the rustic stone tiles, they had been entirely ripped away. Stuck to the wall now was the familiar plain gloss white brand Iain always favoured. Harriet wasn't sure what to say. So, she didn't say anything. Instead, she blinked a couple of times and wondered if she'd somehow fallen down Alice's rabbit hole.

'You're so shocked!' Iain said, looking immensely pleased with himself. 'God, if this small transformation has rendered you speechless I might not bother to up my game for Christmas gifts this year!'

Harriet still didn't know what to say, because she didn't know *how* this had happened. As far as she knew they had only got the keys *today*. But it was obvious, from the brand spanking new fixtures and fittings in this room, that *someone* had had prior access. And it didn't sit well. Why had Iain done this without her? Without even *talking* to her? *Now* it was time to speak. Now, when she was stepping towards the frankly *too* cheap blind even *she* wouldn't have considered putting in this property they would only own as long as it took to sell. Pressing a finger to one of the slats it bent so easily. Perhaps it was foreshadowing her role in this relationship. Easily manipulated. Sometimes fragile to the touch. Not fully committed? She swallowed, wishing her brain hadn't offered those suggestions.

'Iain, when did you do this?' Harriet asked, turning back to look at him. She silently prayed that he wouldn't lie to her. Two years and five months together and somehow, as much as she thought she knew his likes, dislikes and opinion on Lorraine Kelly, she still didn't feel she knew his soul.

'What?' he asked. He was digging hands into his coat pockets now and giving her that small smile he put on when he was channelling naughty yet trying-to-be-endearing schoolboy. 'Don't you like it?' He pressed a hand to his chest. 'Don't tell me you *liked* the green? Christ, Harriet, the green was like... the colour of one of those hideous mind-clearing drinks your dad made us in Spain.'

So, Iain *hadn't* lied, but he hadn't answered the question either.

'*When* did you do this?' Harriet repeated. 'Because I thought you only picked up the keys today.'

Iain laughed then and reached out to put his hands on her shoulders, then seemed to think better of making actual contact. 'Don't you like my surprise?'

She used to like surprises, but she'd learned in life that

7

they weren't always nice. Some of them even broke your heart. Now, sudden changes in routine had the ability to throw her off her game. And Iain wasn't usually the surprise-facilitating type. And definitely not since the disaster of the Quorn skewers meet Jerusalem artichokes incident. It had been a whole lot less *Just Eat* and a lot more just pray.

'Iain,' Harriet said, sighing. This felt all wrong and any delight in the reveal was quickly being destroyed. Had he done other rooms? Was she going to go downstairs and find the kitchen replaced already? Why was she so angry about this? This was a place like any other. Why, now, did it matter?

'What?' Iain asked, dipping his face into her space a little. 'Don't you like it? I thought, with Christmas and everything, it made sense to get a head start. You don't want to spend the whole holidays coated in dust and debris, do you?'

Didn't she? She hated the fact everyone seemed to switch off for the holidays. Apart from consuming all the delicious food on offer, Harriet craved the rush of a new year and fresh projects like others yearned for slowing down and re-runs of *Only Fools and Horses*. Iain didn't wait for her to reply before he was putting arms around her and pulling her a little nearer until she was face down in his tweed coat and he was patting her back. This was as physical as Iain got outside the bedroom. Yet that familiar scent of his expensive aftershave tickled her senses and she could feel her annoyance wane a little. Iain *had* put a smile back on her face when she had started to wonder whether she would ever smile again. She shouldn't ever forget that. She should value it and hold on.

'Mickey had a few days free and we completed so I thought, why not get this one room done,' Iain continued.

They'd completed days ago? And one of their contacts who helped them renovate had known before she had? Now Harriet tried to inch herself away from Iain. He needed to understand this really wasn't on. They were supposed to be partners. In this business *and* in their relationship. Who withheld info like that from someone who valued honesty and frankness above all else?

'Come on,' Iain said. 'This was supposed to be a nice surprise and you're acting a bit like…'

'A bit like what?' Harriet asked, riled again. Because at the moment he absolutely was treating her like she was the flimsy venetian blind he was poking with a big, fat finger.

'A bit like I've done something wrong,' Iain finished.

He gave her the benefit of a look he usually reserved for occasions when he really *had* done something wrong. Like when he'd crashed her car and blamed it on her hanging air freshener blocking his vision. But… maybe she *was* being harsh. This house shouldn't matter that much. It *didn't* matter that much. It was a money-maker, pure and simple. It wasn't as if Iain had walked into her and her best friend Jude's apartment and ripped their bathroom out and replaced it with something cheap and sterile. Clean lines and neutral finishes *were* what most people looked for when they were buying a house. As long as they could *imagine* comfy sofas, rose gold accessories plus their family pics, what did it really matter about quality? People changed things to suit them. Perhaps being slightly resentful was a complete waste of energy. And Iain did tend to sulk for days after a disagreement…

'I'm sorry,' Harriet said with a soft sigh. 'It's fine. I just wasn't expecting it, that's all.' She forced a smile.

'Phew!' Iain said, wiping a hand across his brow. 'I thought for a minute there I was going to have to get Mickey to come and put the green suite back in.'

She smiled again, but she really didn't know how to move this conversation on. She was still feeling frustrated with Iain's lack of communication about a business transaction that was as much hers as it was his. But maybe all that mattered was that the deal was done. In a couple of months this house would be on the market again and they would hopefully be looking at a tidy profit.

'Come on,' Iain said, directing her towards the threshold. 'Let's go and check out the kitchen. Mickey says his supplier has a good end-of-range deal that might have enough units for the space.'

'OK,' Harriet agreed.

'That's the spirit!'

Her eyes went briefly back to the blind and she watched it sway with the draught from Iain's breath. Somehow, it was completely relatable.

Two

The Potter's Heron, Ampfield, Hampshire

It wasn't even December and Harriet was choosing from a festive menu. But turkey and all the trimmings couldn't ever come too early, could it? Not in her opinion, that's for sure. A butter-basted bird front-crawling in thick gravy and accompanied by crispy-outside-fluffy-inside roast potatoes, carrots, broccoli, sprouts and stuffing was *the* holiday highlight. Even Iain put his vegetarianism on hold and ate turkey on Christmas Day. She couldn't help licking her lips now as she read the words 'pigs in blankets'.

'I think I'll have a salad.'

Harriet's stomach dipped at her dad's choice. 'Are you sure, Dad? It's freezing outside. How about something hearty for a change?' Her dad always seemed to have a grey colour palette in the UK, unlike the rosy glow he picked up from his frequent visits to Spain. Today he looked particularly ashen and his shoulder-length hair seemed a tinge more silver.

'The salad's hearty,' Ralph answered. 'It's with figs and

halloumi.' He rubbed his hands together, stretching them out into the space to his right. 'And we're sat right by the fire.'

That was true. A fat wooden mantel covered in chunky turquoise tinsel and surrounded by warm fairy lights sat over the iron wood-burner that was burning brightly. But her dad still looked as if he needed fattening up like festive game. Harriet knew 'clean-living' in all respects had always been her dad's life mantra, but sometimes she wished it involved more than alfalfa sprouts and hemp seeds. Sometimes, especially since her parents' divorce when she was seventeen, she wondered if her dad used the health vibe and let's-all-eat-more-plant-based-products stuff, to camouflage how he was really feeling. Perhaps, exactly like her, he needed a focus to distract himself from something else that was going on under the surface…

'Well,' Harriet began. 'I'm going to have turkey with all the trimmings. Shall we order?'

'Not yet, sweetheart,' Ralph said, stopping her hand from raising to call the waitress. 'We're waiting for one more.'

What? Someone else was joining them for lunch? *Iain?* Harriet swallowed as her stomach changed from ridiculously ready for a roast dinner to being peppered with anxiety. Iain was supposed to be going to see a property in Fareham right now. Despite him bringing up the idea of slowing down on purchases for the holiday season over a steamed seabream and a bottle of Shiraz last night, Harriet had found this flat at four a.m. when she couldn't sleep. She thought it was a hidden gem, boasting river views. She'd be there herself if it wasn't for meeting her dad. She was just about to ask her dad the question of who, when all became apparent.

'Before you say anything, I'm not late,' Marnie Cookson announced, unwinding a leopard print scarf from around her neck and simultaneously slipping down into the seat next to Harriet. 'It was the taxi driver.' She huffed a sigh. 'I made it quite clear I didn't want any chit-chat but no, he insisted on telling me the intricacies of his home life and what all six of his children are "starring" as in the school Christmas show.' She leaned in and smiled at Harriet. 'Hello, angel.' Then she set her back into her chair and nodded towards Ralph. 'Ralph... you're looking reasonable. It's nice you're not wearing a smock.'

'Thank you, Marnie.' Ralph sent a smile back across the table. 'And I have told you before, it's called a *kurti*.'

Something was wrong here. Her parents, although they didn't *hate* each other, were definitely not on let's-catch-up-and-have-a-bite-to-eat terms. Despite the slight swipe her mum had made, it was still altogether too good-natured. And Harriet couldn't remember the last time her mum had ventured away from daytime television. Marnie classed Ben Shephard and Bradley Walsh as personal friends. She had made an effort with her outfit too – a classic Marnie-when-she-used-to-party pleather A-line in brown and a black roll-neck sweater. It looked like she'd also crimped her hair. Harriet felt like the child who'd forgotten it was non-school uniform day dressed in her plain black jeans and a light grey sweater.

'Mum, what are you doing here?' Harriet asked as Marnie swiped up a menu and ran a finger down the options.

'Ooo, salmon! Don't mind if I do! You did say you were paying, Ralph, didn't you?'

'I did,' Ralph concurred.

'I bet you're having something that looks like it's been pulped,' Marnie cackled. 'Something with all the calorific content of a turnip.'

'Mum,' Harriet breathed, eager to make this weird interchange stop. 'Dad. Tell me what's going on and why you're both here being borderline civil with each other.'

'I think we should get some grub ordered,' Marnie said, dipping and diving her head like a mad ostrich in a bid to get the attention of a server. 'You know what some places can be like when they start busying up at this time of year. It's either making you eat at the speed of light so they can clear your table for the next guests, or it's an hour-long wait because Chef's burned the first batch of Yorkshires.'

'Marnie,' Ralph said stiffly. 'This is my local. It's always very nice. And Harriet likes it.' He then engaged in a slightly awkward head-bobbing action of his own, as if he might be talking in tics to his ex-wife.

'It's only your local when you're not gadding off to Lake Vinuela,' Marnie said, sounding irritated.

Harriet sat back in her chair and folded her arms across her chest. 'Well, I'm not ordering anything until you tell me what this lunch is all about.' She looked to her dad. 'I thought this was our monthly catch-up and you were going to tell me you were going to Spain for Christmas again. Which is obviously fine because I'm a grown-up and I don't need you to pretend to be Santa anymore.' And Christmas was just another date on the calendar, just with extra pâté, prosecco and party poppers. She and Iain hadn't made any plans yet, but Harriet assumed, like last year, they would most probably visit his parents in the morning and have turkey for two in front of whatever ITV were premiering. By Boxing Day she would be ready to get one hundred per cent refocused on the business, striking to snap up any winter bargains that had hit the inboxes of their contacts at the estate agent's, or preparing to market the homes they'd already purchased and overhauled.

'Well,' Ralph began, looking a little out-of-sorts now. 'It's partially about Spain but... there's something else.'

Harriet now began to worry. Her dad's eyes were focusing on anything but hers – the large bright white snowman in the corner of the room, the fire, the menu he had already made his selection from... This was something serious and there was now a gnawing in her belly that she didn't like the feel of.

Her dad put his hands into his hair then and took a deep breath. 'OK,' he said, seeming less than OK himself. His hands were shaking a bit and even Marnie wasn't chipping in with all the flippant.

'Angel,' Marnie said, grabbing Harriet's hand and clasping it in her own. 'Your dad's had some... news. And he asked me to be here when he told you.'

'News? What news?'

All Harriet's emotions were stalling now, like they had suddenly been dropped into a barrel of molasses and were finding it was impossible to stay afloat. Was it *bad* news? Her dad didn't seem able to look at her. And here she'd been sitting, internally complaining about his lunch choices and salivating over the thought of little sausages wrapped in bacon.

'What is it?' Harriet forced the words out as her mum continued to hold her hand. 'You need to tell me.' Half of her wanted to know immediately, the other part wanted to hide in the hotel's pile of seasoned logs and *never* know whatever this was.

Ralph cleared his throat as if he might be going to make a speech. But not the encouraging or uplifting kind. Harriet held her breath.

'There's no easy way to say this,' Ralph started, his words catching a little. 'But... my... your nana... Lorna. She passed away yesterday.'

Harriet felt as if someone had pressed halt on life's stopwatch as her dad's words rained down on her like the hardest, skin-jabbing, cricket-ball-sized hailstones. 'I... don't understand,' she blurted as tears fell without compromise. 'How could she? I... only spoke to her last week. She can't be...'

'Oh, angel, it's alright. You can cry if you want to,' Marnie urged, letting go of Harriet's hand now, but patting the back of it over and over as if she was keeping a beat in place of a metronome.

You can cry if you want to? The tears didn't need permission. Harriet was trying hard not to full-on sob, her breaths catching in her throat. But the shock was taking over, moving through her, as the room began to shrink. The Christmas cocktail jazz now sounded like it was on the off-beat more than was meant, the laughter from the group of twelve wearing paper hats and firing long party balloons across the dining area muted, and her heart pounded hard and heavy in her chest. Her Nana Lorna. Her lovely, sweet, strong, grandmother with hair like bright white, fluffy candy floss and always the biggest, most garish earrings. She could hear her laugh, loud, raspy and full of mischief. Her soft voice imparting her own brand of wisdom on all things. The sweet smell of the soft powder she puffed on her cheeks… She couldn't be gone. She just couldn't.

'I'm sure it was quick,' Marnie jumped in. 'I mean… no one saw it coming, did they? She wasn't ill, was she, Ralph?'

'I… don't know. Madame Scarlet didn't really say.' He dropped his eyes.

'I know she wasn't ill,' Harriet snapped at her mother. 'I speak to her every week.'

Spoke. Now it was 'spoke'. And that didn't feel right at all. 'Do they know what it was?'

Now she could hear the raucous balloon-warring again and it was starting to spar with her nerves. 'Fit and healthy people don't just die.' And her nana *had* been fit and healthy. Lorna had never smoked, yes she enjoyed the occasional rum tipple and loved to bake the most delicious treats, but surely that hadn't been enough to have contributed to her demise. Harriet blinked the tears from her eyes, remembering all the walks they'd taken together along the beach nearly every summer for as long as she could remember, the wind and sand sometimes blasting their cheeks like an aggressive Mother Nature facial, then back home for creamy hot chocolates topped with s'mores…

'She was *very* old, angel,' Marnie said, still patting.

'Not that old,' Harriet retorted, whisking away the tears from her cheeks with her fingers. 'And why didn't you call me last night? If you knew yesterday, why didn't you *tell* me yesterday? Why didn't Madame Scarlet call *me*?'

'Well,' Ralph began. 'Madame Scarlet did try to call you

and I did ring yesterday and I spoke to Iain. He said that you were going to see a new property you'd bought and I didn't want to spoil it, so I—'

'—Dad, I know, for whatever reason, you don't get on, but it's my nana,' Harriet bleated sharply. 'Nana means more to me than a stupid property with pebbledash.' Her voice cracked at the end of the sentence as the news began to really sink in. She drew her hand away from her mum's incessant tapping and pushed her hair behind her ears. Bloody Iain! Why hadn't he said her dad had called? Did he just forget? Or did he somehow decide it wasn't important enough to tell her? This was a little like the new bathroom she'd had no say over…

'I don't think Lorna would have wanted you to spend all last night crying and missing out on something nice,' Marnie said, picking up the menu again. 'Is it a proper house you're buying this time? One for you and Iain to actually live together in at last?'

How did her mum know what Lorna would have wanted? Her mum barely knew her nana and grandpa at all. And that's the way it had always been. Her dad had always been estranged from them and, as Harriet grew up and started to realise this, she got inquisitive. Except her dad had never been willing to impart the details. And neither had her nana and grandpa. All she knew was her dad had left the family home in Montauk in his late teens and had never been back since. In the end she had simply stopped asking and just felt grateful that she got the chance to spend each summer overseas with two of the loveliest people on earth. Harriet shook her head to re-order her thoughts. She needed to make plans. She wanted to know exactly what was going to happen next. She focused on her dad. No matter what had gone on in the past, Lorna was his mum. Her dad was the only child. And Grandpa Joe had let his wife manage *everything*. Harriet's heart broke anew thinking about her grandpa. What was he going to do now without his soulmate? Miles away. Alone.

'Have you booked a flight yet?' Harriet asked her dad. If he hadn't, then *that* was something she could take charge of. *Organising*. That's what you did in times like these to get through. You organised, you compartmentalised and you... bought another house or three.

'To Spain?' Ralph replied.

'Not to Spain! To Montauk! To see Grandpa.' Harriet picked up her water glass and took a quick swig. 'He must be... devastated. Nana, she did everything for him. He won't know the first thing to do for anything, and especially for the... funeral.' She stalled at the last word. This still felt surreal and unwelcome. Those glittering decorations around the fireplace, speaking of all things festive, seemed way too merry and bright now. Her nana had always been so vital, so energetic and enthusiastic. No matter her age, Harriet had never envisaged her bright burning flame being able to be snuffed out without any warning.

'Well,' Ralph started. 'Harriet, you know things have always been... difficult between us so...' He stopped to clear his throat before he continued, his voice sounding a little stronger. 'And I actually have ten people coming for an aura cleansing retreat in Andalusia next week.'

'What?' Harriet bit. 'You're not going to see your dad? And you're not going to help him arrange your mum's funeral? Or attend?' The words were getting caught in her throat like each one might have been coated with a sticky Christmas pudding mix containing a few too many large nuts. Whatever had blighted their relationship, surely it stopped now! She couldn't believe this!

'Harriet, you know things have never been easy between your dad and his parents,' Marnie chipped in.

All Harriet knew was they had never visited as a family. It had always been just her. But, whatever the situation, this was *family*. Every memory she had was running through her mind right now – sweet summers at her grandparents' tiki bar on the beach in the Hamptons, fishing in the ocean, riding horses bareback across the shore and rapidly growing up while school was out. And Nana Lorna and Grandpa Joe had both always shown her so much love, the distance between them in the everyday wiped out the second she landed in New York. No, she wasn't about to turn away just because a trip overseas wasn't *convenient* to a group of hippies needing a mind and body reset. Nana Lorna was gone and Grandpa Joe, well, he would need someone. Well, she had decided, he would need *her*.

'You understand, don't you?' Ralph asked.

'No,' Harriet stated, hard. 'I don't understand at all. I never have.'

'Harriet…'

She got to her feet. 'Just don't bother.'

Marnie sighed. 'Awful dying just before Christmas, isn't it? Upsets the equilibrium for everyone.'

And on that note, as she headed towards the toilets to the sound of a yellow rocket balloon whizzing across the dining room and Kylie's version of 'Santa Baby' trying to compete, Harriet knew she was going straight home to book a flight.

Three

Anglewood Mansions, Westbourne Close, Bournemouth

Three days later

Harriet wet her lips, turning her head on the cushion. Carly Rae Jepsen was playing. It looked hot and dusty, the heat moving the air, particles of sand floating in front of her vision, the scent of canvas, rubber and sweat. There was a whole lot of camo. Then... *those green eyes*.

Harriet had only actually seen them once and they weren't a crystalised emerald colour of romance stories. No, these were soft, a mossy wine gum kind of a green that had literally taken her breath away back then.

His hair. She could see *that* now too. Short curls of almost auburn, yet somehow also tawny and blond, in a contrast to the shaved sides. Harriet smiled, wriggling a bit in appreciation, her mind reaching out for more.

His smile. That was even better than his eyes. It was just *perfection*. The second he had widened his mouth into a smile, he had owned her heart a little bit more. She hadn't been able to take her eyes off those lips as he spoke. That American twang to his voice had her wanting to reach out and bring him closer so she could feel his mouth all over hers the way they had talked about…

'Harriet! Wake up! You're doing all the porno noises again and it's the middle of the day!'

Harriet jumped, eyes flashing open, hands coming down onto the fabric of her sofa. She wasn't somewhere hot, sandy and all the dirty. 'Jude, God, you scared me.'

Her flatmate was standing over her, cradling a porcelain bowl that looked like it contained a whole carton of After Eights. 'I know you weren't dreaming about Iain.' Jude plucked a dark chocolate square from the bowl and put it into her mouth, crunching down.

'I wasn't dreaming about anyone,' Harriet lied, sitting herself up and immediately scattering the paperwork she'd obviously dropped onto her midriff when she'd nodded off. She began collating it together and screwed her nose up at the printed-out details of a bungalow for sale in Surrey Gardens. Why had she committed that to coloured ink? The roof looked like it needed replacing and there was a big garden with plants their millennial target market wouldn't even recognise.

Dark-haired Jude sat down on the vacant end of the settee now, crossing one dungaree-covered leg over the other and resting the bowl on her knee. 'Yeah, lies. You were dreaming about Soldier Boy. That's the only time you make noises of appreciation like that,' Jude said. 'When Iain stays over, the only sound is him on Zoom saying "can you hear me now?" or my very favourite "you're muted, Dave. Dave, mate, you're muted!".' She laughed. 'Pillock.'

'Iain's not a pillock. And, seriously, Jude, who uses that word anymore?'

'You know I like underrated insults.'

'Well, I don't like you making fun of my boyfriend or commenting on my sleep noises.' And the second after a moment of weakness – when Jude had got out a bottle of Bailey's Red Velvet Cupcake – Harriet had instantly regretted telling Jude about the man who haunted her dreams. Jude had a memory like Shaun Wallace and Harriet knew nothing good could come from dwelling on that part of her past. It was done, if not completely forgotten.

'Here,' Jude said, bending down and reaching for a piece of paper Harriet had missed. 'What's this? Flight details? For tomorrow?'

'I told you about it,' Harriet said, taking the paper from her friend. 'Please don't forget to water the plants and, should anyone call the landline about the business, just give them my mobile number or Iain's mobile number. They're both written on the pad if you lose your phone again.'

'Oh, I didn't realise you were serious,' Jude said, biting into another minty square.

'Jude, my nana died.'

And things didn't get any more serious than that. Speaking to Grandpa Joe on the telephone hadn't been easy at all. Her grandad was deaf at the best of times and, even on her last visit, some three years ago now, he had done a lot more reading of lips than actual hearing what was being said. But, during this call, it had been Harriet who had done most of the listening. She had wanted to know all the details of her gran's last moments, needing to understand why it had been her time to go. Though there didn't seem to be any real answer to that yet. There was going to have to be a post-mortem and, until the results were received, nothing could be arranged with the funeral. Although it wasn't a nice thought, it did, at least, give Harriet time to get across the Atlantic. And she was booked. Tomorrow. An early flight to JFK, then almost three hours in a car. She wasn't relishing the drive, as the weather was set to be only a touch above freezing, but the alternative was an expensive taxi. However, on the positive side, she had never visited the Hamptons in the winter. It would be good to see how different the area was when it wasn't full-on sunshine. Maybe the climate forcing her to drive slowly would mean time to breathe in the scenery. And the scenery was spectacular. You went from the hubbub of the Big Apple, with its glass and metal giants, to what most people considered the start of the Hamptons, the Shinnecock Canal, with its boats along the water and places to stop and eat.

'You were serious about that? Sorry. I thought it was one of those excuses to get out of things. You know, like, "I'm washing my hair tonight" or "I'm going dancing with my cat".'

Harriet had never heard the cat excuse before. She shook her head. 'No, it was real.' She sighed, grief rolling over her again. 'I meant it.'

'Damn, sorry,' Jude said. Then paused before adding: 'You OK, hon?'

Harriet smiled at Jude's attempt at humour. Her friend had never been the best at compassion, but she was, at least, always honest. Was there a better trait to have in a friend and flatmate? They had lived together for two years now and had met back in 2016 at a dreadful clothes party

Marnie had insisted Harriet came along to. Harriet didn't ordinarily 'do' anything with her mother – back then living with her was enough – but, on the odd occasion, she would be struck by a fit of guilt whenever an offer was pushed her way and feel compelled to accept.

The clothes had been very Marnie and her friends – pleather trousers and striped tunics that wouldn't have looked out of place in the costume wardrobe for the cast of *Ashes to Ashes*, tight-fitting business dresses Harriet had been sure wouldn't flatter *anyone* and lots of clinging knitwear. Jude had been brought along by a friend from craft club and had looked disdainfully at everything the party planner had dressed the foam mannequin in and described in the most minute detail. They had got talking over snacks that looked as Eighties as the clothes – cheese and pineapple on sticks, Skips crisps and bowls of crudités and mayonnaise dip. That first conversation about how dreadful the fashion was spurred the beginning of their friendship and when Jude's flatmate moved out in 2019, Harriet finally left Marnie's and moved in. Living independently for the first time at aged twenty-seven…

'Hang on, though,' Jude said, pointing with the bowl. 'You told me your gran was the reason you were able to buy your first investment property. You said you used inheritance from her to do that.'

Harriet watched Jude give a knowing nod like she might have caught her out in a lie. She sighed. 'That was my *other* gran and… I never actually met *her*.' And Harriet benefitting from her grandmother Gracie's will was still a bone of contention with Marnie. Sometimes, when her mum had sipped one too many gins with *Coronation Street*, there would come a phone call where Marnie would vent her wrath at being 'passed over' in favour of Harriet and the local bingo hall... Harriet *had* offered her mum the not inconsequential sum, but Marnie had flatly refused and commented that she wasn't about to accept sloppy seconds. Besides, her mum was pretty much set up after the divorce. She had her own apartment, the biggest TV known to Sony and all the Oribe hair products...

'So this one... the one you *had* met... lived in America?' Jude asked.

Harriet nodded, immediately realising that she hadn't ever told Jude about her family who lived across the Atlantic. Why was that? She suddenly felt incredibly guilty, as if she had wiped them out of part of her life – a little like her dad had all but eradicated them from his. 'Montauk,' she answered. 'At the end of Long Island.'

'New York?'

New York was Jude's reference for the USA as a whole. Harriet was convinced her friend thought the whole of the United States was as small as the Isle of Man and basically only contained one dirty blues bar, an all-day diner and a man selling hot dogs out of a cart next to the Empire State. But, in this case, she was sort of right.

'It's part of New York State, yes,' Harriet said.

'Cool,' Jude said. 'Yellow cabs and gherkins with a side of Times Square.'

'Really it's more sandy beaches, cool restaurants and a really lovely lighthouse.' Harriet gently sighed. She should have visited more. Made time. Now it was all too late. And the idea of this trip was emotionally pulling her every which way. She took a breath, her skin under her jumper reacting to the thought of those seemingly endless summers filled with sunshine days, ice cream sundaes and her nana's homemade cranberry juice. Perhaps that was why she had never told Jude. Maybe because the last time she had *really* talked about Montauk had meant the end of something she had cherished...

'There'll be turkey though, won't there? On Christmas Day.' Jude bit into another square of chocolate. 'Are you staying there the whole of Christmas?'

'I don't know,' Harriet admitted. She hadn't thought that far ahead. And she did need to think a *little* further than simply throwing her warmest clothes into a suitcase and downloading the Lyft app. She needed to think about the business. She needed to make sure that work on the finishing touches of the two apartments they were selling next continued in her absence. Then there was getting the pebbledash house ready. It still irked her a bit that she never got to rejuvenate those tiles. But, she guessed, she had other priorities at the moment. She was going to make sure Grandpa Joe was OK and give Nana Lorna the send-off she deserved.

'I don't know what December is like there at all,' Harriet admitted, pinching one of Jude's chocolates for herself. 'I've only ever been in summer.'

'Well,' Jude said. 'There's always a friendly diner in New York.'

Harriet couldn't help but grin. 'There's also a fantastic tiki bar.'

'What?'

She nodded. 'That's what my grandparents do... well... just my grandad now I suppose.' She battened down her emotional hatches. There would be plenty of time to shed tears when she put her arms around her Grandpa Joe. 'They own a tiki bar on the beach.'

'What's a tiki bar?' Jude asked, her mouth stopping mid-chew. 'Is it like one of those huts they put up in the square at Christmas with expensive cocktails and patio heaters to pretend it's Brazil instead of Bournemouth?'

'It's a little more tropical than that.' She pulled down from her memories – the chunky pottery cups shaped like fish with their mouths open containing Zombies or Mai-Tais expertly mixed by Grandpa Joe, the little paper umbrellas she had worn in her hair, the stools around the bar she had always seemed too small to be able to climb on...

'My grandparents had an old Ford Cortina,' Jude began. 'And they used to drive it – slowly – to collect their pension. That was the extent of their excitement. There was no running beverage establishments on the sand.'

Harriet smiled. 'Well, my family has never really done ordinary. My dad thinks he's a health deity and my mum exists in a world where the Rovers Return is a real pub and she's secretly related to Bev Callard.'

Jude nodded thoughtfully. 'When you say that it makes running a tiki bar seem quite normal.'

The doorbell chimed and Harriet jumped. 'Are you expecting anyone?'

'Oh yeah,' Jude said straight away. 'I offered to host soap carving club here.' She tutted. 'I didn't know you were going. And the only plans I have involve true crime on Netflix.'

Harriet winced. Soap carving was possibly Jude's craziest hobby attempt ever – and there had been many since she'd moved in. There were still three seahorses, an owl and a very poor attempt at a snail waiting in the bathroom to be used or 'gifted' to someone. She got up and headed to the door, slipping the chain on before opening it.

'Surprise!'

It was Iain. Harriet frowned. He was supposed to be meeting with a new carpenter they'd contacted because their usual one, Jamie, had suddenly decided to move to Leeds.

'What are you doing here?' Harriet asked. 'I thought you were meeting…' What had his name been? 'Willie?'

'It was Wally, actually,' Iain answered with a smile. 'I messaged him. Got him to meet me an hour earlier so I could come over here.'

'But… I've got some paperwork to go through for the central heating in the Branksome flat and I have to get an early night before the flight tomorrow.'

'Harriet, it's only four o'clock,' Iain said, still smiling. 'And aren't you going to take the chain off the door now?'

'Oh, sorry,' Harriet said, quickly pushing the door forward, releasing the chain and opening it wider.

'And actually… we're *both* going to need an early night,' Iain announced, stepping over the threshold. 'Hey, Jude.'

'Oh, Iain,' Jude said with a knowing shake of the head. 'That joke never gets old.'

It was then Harriet noticed the cabin case on wheels plus a backpack over her boyfriend's shoulder. Something told her these weren't full of tile samples or laminate worktop…

'Iain, why do you have a suitcase? And your weekend away bag?' Harriet asked him, the front door still wide open.

'I'm not going to let you travel to the other side of the world on your own when you're grieving. I've booked a ticket on your plane. I'll sweet talk one of the cabin crew to get us seated together but… I'm coming with you.'

All Harriet could hear as Iain dropped the bombshell was Jude beginning to choke on the mint chocolate thins.

Four

Montauk, Long Island, USA

'Scooter, quit it!'

Mack Wyatt closed his eyes again and tuned in to the rain falling outside. It was hard and fierce and it was hitting his boat like someone was firing tennis balls at it. Usually he found rain therapeutic. It cleansed and renewed, how could that not be a great thing? But, right now, he simply craved more sleep. Slowing his breathing, he tried to settle down into his body and relax into the gentle drift of the ocean here in the harbour...

Scooter gave another growl and Mack's eyes opened a crack. His dog seemed to take this as a sign he was fully awake and ready to get out of bed. With one big spring, the hound was up and on the mattress, his nose wet against Mack's cheek and Scooter's mouth was clasped around something it shouldn't be.

'Scooter! What's happening here?! What did you do?'

Mack plucked the polyurethane liner from his jaws and let out a sigh as his dog licked his face. 'You know this is gross, right? You know I've gotta get another now or smell like you for the rest of the day.'

He sighed, pulling himself up a little on the bed and trying to ignore Scooter's attempts to seek more attention. Through the porthole, Mack could see just how hard the rain was driving. He put fingers to the condensation and rubbed, looking again. The water was beginning to turn a little from relative calm, its surface rippling in response to the assault from the sky like the skin of a drum. He blinked, putting his face closer to the glass and focusing on the wooden dock. Was that... someone out there? In this? He looked harder. There was definitely a figure standing out there in the half-dark, without a coat.

Scooter barked and the liner was between his teeth again, as he began nudging Mack incessantly with his head. And then Mack understood. He was needed. He patted his dog on the head. 'OK, buddy. I hear you.'

Taking the liner from the dog, he shifted his body across the mattress, then reached for his prosthetic leg.

'Hey! Are you OK there?'

The wind was getting up, nature deciding now was the perfect time to whip up a little concoction of waves and splash just as Mack came out into the elements. He steadied himself at the edge of his boat, before taking the big step off. Most of the other boats docked were covered, those absent had been dry-docked for the winter. The tackle shop was closed, as was Madame Scarlet's Emporium and Skeet's Surf Shack. The only businesses open now out on this limb, which was ordinarily so buzzy in the summer, were those that served food and alcohol.

Scooter went sprinting past him, up the length of the platform, and then the dog began turning circles around the person standing at the very end of the dock. The figure was wearing jeans, a red-and-black plaid shirt and a baseball cap over their head. Mack couldn't tell right now if it was a man or a woman. And they hadn't responded at all to his calling out. He began walking and tried again.

Putting a hand around either side of his mouth, he hollered. 'Hey! You really shouldn't be out in this! It's close to freezing and I think it might turn into a real storm!'

Scooter was jumping up at the figure now, paws on the person's legs, making a sound Mack hadn't heard him make before. It was a whine, and then an even higher pitched whimper. Next, before Mack could do anything else, the person in plaid was suddenly tumbling off the wooden pontoon and into the icy sea.

'Oh shit! Shit! Help! Somebody help!' Mack screamed.

At least a million thoughts were zipping through his brain as he awkwardly tried to sprint the rest of the way up the wooden planks. He had to dive in. There wasn't time to remove his leg. But what if no one came? Was he strong enough to keep hold of the person and ensure neither of them froze to death? There was no doubt. He needed to get in the water. Now.

Mack jumped off the pontoon and said a silent prayer as his body hit the freezing water and he pumped with everything he had to bring himself back to the surface. Eyes stinging, nose streaming, he emerged, hoping the person had appeared before him. For a second everything was suddenly silent, except for the wind and the churning water. Mack knew it was early, not quite light, but surely there was *someone* around. An eerie feeling began to creep inside of him and he was flung back to years before…

The smell of hot sand and burning flesh, grit in his mouth, the metallic taste of blood on his lips. His heartbeat had somehow felt so loud inside himself, while all the other sounds of his harsh environment fell away, quiet compared to the ringing in his ears. Panic. Then brightness. All the sounds. Absolute agony.

Scooter's barking from the edge of the dock brought Mack to and, just ahead of him, someone surfaced. The hat was gone, the hair was grey and the ashen face, mouth open, belonged to someone he recognised.

'Joe!' Mack called, furiously swimming toward him. 'Hang on, buddy.'

Within a few strokes he was able to reach out and grab the elderly man, ensuring his head stayed above water. Why was there no one here? At seven a.m., even in the winter, there were ordinarily some boats ready to go out and fish. Granted the weather was shaping up to put paid to that, but usually there was someone getting ready for something or, given the conditions, battening something down.

'Joe, how you doing? Can you talk?'

It was taking horrendous amounts of energy for Mack to swim just a few yards with this old man in his charge. His leg was going to be ruined after this. Submersion in water was going to play havoc with the components. He was really going through legs at the moment. The last one he had cracked climbing a tree to rescue Scooter only two weeks ago.

There was no reply in words, but Mack could feel and just about hear Joe was breathing over the howling of the wind. He had to get him out of the freezing water. Soon. He kicked with everything he had, steering them closer to the wooden pontoon and the steps up.

'Mr Mack! Oh my God! Mr Joe!'

It was Lester. His friend. And his voice was like a welcome drop of smooth, sweet honey into hot, dark coffee. Mack, getting out of breath now, could see the tall, dark bartender on the dock, dressed in a bright yellow cagoule, hood over his head, only his face visible. Scooter was at his feet.

'Lester, you're gonna have to help me out, man.'

'You want me to jump in?' the young man asked, eyes popping out in horror at the suggestion. 'I would never! I cannot. No way.'

'No!' Mack yelled back. 'Just... help me get Joe outta the water.'

'Is he breathing? Should I call a medic? I... don't wanna fall in.'

Jeez, Lester was panicking. That was all they needed. Mack had momentarily forgotten that as good as the guy was at mixing cocktails, he was shit-scared of spiders, the dark and – ironically when he lived here – water.

'Lester!' Mack yelled, struggling to keep his limbs moving in the freezing water. 'Focus! This is Joe!'

Mack had no idea how old Joe actually was, but the guy had to be on the wrong side of seventy. And if Mack – at thirty-one – was finding this demanding, then the old dude had to have it worse. He kicked beneath the surface, pain in his residual limb, praying his prothesis didn't come off and get lost to the waves.

'I am focused,' Lester called above the wind, moving to the top of the steps and leaning cautiously. 'I am not gonna fall in. I am not gonna fall in.' He gave a shriek. 'I want to close my eyes.'

'Keep 'em open, Lester. Come on, lean out a little farther and you can grab him. I'll hold him too. And we can get him out of the water and onto the dock.'

'I will pretend that his life depends on me. Like I am the saviour in a Hollywood film alongside Tom Hanks and—'

Mack knew Lester was talking because he was terrified. He had had a guy in his troop exactly the same way. Whenever they were gearing up for an engagement with the enemy, Jackson Tate would start talking about the biggest pile of crap, from his damn hometown baseball team to his opinion on Milk Duds.

'Lester! Joe's life *does* depend on it. Get him outta the water!'

Although Lester gave a whine not unlike Scooter when he wanted more food, Mack's bark seemed to have got the message across. With a huge push from below and a heave upwards from Lester, Joe flopped out onto the dockside, still, pale, but definitely breathing.

'OK, Lester,' Mack called from the water, taking a moment to catch his breath. 'You've gotta get him over on his side so any water he's taken in drains right out.'

'I have to touch him more?' Lester queried, staring down at the old man as if hoping the casualty would move himself.

Mack cursed under his breath and started to haul himself up the ladder, the waves crashing around him, the wind bitingly cold now. 'Just roll him onto his side, Lester. I'll be right there.' He put his foot on the step and, as he continued upwards, his other leg left his body and dropped down into the sea.

'God damn it! Argh! I'm fucking cursed, I swear it!'

Mack watched the prothesis being mashed by the waves, disappearing into the white foam then being thrown up again. It wasn't worth getting back into the water for. He'd just have to hope that Dr Jerome wasn't going to laugh him out of his office when he said he needed another replacement made.

Using his arms on the side of the ladder, Mack clambered up the rest of the way, then hopped to Joe, keeping his balance as best he could.

'Ah! Mr Mack! Your leg!' Lester exclaimed, hands going to the side of his hood, eyes bulging.

'Eyes up on the gun show, Lester,' Mack said, flexing his muscle before awkwardly dropping onto the floor and getting close to Joe. Quickly he rolled the old man over onto his side and positioned his body into the recovery position.

Lester was already removing his cagoule now and laying it over Joe like a thin, already-soaked, blanket. The old man gave a cough and spat water out onto the boards. It was only then that Mack took a deep breath of relief. They were all OK. But, as Scooter laid down next to the patient, making concerned noises, Mack began to realise exactly how freezing it was and that the danger really wasn't past. They needed to get out of this weather.

'What in the hell is going on out here?!'

'Oh, shit,' Lester said, dropping his head.

'Oh, hey, Ruby!' Mack called out to the approaching woman wearing a long black anorak, over tight jeans and a sweater.

'Are you two moronic or something? There's a storm coming in and... oh my Jesus, Joe!'

The young woman dropped to her knees on the floor beside the man and began to stroke his hair so gently. Joe's eyes fluttered open a little but his whole body was shivering.

'What in the hell happened?' Ruby asked, almost accusing.

'I don't know yet,' Mack answered. 'But we need to get him warm.'

'Lester, come on! Help get Joe up and back to the bar,' Ruby ordered.

'I would help but...' Mack said, indicating his residual limb.

'Oh, Jesus,' Ruby began. 'Half naked again?' She shook her head. 'How many legs you gonna go through before the year is out? Do you even have any left?'

'Two,' Mack answered. 'And one's from 2016.'

Ruby got to her feet and offered her hand out to him.

'I'm good,' Mack insisted. 'You take care of Joe. Scooter'll see me back to my boat. I'll get fixed up and I'll go get the doctor.'

'Here!' Lester said, grabbing something from behind them. He began pulling fishing nets and baskets out of the wheelbarrow and stood behind it as if ready to drive. 'We can put him in this.'

'If Lorna could see us now,' Ruby said with a sigh, eyes going to the sky.

Once Joe was safely in his transport and Ruby was

fighting Lester for control of the barrow as they headed up the pontoon towards the buildings on the beach, Mack turned his attention back to Scooter.

'OK, boy, so I haven't done this in a while. Let's see if I've still got it.'

Scooter gave a bark and got up on his paws, looking at Mack, tongue hanging out as the rain began to drive even harder.

This was his party trick. The thing that impressed people once they'd got used to him not having a portion of his left leg. He made a move then, going seamlessly from balancing on one leg to standing on his hands. He began to walk, palms picking a path, the blood flooding to his head. Perhaps this wasn't such a great idea given the weather…

'OK, Scooter, I'm good,' Mack told the dog as Scooter tracked his progress with diligent eyes. 'But watch my six. OK, buddy?'

Scooter gave a bark of understanding.

Five

The Rum Coconut, Montauk, USA

'I don't know about you, but I'm having another one.'

Ruby was behind the bar of Joe's restaurant on the beach pushing another whisky glass to the optics and reaching for Mack's empty glass on the bar. She'd taken off the long coat and her trademark dark head of tight black curls was now even more of a cloud of frizz as she warmed everyone up with alcohol. She might be younger than him, perhaps mid-twenties, but when it came to this bar she was definitely the boss now. A pocket rocket with as much streetwise sass as she had ingredients for home-cooked meals. If it wasn't her business, she made it her business and no one seemed to argue.

Ill-fitting spare leg attached, Mack had called the doctor first, then towelled himself down, re-dressing in something dry, before coming over here to check on Joe. That poor guy. He had really been through it lately. Losing his wife and now this...

'Yeah, fill me up,' Mack agreed, nodding. 'How's he doing?' His gaze went to the log fire, crackling away underneath a wall decorated with palms, wooden tiki masks and colourful leis, Dr Ambrose checking Joe over. On either side of the fireplace were two tall real fir trees, as yet plain and unadorned.

Ruby let out a sigh and took a swig of her neat whisky, passing Mack's along to him. 'He didn't know where any of his clothes were. Lorna, she did everything for him.' She shook her head. 'She told me a couple of moons ago that she'd always picked out something for him to wear their entire life together because he had a bad eye for colour.'

'It smelled like he'd been wearing that plaid shirt for a few days,' Mack said.

'You see I've put him in green,' Ruby said, looking over at Joe now showered and dressed in a dark jumper and matching corduroys. 'Lorna loved him in green. She said it reminded her of his days in the army and how smart he looked in his uniform.'

'I've seen the photos,' Mack answered. There were some up on the wall behind the bar. Joe and his friends from his regiment. Joe and Lorna on their wedding day. A boy Mack had always presumed was their son, naked in a bath when he was a toddler, trying to eat a bar of soap. Mack took a drink. 'When's the funeral?'

'Thursday,' Ruby said. 'Dr Ambrose got the post-mortem prioritised and Joe wanted to get it done, so…' She took a breath. 'Their granddaughter's arriving today. That's where Lester's heading. Got to pick her up from JFK.'

'The kid who got stuck on the Ferris wheel?'

Ruby laughed. 'Lorna loved to tell that story, didn't she?'

'I've only been here two years and even *I* know it word for word.'

'Well, she's not a kid anymore. Last time she came here to visit was just before I started working here. But I met her at The Lobster Roll.' She sipped at her drink. 'She lives in the UK. Lorna told me she used to come here a lot when she was younger.'

Mack nodded and let himself warm up in the familiar surroundings. This was his favourite bar around here. When he first arrived in Montauk with literally only the rucksack on his back and the army pay-out in his bank account, he had come just for the booze. But now, a couple years on, he couldn't deny he liked the company. Apart from Scooter, he had been pretty much devoid of company since his leg had parted with the rest of him. It had been his choice. And, for a while, friends here at the bar were left at the bar. But now, somehow, without him really knowing it, he had become part of the community.

'Their son, Joe Junior, he ain't coming,' Ruby said with a shrug. 'And as much as Lorna loved to talk, God rest her soul, she never wanted to talk about him in the present.' She sighed. 'The stories all stop around high school. It's kinda weird. But if I asked she got all kinds of peppery.'

'Families,' Mack mused. He could relate. He had left his as far behind as he could when he joined the army and there had been only one visit after he'd been medically retired. It hadn't gone so well. And if his parents were right here looking at him now, there would definitely still be a string of I-told-you-so's falling from his father's lips. The military meant nothing to Adrian Wyatt because it stood for everything he wasn't. Stable. Strong. Unified. From the second he'd told his father he was enlisting, their relationship went to a place there was no going back from. Mack had chosen a future with risks, yes, but they were risks he considered to be for a greater good. Adrian's risk-taking involved too much cheap vodka and a cell phone full of the numbers of loan sharks.

Mack watched Dr Ambrose close his black leather doctor's bag and leave Joe by the fire, heading towards the bar.

'How's he doing, Doc?' Mack asked straight off.

'He's… suffering,' Dr Ambrose said sadly. 'Although I suspect that's more from the loss of Lorna than it is from his tumble into the water.'

'He's not hurt though?' Ruby asked. 'Physically like.'

The doctor shook his head. 'No, he's going to be just fine.' He looked directly at Mack then. 'Thanks to you, I'm hearing.'

Mack waved the gratitude away and looked down to the floor where Scooter was curled up asleep by his feet. 'It was more down to Scooter than me. The little dude woke me up because he kinda sensed something was up.'

'Well, thank you, Scooter,' Dr Ambrose said, eyes dropping to the snoring dog. 'Now, do you know if Joe Junior is coming to help with the arrangements for Lorna?'

Ruby shook her head. 'He's not. But their granddaughter's arriving today. Joe spoke with her on the phone.'

'Ah, Joanna,' Dr Ambrose said, smiling. 'She beat me at tennis the last time she was here. It will be lovely to see her again.' He paused. 'A terrible shame about the circumstances.'

'I wonder if she'll get stuck on the Ferris wheel again,' Mack said, winking at Ruby.

'Goodness,' the doctor breathed. 'That was quite the excitement all those years ago. As I recall, it took three firefighters and a lot of cotton candy to get her to be brave enough to be rescued.'

'I feel like the only one who hasn't met her,' Mack remarked.

'Right, I should go,' Dr Ambrose told them. 'Call me if you're concerned. I've made an appointment for him to check in with me next week. Not at the office, at my cabin for a game of cards.' He pointed at Ruby. 'And don't give him any more whisky.'

'This one's for me,' Ruby said, wrapping her hand around the glass.

'Doctor! Doctor!'

It was Joe and Lorna's crazy old parrot cawing from its cage as the medic made his way to the door. It was a scarlet macaw, predominantly red in colour, with a cloak of yellow and green below and all its feathers turning bright blue after that, right down to the tips of its wings. It always had too much to say. Mack shook his head and took a swig of whisky. 'How old is that bird?'

'Lorna and Joe's granddaughter? I don't know. Maybe twenties? A little older than me? Definitely not as hot.'

'I was talking about Meryl Cheep,' he answered. Yep, the parrot was really named after a movie star. Lorna had loved telling the tourists its name and getting it to do tricks...

'Oh, I've got no idea,' Ruby said. 'Why don't you ask her?' She finished her whisky. 'I'm gonna see if I can get Joe to eat something. *You* want something? Ham and eggs? Grits?'

'I'm good,' Mack said, raising his glass in answer.

'OK, I'll be clear,' Ruby said, leaning right over the bar towards him. 'Take the bribe. Because someone has to help me decorate those Christmas trees before we're the only place in Montauk not ready for Santa. And I'll have Lorna haunting me if I let things slide.'

'Can't your brothers do it?' Mack suggested. 'Or Lester?'

'Lester has a worse eye for colour than Joe. He thinks orange goes with red for Jesus' sake. And as for my brothers? You know they either set light to everything or eat it. I'm not entirely sure what one they would go for with the trees, but I have courtside seats at the emergency room as it is.'

Mack laughed. 'OK. You've tragic story-ed me into it. I'll take the ham and the grits. No eggs.'

'Coming right up,' Ruby said, smiling before she headed through the back to the kitchen.

Once she was gone, Mack looked over to Joe sitting by the fire. The old man's gaze wasn't on the flames licking the stack of logs, it was toward the bi-fold doors with the amazing view of the shoreline. The glass was getting spattered with rain and sea spray, the wind blowing through the palm trees like their fronds were made of paper. As Mack watched Joe checking out the storm, internally he held onto the hope that the guy had slipped off the dock earlier, or was pushed by the force of the wind. Because it was going to be a whole lot of something else if, in fact, Joe had jumped.

Six

No matter how many times Harriet tapped the screen of her phone it still seemed determined to take longer to turn on than it took to hard boil an egg. They had done passport control, their ESTAs checked and retinas scanned and now they were heading out of the terminal to find a car to hire. Iain seemed to think *he* would be driving, but that would mean no meandering, taking time to check out the views but instead, rather full-force, A straight to B, watching the Google Maps ETA counting down with each acceleration. In past times she had always made her grandpa stop at Southampton Windmill. She loved the windmill with its grey tiles and rumours of a ghost…

'Whoa, it's cold!' Iain announced as they finally came out into the open air and he removed his face mask.

'I did say it would be,' Harriet answered, the home screen on her phone finally making an appearance. 'Do you have a hat?' She dipped her fingers into the pocket of her coat

46

she'd put on as soon as the pilot had switched the seatbelt sign off, and pulled out her gloves.

'I have a hood,' Iain replied, flipping up the rather insufficient fold attached to his coat. 'Right, rental companies.' He clapped his hands together, then put one hand to his brow like he was a boat captain seeking the threat of icebergs.

In her now-gloved hands, Harriet's phone wobbled and beeped as messages started to arrive.

Jude: One of the plants is shedding already!

Jude: I did not feed it Marmite like last time I promise.

Jude: Call when you can.

Jude: I hope you get there OK.

Jude: *rainbow emoji*

Harriet shook her head. Jude always had to start a new thread for each sentence. And she still didn't know why Jude had ever thought putting yeast spread on a succulent was the right kind of plant nurturing.

'Harriet,' Iain called from ahead. 'Are you coming?'

'Just a second.' She took her eyes off the phone for a moment and looked up. Iain was rushing already, when she wanted to breathe in America. Even outside the terminal deserved a minute. Yes, it was only an airport building, but those yellow taxis lined up a few steps away spoke of everything different to Bournemouth, and the memories of when she had made her flights here before came flooding back. One time, a friend of Grandpa Joe's had flown Harriet right into Montauk, landing at the airport that was the most easterly in New York. The light aircraft had been very different to the British Airways flight they'd just disembarked from. A shiver ran through her then. It was a feeling that spoke of mixed emotions. She couldn't wait to give her grandpa a hug but the whole reason she was here was because her nana wasn't. Harriet looked back to her phone even though Iain was pacing on, his hood still up against the cold wind. There was another notification on her screen.

Grandpa: Joanna I am sending Lester topick you up look out for the. Pickup x

Unlike Jude with her need for full sentences, all neat and tidy, her grandpa texted with one finger, zero *intended* punctuation and often the words running into one another, sometimes altering the whole sense of the message. But this one she understood. And, looking past the taxis to the drop-off area, she saw a vehicle she recognised.

'Iain! Iain, come back! We've got a lift!'

She watched Iain stop and turn around, shielding his eyes again, even though there was no sun to be seen, only grey clouds that seemed to be multiplying. She didn't wait for Iain to start retracing his steps. Dragging her cabin case, Harriet approached the old holly-green coloured Ford pickup, its paint and chrome as fresh as the day it had come off the assembly line.

She had almost made it to within a few feet of the vehicle when a hand was on her arm, halting her walk.

'Harriet, what are you doing? This is not a licensed taxi.'

Iain's mask was back on his face now, but his eyes spoke volumes. She mustn't laugh. Iain didn't recognise this truck like she did. For her, this Ford wasn't just transport. During the times she had spent in Montauk it had been a Native American's wigwam, a castle in the clouds, a hospital for sick teddies and Barbie dolls... When the weather hadn't been clear skies and hot sand dunes, Harriet had climbed up into Grandpa Joe's pickup and let her imagination wander.

'This is our ride,' she said to Iain, knocking her knuckles against the passenger window.

The man with short dark curly hair inside jumped in his seat, a hand going to his chest. Harriet opened the door and gave him a smile. 'Hello, I'm Joe's granddaughter. I think you're looking for me.'

'Oh, my, Miss Joanna, you gave me a scare. Let me get out and—'

'No, don't do that,' Harriet said. 'It's cold.' She turned to Iain. 'Could you pop the bags in the back?'

'The back?' Iain said, his eyes going to the open-to-the-elements flat bed of the Ford. 'But—'

'There should be a tarp in the box back there. Wrap it around the cases, tuck it underneath and secure it with the bungee cord.' She pulled herself up into the cab, shuffling along until she was up close to their driver. She stuck out a hand. 'It's nice to meet you...'

'Lester,' the man answered, shaking her hand. 'I work at The Rum Coconut.'

Just someone saying the name of her grandparents' tiki

bar warmed Harriet's insides. In a few hours she was going to be there, surrounded by all the knick-knacks she adored, seeing her grandpa, maybe even sipping a cocktail… and being faced with the realisation that her nana was no longer filling every corner of the place.

'May I say that I am so very sorry for your loss,' Lester said soberly.

Harriet swallowed. No one had said they were sorry for *her* loss yet. She'd phoned her dad yesterday, saying she would let him know the arrangements for the funeral, but she already knew he wouldn't come. Whatever had happened in the Cookson family that meant Joe Junior had changed his name to Ralph and had never gone back to Montauk was serious enough that a son would miss his own mother's funeral. The rift had never made sense to Harriet and it still didn't. Because even in the midst of this tragedy, no one was talking.

'Thank you,' she said. She took a breath and the smell of the interior of the vehicle pinched at her heart. It was brine, leather, her grandpa's cologne and a little bit of sand. She could see grains of it on the car mats. No matter of Grandpa Joe's need to keep this machine in pristine condition, sand got everywhere.

'Is the man getting in here with us?' Lester asked, his gaze going to the rear-view mirror. 'Or is he staying in the back?'

Harriet twisted in her seat, looking through the rear window at Iain attempting to secure their luggage and the tarpaulin – albeit hefty – was fighting him for control. She felt a twinge of guilt that she had asked him to deal with the luggage. Iain had been raised on golf club lunches and was still treated a little like a schoolboy by his mother's influential-in-the-local-business-community friends. She wasn't sure she'd ever seen Iain dirty. Even when they were renovating properties he usually opted for the full protective white body suit rather than an ancient T-shirt and joggers like she did.

'I'll go and help him,' Harriet said, about to get down from the vehicle again.

'No, Miss Joanna, you stay here,' Lester ordered. 'I promised Mr Joe that I'd look after you.' He opened the door then looked back at her. 'And Mr Joe, he says you are not allowed to drive.'

That was typical of her grandpa. He'd never liked her behind the wheel of his beloved truck. Harriet smiled. 'Then you'd better be quick, Lester. It's been a long time since I drove this Ford, but I haven't forgotten how.'

Seven

The Rum Coconut, Fort Pond Bay, Montauk

Lester was truly a terrible driver. And Harriet had worried about *Iain* having a turn behind the wheel! It wasn't that Lester drove too slowly or even too fast, it was instead the way he moved the steering wheel – this way and that – without consideration for anything else on the road. He did say he usually rode a bicycle and really he was treating the steering wheel like it was handlebars. In the almost three hours they had been packed tight inside the cab of the Ford, Lester had swerved to avoid a car, a leather-clad motorcyclist and, what looked like, a hawk. At one point, Harriet had looked to Iain to 'make comment' with her eyebrows about Lester's driving, but he had been eyes down on his phone. She had nudged his elbow at one point, wanting him to look at Hill Street in Southampton – a gorgeous road with a strictly enforced twenty-five miles per hour speed limit – as they were creeping along the tree-lined sections of it, but he'd held a finger up as if to quieten her, thumbs working fast on his screen in what looked to be the composition of an email.

But now they were here. Lester had put the truck in park and Harriet got her first look at the tiki shack that owned a big piece of her heart. She took a breath, glad that the clapboard exterior looked no different to how it had three years ago. From first impressions, it hadn't even had a lick of creosote. Those effigies of tribal art were grinning grotesquely at them and looking a little flaky, and the large reed and palm awning that usually sheltered patrons from the hot sun was drooping over the outside terrace. Everything was wet and windswept. One thing was for sure, it looked nothing like summer. Those gentle rolling waves were white-capped and cresting at quite some height right now, hitting the sand with a smack that was audible from inside the truck. The blue of the ocean she was used to seemed darker and a little more sinister. One thing that comforted her was the porch, just visible, swing seat on the deck. It was perhaps Harriet's favourite place of all, the location of hot nights drinking ice-cool drinks, listening to Keith Urban, sinking into all the cushions, writing letters…

'We are here!' Lester announced the obvious. 'I will get your luggage. I do not think it blew away on the journey.' Without waiting for a response, Lester opened the door and jumped down, a gust of icy, wintry wind invading the sanctuary of the cab.

'He wasn't serious, was he?' Iain asked, finally looking up from his screen and putting his hand on the door ready to get out too. 'Because my laptop is in my carry-on.'

'Wait,' Harriet said, her hand on Iain's sleeve. 'Just, sit with me a minute.' She drew in a breath. 'Take in the view.'

Even with its winter overtones, this stretch of coastline was peacefully beautiful. Montauk wasn't like the rest of the area labelled 'The Hamptons'. Yes, tourists flocked here, but it still retained its traditional charm. Here, overlooking the bay in winter, there was nothing but nature. Not even a fisherman had ventured out. When Harriet was small, she and her nana had built a wooden fort for her dolls out of driftwood and she had cried when it had blown down at the end of the day. That had been her nana. Always giving her time, always patient, always there… Harriet swallowed the lump in her throat, feeling all the more bereft.

'I've checked out some hotels,' Iain said, putting his phone in her sightline. 'One of them looks extremely extravagant but I thought why not have a treat.'

Harriet's eyes fell to a collection of photos displayed on Iain's screen. It was a hotel room, nondescript, white towels on a white duvet cover, a bit like the now-soulless bathroom in the pebbledash property. Snow was falling down over the web page to give it a festive flair.

'What's that for?' she asked. Had she missed a train of conversation while she'd been bathing in her reverie?

'For us,' Iain stated. 'We need somewhere to stay, don't we? On the plane I asked you if you'd booked anything and you said no.'

Iain was looking at her now as if it was her who had lost the plot. She shook her head and looked at him in surprise. 'I haven't booked anything because there's no need. We're going to be staying here.' She opened the truck door then and slipped down onto the sand-coated dirt and grass ground, the wind whipping around her face. It was bracing and she could smell the salt in the freezing air. Maybe she would get Grandpa out for a walk later. It wasn't far to Fort Pond lake. They could maybe get a coffee or visit Madame Scarlet... Except there was the fact that arrangements needed to be made.

'Harriet, we can't stay here,' Iain said, appearing from the car in a fluster of coat and hood. 'It's some kind of... *ghoulish* bar.'

'Yes,' Harriet agreed. 'My grandparents' bar.'

'Oh,' Iain said. 'It... wasn't what I imagined.'

'And you haven't even seen inside yet,' Harriet told him. 'Come on.'

Harriet pushed open the door and was immediately greeted.

'Who's there? Who's there?'

'What the...'

Harriet laughed as Iain almost lost his footing when Meryl Cheep squawked her welcome. He flailed back a little and hit his shoulder on a hanging blowfish that had graced the window in the lobby for as long as Harriet could remember. It was called Hootie.

'It's OK,' she said to Iain. 'Let me introduce you.' She cleared her throat and put a finger through the bars of the cage. 'This is Meryl Cheep.' The bird eyed Harriet's digit like she was trying to work out if it was a tasty treat or something that might poison her. 'Hello, Meryl. How are you?'

'Is it real?' Iain queried, gingerly stepping forward and looking at the bird like it might be battery operated.

'Of course she's real. And still so beautiful,' Harriet said softly. She waited for the bird to drop its head a little and then gently stroked the feathers on the top of her crown.

'Joanna! Joanna!' the bird spoke excitedly, bobbing its head up and down and shaking out its feathers.

'Aw! She still remembers me,' Harriet said happily.

'About that,' Iain began. 'Why *is* everyone calling you Joanna?'

Harriet smiled. 'Sorry, I should have said something earlier about that. It's like a nickname I guess.'

It wasn't a nickname as such. And she knew the name everyone called her here was a known bone of contention between her father and grandfather. But she had never minded. Here in Montauk she had just always been Joanna.

'So, what should I call you?' Iain asked.

The expression on his face was telling Harriet he was a little bit unsettled by this. She smiled. 'You can call me whatever you want to.'

The inner door suddenly swung open and a short woman dressed in jeans, with tight curls of black hair piled on top of her head, appeared in the frame.

'Well, look-y here! It's good to see you again!'

'Ruby,' Harriet greeted with a smile. She was caught between holding out a hand and stepping forward to make an embrace. She had only met Ruby once, but her nana had always spoken really highly about her during their calls. It had sounded like Ruby was exactly the kind of help her grandparents had needed around the place. And now it was just her grandpa, help was going to be required more than ever.

'Bring it in,' Ruby encouraged, opening her arms. 'Come on, let's get shot of all the English right here, right now.'

Harriet put her arms around the shorter woman and found out she had the fiercest of grips and smelled a little like cherries and hair spray.

'I am so sorry for your loss,' Ruby whispered in her ear as those fragrances wrapped around Harriet.

Harriet swallowed. As good as it felt to be back, her feelings were soaked with sadness at the reason behind it. Ordinarily it would have been Nana welcoming her into the bar and telling her what sweet treats she had cooked up. The smells then would have been cake mixture and raisins, apples and pastry...

'Could I trouble you to show me where the toilet is?'

Iain's interruption made Harriet break apart from Ruby, and she swiped an escaped tear with her gloves. Why was she holding in her pain? Because it was the British thing to do? Or because Iain had never seen her cry?

'Pardon me?' Ruby asked, looking at Iain like he had landed from another dimension.

'It's OK, Ruby,' Harriet said. She turned to Iain. 'The toilets are through the bar and to the right.'

'Thanks,' he said, nodding. 'Three hours is a long drive.' He moved past Ruby and headed into the bar room at speed.

'Is he OK?' Ruby asked, turning and watching Iain zip past tables and the stone and bamboo water feature in the centre of the room.

Harriet smiled. 'It's a long flight and we're still on UK time. Where's my grandpa?' She wanted to give him the biggest of hugs and reassure him that things would be OK now she was here to help. She knew she couldn't arrive and simply wave a magic wand but she could tell her grandpa that whatever he was feeling, he wasn't alone.

'About that,' Ruby began. 'Before you go see him... there's something you should know.'

Eight

It was definitely the change in temperature from the cold outside to the warmth here in The Rum Coconut that was making Harriet's eyes smart. It was nothing to do with what Ruby had just told her. Nothing at all. The inner British restraint was still very much intact.

Iain was back from the bathroom and Ruby was thunderously chattering as she made them both one of her 'signature' coffees that apparently people came from miles around to try. Looking around the barely occupied room, a couple of patrons in the comfy padded chairs playing cards, *no* one in the restaurant area, it didn't look like anyone came from anywhere to visit the bar. It was as sparse of customers as Harriet had ever seen it and decidedly more empty without the presence of her nana. Even the décor – usually so vibrant and eclectic, like a fiesta could begin at any moment – seemed dated and faded. And there was no sign that Christmas was coming. Two bare fir trees looked unloved each side of the fire, as if December had forgotten they existed.

Taking a deep breath, her eyes going to the figure of her grandpa, she didn't delay any longer. There was only one way to play this and it didn't begin with a softly-softly approach. It was time to be more Lorna and manage this situation. She was going to take control and be the conductor of this orchestra.

'Grandpa!' Harriet greeted loudly, rushing her steps to get to him.

There was no immediate response, no head turn or even a flicker of recognition that he had heard her. She swallowed and, as she drew closer, tried again. 'Grandpa! I'm here!'

She swept around his chair until she was stood right in front of him, spreading her arms out like she was part of curtain up on a West End stage. He looked so much older than she remembered from her last visit. His eyes were a little sunken into the sockets, far more wrinkles lined his forehead and his skin was sagging and loose, like it might be trying to escape his bones. She smiled wide to belie her concerns as Joe finally shifted a little in his chair.

'Joanna,' he croaked.

'Yes,' she breathed, dropping into the chair next to him and scooting it right up close to his. She grabbed his hands in hers, holding them tight and trying not to notice how bony and frail they felt. Grandpa Joe had always been a tall, strong man, chopping up wood for the fire, helping to lift tractor tyres for a friend, popping her ten-year-old self up on his shoulders for a ride… She swallowed. 'I'm here at last! Goodness, it took a long time but, well, it was certainly worth it to be back here again and seeing you!'

Joe smiled then. At last a hopeful indication that he was in there somewhere. He had a wonderful, warming smile.

Her nana had always said there had been two reasons she had fallen for Joe back in the day. One was his pearly-white smile and the other was his skill on the dancefloor. The last time she had seen her grandpa dance must have been over ten years ago, waltzing her nana to a slow beat on the sand as the sun went down…

'Did you get my message?' Joe asked, sitting a little forward in his seat and looking directly at her at last.

'I did,' Harriet told him. 'Thank you for arranging Lester to meet us. He seems really nice.'

'God awful driver,' Joe said with a throaty chuckle. 'But… I trust him.'

'That's good, Grandpa. It's good to have people working here that you trust. Ruby seems nice too.'

'She has spirit in her, that one… but she's good people. Having to look after those brothers of hers.' Joe shook his head. 'They're more like your father was. Nothing but trouble.'

Harriet frowned, hope dimming slightly. She hadn't heard him speak quite like this before. Perhaps his tip into the water *had* done some damage. Although Ruby insisted that she had made sure Dr Ambrose had checked him over thoroughly.

'How are *you*, Grandpa?' Harriet asked him, giving his fingers another small squeeze. 'With everything.' She internally cursed herself. No skirting around the issue. Arrangements had to be made. 'With… Nana… going.'

Joe hardened immediately, drawing back his hands and sitting poker-straight in the chair like he'd been ordered to by a superior officer. 'I don't wanna talk about it.'

'I know,' Harriet whispered. 'I understand. I know how

hard you must be finding it… how hard we're all finding it but—'

'Hello!'

Harriet shut her eyes in response to Iain's inopportune interruption.

'Who are you?' Joe asked roughly, turning his head to look up at the newcomer.

'I'm—' Iain began, sticking out a hand.

Harriet shook her head, suddenly irritated. 'Grandpa, this is Iain. I've told you all about him on the phone. Well… I told Nana and…'

'It's nice to meet you,' Iain said, persisting with his outstretched hand.

'I gotta go,' Joe said, looking at his watch. Suddenly and quickly he shifted himself forward in the chair and then stood up.

'Go?' Harriet asked. 'Go where?' Her eyes went to the large windows, the wind whipping the awning, the sea all white horses and angry foam. Surely he couldn't mean outside. Particularly after this morning's incident.

'I just gotta go,' Joe repeated. 'There'll be things needed for the menu.'

Harriet watched her grandfather wringing his hands and looking uncomfortable, exactly like he didn't know what to do with himself. It was the saddest thing… and she wasn't sure how to handle it. What should she do? She looked to one of her favourite photos of her nana and grandad hanging on the wall. Dressed in Fijian dress, a pink orchid in her nana's hair, their smiles seemed to tell the secret of their long marriage…

'I could get things for you,' Iain jumped in. 'Point me in

the direction of the nearest shop and I'll get whatever you need.'

Harriet knew Iain was trying to be helpful, but she wasn't sure this was exactly what her grandad needed when he wasn't quite himself. But what did he need? She was feeling decidedly lacking and unprepared.

'You know your way around a weakfish?' Joe asked, facing Iain and looking suspicious.

'I have no idea what that is, but if you make me a list, I'll do my best to get everything on it,' Iain assured. 'If you'll allow me to drive your vehicle.' He swallowed. 'Sir.'

Joe seemed to be musing over the idea, but Harriet knew the restaurant couldn't need ingredients that desperately. Her nana had always kept stock in order and she was certain Ruby was the type of character who would be on the ball when it came to keeping things ticking over. On first impressions the place was as tidy as Harriet had ever seen it and she had no reason to think that organisation didn't extend to the pantry.

'Grandpa,' Harriet said, slipping her arm through his. 'Iain can get the list from Ruby. Why don't you show me up to Nana's sewing room and I can unpack my case.'

Joe's eyes seemed to brighten then. 'You're staying here?'

'Of course,' Harriet said, leading him towards the door that went to the rooms above. 'Where else would I want to be?'

'Well, by the looks of that guy you're with, I was reckoning on you staying at one of them fancy hotels in Sagaponack.' He gave a throaty chuckle and Harriet didn't dare look at Iain in case he had overheard.

Nine

Fort Pond, Montauk

Mack raised a hand and knocked on the bright purple painted front door of the tiny cottage a short walk from his mooring. There was a wreath hanging beneath the knocker, made from ivy, fir and random twigs, interspersed with red and white berries, pine cones hanging from gold thread. While he was distracted looking at the festive display, suddenly all manner of lights illuminated the porch. Bright white, red, gold, a crazy pink, all started to flash like he might be about to become part of a Christmas extravaganza stage show. Instead of barking his dislike, Scooter whined and hid behind Mack's legs. Wow, Christmas was locked, loaded and ready to go here!

The door swung open and the heavy scent of every fragrance he imagined coming from the inner sanctum of the boudoir of a circus performer hit his nose. Make-up, patchouli... gunpowder? And then there was the undeniable presence of Madame Scarlet, dressed head-to-toe in her trademark red. This outfit was a cross between ready for a costume party and a sixty-something's bedroom fantasy. She was as stout as she was short, with rapidly changing hairstyles – all variations of red – that no one dared to suggest were wigs. But she could go from having tresses like Rapunzel one day to a little bit Liza Minelli crop in *Cabaret* the next. But all of them suited her fierce yet motherly, seasoned chorus girl disposition. Tonight it was a little bit Marge Simpson…

'Madame Scarlet,' Mack began. 'Did we not have a talk about that chain on your door?'

'Oh, Scooter, my darling. Don't you like my lights?'

Mack shook his head at his friend ignoring the question, watching her bend down to muss Scooter's brown furry coat. He waited for her to be upright before he tried again. 'I put the chain on for a reason. So you can check who's at your porch before you open it.'

Madame Scarlet flapped a hand in the air. 'I knew it was you. Who else would skulk around in the half-dark carrying a—' She stopped talking and plunged her nose forward, inhaling deep. 'Is that what I think it is?'

Mack smiled and offered the crockpot forward. 'My special meatball Mack 'n' cheese.'

'Oh my, darling boy!' Madame Scarlet exclaimed. 'You are the answer to an old woman's prayers. Come in!'

'No, we're not here for an invitation,' Mack began as Scooter started trotting forward. He held his lead tight and halted his progress. 'I made the food for you and—'

Madame Scarlet scoffed. 'I know I've got a big appetite but not even I could eat that whole dish by myself.' She smiled. 'Get along in! It's freezing out here!'

Mack loosened his hold on Scooter and the dog rushed

into the little house that was like a second home to him. Immediately he started barking, jumping up and down at the sight of a large, decorated Christmas tree in the lounge area. Only a few steps from the front door, this snug homely room was Madame Scarlet's own personal brand of decadence. And now it was awash with festiveness like Santa himself had descended and filled it with December goodness from his North Pole hideaway. Mack had always felt comfortable here. Yeah, it was part mystical tent but it also reminded him of a TV show depiction of 'home'. Life happened here – it was a little bit chaotic, but it all came together in the end.

Madame Scarlet took the pot from Mack's hands, swinging around to the small kitchenette as Mack unleashed Scooter and the little dog immediately forgot the tree and leaped up onto one of the two sofas squeezed into the space and covered with more cushions than a furnishings store.

'It'll only need a couple minutes,' Mack called to her, settling himself next to Scooter and pulling a V-shaped stick out from underneath him. What was that? He put it down on the arm of the sofa.

'You think I'm gonna wait to heat it up? I've been busy all day putting up that!' A hand pointed through the arch from kitchen and over the breakfast bar to the monumental tree, whose branches were dangerous close to the glass-fronted door of the wood-burner that was heating the area up nicely. There were a few too many baubles and ribbons that would have looked gaudy and over-the-top in any other space, but here they fitted into the general Madame Scarlet craziness.

'It looks… like it should have its own room,' Mack remarked.

'Ha!' Madame Scarlet laughed. 'I'm pretty sure I can find you something that will fit in your boat.'

'Oh no,' Mack said straight off. 'We don't do Christmas on *The Warrior*.'

'Well,' Madame Scarlet said, whisking in, long crimson dress breezing around her, a bowl in each hand. 'You know I love a challenge. Oh, you found my water diviner! I'd been looking for that!'

She passed a bowl and fork to Mack, then plumped down on the sofa opposite. Only the width of a dark wood coffee table burning cinnamon candles and incense sticks, an ornamental elephant and a porcelain black cat wearing a tiny Santa hat, was between them.

Mack took a fork full of the meatball Mack 'n' cheese and, as the creamy cheese and spiced beef hit his taste buds he realised exactly how hungry he was. It was close to nine p.m. now and he hadn't had anything since the ham and grits at The Rum Coconut. The weather had put paid to anything much outdoors, so instead he'd worked out, slept a little, made the meal and put off taking Scooter for a walk until now.

'So,' Madame Scarlet said, pausing in her eating. 'You're here to ask me about Joe.'

Mack shook his head. 'Don't do that.'

'What?'

'Don't try and read my mind. You know it freaks me out.'

'But I am right. Right?'

Madame Scarlet's skills were legendary around these

parts. She might ramp up the crystal ball illusions for the tourists, but she did seem to have some kind of talent for intuition, if not really able to connect with the other side like her posters outside her business premises claimed.

'I dunno,' Mack said, sighing. 'It's not my place but—'

'Darling, it's all our place. That's why we live where everyone minds everyone else's business.'

He shrugged his shoulders, feeling a little uncomfortable with her suggestion of community and neighbourhood. That had been the very last thing on his mind when he'd landed here. He didn't know quite *what* had been his thought process except going somewhere no one knew him as he used to be. Somewhere beautiful. A place he'd learned about from *someone* beautiful. But now he was embedded here, he couldn't deny it was true. Everyone knew everyone's name and what they liked to eat for breakfast. And, he guessed, if he'd really wanted to be more isolated than living on a boat, he could have found a home way out in the mountains... in another country.

'Lorna was his everything. Always had been. I remember the very first time she told me about him. There was this ethereal glow about her.' Madame Scarlet shuddered like she might have just been possessed by a dearly-departed spirit wanting to talk. 'Love owns you,' she continued. 'Whether you like it or not, it dives deep into your soul and it gets its hooks in there and never lets go.' She smiled then. 'Lorna and Joe, they'd have both needed exorcising to get that kind of love out of them.'

Mack nodded, but in truth he felt more uneasy talking about love than he did talking about being neighbourly. He put his bowl down on the coffee table and steepled his fingers together. 'This morning, when I found him down on the edge of the dock... it looked like... I mean, I could be wrong but... it kinda seemed like he jumped.'

Madame Scarlet let out a gasp that Scooter reacted to. The dog's ears spiked and he turned, looking at Mack for confirmation that it was safe and he should curl up again and close his eyes. Mack put a hand on the dog's back and, content all was well, he rested again.

'Are you serious?' Madame Scarlet whispered, as if people might be listening.

'I dunno,' Mack admitted. 'But the more I thought about it and the more I looked at him sitting in that chair by the fire in the bar... He just seems so far away.'

'I see it too, honey,' Madame Scarlet said with a sigh. 'His whole life after the army was Lorna. They were two pieces of the same cake.' She dug her fork into the meal. 'I'm hoping with Harriet coming over she can help him get more involved with The Rum Coconut again. I mean, it's Christmas coming. You know how much Lorna loved Christmas.'

Harriet. Harri. He remembered that beautiful girl again then. Suddenly Mack was flung back in time and the cosy room and that heat from the wood-burner started to feel a little too much. Years had gone by. He shouldn't still get that gnawing in his belly when he thought about her. It had been his choice. But three years of correspondence had meant *everything*. All those letters and that one video call. Twenty-three minutes and seventeen seconds before the connection had been lost and she'd been frozen smiling on the screen of the laptop. And he'd never felt that way about anyone else since. He dug his fingers beneath Scooter's collar and held on.

'Ruby said she'd arrived when I called to check on Joe earlier. She's staying there too, which is good. She can keep a close eye on him then. I'll go over there in the morning.'

'Who is… I don't…' He couldn't even bring himself to say this woman's name, whoever she was. What was the matter with him? There was always going to be a time when he had to hear or say the name Harriet at some stage. OK, now even *thinking* the name was threatening to bring him out in goose bumps.

'Joe's granddaughter from England,' Madame Scarlet said like Mack was brainless.

'But I don't get it,' he said. 'Ruby said her name was Joanna.'

As the words left his mouth he didn't need Madame Scarlet to make any response before finally it all clicked together and his heart began to thunder in his ears.

Harri.

Joanna.

That very first piece of correspondence. The letter passed to him by Corporal Gonzales. He'd almost forgotten. Because there had been so many other letters after that, the ones that had really owned his heart. His fingers gripped Scooter's collar as the warmth of the room became oppressive. It was almost like flames licking his cheeks now and that thought began to bring back a whole different set of memories and images to the fore. It just *couldn't* be her. But the prickle of a cold sweat on the back of his neck was saying otherwise.

'Well,' Madame Scarlet said. 'In that family there's always been a bit of an issue with names. Ever since Joe Junior took off. Lorna never talked about the reason behind that, not even to me, and believe me I knew more about that woman than she knew about herself. But no amount of asking the spirits gave me the answers either.' She forked up a meatball. 'Anyway, her birth name is Harriet. But us folks here, we've always called her Joanna.'

God, this couldn't really be happening, could it? Mack's thoughts were spiralling like the menagerie of different coloured strands of tinsel wrapping around Madame Scarlet's tree. Was Harriet really *his* Harri? And was *his* Harri, Lorna and Joe's granddaughter?

His mouth was now drier than the sand on the nearby beach in the summer as he frantically recalled all the things they'd talked about in their letters. Yes, Harri had told him about Long Island and her holidays there, that *was* one of the reasons he was here. Her language in her letters had been poetic. She had described the place as 'somewhere you don't have to go looking for peace, somewhere where peace simply finds you'. But had it been this *very* spot she had been signposting all along? The *exact* town he was finally deciding to make his home?

'Mackenzie?' Madame Scarlet said quietly. 'Are you OK, honey?'

He wasn't OK. He was as far from it as he'd felt the first day after his surgery. He was terrified and thinking of all the things that could go wrong and whether there was still time to make a run for it. This was… surreal. And he still couldn't believe that Fate was ready to kick him around all over again.

'Yeah,' Mack answered in a rush, taking his hand from Scooter's collar and picking up his bowl of food. 'Yeah, I'm good.' Except he had now completely lost his appetite.

'Why don't you come over there in the morning with me? Meet her?' Madame Scarlet suggested. 'We could make a low-key suggestion that Joe might benefit from someone having a quiet talk to Dr Ambrose about more than a touch of frost bite.'

Mack was shaking his head before Madame Scarlet could even get to the end of the sentence. 'No, I... can't tomorrow. I've got... people... coming to the boat.'

'For what?' Madame Scarlet asked with a raise of those almost carnival pencilled-in eyebrows. 'Sightseeing? Honey, no one wants to see the sights by boat in the wintertime.'

He was shaking his head again. He needed to make it stop and keep his cool. 'No... they're friends... Lester's friends. Visiting. Just wanting a short tour.' What the hell was he saying? Making shit up never solved anything. He needed to get his game together.

'After that,' Madame Scarlet said, digging back into the Mack 'n' cheese, 'I've got some things I want to talk to her about concerning the funeral.'

Mack opened his mouth to say something – anything – that would make it clear he was likely not going to set foot in The Rum Coconut until this situation had been rolled around his mind a million more times, but he thought better of it. Instead he shovelled some food into his mouth and felt it go sour.

Ten

The Rum Coconut

It was early morning and Harriet hadn't slept at all. Iain, on the other hand, was still in bed, snoring and making noises like he was part walrus. She could feel she was exhausted as she sat curled up in the window seat of Nana Lorna's craft room, but her body was also pulsing with the enormity of what she had to do while she was here. Organise a funeral. Make sure Grandpa Joe was really OK. Find out if the bar was going to be able to survive without her grandma. She palmed her face, her skin dry and etched with salty paths where the tears had flowed the second she had got into the fresh flannelette sheets last night that smelled of a crisp new day thanks to the fragranced beads her nana had always added to the wash. Light lavender and fresh lemon. Lorna would have washed them with care and hung them out to dry so they billowed in the breeze, making shapes they'd tried to identify when Harriet was younger. And then Lorna would have collected them in to neatly iron – because wrinkled sheets were the mark of the

Devil – before folding them and popping them into the airing cupboard. Every detail of life had mattered to her nana. It had always been about the little things.

Looking out over the terraced area towards the water now, it certainly looked a better day than yesterday. The wind had died down and the sea seemed almost calm, but there was frost on the windshield of the Ford and a sheen of white on the grass that definitely said 'winter'. Harriet took a breath and looked back into the hobby room her nana had spent so much time in. It looked exactly how Harriet remembered it from her last trip back. The wallpaper was pink and floral – roses, lilies and daisies – and the furniture old and a deep walnut in colour. A rocking chair sat in one corner, three plump cushions resting in it and a plum-coloured crocheted blanket hanging from one arm. Harriet thought back to the times Nana Lorna had rocked in that very chair, some needlework in her hands – cross-stitch art or a repair on one of Grandpa's shirts. Harriet would always sit on the double bed, a sewing challenge of her own in her hands, marvelling at her gran's skills compared to her own as Nana Lorna gently rocked back and forth, sharing gossip or imparting life wisdom. Nana Lorna might not have been as present in her everyday as she could have been had she lived nearer, but with her other grandmother unknown to Harriet and her mum and dad being very hands off when it came to doling out affection, Nana Lorna had been the one who cuddled and coddled and soothed worries whenever they had spent time together. Harriet tuned into some of those scents her nana had worn on her skin – talcum powder, lipstick and wool. Evidence of each of those was scattered around the room. She had a second dressing table in here filled with tiny bottles and atomisers, a pot of powder with a big orange puff, plastic curlers and a heavy wooden hairbrush. And next to the dressing table was a craft area with boxes spilling samples of material, ribbons, beads and skeins of different shades and thicknesses of wool. This was a place still so full of life, bursting at the seams with all these signs of activity. It seemed so wrong that the integral part of this space, the person who had lit every corner, had been extinguished.

Harriet looked again at the photo album resting in her lap. It was one of those really old albums with the sticky pages and clear film that you had to pull back to insert printed pictures. She had always got this album down from its place on the shelf in the cupboard of this room whenever she came to visit. It never failed to make her smile as each photo represented a different era of the Cookson family. There were sepia-toned photos of Grandpa Joe in his US army uniform looking so smart and so young in formal pose, then others where he was hanging from a green utility vehicle in more relaxed combats with other soldiers. Faded pictures from Nana Lorna and Grandpa Joe's wedding, both of them with smiles as wide as the Atlantic Ocean, holding hands, feeding wedding cake to each other, waltzing around the dancefloor as a live band played. There were a few of Harriet's dad – Ralph holding up a fish he had caught on the beach, more gums than teeth, and another where he looked about ten doing a mean and moody expression to the camera astride a Chopper bicycle. And there were photos of Harriet too. She smiled as she grazed fingers over the familiar picture where her eyes were nearly popping out of her head the first time she had tried lobster. She was dressed in nothing but a nappy, Minnie Mouse sunglasses balanced on her head of bright blonde hair. She still *loved* lobster but it never tasted quite the same anywhere else. She'd get some here as soon as she got a minute.

Turning from her toddlerhood to a few more of her over the years – her first bikini when she'd finally got boobs, Nana Lorna showing her how to ice cupcakes, Grandpa Joe toasting marshmallows in a bonfire – she lifted the last page that spelled the end of this collection.

Except this time, unlike all the other times she had pored over the album, it wasn't the end. On the next page, under the sticky plastic was a letter and it was addressed to her... The sight of her nana's handwriting up-tipped her heart and she traced her fingers across the film, swirling over the letters in her name. Tears spilled again as her loss hit hard. How could this be the end? She had never got to hold her one last time or share another big dose of laughter over a baking disaster her grandpa had had a hand in. Wiping at her eyes, she started to read...

My dearest Joanna...

'Morning!'

Harriet almost jumped out of her skin at the sound of Iain's greeting and the photo album slipped off her lap and onto the floor. Quick as a flash, she was up from the window seat, picking it back up and popping it down on the cushion her bottom had just left.

'Morning,' Harriet answered, pulling at the sleeves of her sweatshirt and stepping towards the double bed. It was as pink as the rest of the room, covered in a heavy seersucker eiderdown. 'How did you sleep?'

'Terribly,' Iain answered with a yawn. He then began rolling his shoulders around like he might have spent the night on a rough boardwalk instead of this large soft-mattressed bed.

She didn't reply as she waited for him to stop manipulating his muscles and perhaps ask how *she* had slept.

'You're dressed already,' Iain remarked. 'What time is it?'

'It's still early,' Harriet told him. 'You can go back to sleep if you like. I'm going to make a cup of tea and check on Grandpa.'

'Harriet,' Iain said, as she made to leave the room.

She stopped by the bed, looking at Iain covered by the pink bedding. Maybe this was the moment he was going to take her in his arms and ask her how she was feeling about being back here. Perhaps want to hear some of her stories about Montauk and what her grandmother had been like. 'Yes?'

'You couldn't get my phone charger, could you? It's just in my rucksack over there.' And as Harriet's face fell at this request, Iain was already turning away and plucking his phone from the nightstand.

Eleven

'Rufus! You don't take what's not yours! How many times do I have to tell you?'

Harriet smiled at Ruby as she entered the bar and restaurant. A banquet of hot items – bacon, eggs of all kinds, hash browns, grits – were being set out under the heat lamps. And along from that was a basket of fresh fruit, mixed berries in an urn with a ladle, and pots of yoghurt. Two young dark-haired boys seemed to be alternating between helping Ruby set plates out and plucking items from the serving dishes and cramming them into their mouths.

'Good morning, Joanna,' Ruby said quickly, ushering the boys away from the food. 'I didn't think you would be awake this early.'

'Well,' Harriet said, stepping forward and watching the boys eye her with interest. 'I couldn't help but smell the bacon. Jet lag or no jet lag.' She grinned at the boys. 'Hello. I'm Joanna or… Harriet. I don't mind which.'

The boys simply continued to stare. They were identical

in their features and had to be twins. Each was wearing dark trousers and long-sleeved cotton shirts that were half tucked in and half not.

'Rufus. Riley. Where have your manners got to?'

'Good morning,' one of the boys parroted. The other boy raised a hand in acknowledgement.

'They're not mine,' Ruby started. 'I mean, they are mine. My brothers. But they're not here every day.' She wiped her hands on the front of the striped apron she was wearing over her clothes. 'My neighbour usually takes them to school but she's got someone staying with her right now so I came in early to get the breakfast ready before I go drop them. Lester'll be here soon and—'

'Ruby,' Harriet said, breaking into her monologue. 'Why don't you sit down and I'll pour you some coffee.' She could see the urns were there ready for action already. This is what her nana would always do. Get stuck in. Help someone else take a load off.

'I don't have time for coffee,' Ruby said, still arranging food items and moving things back and forth while the boys pinched and pushed each other. 'I gotta get this set up how Lorna likes it to be and if I don't make breakfast then Joe won't eat anything.'

'Ruby,' Harriet said, reaching out and putting a hand on Ruby's shoulder. 'Please, come and sit down with me for a second.' She looked to the two boys. 'Why don't you two take a plate each and have one of everything.'

'Joanna, there's no need. I…'

'Come on,' Harriet insisted, taking Ruby by the arm now and leading her to a table by the window. Rufus and Riley were now filling up plates with sausage and eggs in a state of excitement. But as Harriet poured two mugs of coffee they did appear to be adhering to the one item rule.

She joined Ruby, putting a mug down in front of her and sitting opposite. It was a little cold in the vast room with no fire lit and the central heating probably not yet kicking in but there was a weak sun appearing outside that would hopefully melt away the frost.

'I added milk. I hope that's OK. And I didn't know if you take sugar.'

Ruby shook her head. 'White and none is just fine.' She cupped her fingers around the mug and took a sip. 'I'm sorry. Things are kinda chaotic around here since…'

Ruby didn't end the sentence and there was no need to. Because there were those tears in Harriet's eyes again, welling up before she could check herself. She swallowed, blinking, and trying to get them to retreat. Nana Lorna had been the driving force in this place. Hospitality had always been her nana's dream. Being among people. Feeding them and making them smile. From the breakfast buffet, to the cocktails, to the themed dinners, Lorna had always made things run like clockwork. And she had done it all so effortlessly. Her nana had been one of those people who always moved from one task to the next in seamless organised symmetry.

'Ruby,' Harriet said softly. 'I don't fully understand the extent of your role here yet, but I know it shouldn't include *everything*. Especially now I'm here to help.'

Ruby shrugged. 'You are our guest.'

'No,' Harriet said firmly. 'I'm family.'

'I apologise. I didn't mean…' Ruby began.

'Don't apologise,' Harriet breathed. 'I didn't mean that

quite how it sounded.' She put a flat hand on the table, wanting to feel the solidity of the wood beneath her palm. 'I just meant… tell me how things are going. And tell me what to do. I want to help.'

Ruby shook her head, her dark curls bouncing across her forehead. 'I'm… a little bit scared.' Harriet could see there were tears brewing up in the woman's eyes too now. This wasn't the brave and ballsy individual her grandma had described in their telephone calls. This was someone with real worries.

'What are you scared of?' Harriet asked in gentle tones.

'I should not be telling you this because you're grieving… and Lorna passing away like that is bigger than anything but…'

'But?'

'I *really* need this job,' Ruby blubbed. 'I'm on my own with Rufus and Riley and if I don't work here I'll have to go back to working at the casino and that ain't the most civilised of hours with two kids who don't know where their off switch is.'

'Ruby,' Harriet said, taking the woman's hand in hers. 'Goodness, whatever made you think that your job was in danger?'

'Well, I dunno.' She sniffed and wiped her eyes with the back of her hand. 'I guess I was thinking Joe isn't gonna run this place like Lorna did and, with you coming here from the UK, I thought you might be here to say your pa was gonna sell the place.'

Harriet's heart contracted at Ruby's words and her eyes did a sweep of the tiki bar and all its eclectic paraphernalia. Sell it? *Never*, was her first reaction. This was history, a whole life's work – two sweethearts intertwined in a beautiful, enduring marriage with a business to match – it wasn't something to be put on the market and sold to the highest bidder who wanted to make a quick profit. And then that thought jarred her mind as she tried desperately not to make the connection to the whole basis of her and Iain's business. Taking homes and turning them back into a neutral palette…

'Ruby, I *love* this place,' Harriet told her. 'I would never let that happen.'

Ruby shrugged. 'I'd understand, you know, if you had to do that. But I'm just asking for as long a head's up as you can give me, is all.'

'Ruby,' Harriet began again, curling her fingers around her mug of coffee. 'Right now, I really need you. *Really* need you. This may be one of my favourite places in the whole wide world, but I get the feeling you know so much more about the running of it than I do. Tell me, are we going to get people in here for breakfast today? Or is this buffet a little hopeful?'

Ruby sat up a little straighter in her chair, jutting her chin out and transforming back into that dynamo who could ass-kick the world. 'We have five bookings this morning and there's always half-a-dozen walk-ins… *at least.*'

Harriet nodded at her enthusiasm. But she couldn't help thinking that perhaps the bar and restaurant did need to be invigorated somehow. When she had got over the awfulness of having to contact a funeral director, she would throw herself into The Rum Coconut, maybe not quite stepping into her nana's shoes exactly, but perhaps continuing

CHRISTMAS BY THE COAST

her legacy in some way. At least for the time she was in Montauk.

'Ruby, this is a horrible question, I know, but... do you know the best person to contact to... arrange my nana's funeral? I could look up funeral directors on the internet but...'

Ruby's hands went straight to her face then, her cheeks flushing with colour. 'Oh my Jesus.'

'What is it?' Harriet asked, all sounds from Rufus and Riley hungrily devouring breakfast silenced.

'The funeral,' Ruby said, lips wobbling a little over the words. 'Everything... it's been arranged. Joe said that Lorna would want it done quickly so it didn't... get in the way of Christmas. So, Joe and Madame Scarlet and me, well not much of me really, just for the food... well we made the plans and... it's tomorrow.'

Harriet felt her heart thud to the bottom of her boots. She should have been here even sooner. She had envisaged helping to select some songs, maybe do a short reading of her own. And what was her nana going to be buried in? Had someone chosen that too? When Harriet thought about her now, she saw her resting in her cream A-line dress with the palm tree print and perhaps her favourite shawl with the parrot decal. She swallowed the disappointment down. At least her grandpa had had Madame Scarlet and Ruby by his side in this. She nodded at Ruby, not letting her feelings show. 'OK.'

'I thought Joe would've told you,' Ruby began. 'If I'd have known, that you didn't know, I would have said something sooner.'

Harriet shook her head. 'It's OK. Thank you, Ruby. Thank you for being here for my grandpa.'

Just then the main door opened and Meryl Cheep announced an arrival.

'Scarlet lady! Scarlet lady!'

Harriet smiled as she took in her nana's lifelong friend, the incomparable Madame Scarlet, dressed head-to-toe in red, as always, not looking a day over whatever her latest bio on her website said. Today's hair arrangement was Medusa meets Daenerys from *Game of Thrones*.

'Well, who do we have here looking even more beautiful than I remember?' Madame Scarlet announced, spreading her arms out wide. 'Come here, honey! Let me hug you hard!'

Harriet stood up and didn't need a second invitation to rush into the woman's embrace.

Twelve

The Warrior, Fort Pond

'You know this is a piece of junk, right?'

Mack had a wrench in one hand and the inner workings of Lester's old bicycle in the other as they sat on the deck of his boat – *The Warrior*. Apart from the meal he'd bought at The Rum Coconut – steak and eggs – *The Warrior* had been his first purchase here in Montauk. It had been worn around the edges, in need of a thorough overhaul, but something about its rusty exterior and fraying insides had struck a chord with him. The boat had needed a new start, just like him. Mack was on the floor now, investigating the repair needs while Lester was sitting on an actual seat. Thankfully the weather was a whole lot better today. It was still cold, but that biting wind that had whipped up the water yesterday had gone. It had been replaced by frost, a mainly blue sky and the sun trying its best to heat up the early morning. Scooter was chasing a rag that Lester was trailing along the deck to amuse him.

'What can I say?' Lester replied with a shrug.

'You can say that you'll invest in a new one so I'm not doing this every couple weeks.'

'I do not have the money. And what would *you* do?' Lester asked, Scooter catching the material between his teeth and growling. 'You would forget how to fix things. You would become bored in the wintertime with no tourists to take on a tour.'

His stomach knotted together then. *Harri*. He had spent all night churning over the fact that she was here. *Might be* here. It still wasn't a given. How could it be? Yeah, Madame Scarlet had kinda connected dots but… really? Was this *really* happening? He wouldn't be able to believe it until he'd seen it with his own eyes. Seen *her* somewhere other than his memories. Except the thought of seeing Harri *in person*… even now the idea of it was drying his mouth. How many times had he wished for exactly that? How many months had he thought about what it would be like to see her smile and hear her laugh right in front of him. He'd had to lie to Madame Scarlet just to get out of going to The Rum Coconut today, but he couldn't avoid it forever. Tomorrow was Lorna's funeral and he wanted to pay his respects to the woman who had mothered him a little ever since he arrived here…

'Listen, Lester, I need a solid,' Mack breathed, oil on his fingers as he attempted to loosen a part that was obviously jammed.

'Oh no!' Lester said immediately. 'The very last time you said that I had to dress up as a fish.'

Mack couldn't stop the smirk forming on his lips. He'd paid Lester to get into a giant shark outfit to boost business for his fishing trips. And despite this comment now, he knew

Lester had loved it. They had cleaned up big over those weeks last season and he had given Lester more dollars than they'd shaken the deal on. But life didn't come cheap.

'This doesn't involve dress-up,' Mack said.

'Oh.' There was a definite note of disappointment in Lester's reply.

Now, how did Mack word this? Quickly, he decided. Without too much thinking about it. 'If anyone asks, today, could you tell them you have friends staying with you and I'm taking them out on the boat?'

There. Easy. No costumes involved. His lie to Madame Scarlet covered. He focused his eyes on the oil-covered metal in his hands, hoping Lester would just agree.

'Who is gonna be asking me that?'

Apparently he wanted details. Mack shifted his body forward towards the bicycle frame and his leg sent out a pulse of pain. This fucking spare was not all that. He'd phoned Dr Jerome earlier and the doctor hadn't laughed, he'd sucked through his teeth in disbelief. He'd also told Mack that he'd never had any patient go through so many prosthetic legs in such short a time. It was unlikely he was going to be able to get a new one before Christmas.

Mack shrugged. 'I dunno. But, you know, if anyone does.'

'If anyone does,' Lester began, taking the rag from Scooter's mouth and starting their play-fight anew. 'And if I tell them I have friends staying with me, they will laugh and they will not believe it.' He shook his head. 'Mr Mack, I live in a caravan with one bedroom and a broken shower.'

'Your shower's broken?' Mack queried, finally looking up. 'Why didn't you ask me to take a look?'

Lester shrugged. 'Because my bicycle is more important.

It gets me to work.' He checked his watch. 'And that is where I should be.'

'Listen,' Mack said. 'Leave the bike with me. I'll fix it. You can get it later.'

'Really?'

'Sure,' Mack answered. 'And then I'll come round and fix up your shower. No arguments.'

Lester beamed. 'Thank you, Mr Mack. I will do my best to lie for you.'

Mack didn't answer and Lester was already sprinting up the dock towards the road that led to Fort Pond Bay and The Rum Coconut. But halfway up the pontoon, Lester slowed, waving a greeting, before running off again. And then Mack's eyes homed in on the people Lester had said 'hi' to. Two people. One of them in a long green coat, both heading his way. Suddenly he felt breathless, but he knew he had to act and quickly. Using the edge of the seat to drag himself up from the floor, he grabbed Scooter by the collar and rushed him into the cabin, heading down the steps to below decks.

It was Madame Scarlet. Without a doubt. But was it Harri too? He closed his eyes. He shouldn't keep saying her name, even in his head. It was torture mixed with fear and speckled with something like hope. He held his breath, feeling like an intruder in his own cabin home as he ducked down on his sofa seat, just able to see enough of the dock above the small window. His heart rate gathered pace again as he heard voices. Scooter whined, jumping up next to him and panting because this was unusual behaviour. He petted his dog on the head and listened hard, trying to make out the conversation…

Harriet took a deep breath, inhaling the freezing cold air and the stillness. The years were rolling back as she gazed over the water and took in the little piece of Montauk that felt like home. There were the waterside restaurants, a smattering of boats still in the water and there were the places that really hit her heart. Skeet's Surf Shack, the fishing tackle shed and Madame Scarlet's Emporium. The surfboard and shark head outside the shack were a little weathered, the chain on the tackle shop sign was even more rusted and perhaps Madame Scarlet's snug hut could do with its red exterior brightening up a bit, but everything was familiar. There were no massive rebrands here.

'It hasn't changed,' Harriet said.

Madame Scarlet let out a hearty laugh. 'You think things change in three years, honey? I'm telling you not much has changed here in my lifetime.'

'That's good though, isn't it?' Harriet said, as much to herself as to her companion.

'Are you asking me?' Madame Scarlet said. 'Or telling me?'

Harriet sighed. 'It feels good to be here.' It was the truth. Montauk was wrapping its arms around her like it always did when she returned, but the biggest piece of that community, the Nana-shaped part, was missing. 'But... I feel guilty for feeling that way.'

Madame Scarlet put an arm around her shoulders as they continued their stroll down the dock. 'I know,' she breathed. 'I hear you, honey. Things feel, I don't know, off balance a little.' Madame Scarlet sighed. 'That's what Lorna did around here for most people. She evened us all out.'

That was a really accurate description of the pint-sized

force to be reckoned with who got things done with words of kindness as well as a kick up the rear end if you needed it.

'But Lorna would be so glad you're here. And she wouldn't want you getting maudlin about it.'

'It's hard not to,' Harriet admitted, tucking her hair into the bottom of her hat. 'I should have been here more. I should have phoned more often. I shouldn't have let—'

'—Life get in the way? Oh, honey, we all get a case of the "what ifs" every now and then. There's absolutely nothing to be gained from going over what we coulda or shoulda done. You're here now, for Joe, that's what's most important.'

Madame Scarlet drew them to a halt then, her eyes going to one of the boats moored in the water. It was white with a dark blue trim, a nice deck area with seating around and the captain's section behind the wheel was enclosed. From the portholes above the waterline it looked like there was a whole cabin downstairs.

'Hmm,' Madame Scarlet mused. 'That's funny.'

'What is it?'

'I was hoping to introduce you to someone.'

'Oh?'

'He's been here a couple years now. Been real good to your nana and grandpa. In fact, he was the one who pulled Joe outta the water yesterday.'

'Goodness, I really need to thank him for that. Who knows what might have happened if he hadn't been there.' It really didn't bear thinking about. Her poor fragile grandpa who had only just managed to cut a piece of toast in half at breakfast.

Madame Scarlet moved closer to the boat, squinting her eyes and trying to peer inside.

Mack held his breath and clamped a solid, hopefully calming hand over Scooter's jaw as they both cowered on the sofa like criminals hiding from an impending police raid. He was shaking. From the bottom of his good foot, through his residual limb, something was spiking his gut and zooming into his heart. It was her. *Harri*. He'd know her voice anywhere, despite only having heard it that one time. And anywhere was here. Right outside his boat. His home. Turning his head slightly, he looked to the porthole, part of him wanting to see, the other half of him terrified to look. Brown winter boots led up to black jeans and a green coat. He couldn't see anything else. And suddenly he *needed* to see her face like his whole life depended on it. He shifted Scooter a little, bending his body, getting his face as close to the small circle of glass as he possibly could without being discovered. Because, for some reason, he still didn't want to be seen. He wet his lips, twisting his neck into positions not even a circus performer could hold. He remembered her hair was just longer than her shoulders, the colour of sunshine…

'I guess he's really not in.'

And just like that the boots and the jeans and the green coat disappeared from Mack's view. *Please speak. Please say something more so I can hear your voice again.* He closed his eyes as Scooter began to nuzzle his hand, face warm, teeth teasing the skin a little.

'Is he coming to my nana's funeral?' came the question from the outside. 'I can thank him then.'

Mack screwed his eyes up tight and let the memories flood all over him.

Thirteen

The Rum Coconut

My dearest Joanna,

I've always thought that letters are the most personal form of communication. Words written down have been carefully considered and thought about before they're committed to ink and paper. But once they are committed there's no pressing buttons on a computer to erase them. There they are and the writer's only choice is to send the letter or not. I'm not going to send these letters to you, Joanna. Not because I don't want you to read them, but because I want you to read them at the right time. And, if you're reading this first letter now then it must be that right time.

So, what is it I want to share with you? Well, my sweet girl, let me start by telling you all about a Montauk Christmas...

'Well, this is nice, isn't it?'

Harriet took a deep breath and held it in response

to Iain's remark. She knew conversation with her grandpa was more trying to get any words out at all, than it was naturally flowing property talk over a nice bottle of chenin blanc, but to say it was 'nice' felt even more awkward and inappropriate. And, as well as not talking, Joe wasn't eating any of the evening meal either. He was dressed in baggy denim overalls over a grey T-shirt that had seen better days.

It was almost seven p.m. and Harriet had suggested this dinner together after she had read the first note from her nana stuck in the photo album. It had pulled her heart all over again, slipping the notepaper out from under the film in the album and holding it in her shaking hands. She had imagined her nana sitting at her sewing table perhaps, or even on the swing seat on the porch, proper ink pen clasped between her thumb and finger, deep in thought. Now Harriet's eyes couldn't stop looking at those bare pine trees each side of the fireplace…

'The pork's cold,' Joe said, putting his fork down with a clang.

'It's lovely though,' Harriet said. 'Shall I get Ruby to warm it up for you?' She put her fingers on the rim of the plate, but Joe edged it away from her quickly.

'It's not the same as Lorna makes.'

'We could go somewhere else for dinner,' Iain suggested. 'I did a bit of research earlier. Had a look at the locale. There are some wonderful looking restaurants in Southampton.'

Iain still hadn't seemed to realise that this wasn't a holiday but a trip to bury a family member and make sure Joe was going to be able to function without his beloved wife. Earlier, Iain had suggested going to look at property here like they might be open for researching investments.

Harriet knew she was usually the one working twenty-four-seven, but with the funeral the next day she couldn't focus her mind anywhere else.

'You go out if you want to,' Joe said, sitting back in his chair and folding his arms across his chest.

'No,' Harriet said straightaway. 'I'm really enjoying what Ruby's made and I want to spend some time with you. That's what we came here for.' She couldn't help but give Iain a sideways glance.

'What if I don't want company?' Joe said gruffly.

'Well, I...' Harriet knew her grandfather could be a little on the brusque side when he felt like it, but he'd never really turned down the opportunity to spend time with her. Seeing him like this was so hard. She just wanted to magically have her nana back with them. Instead she was holding her grief in and trying to keep things normal. But things weren't normal. Perhaps pretending they could be was a mistake.

'Do you want Harriet and I to leave you alone for a bit?' Iain suggested.

Harriet held her breath. She might have told Iain he could call her whatever name he wanted, but her grandpa *never* called her Harriet and, for some reason, he didn't like it one bit.

'Joanna,' Joe barked. 'Her name is Joanna.'

Joe looked agitated now, was picking at a thread on the dungarees. Harriet turned in her seat a little and faced Iain. 'Do you want to go for a run or a walk or something? Or, if you want to see Southampton, I'm sure Grandpa will lend you the truck.'

'I don't want to go out,' Iain whispered. 'I want to spend some time with you. Being here for you.'

'Iain,' Harriet said softly. 'It's my nana's funeral tomorrow. It's not the time to… drink fine wine at a fancy restaurant, no matter how lovely the idea might sound.' She was trying to let him down gently, but the truth was it didn't sound like a lovely idea given the circumstances. She was super-tired, her eyes were burning with all the crying she'd done and she just wanted to get her grandpa through the evening, into bed and ensure he was as relaxed as he could be before the following day. She also wanted to speak to her dad. Although she knew there was no chance of him making the funeral tomorrow, she wondered whether now might be exactly the right time to find out what this family rift was all about and end it once and for all.

'Is he OK?' Iain asked as Joe got up from the table and shuffled towards the bar area.

Harriet took a breath. 'His wife has died. The person he loved most in the whole world. The ground has been taken from under him and he doesn't know what to do.' If that didn't explain it to Iain she wasn't sure what would. She watched her grandpa moving so forlornly, like all purpose had left him. Yes, her nana had always been the bright, loud, sorter-outer of the partnership, but Joe had always been the strong backbone who perhaps didn't talk as much as Nana Lorna, but definitely dropped in the words that needed to be said at the right time.

'Do you think you should…'

'What?'

'I don't know… maybe get him to see a doctor?'

Harriet bristled. He still didn't seem to get it. 'Dr Ambrose saw him this morning. He said he was doing surprisingly well after his fall into the sea.'

'What?!' Iain said. 'He fell into the sea?'

She'd forgotten she hadn't told Iain that. She swallowed, suddenly feeling guilty that she'd held it back from him. And why had she? Maybe because she knew somehow he would judge. 'The doctor said he was fine.'

'But why did he fall in the sea?' Iain asked, a little too loudly for Harriet's liking. 'Is he unsteady on his feet? Has he got a condition no one knows about?'

'Iain, stop,' Harriet begged. 'Please, we've only just got here. My nana is being buried tomorrow. I just need some time to get my head around everything.' Her head was actually starting to hurt now. She knew it was mainly jet lag and the fact she hadn't slept at all last night, but everything Iain was saying was grating an already fractious nerve.

'I'm only trying to help,' Iain answered.

'I know,' Harriet said, sighing. She was being mean. He had travelled across the Atlantic to be here as a support to her and she was shutting him down any chance she got. 'I'm sorry. It's just—'

'I get it,' Iain interrupted, sounding slightly bruised. 'It must be hard, someone dying, coming back here, being called by an entirely different name. I tell you what, I'll leave you to it. I'll catch up on some work.' He pushed his chair back and stood up.

He was getting bolshy now and Harriet didn't know whether to stop him or let him go. 'Iain, I didn't mean—'

'It's fine,' he responded, a little less brusque. 'I should probably check in with Mickey anyway.'

Harriet nodded. 'OK.' She would patch it up with him later when her grandpa was asleep and she had one less thing on her mind. Her focus was already back on her grandpa as Iain left. Thanks to the words in her nana's letter, she knew exactly what she had to do.

Fourteen

'Pass me the pink baubles,' Harriet said, stretching out a hand. Her tongue was sticking out of her mouth now as she concentrated on the task in hand. She was kneeling by the fire with her grandpa supervising from a chair, trying to decorate the two fir trees in as many festive ornaments as she could. Her mum and dad had never been big into the whole Christmas thing. They'd had a fake tree they got down from the loft every year and Harriet always had to decorate it, but that was the extent of the efforts – no festive baking or strings of cards around the room, definitely nothing attached to any of the windows that might tell the street they were celebrating a holiday. And Harriet had never been able to imagine what the tiki bar would look like at this time of year. To her it had always been a summer sunshine destination, her nana adorning every person she welcomed through the doors with colourful leis, the warm breeze filling the space, with the bi-fold doors open to the ocean. In her mind it was always surfers and fisherman, reggae and coconuts.

'Not the pink yet,' Joe growled.

'Why not?' Harriet said, pausing.

'Lorna always liked the pink on last.'

Harriet turned away from Joe so he didn't see the wide smile that had arrived on her lips. She *knew* her nana would have wanted the pink on last. It had been a small test that Joe had passed with flying colours. And the pink baubles going on after everything else was one of the things Harriet had learned from the first letter she had read in the photo album.

'So,' Harriet said softly, picking a piece of red tinsel from the stash of decorations. 'Are you... ready for tomorrow?' The words had caught in her throat. Was anyone ever really ready for saying goodbye to a loved one?

'Tomorrow? What's happening tomorrow?' Joe responded.

Harriet's heart sank further. So much for thinking that her grandpa was fully *compos mentis*. Surely he couldn't have forgotten the funeral? But blocking things out was what this family seemed to do when a crisis hit. Like with whatever happened here in Montauk with her dad. Better to pretend and make things as Disney as possible than address the root of something. Except that ordinarily wasn't how her nana operated. She was a truth-seeker through and through, a resolver of problems. It seemed at odds to think she had been estranged from her only son without trying to ever make peace.

'Grandpa, we're... saying goodbye to Nana tomorrow.'

Harriet watched his lips turn into a hard, thin line and he turned his face away from her.

'I don't wanna talk about that,' he muttered. 'I thought you were gonna tell me about something nice.'

'Well,' Harriet started. 'As hard as it's going to be, I was thinking that we could *turn* it into something nice.' She shook the band of tinsel towards him. 'That's why we're doing these trees now. Because…' She took a breath, hoping her grandpa was going to re-engage with her if she paused long enough. 'Because…'

Finally he turned his head a little and so she blustered on. 'I thought we could have the Christmas tree trimming competition the day after tomorrow.' She didn't wait for her grandpa to say or do anything because she had already decided it *had* to happen. The competition was apparently an event her nana had run here at The Rum Coconut and Harriet knew finding these letters right now was serendipity. It was going to gift her the memories of all those Montauk Christmases she had missed out on. And perhaps give a little part of her nana back to her.

And her grandpa still hadn't said anything.

'We can tell everyone about it at the wake and they can come along and have fun remembering Nana,' Harriet told him, brightly.

Joe blew out a breath. 'I dunno.'

'That's OK,' Harriet said, putting down the tinsel and reaching for his hand. 'Because I *do* know. Nana wouldn't have wanted things to be any different around here. She's probably up there right now, looking at these trees and getting cross because we haven't done them quite right.'

Joe cracked a smile then and a wheezy laugh came from his chest and met the air. 'They call her Mrs Claus around here.'

'Really?' Harriet said, shifting on her knees to get a bit

closer to him. 'Tell me. Because I want to get this place as close to how she would have wanted it.'

'She makes a special cheesecake,' Joe began, wetting his lips and sitting forward in the chair.

'Really? For the tree trimming contest?'

Joe shook his head. 'No. The cheesecake is for the winner of the Christmas cocktail making competition.'

'Goodness.' It seemed there was much to learn.

'That's three cheesecakes in all,' Joe continued, becoming as animated as she had seen him since she'd arrived. 'One on top of the other, using columns and making tiers like a wedding cake.'

'Do you know the recipe?' Harriet asked. She hoped so.

He shook his head. 'No.'

'Oh.'

'But maybe Ruby knows,' Joe suggested.

'I will ask her.'

Joe squeezed her hand tight and a different expression came over his face now. It was pain and sadness. It was someone reaching out for comfort. 'They said it was quick,' he whispered. 'They said she knew nothing about it. That she went to sleep and the heart attack just took her.'

There were tears in her grandpa's eyes now and Harriet had a feeling that he had been holding these in until this very moment. 'It's OK,' she whispered, her own eyes brimming as she looked at him. 'I'm here now, Grandpa. And, I promise, everything's going to be alright.'

'Oh, Joanna,' Joe said as tears began to dampen his cheeks. 'What am I going to do without her?'

Before Harriet could even think about replying or putting

her arms around her grandfather, there was a squawking and some fluttering and Meryl Cheep landed on Joe's shoulder. The bird bobbed its head and padded about on its new landing strip.

'Jo-seph! Jo-seph!'

'What are you doing out here, you crazy old bird,' Joe said, putting his hand out to take the bird down. The parrot duly complied, stepping onto the man's gnarled fingers and pressing its beak to his skin.

'Maybe she sensed you needed her,' Harriet suggested, raising her hand and petting the parrot on the head.

'Joanna! Joanna!'

Joe smiled. 'She remembers you.'

'I know,' Harriet said. 'Parrots have impeccable memories. I looked it up once when Nana said Meryl recognised the son of the log delivery man who had only been here twice before.' She stroked under Meryl's chin. 'You're such a clever lady.'

'And you're a good girl, Joanna,' Joe said. 'You've always been a good girl.'

Harriet rested her head on her grandpa's knee and closed her eyes. All she wanted was to ease his grief but with the brightest personality ripped from their midst, she wasn't sure exactly how easy that was going to be.

Fifteen

Madame Scarlet's Emporium, Fort Pond

'Lester, honey, stand up straight and let's get that shirt tucked in.'

Mack was standing in front of a full-length mirror, behind the curtain in Madame Scarlet's fortune-reading premises while Lester got dressed on the other side, apparently with the spiritualist's help. If he moved at all Mack was in danger of clashing elbows with numerous candles, joss sticks and maps of the chakras. There was also a large box of Christmas decorations on one shelf that looked ripe for the toppling. He was glad he'd left Scooter at *The Warrior* until after the church service. His dog would have been nose-deep in every cardboard offering, given the opportunity.

As Lester let out a string of moans and gripes Mack took a deep breath and regarded himself in the army dress uniform he hadn't worn for years. He was wearing it today for a few reasons. Firstly, he didn't own another suit of any description and jeans and a sweater weren't really the mark of respect. And secondly, it was a funeral. It was not only a chance to say goodbye to Lorna, he would also take a minute to remember everyone else who had passed. His friends. Every soldier who had served. *All* the fallen. Including the one person he could never shake from his mind. The one who had saved him. He swallowed. He was a portion of one leg down but, the truth was, he shouldn't even be here at all. He closed his eyes and right away his mind flew back there without permission. Snapping his eyes back open, his hands started to shake. He took one in the other and held on tight until the feeling diminished and Madame Scarlet and Lester's bickering became the only thing he could hear again.

Putting his hand to his tie he straightened it a little before his eyes found the Distinguished Service Cross pinned to his chest. Fingers moving over the ribbon they stilled on the gold cross and eagle that hung below. He might own it but in his mind it had never been his. He didn't believe he was deserving. And, apart from his disability, that was what he had a hard time living with the most. But, he had accepted this medal out of respect for everyone who was no longer here. Because *they* were the brave ones, the servicemen who had paid with their lives. He was simply who was left from what had always been, and would forever continue to be, a team effort to serve the United States of America.

He brought his hand down and his elbow snagged the ornaments, knocking the contents to the ground and all over his feet.

'Mack, honey. Are you OK in there?' Madame Scarlet called.

'Yes, ma'am,' he answered quickly, bending to pick the tinsel, baubles and half-a-dozen nutcracker figurines off the carpet. The last thing he wanted was Madame Scarlet to part the curtain and start messing with him like she was messing with Lester. Besides, this suit had been sitting in plastic wrap in his wardrobe since the last time he had put it on. Dry-cleaned and crinkle-free. Picking up the last escaped decorations, Mack returned the box to the shelf, then pulled down one of the sleeves of his jacket and made sure he was happy with the look. As his hands went to the curls on his head he realised his fingers were still shaking. No matter what he did, no matter how many times he told himself not to think about Harri, she was there, deeply rooted in his thoughts. What was he going to do? Could he still go to the funeral and maybe avoid seeing her? He wet his lips, toying with one of the gold buttons on his suit. Except Lorna was her grandmother. The Montauk community were grieving the loss of someone who had been the beating heart of their daily lives, but how must *Harri* be feeling? He could feel his own heart almost trying to work out how to behave. This was *Harri*. The girl he had thought about every day since the end of 2012. But somehow he was going to have to try to put that aside. Except he had thought about her *so* many times, the idea that it was about to happen was as confronting as it was the stuff of dreams. How did you dumb down feelings like that? What were you supposed to do when all your senses were popping at you like enemy gunfire?

'Mack, honey, are you *sure* you're OK in there?' Madame Scarlet called again. 'Only inhale the bergamot and chamomile. Anything else in those boxes isn't appropriate for today's sentiment.'

He needed to get over himself. He wasn't the same

person as he was back then. So many years had gone by and every one of them had left their mark. Perhaps all this panic and reverie was for nothing. Maybe Harri wouldn't even remember him. And that thought internally floored him.

He swiped back the curtain and a laugh got caught in his throat. Lester was dressed in a plain black suit, but his tie was the keyboard of a piano. It was the reality check that he needed but he didn't want to come off as rude.

'Why is Mr Mack laughing?' Lester asked, wide eyes going to Madame Scarlet for an answer.

'I have no idea,' Madame Scarlet replied, stepping forward into Mack's space. She had a can of hair spray in one hand, which Mack hoped wasn't going to find its way anywhere near him. She gave Mack one of her special looks he knew was reserved for customers who needed more than a small dose of convincing about her spiritual powers. Then she stage-whispered. 'It was the only tie I had.'

'Do I look like a piano player?' Lester asked, lifting the tie up and looking at it with such intent it was possible he was counting each note. 'Argh! Is that a spider?!'

'No, honey, that's a hair net,' Madame Scarlet reassured. 'You both look so smart.' She patted Mack's arm. 'Lorna would be very proud to see you dressed up like this.'

Mack checked his watch. They had an hour before the service and his stomach reminded him that no matter what he was trying to convince himself of, today was not going to be easy in any way.

Sixteen

Montauk Community Church

It had felt surreal seeing the Christmas decorations in the windows of houses and on front lawns on the route to the church, following the car that contained the coffin of her grandmother. Reindeers and quirky-looking penguins lit up rooftops, Christmas trees twinkled behind windows of diners and coffee shops advertising wintry specials to warm the body as well as the soul. But, after the first few tears had left her eyes, Harriet started to see the festivities as a sign that it was so important they should celebrate everything that Lorna had meant to everyone closest to her. She had decided she was going to find a quiet moment alone to read another of her grandma's letters later. But, here, now, standing outside the beautiful little church with its stone façade resemblant of a small castle battlement, there were vehicles packed into the car park and flakes of snow floating in the air.

'Are you OK?'

Harriet knew she was shivering but she moved away a

little as Iain tried to put his arm around her. 'I'm OK.' She gave him a small smile and hoped it was enough because it was literally all she had. 'But... I need to make sure Grandpa's alright.' She took a few steps forward then, moving closer to the hearse.

Despite Joe being meant to travel in the same car as her and Iain, instead, at the last moment he had demanded to travel with Lorna. One of the pallbearers was ousted from the vehicle so Joe could take his place and Harriet had watched her grandpa turn in the seat slightly, spreading his fingers out over the top of the white wooden coffin decorated with arrangements of seasonal floral tributes. Joe hadn't let go until the hearse had parked up here.

She smiled at her grandpa as she approached. Ruby was next to him now, straightening his collar and trying to run a comb through his sparse grey hair, much to Joe's disgust. He'd wanted to wear his army dress suit today but when Harriet had got him to try it on late last night it was obvious it was way too big on a frame that had withered with age. This alternative suit was light grey in colour and Harriet had picked him out a tie she knew her nana had always liked. She remembered it from one of The Rum Coconut's infamous summer jamborees. The bar and restaurant had always come to life for the fourth of July, with live music including a steel band and Tahitian dancers, and Nana Lorna had firmly insisted everyone wore their very best clothes – or sometimes even fancy dress. This cream tie with delicate pink roses was something her very masculine grandfather would never usually have donned, but on special occasions and when he knew agreeing would make his wife happy, he would put it on with a smile.

'There,' Ruby said, taking a step back. 'You look great.'

'Why are there so many people here?' Joe asked, eyes scanning the groups loitering in the parking lot.

'Grandpa, Nana had so many friends, you know that,' Harriet reminded him.

'But the church is small,' Joe fussed. 'There won't be any seats.'

'Let's let the pastor worry about that,' Harriet said, putting her arm through his. She looked to Ruby. 'Will you sit with us?'

'Oh, I don't know if—'

'Please? And Lester too.' Harriet swallowed. She was desperately trying to make up for the fact that the first designated 'family' row was going to be without her dad. She'd spoken about that with Madame Scarlet yesterday, thinking she needed to say something about her dad's absence but before she could make any excuses, Madame Scarlet had just waved a hand and said 'why change the habit of a lifetime' and then quickly moved the conversation on to another topic. Harriet was starting to wonder if her nana's closest friend knew more about the falling out than she had ever let on.

'Would you like me to do anything?' Iain asked.

He was beside her again and it was at that moment she suddenly felt so alone and the weight of the loss was hanging so heavily it was too much to bear. Everything hit Harriet full force. She was standing in the car park of the local church, about to go to her nana's funeral service and she was the only other relative there. There were no siblings on Nana Lorna's side and Grandpa Joe's two brothers had died some years ago. What must everyone think of them as a family? How could this woman who was so cherished by all her friends be without her only son on this day? And there was her grandpa, at a complete loss and looking so depleted.

'Iain... I... don't feel very well,' Harriet breathed, her legs wobbling a little, her arm falling from Joe's.

'OK,' Iain said, his tone telling everyone around that he was taking ownership of the situation. 'Let's get you inside.' He put a hand to her elbow.

However, as weak as she felt, she couldn't crumble in this situation. No, it was up to her to be strong for Grandpa Joe. That was the whole reason she was here. And that's what her nana would be expecting...

'Just... give me a minute,' Harriet said, firming up her stance and stopping Iain from propelling her forward like she was a paparazzi-chased star seeking shelter.

'Joanna?' Joe said, looking confused.

'Do you want a breath mint?' Ruby asked, quickly getting a packet out of the pocket of her coat and holding it towards her. 'Rufus knocked them onto the floor of my car, but I think they're good.'

Harriet's gaze went to the door of the church again. People were still filing into the building in their dozens. There was Maggie from the florist's her nana loved to get sprays of lilies from to decorate The Rum Coconut. Howard, the local mechanic, who had seen almost as much of Joe's Ford on Harriet's visits as she had. More faces she recognised but didn't know the names of – patrons of the bar who had seen Lorna far more frequently than *she* had. In some ways, this loss was more Montauk's than it was hers. She found herself reaching for one of Ruby's sweets and popping it in her mouth.

'OK?' Iain asked, looking a little like he would be embarrassed if she wasn't.

The mint was quite hot and Harriet began to wish she hadn't accepted it. As she moved it around in her mouth she was about to nod an agreement to Iain's question until Madame Scarlet caught her eye. Just coming up to the door of the chapel, a vision in one of her quintessential red outfits – no mourning black for her – and a hair-do that was swept over one side of her face. Lester was beside her and... someone else. Suddenly the mint felt like it was clogging her throat and she couldn't catch air. *The khaki. The hair that was shaved at the sides with curls on top.* Her heart was pounding as she desperately tried to make any kind of sense of what she was seeing. She could almost hear Jude's voice in her ear whispering. *Soldier Boy.* Harriet closed her eyes and opened them again. It couldn't be...

'Joanna,' Joe said, taking a grip on her arm and shifting in front of Iain. 'It's OK. I can look after you.'

She turned back to her grandpa and quickly regrouped. This jet lag really was knocking her for six. She was exhausted, her mind was a mess, and here her grieving grandpa was saying he was going to prop *her* emotions up. Giving him a smile, she clasped his hand and steeled herself for the service to come.

'I'm OK, Grandpa.' She gently squeezed his fingers. 'Come on, let's look after each other, shall we?'

Seventeen

The Rum Coconut

Mack was loitering without intent. If he *had* intent he wouldn't be loitering. Did that make any sense at all? Snow was still in the air, the type of wispy flakes that were sticking in his hair but not actually making any impact on the surroundings. The sand was still wet from all the rain in the storm, giving no chance of anything settling for the meantime. And, as the weak sunshine tried to give a little light to the wintry beachfront, Mack kept on loitering as Scooter ran up and down the sand, bringing him a stick and happy-drooling with each capture of the long wooden branch. Mack rubbed at Scooter's head before throwing the missile again and wishing *his* life was only as complicated as wondering where the next bowl of kibble was coming from.

He'd seen Harri outside the church and it had been all he could do to keep putting one foot in front of the other. If it hadn't been for the fact that Madame Scarlet had his arm in a tight grip, he would have high-tailed it out of the parking lot and not even gone into the church. As it was, he had walked Madame Scarlet to a pew, then scurried toward the back of the building like a fugitive trying to avoid capture. He'd hidden himself in the smallest corner and willed himself invisible. He was still part of the service, able to pay his respects to Lorna, but no one could see him. And by *no one* he really meant Harri.

But while wishing himself invisibility, he had carefully sought her out, needing to drink her in. He'd watched her accompany Joe to the front of the church, sitting down beside her grandfather and Ruby, and it was then he noticed the guy. He was tall. Dark-haired. Kinda preppy. Mack wanted to believe he was a brother, or a cousin she had never mentioned, but in his heart he knew. And what had he really been expecting? All these years on for the world to be exactly the same? Rotating just right to enable him to get his shit together?

'Mackenzie!'

He closed his eyes as the voice calling his name swirled around with those snowflakes. He couldn't avoid this situation unless he really *did* want to hole up on *The Warrior* until Harri went back to the UK. And he didn't know how long that was. Maybe she would be gone as soon as this wake was over. Perhaps their paths really wouldn't have to cross… if that's what he wanted. The thing was, he didn't know *what* he wanted. And he had never thought he would ever have to think about it again. That door had closed and it had stayed shut because *he* had locked it.

'Mackenzie, honey!'

And he had to answer Madame Scarlet before her bullhorn vocals gave him up anyway. He called Scooter to heel and turned around, forcing a smile. 'Yes, ma'am.'

*

'Thank you so much for coming,' Harriet said, smiling at another guest as she busied herself handing out cups of coffee and trying to remain upbeat in accordance with her nana's wishes for the wake to be 'full of laughter'. If Lorna's death was unexpected, it certainly wasn't without prior planning. It seemed that actually her grandpa had had very little to do to make this service happen. Lorna had chosen the songs for the church, the food for this party, even creating a bespoke cocktail called 'Lorna's Last Sundowner' that Lester was having to quickly perfect after the recipe had been slipped across the bar by the undertaker once they'd arrived back here. Harriet couldn't quite bring herself to drink one yet. When she had gone upstairs to freshen up and wipe her eyes for the millionth time after the service, one of the doors of her nana's wardrobe had been slightly ajar and peeking out of the gap had been one of Lorna's blouses – the bright blue one with the large pink polka dot print. It had three-quarter length sleeves so had been an option for warm days and cooler ones. Harriet hadn't been able to help herself. She had opened the doors wide and started a trip down memory lane of her nana's outfits. The cardigans, never without a sequin or pearl embellishment, smart black trousers but with a comfortable elastic waistband, creases ironed in just so, dresses from yesteryear – some thigh-hugging, others with flared skater-style skirts. Harriet had lost herself to the tears the second she found the collection of swimming hats Lorna always used to wear when they went into the sea together. Right now, as lovely as the memories were, they were equally painful to recall.

'How are we doing?'

It was Iain, arriving at her side now with a tray of empty cups and saucers.

'I don't know really,' Harriet said, exhaling and putting her own tray down on a table.

'Big day,' Iain said, clapping his hands together.

'Mmm,' Harriet answered. She wasn't quite sure making her nana's funeral sound like the culmination of a big grudge football match where only one team could progress to the next round of the FA Cup was the right sentiment. What didn't Iain get about loss? She shook herself a little. Perhaps he had never been through anything like this. Maybe he *didn't* understand.

'Maybe you should go up and have a nap,' Iain suggested. 'Get your head down for a bit. I can help around here.'

Leave her nana's wake? To sleep? As exhausted as she was, as weak as she was feeling having not been able to stomach anything except black coffee, she wasn't going to leave Joe in the middle of this.

'No,' she answered a little bluntly. 'I didn't come all this way to have a nap. I came here to spend time with my grandpa and to… remember my nana.' The words were catching in her throat as the tears pricked her eyes again. She couldn't let her nana down.

'Harriet,' Iain said softly. 'I'm sorry. I didn't mean to sound insensitive.'

And really it was *her* who was being insensitive. He had come all this way too. To support her. She swallowed. 'I'm fine, Iain. Honestly.'

'Well,' he began. 'Can I get you something to eat? I've had some of the fish tacos and they're really very good.'

Ordinarily the idea of the fresh flaky fish combining with lime, paprika, chilli plus a slaw of purple cabbage, lime, coriander, honey, jalapeno and mayo would have made her taste buds tingle, but right now the thought of having anything in her stomach wasn't appealing.

'I don't think I—'

'Humour me,' Iain interrupted. 'Let me get you a plate while Joe is happy with his friends over there, and just try and have something.' He smiled. 'For me.'

Harriet nodded. Sometimes it was easier to agree. 'OK.'

Iain smiled and turned away, heading for the buffet table across the room where Ruby and one of the waitresses were both serving with a smile.

'So, how are you holding up, honey?'

Harriet turned around to greet Madame Scarlet, but her nana's dearest friend wasn't who her eyes found first. Standing next to the woman in red – wearing the khaki dress suit of a military man, ribbons and a medal on his chest, his head covered with a hat – was the guy from her dreams. Her heart both lifted off and crashed to the ground, seemingly not knowing what it should do. This could not be real. It made no sense. Was this what the combination of grief and jet lag did to you? Was it similar to being in the desert and your brain conjuring up mirages as it alternated between shutting down and keeping going? And she hadn't responded to Madame Scarlet at all. Did she even have the breath to make a reply? It felt like the bi-fold doors were folding in on *her* as the tiki bar began to shrink. It was then, at that moment, the man took off his hat, popping it under his arm, those short tawny-coloured curls revealed. There was absolutely no mistake now.

'Are you OK, sweetie?'

It was Madame Scarlet again. Speaking because Harriet hadn't. *Couldn't*. She nodded. Why had she nodded? Nothing about this scene deserved a nod. How could *he* be standing here? How?

And suddenly, like it had taken a full minute for her body to catch up to what was happening, all her senses went into freefall. Madame Scarlet was still talking but Harriet couldn't make out any of what she was saying. It felt like her eardrums were vibrating with white noise caused by panic, humming and buzzing and echoing as if she was drowning, trapped at the bottom of a deep, dark lake, her head filling with murky water…

Her mind was drifting now and physically she was swaying, her eyes connected and uncompromisingly attached to those beautiful green irises that belonged to him. She had to make this stop.

'I,' she began. 'Sorry.'

'Sweetie, you don't look so good.'

Harriet couldn't wait any longer. If she didn't leave right now she couldn't promise she wasn't going to vomit. Finally dropping her eyes away from the man in uniform, she ran for the door.

Eighteen

Harriet couldn't catch her breath. It was getting stuck somewhere between her lungs and her windpipe, and it didn't feel like it was actually making it to where it was supposed to be. She tried harder, eyes on the ocean, boots pressed into the sand, attempting to time her chest inflation with the rhythm of the waves, thoughts somewhere between Montauk and Afghanistan.

'Harri.'

She closed her eyes up tight and tried to pretend the voice wasn't ripping right across her heart. Seeing him had been one thing. Hearing him was something else altogether. She had only heard his voice for the duration of one too-short video call but it was etched into her somehow, immediately recognisable and containing an air of deep familiarity it had no right to.

'Harri, please.'

No, she couldn't do it. She couldn't even look at him. And then she yelped as touch arrived. But it wasn't human, it was damp fur brushing against her tights. She opened her eyes and greeted the face of a little patchwork dog, tongue lolling from its mouth, eyes a soft brown. It nudged her with its nose and, such was the jolt, Harriet was momentarily distracted from the plummeting of her emotions. She bent slightly and gave the dog a pet on the head. 'Oh, hello, you.'

'Scooter, heel.'

It was his voice again. She didn't even want to *think* his name. It had taken years to flush him out of her system and now here he was. The dog left her side, presumably obeying orders. She still couldn't move, couldn't even look. Perhaps if she just stood here he would leave, or maybe evaporate.

But then he was right in front of her. And she could *smell* him. She had never smelled him before. And why had that thought hit her straight in the solar plexus? Because it was the scent of evergreen fir, fireside logs and a musky aftershave. Some of her very favourite aromas and possibly exactly how she had *imagined* him to smell. And she *had* imagined it. So many times.

Her eyes travelled from his mid-section and upwards, taking in that broad chest and shoulders, that angled jaw and Ryan Phillippe nose, until there were those eyes again…

'You,' Harriet began, voice quivering over that one short word and she hated herself for not being able to stop it. 'You have… no right to be here.'

'Harri,' he half-talked, half-breathed. 'You look… incredible.'

'Stop talking,' she begged as he took a step closer. 'You're not here. You can't be here.'

'But here I am,' he whispered. 'Here *we* are.'

And then suddenly she was filled with pain and it was rising up inside her like boiling water about to burst its pan confines and flood the top of the stove. She lashed out, her fist tight, a desperate burning need to strike.

Before Harriet could make a connection he blocked her. Grabbing her hand and stopping the punch, he held on tight, with his fingers *and* his gaze.

'Good work,' he rasped. 'Fingers locked and thumb secure. Just like I taught you.' He gave a half-smile then. 'I have to level with you. That wasn't how I imagined the first time I got to touch you would go.'

And Harriet was more than aware that his fingers were wrapped around hers. So often she had imagined him touching her, a lot more intimate places than her hands if she was honest, but just feeling his skin on hers was indescribable.

'You cut me off,' Harriet said through trembling lips.

'I…'

'You lied.'

'I know.'

'And you were there today,' Harriet said, still feeling that she was fighting for air. 'At my nana's funeral. I saw you.' That imagining of him hadn't been all in her head. She hadn't conjured him up like a comfort blanket to get her through the distress of the day.

'To pay my respects to someone who's looked out for me since I came to town.'

Harriet shook her head. 'This is crazy.'

Suddenly the dog barked and the sound made a small

tear in the tense atmosphere like a fizz of lightning through a thunderous sky. She ripped her hand from his as if the touch had turned toxic.

'And this is Scooter,' he said, dropping a hand to the dog's head and giving his fur a muss.

Her heart wasn't letting up. He was here. Right here. With her.

'Harri.'

Him repeating this version of her name sent crisp crackles of heat down her spine every time it happened. He had been the only person ever to call her Harri. The only person who had ever suggested it.

'We should talk,' he continued when she hadn't replied.

'I have nothing to say.' And what was there to hear? She might not have been able to stop him invading her dreams when she was tired or stressed or overworked, but she had tried desperately to wipe him from conscious thought a long time ago. Because she'd had to. Because how else did you manage to carry on – survive – unless you made a clean break? She had loved him. Like she had loved no one else. And he had ghosted her before ghosting was even a thing.

'What if *I've* got something to say?' he replied. 'What if I have *so much* to say?'

Harriet met his eyes and saw possibly a thousand stories written within that whirl of colour. But the only tale she knew was her heartache. And what someone called Jackson Tate had written to her…

'It's too late,' she told him, injecting all the bitterness and hurt she'd felt into her tone now. Him being here changed nothing. He was not a part of her life anymore. He didn't even deserve to be part of her memories. He had said he loved her time and time again and then, just like that, out of nowhere, he'd moved on. She turned away, willing her legs to take her back over the sand towards the tiki bar and away from this situation. She'd regroup with Iain and her grandpa, immerse herself in stories about her nana… Those solid, real reasons for being here.

'I can't believe that,' he answered, soberly but firmly.

She turned back, facing him with as much strength as she could muster. 'What?'

He took a step closer and there was that aroma again battling with her common sense, which was reminding her this was a long time finished.

'OK,' he breathed deeply. 'Maybe… I don't wanna believe it.'

'Too bad,' Harriet snapped her reply. 'Because it's not your choice.'

She made to turn away again but this time he took her hand, sliding his fingers in next to hers, holding on.

'Just tell me,' he whispered. 'Tell me, you're not feeling the exact same way I am right now.'

He was holding her hand. And she wasn't letting go. Why wasn't she letting go? Or saying anything.

'My heart doesn't know where it is right now,' he continued. 'And it's thumping so hard.' He moved his fingers against hers. 'I want it to stop. But then again… I don't.'

And, like it or not, Harriet's body and mind was telling her she felt exactly the same…

'Harri, please, give me a second to try to explain.'

It would be so easy to agree. Hadn't she always longed for clarity? Didn't she deserve full and final closure if nothing else? But, then again, did it matter what he had to say? What would it change? He'd given up on her. He'd given up on *them*.

'I'm sorry,' she breathed, taking back her hand. 'But, the answer's no.'

She turned away then and bolted back across the sand.

Nineteen

Outside The Rum Coconut, Montauk

There were thirty of them altogether and Harriet had been shifting them around for over an hour. Christmas trees. In pots. Delivered at just after six a.m., as she'd requested last night. Yes, she might have had one too many Lorna's Last Sundowners listening to everyone at the wake regale their stories of her nana in her many heydays, but the call for the firs hadn't been without thought. This was what she had advertised at the funeral tea, with the help of some squawking and wing-flapping from Meryl Cheep – her nana's annual Christmas tree decorating contest was happening. And it was happening today.

Morning was just about to break. Darkness was receding and there was the hint of blue sky behind the winter clouds. It was cold though. Harriet was dressed in denim dungarees with a jumper underneath and a gilet over both. Her blonde hair was loose with a beanie on her head and, as she pulled another pot into position, in the garden area just before the sand began, her boots slipped on a glaze of frost.

'Whoa! Steady there!'

Iain supported her arm and held her still.

Harriet gained traction and got hold of her momentum.

'What are you doing out here?' Iain asked. 'It's freezing and it's barely light.'

'I told you last night, it's The Rum Coconut's Christmas tree decorating event and I needed to get the trees here early because people will be coming at ten.'

'Well,' Iain said, clapping his hands together and rubbing them like he might be a massage therapist ready to give healing treatment. 'They might but, you know, it's cold and...'

'And?' Harriet asked with a frown.

'Well, people came here yesterday, didn't they?' Iain continued. 'Maybe they won't want to...'

Harriet was narrowing her eyes a little now, almost challenging him to end the sentence. His words tailed off until:

'I'm just suggesting, well not suggesting, just saying that, you know, if people don't turn up right away then... don't be disappointed. That's all.'

'You don't think people will come?'

Harriet was caught between being cross that Iain had even made this suggestion and wondering whether he might be right. Nana Lorna had spoken with such joy about this event in her letter, talking of scores of people attending, local families making teams and descending en masse to create the most festive tree, the prize being a free meal at The Rum Coconut. Last night she was worried thirty trees may not be enough but now perhaps she would end up decorating half of them herself... Maybe these events just wouldn't have the same impact now as they had when her nana was at the centre of things. But what did that mean? That it was all over? That they shouldn't try and recreate the past?

'I'm just saying, perhaps don't put *all* your energies into this. Focusing on one thing isn't always a good choice, remember?' Iain said.

Harriet swallowed. Now *Iain* was surreptitiously bringing up the past. And she couldn't let that take over. There was no going back. Throwing herself into projects was the only way to work through it – just like before.

Mack watched. He'd been watching for the past ten minutes since his run had led him on the route that went by The Rum Coconut. Despite Harri taking off yesterday and his decision not to rejoin the wake, he couldn't get her off his mind. More so now he had actually been in her company again. *He'd held her hand.* It felt like the most momentous event. And here he was now, ducked a little behind a tree, looking like he was casing the joint. And there was that guy again. So close to the woman Mack had never been able to move on from, despite everything he had controlled to give the very opposite outcome. Why had he hurt her like that? What did he think she was going to do when the letters were returned? Forget him? Move on? No, the Harri he knew as well as you could know anybody was always going to dig deeper and ask questions...

He kicked his blade at the ground a little and instantly regretted it as spasm of pain rolled through his leg. What was he doing here? Creeping around in bushes. Being places he was no longer welcome?

'Oh my God! The soup!'

It was Harri, yelling at the top of her voice. Mack watched

her put her hands to her hat and stamp her boots on the icy ground. He knew it was frozen as he'd almost had a coming together with the tarmac earlier.

'I was thinking so hard about having the trees ready I forgot to check with Ruby about the ingredients for the soup. How long does soup even take to cook?!' Harriet exclaimed.

Mack didn't wait to hear any more. He had some calls to make.

Twenty

The Rum Coconut, Montauk

'How many teams do you usually get?'

Harriet looked at her watch. It was just past ten and there were only six teams assembled in the space she had designated for tree decoration. The sun was finally providing a little warmth and defrosting the ground and the fir trees were looking perfectly ready to receive some tinsel, baubles or whatever people had brought for decoration. However, some of the groups only consisted of two people and one was a lady accompanied by a rabbit on a lead. It wasn't the buzzing extravaganza her nan had outlined in her letter of reminiscence.

People come from miles around, Joanna. The car park is always overflowing and sometimes we have to let cars spill over onto the sand. Because no one does anything like this on Long Island. Of course people trim trees, but usually only their own. I started this competition because you can never have too many chances to get the community together and raise money for charity. The Mrs Claus in me simply loves to see the smiles on children's faces. I remember the first time your father was old enough to appreciate a Christmas tree. There was no getting his chubby little hands out of the box of decorations. Then every year he liked to put three or four ornaments on each branch. And as much as I wanted to straighten things out a little, I never did. And that's what I always have in mind when I judge this competition. Your father and those full bottom branches. The decorations can be anything, Joanna. Some people don't have a lot of anything around here. And the trees don't have to be a magazine cover's idea of perfect. It's all about the doing, not the end result.

Hearing about her dad decorating real trees had brought a tear to her eye. There was no artificial relic dragged down from the attic. Little Joe Junior once embraced Christmas and spent quality time with his mum. How had things turned so sour?

'I couldn't put an exact figure on it,' Ruby answered. 'It's not the same every year but... Lester's fixing a big ol' cardboard sign to the fence out front, catch passers-by, you know.' She finished the sentence by waving a hand to the empty car park and the quiet road.

This was a mistake. Because she wasn't her nana and because events needed planning. Harriet knew that. Before she'd gone into business with Iain she'd worked for a tile company. Her main jobs had been invoicing and accounting until Terence had taken early retirement and she'd been thrown head-first into promotion and marketing. If you wanted to get the most out of a price-drop or flash sale you had to get the timing right. And she had told everyone about this Christmas tree adornment only yesterday. No notice. No time to make flyers to push through people's doors or drop into the coffee shops and restaurants of the area. Why had she insisted this had to be done right now? Today. Instead of keeping her nana's legacy going, she might have unwittingly thrown it onto the pyre. Jude had said as much in their last text exchange. Yes her friend had been all positive about the *idea* of the event, but she had also sent the 'shocked face' emoji and ended it with a full stop when Harriet had said it was today.

'Where's my grandpa?' Harriet asked suddenly. She had been so busy trying to prepare for this she hadn't seen Joe since she'd made him eat at least a few spoons full of porridge earlier.

'I will go see,' Ruby said, putting her hands into the pockets of her apron.

'No... I'll go,' Harriet said, really needing an excuse not to be looking at all those trees that were starting to look sorrowful as well as bare. She was about to turn but checked herself. 'Should I check on the soup too?'

'Oh, no, you don't need to worry about the soup.' Ruby nodded and put fingers to her curls. 'That's all taken care of.'

There was something about Ruby's tone and the expression on her face that was saying something in addition to the words that were coming out of her mouth. But she didn't have time to think too hard about it. She wanted to make sure Joe was OK.

Mack was, he admitted, an inexperienced soup maker. But he was sure the quantities they were going for, following

Lorna's recipe, were going to be more than generous for the amount of people currently outside The Rum Coconut. But Madame Scarlet was insistent as his sous-chef. You didn't mess with Lorna's recipes. Ever.

'I'm sure there's something missing,' Madame Scarlet said, finger by her mouth, glittery glasses resting on her nose as she perused the handwritten recipe. As she leaned in over the vat of ingredients Mack was stirring, the lenses began to steam up.

'We triple-checked everything,' Mack reminded. He'd had to shout a little. When Lorna made this festive soup she had always done it to the background sound of Christmas music. Currently, the old-fashioned radio on top of one of the fridges was belting out a rousing rendition of 'Sleigh Ride' by The Ronettes.

'Let's go through the list one more time,' Madame Scarlet suggested, taking her glasses off and wafting them in the air to demist them, hair in a ringlet style today.

'But this is kinda already cooking, right? It's gotta be done in an hour,' Mack reminded. And it felt like he had mice nesting in his stomach. Sensations were crawling around like his insides were part of a carnival ride. Because he was all too aware it was only a matter of time – maybe minutes – before he saw Harri again.

'Sage! It's written here in big letters! How could I forget the sage?!'

Madame Scarlet jumped like maybe the floor of the kitchen had turned into hot coals. And the next thing Mack knew, the woman was slipping on her thick coat, the recipe book discarded on the counter, dangerously close to the flames of the hob.

'What are you doing? You can't leave me here.'

Mack knew he sounded as panicked as he felt but this wasn't the plan. The plan had been to organise the soup but with Madame Scarlet as a big red buffer. Without Madame Scarlet here with him, he kinda looked like he was getting right up in Harri's grill – literally. And, yesterday, she had made it very clear she didn't want to talk, but maybe if he did this right, surely she would give him an opportunity to tell his side of things. Even if nothing changed.

'We need the sage, Mackenzie! I can see Lorna flipping over in that casket if we make the seasonal soup without it.'

'There's gotta be something here, right? I mean, there's every kind of herb and spice in that cupboard over there. I'll go look.'

Mack rested the spoon on top of the pan and moved across the kitchen as the music changed to a bit of festive Kelly Clarkson. *Bay leaves. Cinnamon sticks. Garlic powder. Oregano.* As organised as it seemed to be, he still carried on rooting around among the pots, praying harder for the miraculous appearance of the herb than he had prayed during the Pittsburgh Penguins' last game.

'It has to be fresh. I have some at home. I'll ask Joe to drive me. It will make him feel useful, and I won't be a minute.'

Mack opened his mouth to respond but Madame Scarlet was already leaving, coat whisking out of the door before he could even draw breath. And then his shoulders raised in response to what he could hear from the bar. He shifted a little closer to the oven, picking up the spoon again. Someone was coming and he didn't need a diploma to work out who it was going to be.

Twenty-One

Harriet's cheeks were flaming hot in a combination of the cold from outside and the news that *he* was in her nana's kitchen. She had told him in no uncertain terms that she didn't want to speak to him. And he hadn't listened. Instead he was inviting himself into her space. Well, she wasn't going to have that! How dare he! Three more stompy steps and she would be in the kitchen and it would be time for confrontation. Not that she really had time for this! Joe was going off with Madame Scarlet, Lester was in charge of bar/restaurant and Ruby was flitting between the car park – where a few more teams had arrived to take part in the contest – and Rufus and Riley. The boys were gathered under the television on the wall, loudly commenting on a NASCAR race. Iain had wanted to be on hand to help but she'd snapped at him when he'd made another comment about the number of trees she'd bought. She presumed he was upstairs on his laptop, alternating between working and stewing.

Harriet stopped before the doorway and took a deep

breath. Although she was shaking on the inside, perhaps confrontation wasn't the way to handle this. Getting hot under the collar showed emotion, didn't it? If she thundered into this kitchen and displayed what she was feeling, then the game was up. It would prove that he was right and something *was* bubbling away under her surface. Indifference was what she needed now. She should make it all about the soup and nothing else. Because nothing was more important than making this first festive event a success. She felt her temper cool just a touch and then she stepped in. It was her chance to be in control.

'Madame Scarlet said you're making the soup.'

No greeting, just a fact. She stood close enough so she could see inside the pot, but not too close that connection could occur.

'Yes, ma'am,' he replied.

'And what makes you qualified?' Harriet internally cursed herself. It sounded a little too tart.

'I used to help my grandma make her famous cherry pies for the neighbourhood back in Pittsburgh. And, I got a few years interfering with a kitchen in Afghanistan… if you remember.'

He looked up from his stirring and caught her eye. *Those eyes*. And he *had* told her about the kitchen in Afghanistan. Under canvas, sometimes in intolerable heat, lines of metal trays filled with literally gallons of food filling the space. He'd brought the scene to life in his descriptions. She remembered lying on her bed, holding his letters in her hands, reading and then imagining, closing her eyes and trying to recreate every nuance of it in her mind.

'And this is not my first festive soup gig,' he continued.

'Not that I'm trying to say I am in any way as skilled as Lorna was.'

Harriet quirked a little. Was he saying he had made *this* soup before? With her nana? She had to ask.

'You've made this recipe before? Here? At Christmas?'

Wow. Three questions. That was emotion right there.

'Harri…' he began, turning his body towards her.

'Just answer the question.'

'Which one?'

She tutted at his reply and folded her arms across her chest the same way she had done when she was six or seven and Marnie had outlawed ice cream in favour of low-fat yoghurt.

'I've helped,' he admitted. 'The first Christmas I was here. Lorna insisted and… well, she was a pretty hard woman to refuse.'

That comment made Harriet smile. Yes, he had got that right. No one really got to say no to Lorna Cookson without good excuse, and sometimes even a good excuse wouldn't do. Harriet might not have been here for Christmas before but she *had* seen her nana's enthusiasm always running on the very edge of being overbearing.

'But, you know, I'm not sure this is gonna turn out as perfect as she made it.'

And Harriet had *never* tasted this acclaimed winter soup. On the one hand maybe it was good she didn't have anything to compare it to, but then there was the other side, the side that said there was a lot about her nana's life she had missed out on. It might be too late to make more memories with the woman herself but was it too late to get in the midst of it?

She took a breath. Could she do this? Could she separate one thing from the other? Help him with this soup for the sake of the event. Forget that he had shattered her heart.

'Do you need—'

'Hey, Joanna, I think you should come outside.'

It was Ruby arriving in the kitchen, her brothers at her tail. Harriet couldn't tell if she looked excited or fearful. That was often the case with Ruby's expressions, she was finding already.

She stepped away from the cooker. 'Coming.'

Twenty-Two

Harriet couldn't believe it. Now, just thirty minutes later, all the trees were starting to be decorated and, to avoid a disappointment that there were no firs left, she had had to allow one team to decorate Meryl Cheep's cage instead. Yes, Meryl was constantly pecking at the tinsel and making the baubles jingle, but the mother and child who were in charge of making it winter-pretty seemed to see that as an added bonus.

The fenced garden area next to the beach had been turned from a barren, half-empty non-event into an almost festive wonderland. Lester had found some reindeer bunting to attach to the trees and decorate the frontage of the building, there were faces Harriet recognised from the church yesterday, all singing carols together and everyone was getting busy making their chosen evergreen as beautiful as possible.

'This is a good turn-out,' Joe said, nudging Harriet's elbow with his. 'I think it might even be more than we had last December.'

'Is it?' Harriet exclaimed, her heart soaring a little.

Joe gave a slow nod. 'Well, last year was distance and masks and what not. No one allowed to touch anything anyone else had breathed on.'

Harriet nodded. 'I remember. It was the same in the UK, Grandpa.'

'You know how your nana loved to hug.' He smiled. 'It half-killed her to not be able to do that.'

Joe ended the sentence with a sound of realisation that perhaps 'half-killed' was a little inappropriate. Harriet put an arm around his shoulders and steered him towards Madame Scarlet, who seemed to be caught between helping a group wind battery-powered lights around their tree and giving a palm reading.

Mack couldn't stop watching Harri. He was soaking up every nervous smile, every laugh, each tiny interaction she had with the locals, like each one of them was a precious commodity to be securely pocketed in case he might never have the chance to experience them again.

'And here I was thinking that you would be spending your time worrying about letting my brothers take Scooter for a walk,' Ruby said, sidling up beside the counter from which he was going to be dispensing the soup.

'I am thinking about that,' Mack replied, messing with the tin foil covering the soup that was now simmering on a camping stove.

'Uh huh.'

Ruby had said it in a way that sounded like a high school teacher uncertain of the truth in an explanation of missing homework.

'What?' Mack asked.

'I see you checking out Joanna.'

Right away he was dropping his eyes to the table as if he was twelve and had been caught with a top-shelf magazine. He lifted the foil from the soup. 'I don't want this soup to get a skin on it.'

'You know she's with that guy, right?' Ruby continued. She grabbed a slice of bread from under the plastic cover and bit into it. 'Iain.'

Mack tried not to let the unease show in his demeanour. He had no right to feel this way. He deserved Harri's indifference. Although he really did hope it didn't run right down to her soul. There had to be a possibility he could make things better, if not completely right. And that's what he was focusing on. Making things better. Helping. Starting with this soup.

'I know her,' Mack found himself admitting.

'Wow,' Ruby replied, chewing on the bread as two children skidded past her, chasing each other with spray cans of fake snow they were squirting into the air. 'She's been here a couple days.'

'No,' Mack said, folding the foil tight again, as his eyes strayed back to Harri, now helping her grandpa decorate one of the parasols in the centre of a table. 'I mean, I know her… from way back.'

He didn't know whether this was a good idea or not, but getting this out to someone here in Montauk felt like the right unburdening path to take.

'Catch me up,' Ruby said, still chewing the bread but now completely focused on whatever he was going to say next.

'I...' And now he was already beginning to regret it. What could he say?

'Lived in England for a time?' Ruby asked.

He shook his head. 'No.'

'She grew up in Pittsburgh?'

Ruby was frowning now and he knew the only choice he had was honesty. Say it. Speak his truth.

'We wrote one another,' he said. 'When I was on tour.' And there it was in his mind's eye. The mail arriving. That anticipation – adrenaline as well as desperate fear – longing for more of Harri's words written just for him, but still crazy worrying that she'd decided not to write him back. He used to trace his fingers over the ink when he'd finished the first read of the letter, touching where her pen had touched, where her fingers might have trailed. His heart padded in time to the timbre of what he imagined her voice to be like...

'You wrote one another,' Ruby parroted.

'Yeah,' Mack answered. 'For three years.'

'What?!'

And he still had every single one of the letters. Hopes. Dreams. Hers and his. What they might make together. He gave Ruby a nod. 'Yeah.'

'So, like, what... and how... and I dunno... three years?!'

Mack nodded. 'Yup, shocker, right?'

'You've got that right,' Ruby answered, grinding a crust between her thumb and forefinger. 'So, what's the deal with you two?' Then an expression arrived on her face that suggested thoughts were lining up like the counters in Connect Four. 'Is that why you disappeared from the wake yesterday?'

'No,' Mack said, shaking his head.

'That would have been the first time you'd seen her since she got here.' Ruby raised a finger in the air. 'Did you not know she was Joe and Lorna's granddaughter? All this time?'

Hearing someone saying it aloud hit all the high notes in the craziness stakes. He shook his head. 'No.'

'What?!'

Ruby had squawked the word like she was aping Meryl Cheep when the bird desperately wanted bar snacks. Mack looked back to the soup as Harri herself turned her attention their way. 'Not so loud. If that's even possible for you.'

'Hey,' Ruby said, striking his arm with what was left of the slice of bread.

'And quit eating the bread. We want the donations for the charity box, don't we?'

Ruby waved a hand. 'There's plenty. So, tell me, how were things left between you and Joanna?' She curled a tendril of hair around her finger. 'I mean, did you stop writing? Did *she* stop writing? What?'

Mack let out a sigh as those worst memories came rolling into his brain like a huge ugly tank on a mission to destroy. No, not a tank. Just two soldiers, quietly watching the street, not expecting what was about to blow their world apart. *That smell. That taste.* He felt his heart rate increase and his head start to pulse.

'Mackenzie!'

It was Madame Scarlet calling. Her voice cut through Mack's reverie and broke his opportunity to carry on unloading a little to Ruby. Maybe it was a good thing.

'Can you watch the soup?' Mack asked her. 'I'll go see what she wants.'

Twenty-Three

'They all look amazing, don't they?' Harriet said quietly to her grandpa as they walked the line of completed trees.

'Grand,' Joe whispered. 'Worthy of a home out in Wainscott, some of them.'

Harriet smiled. Wainscott, the area of the Hamptons with some of the most expensive real estate, was one of her grandpa's favourite references when he was calling something 'fancy'. But it was true. The quality and diversity of the decoration was like nothing Harriet had ever seen before and she now knew exactly what her nana had been referring to in her letter. There were baubles of all shapes, sizes and colours, tinsel in silver, gold, and every colour of the rainbow too, one tree had been entirely bedecked in recyclables cut into festive shapes. Another family had made a whole nativity scene out of wool that gently cascaded from Baby Jesus at the very top of the tree, ending with a barnyard chicken and a pot of frankincense. There were rustic materials – wooden stars and clay figurines – amid over-the-top, almost Broadway, flashing lights, spinning orbs and a train set that was powering around the base of one tree to the tune of 'Ding Dong Merrily on High'.

'How do we choose?' Harriet whispered, stopping in front of a tree decorated by a family with three children who had used entirely fruits and vegetables. They had also brought a donkey who had been trying to eat the treats on the tree since the competition had begun. She looked to Joe. 'How did Nana choose who won?' That was one thing Lorna definitely hadn't mentioned in her words.

'Hmm,' Joe began, his eyes roving up and down the entrants like he was sussing them out all over again. 'Your nana did have a particular way of doing things.'

'I know,' Harriet said, nodding. 'And this is all about her. So… what did she do?'

'Well,' Joe said with a heavy sigh, looking back to Harriet. 'It was very difficult for her to decide every year too.'

'Seeing the amount of effort that's gone in, and on such short notice too, I am totally getting that. But did she have some kind of scoring system?' Surely if there was any system in place her nana would have described it in detail in her letter. Harriet then realised that perhaps she should have thought about that herself. In between getting the trees here and panicking about getting literally *anyone* here to take part, and the soup – and then the soup-*maker* – she should have considered the judging aspect a little more.

'We tried that once,' Joe whispered. 'But it got too complicated.'

'So what did you do?'

'Well, we pretend that we've deliberated hard.'

'Yes.'

'And we point a lot.' He poked out a finger towards a tree looking festively beautiful with Barbie dolls through the eras hanging from every branch. He mock-whispered to Harriet and then he pointed again, this time to the tree featuring effigies of Tom Hiddleston.

'And then?'

'Then,' Joe said. He lowered his voice even further. 'We put all the team names in my cap and we pick one out.'

'Grandpa!' Harriet exclaimed. She put her hand over her mouth in case anyone had heard. 'You're not serious!'

Joe chuckled. 'Your nana could never choose. She'd have everyone here 'til sundown while she made her decision if we didn't make it chance not choice.'

'But what if... I don't know... what if we do that and... *that* tree wins.'

She was looking at the late entrant to the competition. It was a bush most likely pulled up from someone's front garden that Rufus and Riley had spray-painted red, green and black and topped with a beanie hat with the motif 'RAGE' embellished on it.

'True,' Joe said. 'And those kids don't need a free meal to win when they eat enough of my food already.' He shrugged then, scuffing his feet against the ground. 'But, then again, they ain't probably won anything in their lives before. And Lorna always believed that what's meant to be will always find a way.'

Harriet swallowed as the poignancy jumped up and down on her like a reckless teen on a bouncy castle. She couldn't help her eyes flicking over to that soup stand and Mack.

There it was. His name. Said in her head. Real. He was here and she had to deal with that. But was she really going to burrow down and ensure she had multiple projects encasing her in her usual classic avoidance practice? Or was she going to... hear him out? God! Where had that idea sprung from? This was Nana Lorna's words from beyond and her grandpa here next to her talking about things that were meant to be...

'Here's my cap,' Joe said, taking it off his head. 'Let's go write down the names and find out who has luck on their side today.'

Mack mussed his hair, seeing Harriet was looking in his direction. *Dick*. Who did he think he was? And she was taken. He should only want the opportunity to make amends.

'I see you,' Ruby said, arriving with more bowls and plates.

'Yeah?' he replied, trying desperately to compose himself. 'That's good because I'm the guy getting ready to serve soup.'

'Your hair's good by the way,' Ruby teased.

'It's the flies,' Mack answered. 'They like the curls.'

'Winter flies,' Ruby said with a wry smile. 'Yeah, can't say I've heard about them. But what I have heard is that you went door-to-door and café-to-café getting people here today for this.'

'And no one needs to know about that, right?'

While he'd been rounding up Madame Scarlet to help him with the soup, he had hit up every place in the area and got permission to entice people down here for this tree adornment contest. It was for charity. It was Christmas time. And he didn't want Harri to be disappointed if no one turned up for her nana's event.

'You don't want Joanna to know that you full-on single-handedly saved the event today and made it a success?' Ruby queried.

'Exactly that,' Mack said with a firm nod.

'I don't get it,' Ruby said, folding her arms across her chest. 'And you never did tell me the deal with you two.'

'I can't help that Madame Scarlet needed my strength and cut me off.' He'd deliberately swerved her question.

'But whatever happened between you, why wouldn't you want the credit for this?' Ruby frowned. 'Soup saviour. Not forgetting rescuing Joe from the water.'

'Because I didn't do any of those things for kudos,' Mack told her. 'I did them because they were the right things to do. Not because I want anyone to think I'm a hero. Because that's the very last thing I am, OK?'

God, things had gotten deep and he could feel that uncomfortable swell in his stomach like when he looked out to sea from the deck of *The Warrior* and could sense a bad tide was about to turn. He just wanted to help her, make her smile, ease some of that grief she must be feeling, make up a little for what he had done to her. But the thought that she would somehow feel indebted to him was not a longed-for scenario.

'Mack, I didn't mean—'

'Don't tell her,' Mack said, looking directly at Ruby and pleading with his eyes. 'Please. Just, let her think that people came because she told everyone at the wake, or that they saw the sign outside or… I don't know, any other reason but me scooping a few people up.'

Ruby shrugged. 'Sure. If that's what you want. I don't understand it but…'

'Mr Mack!'

It was Lester calling now and it sounded almost like a warning cry. He had seconds to take in what was happening until the missile that was Scooter came pounded into proceedings, leash loose, legs moving at speed, limbs and tail thumping against anything in his path.

'Oh, God, the trees!' Mack dashed from behind the stall. 'Scooter! Stop! Get back here!'

Twenty-Four

Harriet was on the ground surrounded by a mixture of boiled sweets, gingerbread men and a Funko POP figure of Loki. On top of her was the dog called Scooter, pushing his nose into her face and licking her jaw like it had turned into rawhide. Rough tongue, super-sloppy drool but there was an infectious air of happiness about the hound.

'Come on! Get off!'

As Harriet caught her breath and took in the situation, Iain was there, grabbing hold of the dog's collar. The dog began to growl, a low ominous noise that sounded like it was coming from the very back of its throat.

'Iain, it's OK.' She started to roll up out of the prostrate position, feeling only minorly winded. And, by a quick look at curious expressions on faces, no one was stressing too much about the loss of a few of their tree adornments. Rufus and Riley, eyes wide, looked positively ecstatic at the interlude.

'It's not OK, is it?' Iain stated, a frustrated edge to his tone. 'This animal is clearly out of control and I'm going to find the owner and have some very strong words with him or her.'

'Iain…' Harriet began, standing now as Iain tightened his grip on Scooter's collar and began to drag him off. The dog was protesting strongly, gnashing his teeth a little. And she knew exactly who the owner was…

'Hey, are you OK?'

And here he was. Mack. By her side. Looking like he might be ready to dust her down if she asked him to. She swallowed, trying not to get whisked into the whirlpool of those eyes…

'I'm fine. Honestly.'

'Sure?' he checked.

She nodded, shaking her arms and legs as if to show him everything was functioning.

Mack turned away then, heading for Iain, who was pulling Scooter towards the teams of people, looking for an explanation to normal – if perhaps a little over-zealous – doggy behaviour.

'Hey, buddy. The dog you're kind of choking there. He's mine.'

Iain whipped around and seemed to look Mack up and down as if he was mentally assessing the newcomer and possibly deciding that what happened next was largely down to his reply and maybe his size. Harriet held her breath. She should shut this down. Take Scooter from Iain and smooth everything back over. Her grandpa was going to be wondering why she wasn't inside with him 'deliberating' on the trees…

'This hound is out of control,' Iain retorted. 'Look at him! Baring his teeth and making that aggressive noise.'

'Yeah, I taught him everything he knows,' Mack answered. 'And he's a great judge of character.' He took a step closer. 'Wanna see what noise *you'd* make if I squeezed your neck like that?'

'Is that a threat?' Iain asked. 'Are you threatening me?' He raised his voice a notch. 'In front of all these witnesses?'

'Just a suggestion, buddy. If you wanna try me.'

'OK,' Harriet said, stepping in between them and taking hold of Scooter's collar. As soon as she had obtained ownership, she moved her fingers to the trailing leash and the dog's demeanour brightened considerably, putting paws up onto Mack's legs.

A lightning bolt of pain shot through Mack's residual limb as Scooter's weight hit a 'sweet' spot. He gnashed his teeth together – a bit like Scooter had when the guy had been holding him too tight – and tried to pretend it wasn't happening. This damn spare prosthesis wasn't cutting it. He was going to have to get on to his specialist again before everything starting shutting down for Christmas. He could wear his blade, which was a far better fit, but it was made differently – for running obviously – and that meant balance for standing still was difficult and that took a real toll on his knees and back. But, right now, none of those things were the reasons he wasn't opting for it. It was because it was harder to hide the abnormality when you had a flipper attached to your leg. If you didn't know, then this leg, hiding under jeans with a trainer over the foot, wouldn't draw a crowd. Harri had no idea yet, unless someone had already told her…

'Here,' Harri said, passing the lead to Mack. 'No harm

done. Why don't you take Scooter inside and get him a bowl of water?'

God, this fucking pain needed to leave right now! It was taking over the ability to think, let alone make a coherent sentence. It would pass, he knew, but it needed to pass right now.

'Are you OK?'

Damn her concern. He didn't want it. And he could feel there was a pulse in his cheek that was certain to be visible. Maybe if he shifted a little it would help. What was the worst that could happen? Apart from the pain strengthening, him falling on his ass and this poorly-fitting leg flipping out on him completely... Harri was still looking at him as if he might be about to stroke out on her.

'Harri,' he breathed, trying to keep his voice even. 'I'm good.'

'Harriet,' Iain's voice broke in between them. 'Joe's waiting for you inside.'

Good. She was gonna leave. All the time wanting an opportunity to be with her and now he wanted her gone. The fucked-up irony.

'OK,' Harri said in response. 'I'm coming.'

She gave him one last look – a mixture of concern and curiosity – before she turned away and started to walk towards the tiki bar.

He held his breath until she'd gone right into the building and then he let it out, crumpling a little and knowing he had to make it to something to hold on to.

'Mr Mack.' It was Lester at his side, taking Scooter's leash from him. 'I am so sorry about Scooter. He saw the rabbit over there and I was paying attention to a pretty person who works at the car wash and before I knew it he was running like a cousin of Michael Johnson.'

'It's OK, Lester,' Mack breathed. 'Just, take my weight a second and help me back to the soup stand.'

Twenty-Five

Babette's, East Hampton

Jude: The plants are still alive.

Jude: Are you still alive?

Jude: If you are still alive, are you still with Iain?

Jude: I still can't believe Soldier Boy is there!

Jude: Have you made dream noises in reality yet?

Jude: I suppose, if you've done that, the answer to question two would be no.

Jude: Please tell me Iain can't override your Face ID and read these messages.

Jude: This time difference is a pain. We need to talk! Don't forget I have Bridgerton Club tonight. Tonight – my time.

Dad: Did the funeral go OK? Beautiful sunshine here in
Spain. X

Ralph's lone text had been accompanied by two emojis.
The sunshine with rays and the face wearing sunglasses.
Did the funeral go OK? The sum total of his interest about
his mother's death and concern as to how his daughter was
getting on in the thick of things with her grandpa and the
bar and apparently the love of her life living here now too.
The *old* love of her life... because here she was with Iain at
a lovely-looking restaurant in East Hampton. It was called
Babette's and was as quaint as anything. From its white
exterior and garden area, which was probably really popular
at a warmer time of year, to this café vibe inside, not a spare
table to be had. Harriet popped her phone back in her bag
and vowed to set a time to talk to Jude tomorrow. She still
didn't know what she was going to say to her dad. At least
he had texted. At least he had asked about the funeral.

Iain had helped her clear up after the very successful tree
decorating event and he'd had to listen to Madame Scarlet's
take on every single one of the entrants including at least
a five-minute undressing of the winner – festive Barbies
through the ages – with special commendations to the tree
with the model train and Rufus and Riley's bush, therefore
Harriet had quickly accepted Iain's suggestion to eat out.
He'd never been to this area before and yes, the circumstances
for their trip might be difficult, but he deserved to have a
break, leave The Rum Coconut for a night and indulge in
a bit of Hamptons magic. And this place was a Mecca for
plant-based eats, Iain had pre-sold her.

'This is better, isn't it?'

Iain sipped at his carrot, lemon, ginger and vodka cocktail he'd ordered them both and Harriet tried not to infer anything about the word 'better'. She knew possibly nobody could love The Rum Coconut as much as she did and Iain, well, he didn't know it properly yet. It was nice here too with its relaxed feel and subtle Christmas decorations – not too much, a reverent nod to the season. Outside on the street was a little different. Festive was everywhere! Red and green swags hung from awnings, fairy lights spiralled around trees, there was even a stall selling wreaths at the end of the street.

'It's very nice,' Harriet answered. But she was going to take it easy on the cocktails so she had the opportunity to drive her grandpa's Ford. It was like she had to rely on subterfuge to get behind the wheel of his beloved truck!

'It's been a hectic few days,' Iain mused, sitting back in his chair a little. 'I don't think I've felt as stressed since we bought those three flats on the same day.'

Harriet remembered that. They'd gone to the auction to pick up this one apartment that had shouted 'bargain' from the get-go and ended up bagging two other properties they'd had to stretch to their very limits to deal on. She wasn't sure it quite compared to being in the Hamptons the day after her nana's funeral, having directed a Christmas tree decorating contest though…

'Sorry!' Iain said quickly. 'Gosh, that sounded so awfully self-indulgent and terribly crass.' He reached for her hands but then stopped. 'And I haven't been in the thick of everything like you have.'

'Yes you have,' Harriet answered. She sighed. 'And if you haven't been there it's because I've ordered you not to be.'

'Well,' Iain began, picking up his cocktail glass. 'It's given me the chance to keep a handle on what's going on at home, as well as look at new opportunities.'

'New opportunities?' Harriet had assumed Iain was just checking in with their renovation team to ensure things were progressing on all of their investments, not finger-strolling down other internet avenues. Although, early this morning, before it had dawned on her exactly what she had got into with the spruces, she had nibbled at Rightmove to keep her mind busy. Like old desperate-to-keep-her-brain-occupied times…

Iain pointed a finger at her. 'I knew you'd be on the same page.'

The same page? She did not have a clue what he was talking about and, frankly, she was feeling a little bit apprehensive right now.

'I've been looking at real estate… around here,' Iain elaborated.

'Around here?' What did he mean? She took a sip of her cocktail and the ginger bit a little.

'It's what we do, isn't it?' Iain asked with a smile. 'Jump on board a bargain train. See potential where others see too much work?'

'We do,' Harriet replied. 'But we also said we would—'

'I've arranged for us to see three places tomorrow,' Iain blurted out. 'God. I was going to wait to tell you until we were eating, because the thought of a new exciting development coupling with a chickpea buddha bowl was almost too much but… there, it's out.'

And Harriet was looking at him like he might be talking

a completely different language. *See three places? Here in the Hamptons? Property he wanted them to buy?* She shook her head a little, like some movement would dislodge the missing pieces of this conversation.

'There's a little house I'm not completely sold on but I'm expecting you to convince me otherwise. An apartment with sea views – perfect holiday letting potential. And there's a large plot of land right on the beach.'

'Iain,' Harriet began. She suddenly felt as if she was on one of those steel walkways at the airport. She was being carried along, the carpet at the end inevitable no matter if you ran, walked or stayed still… 'You've made appointments for us to look at things? Is that what you're saying?'

Iain laughed then and wiped his mouth with a paper napkin as cocktail speckled his lips. 'Sorry. I rushed it out a little, didn't I? I can't help it. I'm excited!' He nodded. 'Yes, that's what I'm saying.'

'But…' Harriet didn't even know what to say next. This felt so wrong and the timing was completely off. Plus they'd never discussed buying property abroad before! How did you manage property from so many miles away? Yes, they could get a team on the ground here, but, when things went wrong – and they did sometimes go wrong – how would they solve problems when they were so far away? And this was *the Hamptons*. Montauk wasn't business. Montauk was pleasure. Montauk was… *family*.

'What?' Iain asked, still smiling. 'Goodness, Harriet, you look like I've just suggested we pull the moon down from the sky.'

'Well, I don't know, I suppose I didn't think we would

be doing this here.' Or right when she was in the middle of grieving for her nana. Or, in fact, *ever*. And her stomach was churning so much she really wished she hadn't ordered the tofu quesadillas. 'We always buy local to us. Properties we can almost guarantee will sell quickly.'

'Speaks the girl who wanted to branch off course and buy that dreadful, poky little cottage riddled with damp because you felt sorry for the frogs in its pond.' Iain laughed.

He always brought up that cottage and used it as ammunition. She had had to force him to even look around that property and it hadn't actually been profit on her mind when she'd seen it on the website. She'd been thinking of them. Everyone said it was long overdue. Even her mother had said it recently and it niggled. She had seen a forever pad, not a do-over destined for someone else. But Iain going around the place tearing apart the quirkiness she found so appealing, laughing at the creaking floorboards and poking his finger into the knots in the wood of the beams and suggesting potential parasite problems, she realised that despite trying to move her heart on and being practical and grateful for the relationship she and Iain shared, they just weren't ready for this kind of permanence. And there were moments like this when she wondered whether they were *ever* going to be ready.

The arrival of the food brought her out of her head and back into the room.

'This looks fantastic, doesn't it?' Iain asked, preparing his knife and fork.

It did look nice but, if she was honest, her appetite had been destroyed the minute Iain had planned her tomorrow for her.

'Mmm, I love butternut squash,' Iain said, forking into his meal.

Harriet looked down at the perfect quesadillas and began to feel as sorry for them as she had felt for the frogs in that cottage pond.

Twenty-Six

The Warrior, Fort Pond, Montauk

Dear Mack,

Hey! Hi! A British hello! So, how long has this letter taken to get to you? Are you sitting on your bed? Is Sanders rapping so loud your brain can't help trying to join in? Is it still hot? Does Afghanistan ever actually get cold? By the way, are you going to tell me what Mack is short for? Maxwell? Maximus? Maximillian? You have to tell me in your next letter if you want to get more Cadbury's chocolate! Or any of the good Haribos! We've agreed that the bears are horrible, haven't we?

Time to confess now. My real name isn't Joanna. I'm Harriet. I put Joanna on my first letter because, well, they tell you to be careful with giving your real details out and Joanna is what some of my family call me. I don't really feel like a Joanna, or a Harriet, but maybe you don't feel like a Maximus either. See what I did there? Is it Maximus? Ha! I bet it is! That's quite a cute name. But are you a cute guy? I can't believe I wrote that! Sorry!

It's just, I sent you a photo and I had to rifle through a lot of pictures to find one where I wasn't pulling a stupid face or wearing awful clothes or both of those things and I'm starting to think that maybe you hated it. And I have no idea what you look like. Some days I imagine you like Leonardo DiCaprio. Other days you're much more Usher. Can you dance? I don't know why I thought that was important to ask, but there you go. Can you?

Feel free not to answer that question when you write back, I'm going the wrong way about trying to find out more about you and what I should be doing is pepping you up with talk about my everyday so you have something else to focus on other than the fact you're risking your life every second you're there. And that last sentence helped no one. Sorry! But please send a photo if you can. I don't care if you look like Leo or Usher or Larry King, just give me a face. I promise to keep on writing even if you look like Pinhead from Hellraiser. I've just realised that if you do look like Pinhead from Hellraiser I've insulted you really really badly and you probably won't want to hear from me again. You could always send me a photo of you and Sanders and I'll guess which one is which. That might be fun and...

Mack sighed and took his glasses off his face, dropping the letter to the countertop and putting one arm of the spectacles in his mouth. Why was he re-reading these? What good could come from it? It wasn't like he didn't know virtually every word of every single one. Except the Joanna/ Harriet thing apparently. He should have seen this coming a few conversations before it had hit him like a train. And

Sanders. They had found a reason to laugh every single day of that last tour. He was the best friend he'd ever had. Mack sighed, eyes going to the dock outside. Morning had broken a little while ago and it was a cold and bright one, frost on the pontoon, crystalised spider webs decorating corners of ironwork, mist rising from the water. He'd seen Lester go past earlier on that excuse for a bicycle, knees out at right angles, balancing hard. Mack had thought for a second that he could breeze on into The Rum Coconut and have a little breakfast. He would do that a couple times a week before all this happened. Lorna dying. Harri arriving. Harri arriving with that jerk she was dating. And nothing could persuade him that this Iain dude wasn't a jerk. Grabbing Scooter like that, being loud and obnoxious in the situation, not helping Harri up from the floor...

But, in between the soup and his crazy dog, she had spoken to him. Kind of conversed in an ordinary way, which was what he had hoped for. It was *more* than he had hoped for actually. But he still didn't know what came next. His eyes went to Scooter, asleep on the other banquette. He wasn't going to get any kind of answer from him right now.

Harriet blew out rapid breaths as she came to a stop at the top of the dock, hands on her hips, hot carbon dioxide mixing with the air. She hadn't done any exercise like this since she stopped the boxing and self-defence training. Her heart pounding hard, she wasn't sure she was going to be able to jog the whole way back to The Rum Coconut. But she did have a few minutes at least to get her breath and reconsider whether she was really actually going to do this.

It had seemed such a great simple idea when she had woken up with it in her head at five a.m. but now she was here, looking down the dock to the few boats bobbing gently in the water, it was an entirely different feeling nibbling at her gut like minnows around a piece of dropped bread.

'You're overthinking it, Harriet. Like you do with literally everything in your life.' She began to pace, her trainers making dark marks on the light frost. 'You are going to knock on his door... do boats have doors?' She looked up at the sky as if expecting divine inspiration. 'Of course it has a door. He lives there.' She shook her head at herself. 'Come on, you're doing this for Nana and for Grandpa. It doesn't have to be awkward.'

Except it was. Because she suspected as soon as she saw him again her heart would be unable to stop itself turning into the consistency of the Christmas soup Mack had served up to everyone yesterday.

'You need to say thank you,' she coached herself as she forced one foot in front of the other. 'And then you just need to ask him for his boat for the sake of Nana's Santa Cruise. Say it was Madame Scarlet's idea.' She nodded to herself like that last idea was a stroke of genius. *The Santa Cruise.* Only her nana could have a festive event that sounded like a California hotspot. And that had been at the heart of the letter she had read late last night, before she'd finally feigned tiredness in order to escape Iain showing her details on his iPad of the properties he had set up viewings for.

You know how much we love the water in Montauk! Well, I decided that boat rides don't have to be just for summer. Although your grandpa's little fishing boat isn't to be recommended. No amount of blankets or flasks filled with hot coffee could stop your bones freezing sitting in that old thing in December. But, despite the cold, your father used to like to fish in the wintertime. He used to say the fish were so hungry they'd eat even the worst kind of bait and because they were so cold they couldn't swim away too fast. I always remember that.

So, let me tell you a little about The Santa Cruise. This one is all about the magic of Christmas for the children, with a Hamptons spin...

OK, she felt a bit more confident. Time to move.

There was a rap on the door and Mack dropped the letter to the table. It would be Lester. That bike's chain having come off for the forty-second time!

Wearing a T-shirt and shorts, no prothesis, he used his upper body strength and his one good leg to move to the door. Then he opened it up. 'Lester... oh.' Suddenly he felt sick. 'You're... not Lester.'

It took maybe two to three seconds for Harri's eyes to move from his face to the rest of him. He held still. There was nothing he could do. And she was looking at him how everyone looked at him the first time they realised he wasn't whole. But what was Harri going to do next? There were usually two paths. The one where someone made an extreme point about it. *God, what happened to you, buddy?* And then he sometimes had fun with the explanations. *A fight with a rattle snake – he came off much worse. This is what happens when you eat too much salt – go easy at the diner, man.* Or there was the other path. Doing everything in their power *not* to look at/mention the limb that wasn't in the room...

'Mack! Oh my God!'

OK, it was neither of the usual trails. It was complete shock. Her hands were at her mouth, her eyes wide and slightly terrified. But filtering through all of that was the fact she had said his name for the very first time since they'd reconnected. That felt good. But he couldn't forget that he was bare in this moment. Revealed.

'You OK?' It was him asking her that. He'd lived with this a long time now. It was what it was. Physically at least. Mentally was another thing.

'What… happened?' Harri gasped.

Mack looked down at himself and gave a shriek. 'Jeez! Where's my leg!' He hopped a little. 'Scooter! Was this you?'

He looked back to Harri then, but she wasn't even breaking a smile at his humour. She was actually looking like she might want to try to thump him again. Or… cry.

'Hey, I'm sorry,' he whispered, shifting forward a little and reaching out to… what? Touch her cheek? He braced his hand against the door frame to stop himself doing anything crazy. 'Listen, are you hungry?'

'I…'

'I'll get myself together and we'll… go get lobster.'

He didn't wait for the answer. He just hoped she'd still be there on the deck when he returned.

Twenty-Seven

South Etna Avenue, Montauk

She was on the back of a motorbike with someone who didn't have both lower limbs. Surely, that was a prerequisite for motorbike riding. A helmet was keeping her hair in check from the wind, but it was her heart that needed the body armour. Her arms were around Mack's torso – holding tight – but all of her felt numb. And she'd said very little since this revelation. At first when he had opened the door of the cabin on the boat, she thought her brain was getting the signals wrong. Pieces of the picture were missing and its information gathering to get to completion was somehow not catching up. But then, in a rush, it all came together quickly. The lower portion of one of his legs simply wasn't there. She still didn't know what to do with that knowledge. Even though it had spun around in her brain as she'd waited for him on the deck, listened to him inside the boat, knocking things around – she guessed getting changed – Scooter barking for attention… The whole time her mind was saying 'he's lost a leg' and then 'had he always been that way and she hadn't known?' But then her memories had dealt her all the letters he'd written – talk of running, climbing on tanks, swimming, swinging from a tyre over a lake when he was younger – and then that one video call. She had replayed that time and time again in her mind. Mack jumping up on a table and he and other members of his troop singing along to Kim Wilde, 'Kids in America'. There had been ridiculous high-kicking, hip-swaying and leaping about until one of them had fallen off the table. She swallowed. Had he moved on with a girl from back home, like she had been led to believe? Or was it this? Was *this* what had changed everything?

He pulled off the main drag and stopped the motorbike outside a blue-and-white painted diner with a large flashing Santa Claus model standing at the entrance. The windows were steamed up a little, suggesting the interior was all the cosy compared to the chill of the air out here. She could smell sugar and cinnamon mixing with chilli and salsa and all those fragrances called to her empty stomach.

Harriet attempted to remove the helmet, but her fingers were so cold she couldn't disconnect the clasp.

'You OK?' Mack asked her, turning a little to check on her. His helmet was already off, fingers in his curls ruffling the helmet hair he clearly didn't even have.

'Yes,' Harriet answered quickly.

He grinned at her. 'Listen, I'll help you with the helmet. If you can get down. I kinda need all the space to get myself off this thing.'

'Oh, yes, of course.' She was blushing now. Of course he needed all the space! Because he had a prosthetic leg! She manoeuvred herself, finding the foot peg and then, using his shoulder as a base, she pushed herself up and off as deftly as she was able.

And then she was caught deciding between watching Mack get off the bike or not. She was oddly fascinated by the mechanics of it all, but also worried that being curious might be construed as insulting. And she still couldn't get her head around it. She focused on Father Christmas instead, winking on and off as his plastic arm offered a plate of plastic mince pies.

'Hey,' Mack said, suddenly next to her, that scent of pine forest and musk filling her nose. 'You gonna eat breakfast with the helmet on?'

'Oh, no,' she answered, hands going back to the tricky catch.

He'd had the same idea and their fingers met in the space under her chin. Harriet quickly dropped her hands away and in one swift move, Mack released the clip, took the helmet off her head and dropped it down onto the back of the motorcycle.

'Come on,' he said. 'I'm starving.'

Mack liked this place because it was simple. Inside it looked part-boat, part seaside apartment, with its shabby chic wood floor and maritime nods in the décor. It was clean, cosy and it did the greatest seafood at all hours of the day. It might not have the sea views of some of the tourist hotspots – or The Rum Coconut – but it had charm. And in December it now had poinsettias and tinsel as decoration as well as palm leaves and nautical knots.

They'd chosen a booth at the back of the restaurant, but Harri was still eyes down on the menu and hadn't said a word except a 'hello' to Tom, the owner, when he'd introduced them.

'I highly recommend the lobster,' Mack said, drawing the menu away from his face. 'But then, *you* told *me* how great the lobster is in the Hamptons.'

'They let you have lobster for *breakfast* here?' Harri asked, her eyes lighting up.

'Sure,' Mack replied, laughing. 'All day menu. All freaking day. And night actually. Lester and I once had a tuna fish sandwich at four a.m. The lifesavers on the wall kind of freak him out though. Lives in the Hamptons and terrified of water, go figure.'

He watched her smile. That was what he wanted from this. Perhaps it was all he needed. Some sort of normalcy in the middle of this crazy situation they'd found themselves in. Except it wasn't the normal he had wanted, for either of them.

'So...' Mack said.

'So...'

'Lobster?'

She smiled again, nodding. 'Lobster.'

'Hey, Tom!' Mack called, turning in his seat. 'Can we get two hot lobster rolls with all the slaw you've got? And two root beers.' He waited for Tom to wave a hand in acknowledgment before he brought his focus back to Harri.

'Root beer?' she asked.

'You don't like it?' Mack asked. 'I can switch it.'

'No... I do like it. But I've never had it before eight a.m.'

'Wow. Really?'

She laughed. 'OK Mr I've-Had-Tuna-Steak-At-Four-A-M. I get it. You've done it all.'

He grinned. 'And now I need to know what I can do for you?'

'What?' She looked suddenly confused.

'Harri, you turned up on my boat at seven-thirty for a reason, right?'

'Oh,' she said. 'Yes. I did.'

'So, let me have it.'

'Well... I know now... that... it was you.' She paused for a beat as if mulling something over in her head. 'Who rescued my grandpa when he fell into the water.'

She looked directly at him then and he felt that fierce, raw connection snap right back into place. It wasn't right to say that they had always had it, because they had only looked into each other's eyes over one video link, but whatever it was they'd conveyed between the lines of those letters was more real than anything he'd felt with anyone before. And this physical meeting was simply intensifying everything that had gone before.

'Yeah,' he answered finally.

She took a huge breath that moved her in her chair a little. 'Thank you.' Her tone was packed full of gratitude and relief.

He shrugged. 'It was nothing. I'm just glad I was there.'

'But, now, I can't imagine how you... did what you did when...'

His leg. Yup, there it was. Or... wasn't. Now she knew, perhaps they would never be able to have a normal conversation again. He wished he could have kept it hidden a little longer. But then it might not have been his news to control. And what good would have come from pretending? When had that really done him any favours?

'Well, it kinda went like this.' Mack grabbed the condiments on the table. He knocked over the pepper pot. 'Your grandpa fell in and me – the salt here – I rushed down the dock and this – the mustard – this is Scooter going crazy.' He barked. 'And then I jumped in – bam.' He moved the salt and pepper together. 'And then this ketchup is Lester.' He pushed the red plastic bottle over. 'He panicked.' He knocked the bottle over then shook it so it wobbled. 'But I guess he did get Joe outta the water.' He straightened the ketchup back up. 'And then Lester took your grandpa back to the bar while I mourned the loss of another limb.'

'What?' Harri exclaimed.

'Don't sweat it. I was talking carbon fibre and thermoplastics rather than flesh and bone.' He smiled. 'My doctor loves me for breaking them. And he loves me even more for losing them to the ocean. I have to remind him I'm adventurous and he always calls me something more intellectual-sounding. He favours "foolhardy".'

'Oh, goodness, I… do you… have others… legs I mean… not doctors.'

'I drove us here, didn't I?'

'You did,' Harri answered. 'Yes.'

She looked uncomfortable again and he hated that. It was everything he had imagined it might be in his head. And that was one of the reasons they were at this halfway house of a relationship. *Friendship.* He had to remember that was all their standing could be now.

'Harri,' he said. 'This shouldn't be weird.'

'Is it weird?' she answered. Her eyes told him she hadn't really needed to ask the question. She had her fingers on the mustard bottle, rubbing at the soft plastic.

'Come on,' Mack said. 'You know it's weird. I admit, the whole thing is crazy. You. Me. Here in Montauk together. But it shouldn't be weird and I really don't want it to be weird.'

'Me neither,' she whispered. 'But...'

He could see a million questions written all over that beautiful face and he wondered which one she was going to ask first. He suspected he knew. Somehow it always ended up being paramount.

'What happened to you, Mack?'

He couldn't help the sharp intake of breath that whizzed through his teeth. It was a big question. *What happened to you?* Where did he start?

'Wow,' Mack answered. 'Still not pulling any punches there, Harri. It's like the time you asked me how big my feet were.' A light laugh left his lips while his brain tried to do a work-around of how to manage this ask. 'Kind of ironic now. If you really were asking about my feet.' He winked.

'Now who's making it weird?' Harri asked with a small smile.

He righted the ketchup bottle and moved the salt and pepper pots back into position, playing for a few seconds. And he had been the one who wanted to talk. That first time he had got her alone and held her hand on the sand...

'I want to tell you,' Mack began. 'But, it's a lot and I haven't really talked to anyone about it so...'

'So talk to me,' Harri told him. 'I know I said there was nothing to say when we were on the beach but that was before...'

'Before you found out I don't have half my left leg?' Mack

shook his head. 'Well, let's bring in the pity party. Let's give Mack the time of day now he's disabled. Is that it?'

'Oh, grow up, you stupid man-baby!' Harri yelled.

Harriet's heart was thumping. She was angry and desperately sad and shaking with the feelings she so very obviously still had for him. He was still all the hilariously funny and sexy and cute from his letters and they still shared this unique connection that had first come from written conversation rather than physical attraction and yet here they were, the spark and crackle of intensity circling between them.

Then Mack laughed out loud and the joyous free-spirited sound almost filled the room. He had laughed on that one call they'd had – a lot – as well as the singing and dancing and the larking around. He'd also whispered and there had been moments of quiet where neither of them had said anything, just looked at each other across the connection. He laughed again, this time holding onto his ribs.

'What did you call me?'

She smiled. 'A stupid man-baby. There. I said it again and meant it twice.'

'Was it an insult? It just sounded real British.'

'Yes, it's an insult,' Harriet told him. 'What, did you expect me not to mention the fact you're missing a limb? It was pretty obvious on the boat when you opened the door in nothing but shorts. But, if you must know, I did check out the way your T-shirt clung a little to your abs before I looked further south.' She drew a breath. 'And, to be honest, I think it would be more insulting for me *not* to have mentioned your leg. If only because it's probably the only thing that's changed about your appearance since the last time I saw you.' She swallowed. 'Same hair. Same jawline. Same eyes.'

'Harri, are you checking me out?' He grinned and there were those cute dimples…

And she had to stop running with this. She had Iain, and Mack was her past. Loving him had almost destroyed her. She straightened a little in her seat as if the change in position would make this interchange more proper.

'I'm saying that despite what I might have said before, when I was shocked to see you, in the middle of a wake I never expected to have for, I don't know, a lot more years…' She waited a beat before carrying on. 'I would like to know… how you've been and where you've been and how you ended up here.' She smiled.

'OK,' Mack answered.

'But first I really need to ask you something. It was the other reason I came to find you this morning.'

'Shoot.'

'Can I book you for The Rum Coconut's Annual Santa Cruise?'

'You just want me for my boat,' Mack said nodding. 'I know all about girls like you.'

'Actually it was my nana who suggested you in a letter she wrote for me. She said that Skeet's guy had sailed a little fast for some of the children last year and that she had struck up a friendship with someone called Mackenzie Wyatt—'

'OK, OK, keep it down. I may have charmed the older ladies of this town with my full name, but that doesn't mean I wanna hear everyone say it.'

'So, can I book you and your boat to take the children and Santa Claus around the bay?'

'You got a Santa Claus lined up?'

'Well,' Harriet began. 'Nana said that Dr Ambrose used to do it, but I thought I might ask my grandpa. What do you think?'

'I think,' Mack started. 'That's a great idea.'

'Two hot lobster rolls with extra slaw and two root beers,' Tom, the white-bearded owner of the diner said as he brought a tray of sustenance to the table.

'Oh my goodness,' Harriet gasped. 'This looks incredible.'

The varying tones of pink lobster meat mixed with mayo and celery were filling a huge, long white roll and there was the most massive portion of coleslaw on the side of the giant platter.

'Don't just look at it,' Mack ordered. 'Eat!'

With her stomach gurgling in anticipation, she didn't need to be told twice.

Twenty-Eight

'Hit me.'

'What?'

They were outside and Harriet had her fist clenched and extended towards the Father Christmas at the door of the diner. And if that wasn't crazy enough behaviour when your whole body felt part-lobster because of the amount you'd consumed, surely striking your dining companion was totally over the top and ridiculous.

'Now you've got your stance right and your fist tight, throw one at me. You've seen the cut of my T-shirt, right?' Mack said, grinning. 'You know I can take it.'

Harriet turned away from Santa and faced Mack. 'I'm not going to hit you. I told you, I don't do the training anymore.'

'Is this a I-can't-hit-the-amputee situation? Because that's discrimination right there.'

She knew he was teasing, but she couldn't help but laugh. And equally she wanted to take the bait. 'I wouldn't want to knock you over.'

'I go over,' Mack stated. 'You're coming down with me.'

All the connotations of that suggestion flooded Harriet's senses and she firmed up her knuckles again, remembering her training and the little drawings Mack had done for her in his letters. What had started out as a little self-improvement in the fitness area had turned into self-defence and a little boxing after one of her colleagues was mugged not far from the tile centre. It had felt good to have the cardio workout and empowering to know she could handle herself. But it had been so long…

'Hit me,' he encouraged. 'Right here.' He patted his abdomen.

'You're crazy,' Harriet told him.

'Always.'

And then she struck him with full force, right in the centre of his gut. He barely flinched.

'Good! Now do it again, but harder.'

She punched out again, this time making a noise as she connected with him, her blonde hair flying out behind her.

'Better. Again.'

'How can I not be hurting you?' Harriet asked, frustrated. 'The guy at my self-defence class taught us moves to maim our attackers. How can I incapacitate someone if you're not even moving a muscle?'

'You forget, I'm a trained assassin.'

'You told me you were a sniper.'

'Only on weekdays. Come on, Harri. You tried to punch me a couple of days ago. Punch me like you mean it now.'

She squeezed her fist tighter and remembered. It was this guy right in front of her who had hurt her more than she had ever been hurt before. Even the uncomfortable situation of her parents' divorce had nothing on the heart-shattering feeling that his loss had created. She'd lost herself back then. Had needed to battle to find her way back. And now she was feeling a little lost again. Her nana no longer here. She channelled those feeling into the squared fist and punched.

'Ow! Jeez!' Mack said, shifting backwards and putting a hand to his midriff.

'What's the matter?' Harriet asked, ducking and diving like she was a champion at sparring. 'Too much for you now?' She hit him again with the same amount of power.

'Seriously, Harri, stop,' Mack said.

'You took the bunny out of the box.' She struck him a third time.

'*Con Air* references? Man!'

He dodged another blow she'd intended to connect.

'Harri, I mean it.'

'Pow!' She struck out her hand, but this time Mack grabbed hold of it and somehow, quickly, before she even had time to realise it, she was on her back on the ground and he was leaning over her. And her bottom lip started to wobble as her psyche went from wound-up to perilously close to breaking down.

'I'm sorry,' she whispered. 'Did I really hurt you?'

He shook his head and those cute curls wobbled with the movement. 'No.' He breathed out. 'But I know now how much I hurt you.'

She couldn't let the barriers down and be emotionally bare with him. She hadn't been emotionally bare with anyone since she'd tightened the strings around her heart. Mack's face was right there, so close she could see those light freckles across his nose and the thinnest strip of pigmentation outlining his top lip. He was still holding her wrist... and it was then she caught sight of her watch. *The time!*

She wrenched herself from his grip and then out from underneath him, scrabbling up from the floor in panic. 'I can't be here! Iain and I are meant to be seeing some properties!'

'Property?'

'I need to get back. I'm going to be late and I'll make us late and Iain hates to be late and...'

'Whoa,' Mack said, getting himself off the ground. 'There's a hell of a lot of "lates" in that sentence. And what does Iain do if you're late? Flip out? Like he did with Scooter?'

'I'll walk.' She simply needed to get moving now and she would call Iain to say she was on her way.

'Harri, don't be crazy. Get back on the bike. I'll take you to the bar.'

She turned back to face him. He was already putting on his helmet and preparing to get back on. Walking would take ages but *not* walking meant getting back on that motorcycle in close proximity to Mack. And close proximity was proving to be an issue. But, what choice did she really have?

Twenty-Nine

Navy Road

The realtor – Denise – was dressed up like she might have a walk-on part in a glitzy TV drama after she had finished with them. From her pristine heeled boots that didn't seem to be coping too well with the part-grit, part-sand of the terrain outside the little house, to her large gold earrings that looked like they could double as dream catchers. She was also really *really* enthusiastic and eager about everything. Plus she had an iPad she kept prodding at with one of her manicured fingernails.

Harriet couldn't deny that this cute property was nice though. It was literally a few steps from the sandy beach, so frontline, and the nearest neighbours were a number of yards away. But it needed work. Quite a lot of work. Like a new roof, and that was just for starters. And the price was way more than they had ever considered spending on an investment property thus far. She was trying to work out exactly what had made Iain pluck this one from the internet.

'It's cosy, right?' Denise asked as Harriet padded into the bathroom that consisted of a seen-much-better days suite with a skylight encrusted with louse bodies and spider webs. Seriously, maybe Denise needed to spend a little more time on the titivating of her properties than she did on her own appearance if she wanted to sell anything.

'It's definitely got potential,' Iain answered.

What? Harriet whipped around as Iain's coat tails disappeared out of the bathroom again and he moved into the living room. This was nothing like any of the houses Iain usually went for. The ones Iain *made* them go for. They had a strict and well-established remit and this house on the beach was not ticking any of those boxes. What was going on here?

'I can see windows that open right out to the ocean view along here. Imagine light drapes and the woodwork all painted white and—'

'Can you give us five minutes, Denise?' Harriet interrupted.

Iain was prowling into the kitchen now. It compromised of a stained sink and three wall units.

'You betcha,' Denise replied. 'I'll be right outside if you need me.'

Harriet waited until the heels had finished striding across the slightly warped old wood floor and departed the building before she spoke.

'Iain, this place… it's—'

He turned around and looked straight at her. 'Do you like it?'

'Do *you* like it?' Harriet returned the question. 'I mean, really?'

'I asked first.'

OK, this was a bit odd now. 'It's not about whether I like it or not, is it? It's whether we think it matches our plans for renovation, and this completely doesn't.' She gave a laugh. 'I mean, Iain, we put in new bathroom suites and change all the cupboard doors in kitchens. We don't rip up floorboards or replace roofs.'

'Not yet,' Iain answered.

Seriously, Harriet was floored. What had got into him? Iain was Mr On-Brand. He always had been. He was stable and predictable. That was what she liked most about him. *Liked*. She shook her head.

'What do you mean, *not yet*?' Harriet asked.

'Well, looking here has to be *slightly* different to looking in the UK, doesn't it?' He strode back into the living space and rested a hand on the wall. 'Here isn't the kind of place for professionals, is it? I'm finding out that here it's all about the holidays. Do you know how much some of these beachfront properties rent out for in the summer?'

'Well, I…' The answer was no. Because it wasn't something she had ever had the need to look into. She'd always stayed with her nana and grandpa when she visited and, although they had spare rooms above The Rum Coconut, they'd never been used for letting as far as she was aware.

'Think over three thousand pounds a week! And that was a quick estimate based on some dates in June. Denise says even more for July or August,' Iain informed.

'Oh.'

Iain laughed. 'Well, that didn't sound quite as excited as I'd hoped.'

She wasn't excited because she didn't understand. Many

a time she had suggested their business looked a little bit more outside the box and considered other types of house. But Iain had never entertained the idea before.

'Iain, I just... this house, it needs so much work and it's already over our price marker and—'

He smiled and reached for her hand. 'Come with me.'

He led the way across the living room floor, into the hallway and then through the door to outside, shooting past Denise who was talking on her mobile phone.

'What are you doing?' Harriet asked as Iain walked them across the road and down onto the sand of the beach.

The wind was getting up now and Harriet really wished she had brought her hat. The icy cold was getting all up and under her hair, freezing her from the top of her spine downwards.

'Humour me for a minute,' he said, walking them a few steps east along the beach.

Finally, after five minutes or so, he stopped and pointed across the sand.

'Do you see that sign down there?' Iain asked.

There was the endless sand, a couple of wooden shacks and a large blue-and-white hoarding that was hard to miss. 'I do.'

'Well.' He paused dramatically. 'That whole section of beachfront is for sale too.'

'O-K.' Where was this leading now? It was like she had landed in Montauk and Montauk had turned into something out of *WandaVision*.

'What if,' Iain began again, 'we buy the entire beachfront and build a whole block of holiday apartments?'

Harriet looked at him, waiting for the punchline. Because

there had to be one, didn't there? Had he said 'build'? Gone from the usual fitting a new toilet and basin through taking the roof off a small house, to laying foundations on a complex? But Iain wasn't pulling any 'fooled you' comedy faces. He was facing her and seeming expectant.

Harriet smiled. 'You must really like that house back there.'

'What?'

'Well, I mean, is this the crazy pitch that's then going to make me think that putting a new roof on that shack is the easiest project in the world?'

'No, this is a serious business suggestion,' Iain said. Now his look said 'dumbfounded' that she was questioning his sanity.

'But,' Harriet began. 'The two things are entirely at odds. We don't rent houses. We renovate and we sell on. And we've never discussed holiday resorts.'

'I don't think I said the word "resort",' Iain answered, as if that was the crux of the matter here.

'Iain, what's going on?'

Harriet had a feeling this wasn't only about property. She swallowed as she watched him put his hands into the pockets of his coat and turn a little towards the sea, his dark hair picking up the breeze.

'I was rather hoping you would tell me,' came his response. 'Shall we start with why you were up and out before dawn and why you turned up at the bar on the back of a motorbike with that... thug.'

Harriet sighed. She wondered why Iain hadn't said anything at the time when Mack had roared them into the parking lot of The Rum Coconut with all the speedway cornering... Iain had been outside with Denise looking ready to depart without her. She had wrenched off the helmet and, all red-faced and straggling hair, she had talked a lot of loose statements and apologies to lessen the look of the scene.

'He's not a thug.' Perhaps she shouldn't have led with that. She quickly carried on. 'And it was about my nana's Santa Cruise. I had to get someone who has a boat and Nana said he had a boat, so I took a run down to the dock and asked him about the boat and then I had to say thank you to him because he was the one who saved my grandpa when he fell in the sea and...' She stopped talking when she ran out of breath as well as the desire to say any more as it looked like Iain's eyes were glazing over.

'I have no idea about anything you're talking about,' Iain said. 'But all of it sounds absurd. Santa Cruz? Your nana *asking* you things? Getting up in the middle of the night. Riding on motorbikes. I mean, Harriet, are you sure you're feeling OK? Do you think you might need to see a doctor?'

Harriet had to really check his expression to see if this was absolutely a question, or if he was going to turn it into a joke. His mouth didn't look like it was about to upturn anytime soon. 'I'm fine.' She wasn't. And perhaps he needed to hear that. 'No... I'm not fine. Iain, my nana has just died.' Saying the words brought tears to her eyes and she wondered if she would ever get used to it.

'I realise that but, you know, the world has to keep turning, doesn't it?'

Iain still didn't get it. She wasn't talking about the loss of a pet goldfish. She was talking about her grandmother who she'd spent six weeks with every summer until very recently.

Someone who had shaped who she was. Someone she would never see again. Iain didn't understand at all because, if he did, he wouldn't have brought her to a freezing cold shoreline to show her land! But here they were and she needed him to see this idea was madness.

'Iain,' she began. 'This land, right on the sea, it can't be cheap and… how much would it cost to build apartments? And then, before all that, there would be planning permissions and we don't know anything about how they do things in the US.'

'But we could find that out,' Iain said. 'Because that's what people do when they have new and exciting joint goals. Something different. Something that scares you a little bit.'

Who was this Iain? Because she was starting to think he'd been cloned and this wasn't the original. And it did scare her. For all kinds of reasons. Mainly because the business they had, operating exactly as it had since they formed it, was her rock. It was solid, familiar, it was what had got her up in the morning when crawling back under the duvet had felt favourable. And now Iain wanted to reshape that? With everything they had in the bank and a whole lot of what they didn't.

'I don't want to be scared.' The words were out of her mouth before she really knew it.

'Oh, Harriet, I didn't mean scared like that.' Iain put his arms around her and drew her into his body. It should have felt like a comforting act but somehow she was sensing entrapment. Her mind was working overtime, her emotions bumping up and down like an office chair with lever issues. She needed to say something. That this was out of the blue.

To ask how long this change of vision had been on his mind. To say this was not the right time when she was destabilised and grief-stricken.

Iain parted them again, a big grin on his face. 'Imagine it, Harriet. Beachfront property! Wouldn't that stick it to Marvin Jeffries?' Iain took her hand. 'Come on, let's go and see the land down there. And promise you'll keep an open mind to the idea.'

She shook her head and wondered when sticking it to Marvin Jeffries from their networking group had been a thing. 'I...'

'Let's go and get Denise,' Iain said without waiting for further comment before he started to stride off.

Harriet watched him go, the freezing wind feeling like it had dropped a few degrees in temperature as it hit her cheeks. Somehow everything in her world felt as if it was sliding in a different direction.

Thirty

The Rum Coconut

The bar and restaurant were busy and that warmed Harriet to the core. When she'd first arrived here and the patrons for breakfasts, lunches and dinners were as sparse as her grandpa's greying hairs, she was worried that the place was no longer viable. But now, as she showed Jude around on FaceTime, there were customers enjoying Ruby's chicken and biscuit sliders, the traditional surf and turf platter that had been a staple on the menu for as long as Harriet could remember and the first festive treat of her nana's apparently infamous turkey and oyster pot pie. There was still so much about these annual festivities she needed to learn. And perhaps through her nana's letters and Ruby's intimate knowledge she would get much more familiar.

Earlier, she had helped Ruby, Lester and her grandpa get more Christmas decorations around the room. While Iain had sat at his laptop with spreadsheets and design tools, his mobile glued to his ear, Harriet had been trying to discourage Joe down from the stepladder he was wobbling around on with arms full of tinsel and lanterns. It looked beautiful now though, everything glittering perfectly with the cosy atmospheric lighting as a hubbub of chatter filled both the restaurant and bar areas and customers enjoyed the food and cocktails. Even Meryl Cheep looked relaxed, bobbing her head in acknowledgement of new patrons arriving at the door.

'I thought you were going to New York,' came Jude's voice through the connection as Harriet propped her phone up on the bar with the help of a container of paper straws and some beer mats.

'Er, yes, but you know New York State isn't all Broadway and Central Park. We discussed this.' Harriet got back up on the bar stool.

'But it looks like you're in Hawaii,' Jude countered, her face getting so close to the screen Harriet could count her eyelashes. 'After Father Christmas has dropped all of Lapland's decorations over it.'

Harriet laughed. 'Yes, well, that's the idea of a festive tiki bar. Do you like it?'

Jude pulled an unreadable expression that wasn't giving any opinion. 'It looks a whole lot more December than the flat. Do I need to make some tiny tiny tinsel crowns to go on your plants? Because I don't want to suffocate them.'

'You don't have to do that.'

'Good. So, now, get to the heart of the matter. Tell me about Soldier Boy!'

Harriet looked over her shoulder as it felt like the volume of Jude's voice had increased ten-fold. No one was paying any attention to her and her phone call. Iain was upstairs in their room. Joe was helping show customers to tables along with the casual staff. Ruby was busy in the kitchen and Lester was behind the bar keeping the drinks coming.

'There's nothing to say.' Oh, that statement was about as far from the truth as anything could be and she internally cringed at her own ridiculousness.

'Oh, yeah?' Jude said, focusing the camera on her eyebrows for some unknown reason. 'So, someone you have wet dreams about, someone who broke your heart into a zillion pieces because one of his stupid mates told you he'd died and another said he was getting married, someone you loved so much, walks casually into your orbit and there's nothing to say? Do you want to re-think that statement?'

And Jude had laid out the situation pretty accurately. Except the bit she didn't know about yet. The missing part.

'He took me out for lobster,' Harriet breathed, a whole truckload of emotions suddenly being emptied into her. 'And… things have changed since we last saw each other.'

'Oh, he's not as hot as he once was?' Jude sighed. 'Well, the years do that to some people. There was this guy at origami club that was cute when I first started but then he left and when he came back again I seriously thought it was a whole different person. His head honestly looked like a giant ugly sprout.'

Harriet put her coffee cup to her lips and bought herself another few seconds of time. *Mack was still as hot as he had ever been. Hotter maybe.* And she should not be thinking that because she was in a relationship with Iain. But it was true nonetheless. And she needed to get her head around the fact he was changed, physically at least. She couldn't imagine what that might have done to the inside of him. And she might never get to know if he wasn't up for discussing it.

'He…' She drew in a breath before rushing out the rest of the sentence. 'Lost a part of one of his legs.'

There, it was out. She'd said it. And Jude's whole face was in focus now, except she suddenly looked very still. Harriet shifted a little nearer to the screen.

'Jude? Have you frozen? Is it the connection?'

'I think so,' Jude said, responding and giving Harriet a close-up of her necklace as she shifted position. 'Because I heard the words "lost" and "legs" and I'm trying to put them into an order that makes sense. So, what did you say again?'

Harriet took a breath. 'Mack has lost part of one of his legs,' she repeated. 'His left leg. Below the knee.'

Jude said nothing for a moment and all Harriet could see was the top of her dungarees until she thumped down onto their sofa with a: 'Damn.'

'I know. And I'm trying not to dwell on the fact that this has happened to him and that it's probably all wrapped up in what happened with us – maybe – and I'm trying to pretend that he's just a local and a friend of my nana but…' She stopped talking because she was wondering where these words were actually going to take her.

'But?'

'It's hard,' Harriet admitted. 'You know, to remain neutral.'

'Because he's still hotter than hot and dream-worthy and you want to know everything that's happened to him since you thought he was dead and then you found out he wasn't. Because now you know he wasn't dead or getting married to someone from the backwoods, but he's obviously been through a trauma and you got angry about him lying to you but now you think you might have been a little hasty and maybe you should have given him a chance to explain himself instead of jumping to a conclusion.'

Finally Jude stopped talking. But everything she'd said had pretty much hit the nail on the head. She was now thinking there had been so much more maybe she should have followed up on. But how much deceit and pushing away did one person put up with before they had to give up to maintain at least some self-respect?

'When are you seeing him again?' Jude asked, breaking into her thoughts.

'He lives just down the road from here,' Harriet said. 'On a boat.'

'He lives on a boat.'

'With a dog called Scooter.'

'Harriet, has your life become a film from *Movies 24*?'

'I don't know,' she answered with a sigh. 'Maybe.' She couldn't even tell Jude that Iain was currently trying to find out exactly how much money the company could borrow from the bank to fund the creation of a gated holiday community.

'So, when are you seeing him again?'

'I don't know. When he captains the boat for my nana's annual festive Santa Cruise I guess.'

'Is Santa Cruz in New York too?'

'No, it's… never mind.'

'So what are you going to do?' Jude asked, popping what looked very much like a handful of Ferrero Rocher into her mouth.

'I'm going to stick to my plan,' Harriet said with a confident nod.

'Come home? Save your plants from certain drought?'

'Not yet,' Harriet breathed. 'I'm going to make sure my grandpa is OK and I'm going to let my nana teach me all about a Montauk Christmas.'

Her grandpa and the bar. Keeping things even and familiar for Joe was going to be her focus. Mack was here, yes, but she couldn't let her past feelings for him cloud her present. What she was going to do about Iain's property aspirations she still didn't know.

'That's all Hallmark-worthy, Harriet. Honestly,' Jude said through a mouthful of chocolate. 'Bravo.'

Thirty-One

Fort Pond

'What if no one turns up?' Harriet asked Madame Scarlet as they trailed in Lester's wake. Lester was pushing a wheelbarrow full of lunch boxes, gift bags and decorations down the jetty. 'Or what if people turn up, but they don't like the food? Or what if one of the kids get sick? Or more than one? Or what if—'

'—A big ol' whale leaps outta the water and snatches one of the kiddies between its slippery lips,' Madame Scarlet suggested with a throaty chuckle, hair in a pixie crop today.

'I'm panicking, aren't I?' Harriet said, blowing out a nervous breath. She knew she was panicking. And she also knew that she, Ruby, Madame Scarlet and Joe had been through the planning for the Santa Cruise meticulously over the past days. The children's parents/guardians had all signed the forms and declarations relating to allergies, a parent/guardian was going to be with the children the whole time, Mack had assured her he had all the relevant licences and permits for this to safely go ahead and her grandpa had told her – at least three times – that no child had ever been lost to the lake in all the years they had been doing the Santa Cruise. Equally, Joe had also told her that this event always raised a tidy sum for charity. The Rum Coconut would take their costs from the ticket price and the rest would go into the charity pot. Harriet swallowed a mouthful of cold air. She hadn't even discussed how much Mack was charging for the rental of his boat.

'You don't need me to answer that question, darling, do you?' Madame Scarlet said.

'No,' Harriet answered. 'But, tell me, what's *Santa and the Pirate* all about?'

'You ain't read *Santa and the Pirate*!' It was Ruby, suddenly at their side, holding Meryl Cheep in her gold-coloured portable cage that funnily enough looked right out of a pirate ship.

'No, I had no idea about it until my nana wrote about it in her letter.'

I know you've never been in Montauk for Christmas, Joanna, but I'm sure your father has read you Santa and the Pirate. *He loved that story when he was growing up. Santa Claus needing the help of a dastardly pirate to save Christmas. I always liked it because it shows that help can arrive from the most unexpected places and teaches that perhaps none of us should ever be too quick to judge. We're all a little guilty of judging too quickly every now and then...*

Both Madame Scarlet and Ruby gasped and looked at her with expressions that said not having heard of this was like not having seen Joe Biden fall up the steps of Air Force One.

'Are you serious?' Ruby exclaimed. 'That book is like as famous as the Bible around here. My brothers would rather poke each other's eyes out than have anything to do with books, but that story, they want it read to them every night through December.'

'I can't believe Lorna never read it to you,' Madame Scarlet said, reinforcing her grip on the two bags she was carrying. 'Or your father.'

Meryl Cheep let out a squawk that seemed to suggest she felt exactly the same way about Harriet's ignorance on the topic. This was the weirdest thing about being here in the midst of all these festive activities. She didn't know anything about life here in December and she was getting the feeling that, for whatever reason, Montauk Christmases had been held back from her. It was obvious her nana and grandpa were at the heart of the community when it came to arranging these events and raising money for charity, so why had she never even heard of them? Why was she only finding out about this now through letters in a photo album?

'Hey,' Ruby said, laying an arm around Harriet's shoulders as Meryl Cheep flapped about in her cage. 'I'm kinda jealous you're gonna get to hear it for the first time.'

'Oh me too,' Madame Scarlet concurred. 'Come on, sweetheart, we are going to put on a Santa Cruise to remember.'

Harriet gave a nod as her phone vibrated in the pocket of her jeans.

'Argh-ha, me hearties!'

Mack leaped out at Lester as he arrived beside the boat and the other man almost fell sideways and tipped over the contents of the wheelbarrow.

'Oh, Mr Mack! I think my heart has stopped beating!' Lester dropped the prongs of the wheelbarrow and put his hand to his chest.

'You think the pirate costume is too much?' Mack asked. He smoothed down his waistcoat and pulled at the sleeves of a white shirt with ruffled cuffs. He was wearing it over jeans and sporting a big belt buckle that probably should have died in the Eighties, along with a pirate hat he used for games on his tourist tours.

'I think you might have to be Santa,' Lester remarked, taking deep breaths. 'Mr Joe was not enjoying the beard when I left the bar.'

'Nah,' Mack answered. 'I have all the credentials to be a pirate. Cute hair. Sexy smile.' He gave Lester his very best blue steel. 'Might wanna romance you. Would fight for you. And, that's before we even get down to my individual leg attributes. I'm a casting dream.'

But, as he saw Harri heading his way down the wooden dock, he knew, if she asked, he would likely dress up in anything she wanted him to.

'And here comes my parrot,' Mack said, stepping down off the deck of *The Warrior* and making to greet the arrivals.

'Good morning, landlubbers!' he said, striding across and into their path.

'Mackenzie!' Madame Scarlet squealed like she might have turned into a fourteen-year-old. 'Look at you!'

'Didn't know Johnny Depp cos-play was a thing round here,' Ruby said.

Harri wasn't saying anything, but she was looking directly at him and suddenly he wished he wasn't in costume. Things between them were level. Kinda business-like, with a friendly undercurrent. But the whirlpool of the past was likely not gonna get discussed unless they swam right into it. And he was still re-running their lobster breakfast and that heavy landing outside the diner, together with those motorbike rides, his body right next to hers…

'Shall we get on board?' Harri suggested, taking a step around him. 'We've got a lot to do before everyone gets here.'

'Hold up,' Mack said, crossing her path a little. 'Where you going?'

'To put things on the boat. To decorate it. Like we agreed.'

'Not *that* boat,' Mack said.

'What?'

She was looking really confused now and it was only then he realised she had never been inside *The Warrior*. She didn't know that in the cabin below deck was a home in miniature and it wasn't where he nestled tourists on sightseeing or fishing trips.

'I *live* on *The Warrior*,' Mack told her. 'But my business is all about *The Warrior Princess*.' He stuck out a hand towards the opposite side of the mooring and presented the more modern and sleeker cruiser that hosted vacationers from bachelor parties to diamond wedding anniversary celebrations. This had been his last big purchase before he stopped nibbling away at his army pay-out, and the investment was paying off.

'Sorry, doll,' Madame Scarlet said, puffing her way forth

with the heavy bags of goodies. 'I thought you knew or I would've said something.'

'Here,' Mack said. 'Let me take 'em.' He lightened Madame Scarlet's load and then turned back to Harri. 'I can take yours too.'

'No,' she answered. 'I'm fine.'

And there was the layer of awkwardness sitting on top of business-like. He needed to do something about that. Perhaps, if things were going to get more open between them, it had to start with him.

Thirty-Two

The Warrior Princess, Fort Pond

Harriet had finally heard the story of *Santa and the Pirate*, which most of the children had known word for word and mouthed along to, and she had taken a second to visualise her nana and her dad reading it together in his youth.

I'm a pirate, hale and hearty
And ol' Santa Claus he ain't no smarty
I'll take his gifts and make them mine
And my Christmas Day will work out fine

But there's no room for presents on my boat
And no one there to see me gloat
What would it be like to try to share?
Can a pirate learn to care?

Mack had done a fantastic job in the pirate role while Joe had struggled a little without his forgotten reading glasses.

But everyone had laughed in the right places and clapped at the end.

Harriet smiled at Joe now. 'How are you doing, Grandpa?'

There were forty children and their parents on board enjoying festive picnic boxes – turkey and cranberry rolls, a seasonal fruit compote, Santa-shaped biscuits and Rudolph's carrot sticks – as they gently cruised around the lake to the sound of Christmassy tunes over the tannoy system. Meryl Cheep was the star of the show, talking to the children and trying to eat the tinsel spiralled around her cage. Harriet was a little bit nervous at having to pick a winner of the fancy dress competition seeing as there were children in costumes ranging from a festive version of Professor Snape to one little girl dressed as the entire nativity scene with a stable exterior, an essence of Mary, Joseph and the three kings, a toy sheep under her arm and a baby doll Jesus gaffer-taped to her midriff.

Still, so far so good. The lake was calm, hardly anything else out on the water except a couple of small boats and a lone fisherman hoping for a bite. There was still green to the vegetation surrounding the water, but it wasn't like the summer with flowers and private landing docks busy with boats and swimmers ready to dive in. And no one was getting lost to the freezing water on her watch. The only issue she had at present seemed to be a touch of reticence from her grandpa about staying as Father Christmas.

'I don't like the beard,' was Joe's reply. He pulled at the white curls, exposing way too much of his face when he was supposed to be impersonating a beloved festive character every child of a certain age – and some grown-ups who possibly should know better – thought was real.

'Grandpa,' Harriet said, quickly pushing the beard back into place and looking over her shoulder to where staff from The Rum Coconut were dishing out paper hats. 'You have to stay in character. We talked about it, remember? You're Santa Claus for the children. You have to stay Santa Claus for the whole trip.'

'Where's Ambrose?' Joe asked loudly. 'He's always been Santa.' He sniffed and patted his stomach. 'He reads better. And he has the natural padding for it.'

'Ambrose had a diabetic clinic today, remember?' It was Ruby slipping in beside them on the banquette seating. They were in the cabin area underneath now to eat, but – as the weather was fair – it was hoped, depending on the wind, that they might do song time back on the deck.

'I always said he ate too much sugar,' Joe remarked, scoffing.

'Grandpa, he isn't attending the clinic as a patient. He's running it as the doctor.'

'I know that,' Joe responded, tutting.

Harriet swallowed. He might be making a joke of it, but had he *really* remembered his friend was a doctor? She tucked the red plaid blanket around his knees and wondered if he was really up for this. Maybe *she* could be Santa if she had to be. She tweaked the elf hat on her head.

'I'll sit with him,' Ruby said quietly. 'You've not stopped since we got everyone on board. Go get a drink and a snack. There's crew biscuits up top. Lorna's recipe. And she always taught me to make plenty of extra.'

Harriet stood up and stretched her legs. It was funny how it only took someone to mention the fact you hadn't rested to make you realise how much you needed five minutes – and maybe a triple espresso.

'I won't be long,' Harriet said. 'I'll grab a coffee and a biscuit and—'

'Don't sweat it, Miss England,' Ruby teased. 'We'll be just fine.'

It was going well. She repeated the words over again in her head as she moved past the groups of children and parents eating the Christmas food, reading the jokes from the crackers and singing along to the songs. She climbed the stairs to where she knew Mack was, on deck, behind the wheel, steering the boat around the lake. But, as she hit the last step she saw someone else was with him. It took Harriet a second to establish the scene. A woman with red hair and a curvaceous figure standing the kind of close formed by familiarity. And Harriet was now simply going to turn around, go back downstairs and find something else to nibble on.

'Hey, Harri, come on up here!'

She turned around with a smile as Mack addressed her and she watched him seem to extricate himself from his closeness to the woman.

'Hello,' Harriet said to them both.

'Are you new around here? I'm Wendy. I know everybody and I don't know you. Are you bar staff? If you're bar staff can you get us a couple of drinks?'

Harriet didn't know what to say or if the woman had finished talking yet.

'Wendy, this is Harri. She's Joe's granddaughter, here from England,' Mack introduced as he kept his eyes on the water ahead of them. 'Harri, this is Wendy. She has a seven-year-old son called Matty who's at the party downstairs and Wendy, you'd better go check on him, right?'

Wendy waved a hand as if she had no intention of leaving any time soon. 'He's with Sarah-Anne.'

'Sarah-Anne?' Harriet queried.

'Yes. You know her already? Works at the garden centre. Well, I'm depressed she met you before I did.'

'Oh, we haven't really been introduced,' Harriet said. 'Someone just said her little boy was feeling queasy.'

Wendy's face dropped from full-on flirt mode to panic-stricken. 'Sarah-Anne has a girl. It must be Matty.' Suddenly she was bolting down the stairs as fast as her high and inappropriate-for-sailing shoes would carry her.

And then the space behind the wheel was just her and Mack, the lake shimmering in the winter sunlight, the sound of the festive tunes filling the air.

'You are so bad,' Mack said, briefly looking at her before turning back to watch the water.

'What?'

'Her son's not feeling sick.'

'No?' Harriet picked up the tub of biscuits and helped herself. 'Is this coffee?' She pointed at a flask on the dash. 'Or something stronger?'

'Hey, I am in charge of this boat and all the people on board. Only coffee goes with that responsibility,' he answered.

She picked up the flask, undoing the lid and taking a big swig. But then she drew it away from her mouth and coughed. 'What's going on? There's no sugar in it.'

'I don't take sugar.'

'You take two sugars. We had a whole sugar versus sweetener debate about it. You did a very poor drawing of a doughnut and I said…' Harriet stopped talking as deep reverie swelled over her, like her own personal lake had turned tidal. She was lending too much weight to their shared past when it needed to lose a few pounds here in the now. Why had she done that?

'Well, all I know is 2013 could've killed my smile if I hadn't quit,' Mack answered her.

'Sorry,' Harriet said, replacing the top and putting the flask back down. 'You probably don't remember the letter and of course, people change.' She sniffed. 'I bet Wendy doesn't take sugar in coffee either. She doesn't look like she takes sugar in anything. No diabetic clinic needed for her.'

'Whoa,' Mack exclaimed. 'Hold up. What's going on here?'

'Nothing,' Harriet said. What *was* going on? She had come up here for biscuits and she had turned into a monster with green eyes. And now the biscuits tasted sour because Ruby had made them to her nana's special recipe and Harriet didn't even know what that recipe was. And she was tired. So, so tired. It was jet lag and grief and Iain wanting to buy land and being right in the centre of her past. Before she knew it, a blub had passed her lips.

'Hey, hey, hey,' Mack said, reaching out and putting an arm around her shoulders, drawing her in. 'It's OK.'

'I'm not doing this. I'm not,' Harriet said, snivelling.

'Doing what?' Mack asked. 'Being human?' He pulled her in a little closer. 'Seems to me that the sugar and the coffee has been holding you together since you got here and you're about ready to burst.'

'I can't burst though,' she breathed. 'I have to be here for everybody else. That's my whole reason for being here.'

She swallowed. *Keeping busy. Blocking out her feelings.* She had almost made a career out of emotional avoidance. Was it time to address that? The thought of facing up to her insecurities instead of drowning them with work noise made her shiver.

'Let me cook you dinner,' Mack whispered.

Harriet shivered again. The weight of his arm was around her, strong yet sensitive. His voice was so gentle, yet a little rough around the edges. It was exactly like how she had replayed it to herself in those dreams. And that was dangerous…

'I can't,' she answered, drawing herself away from him. 'I have Iain.'

'You have Iain?' Mack queried. 'What does that mean?'

'It means… he's my…' *Boyfriend. Partner.* Why couldn't she say any of the words that described Iain's standing in her life?

'Gatekeeper? Warden?' Mack suggested, perhaps a little harshly. 'It was an offer of dinner, Harri, not an invitation to take off my leg.'

What did she say to that? She needed to go back to the party and make sure all their guests had everything they needed and ensure her grandpa was going to carry off his impersonation of Santa Claus. She turned to go.

'Sorry,' Mack said quickly, his hands on the wheel, keeping the boat slow and steady. 'That was a cheap shot. Don't go back downstairs.'

Harriet turned back, meeting his gaze.

'Because, you know, if you do that and Wendy finds out

that you lied about Matty feeling sick then she's gonna be up here turning all "my anaconda do".'

She sputtered out a laugh. 'Stop it.'

He grinned, his eyes firmly back on the water. 'Listen, I'll be making food anyway. It'll be ready around seven. You know where I'm at.'

Yes, she did know where he was at. Looking gorgeous, being that sweet-hearted, sexy guy she fell for over note paper, the person who was suddenly here and making all the heartbreak she'd endured lighten in her memories somehow... Perhaps she needed to remember exactly how tough that time had been on her. So, in fact, the most important question should be... where was *she* at?

Thirty-Three

The Rum Coconut

'I'm calling it!' Ruby announced loudly, swinging Meryl Cheep through the door and putting her portable cage down next to her permanent home in the lobby of the bar. 'It was a complete success!'

'I did not fall overboard!' Lester replied, all smiles as he parked the wheelbarrow outside. 'And nobody was sick!'

'Um, why are you saying that like it's a surprise?' Harriet asked. She had the chocolate hamper under her arm that was meant to be given to the winner of the fancy dress costume competition. She had chosen the nativity scene, but the little girl and her parents had asked for the prize to instead be raffled in the bar's festive auction. A festive auction that Harriet didn't know anything about.

'Oh, there's always one,' Ruby continued. 'Or two... or six.'

'Last year it was seven point five,' Lester said as Ruby installed Meryl Cheep back into her cage and they all moved into the bar room.

'Seven point five?' How did you get half a person being sick?

'Meryl Cheep was sick,' Ruby expanded. 'It was kinda a cuttlefish and millet avalanche that I never wanna see again.'

'There you are!'

Suddenly Iain was in the room, rushing across to her, his suitcase trailing behind him. Why was his suitcase trailing behind him? As Harriet tried to process what she was seeing he was talking again.

'I text you,' he began. 'Thirty times at least. And I called.'

'Oh,' Harriet said. 'I'm sorry. We were so busy with the Santa Cruise and I didn't check my phone… where is my phone?' She put the chocolate hamper on a table and patted herself down. It didn't seem to be anywhere about her person.

'Never mind that now,' Iain said. 'I've got to go.'

'Go?' Harriet queried. 'Go where?'

'Back home,' he replied. 'There's a problem with a gas line and an electrical cable in the garden of the Sycamore Lane property and—'

'What?' Harriet gasped. Gas and electric was never a good mix, was it? 'Well, what's happening? What do we need to do? Is someone there now? Should we call for…?' She bit back the words 'emergency services'. If the emergency services were required then Iain would already be on to that.

'Relax, Harriet. Take a breath. I phoned Martin and he's on the ground coordinating things, but one of us needs to be there to make sure things are done properly and that there isn't going to be any issues with the slabbing of that lawn going forward.'

Yes, that was sensible. Obviously. But he was leaving *now*. Right now? Suddenly the reality of his imminent departure hit her.

'You're going now?' she asked.

He nodded. 'I managed to get a seat on a flight tonight. I've got a cab arriving any second.'

And what would he have done if she hadn't arrived back now? Would he have gone without saying goodbye? Left her a note? Should she be going with him? All those thoughts vibrated through the layers of her like this news was triggering a reaction from an inner fault line.

'I would have got you a seat too,' Iain continued. 'But I couldn't get hold of you and I didn't know if you were ready to leave quite yet.'

Harriet swallowed. Here was her reality check. She knew, even if Iain had been able to reach her on the lake, she wouldn't have wanted to leave now. She still didn't know how long she was going to stay. She knew it wasn't sensible to think she could stay indefinitely, or even until Christmas, but she did want her grandpa to be showing signs of settling into a new routine without her nana before she left him. And there were all these festive events to make happen. It felt like she would be letting the whole community down if she wasn't here seeing them through, making them happen even a little bit close to the way her nana had.

Iain put his backpack on his shoulder. 'You're almost done here though, aren't you? Joe seems OK, doesn't he?'

Harriet's eyes went to the door of the lobby where her grandpa and Madame Scarlet were just making their way through. Joe was holding the fake beard he had broken the elastic on moments after the last child had received their gift from Santa and told him what they were wishing for this year. The red trousers were too big on his skinny frame and Madame Scarlet appeared to be doing a bit of coaxing to get him moving. 'OK' wasn't quite how Harriet would have described it. She needed to speak to Dr Ambrose.

'And the land we looked at,' Iain continued. 'On Navy Road.'

'Mmm,' Harriet said, just so she was saying something. A noise was all she could muster.

'I want you to have another look. Take a trip down there and try and see what I see in it.' He smiled at her. 'I know sometimes you're not the greatest at seeing the full potential and I know you know you can often get bogged down with the thought of snagging issues before they've even materialised.'

She wasn't the greatest at seeing full potential? What?!

'Miss Joanna, there is a car blaring the horn outside.' It was Lester next to them and Harriet had almost never been more grateful for the interruption. She wasn't sure what she might have said if the bartender hadn't beaten her to it.

'That will be my taxi,' Iain said. He smiled at her, then leaned forward and gave her the briefest of kisses on the cheek. 'Look at the land with fresh eyes. Imagine luxury apartments netting us a small fortune.'

Harriet opened her mouth to say something, even if it was only 'goodbye' but Iain was already heading towards the door. What was going on? She rushed after him, flying past Meryl Cheep who squawked an irritated 'Joanna' as she flew off her perch.

'Iain, wait,' Harriet said, her feet meeting the sand-cum-soil at the edge of the car park.

He was already at the taxi with his case, the driver out of the front seat, preparing to stow it away in the boot. He looked at her and she felt her heart drop. Whatever she had been going to say fell away from her mind because as she took him in – the tall, dark, handsome figure who had helped her get her life back on track – she felt absolutely nothing. He was about to head across the Atlantic, without her. What she should be feeling was a little bit empty, to know she was going to miss him, to be saying 'safe travels' and demanding that he message her as soon as he landed and have the anticipation of that text gently nibbling a little at her heart and belly until it was received. There was something missing from their relationship and Harriet was starting to think that it might be her.

'Bye!' Iain called like she could just be someone from Marvin Jeffries' networking group.

She should say something meaningful and mean it...

'See you,' she replied with a wave of her hand. 'Let me know how it goes with... the utilities.'

Inwardly she cringed, knowing that perhaps that one sentence was the very beginning of a conversation she was going to have to have in the future. Maybe with herself first before Iain. And as the taxi pulled out of the car park on its way to JFK, Harriet knew exactly where she was going to look for answers.

Thirty-Four

The Rum Coconut

How old was he? Fifteen? The air was freezing and Mack was standing outside the door of The Rum Coconut with an earthenware pot full of sausage and bean casserole in his hands. No, at fifteen he had bravado already. At fifteen he knew life could be all kinds of rotten with his alcoholic father and his mother who never knew where Mack was, nor ever seemed to care. He'd known *exactly* where he was heading at fifteen. Out of Pittsburgh and into the army. He had an aim, a goal. He was going to get out of that house and travel as far away from the yelling and the thumping and the chaos as he could. He shook his head. How ironic was that? To swap the noise and the assault for something so similar with his regiment. Except it hadn't been anything like the same. The army had taught him discipline and respect – the value of friends. People did care. That's what he had learned the most. He was part of a crew predominantly protecting the citizens of the United States of America. But there on the ground it had simply been about watching each other's backs. Fighting as one body. Being brave. Yet, here, in the dark, feeling a bit like someone who had been dumped seconds before prom night, he had exactly none of that bravery left and he wondered whether he should simply turn around and go back home to Scooter and a bottle of Bulleit.

He looked through the glass in the door, past Meryl Cheep's cage where the bird seemed to be having a rather thorough wash, plucking at her feathers and digging deep with her beak. He could see Harri and Joe, sitting at a table close to the fire, playing a game of dominoes. The lights were low, a few people sat on bar stools drinking beers, Lester was stacking bags of peanuts, the festive decorations were almost swamping the Hawaiian flavour the place was known for the rest of the year round. A memory spiked him then. A small Afghan pine tree in a pot his troop had gone crazy decorating with any shit they could get their hands on. Bottle tops. Socks. Panties sent by Jackson Tate's girlfriends. It hadn't been any kind of traditional, but it had made them happy to feel as if they were still attached to the everyday of the world. Still normalising what they were doing.

And yes, he couldn't help himself, he was checking Harri out exactly the same way he had when he'd received that first photograph of her. He remembered having to force himself to breathe when he'd opened that letter and the picture had fluttered down onto his camp bed. Blonde hair that reached her shoulders. Big blue eyes. A wide closed-mouth smile that said 'happy' but didn't exude super-confident. It had been the image of exactly the kind of person he was beginning to form a deep affection for from their correspondence. He shook his head at himself and saw his reflection give it back to him. Deep affection. He had *loved* her. Still did...

He pushed the door with his free hand and walked in.

As he headed towards Harri and Joe's table he mentally gave himself a motivational talking-to.

You just made too much food. You're not pissed that she didn't come to the boat. Remember what you said about it being only dinner and not an invitation to take off your leg. Yeah, that was still dumb as.

And then he was right there.

'Hey,' he greeted breezily. 'Wow, dominoes.'

Somehow he had made it sound like he was ordering a pizza and not talking about their game play. And neither of them had even looked up.

'Sshh!' Harri said as if his intrusion had been a roaring number by the Foo Fighters at the top of his voice and the bar was in fact a library.

'You wanna sit down then sit down!' Joe said a little gruffly, kicking a foot at a vacant chair, gnarled fingers around a tile he was being careful to hide the spots on.

'Whoa,' Mack said, hooking his good foot around the leg of the chair and moving it out from the table while balancing and holding the crockpot. 'This doesn't sound like a game. This sounds like war.' He sat down.

'He's always been a bad loser,' Harri remarked, placing her tile into the game play. 'That's why he's so desperate to win tonight.'

'And you never learn your lesson, Joanna,' Joe said, a grin spreading across his papery lips as he placed down his last domino in victory.

'How?! How did you win?!' Harri exclaimed.

Mack watched her do shocked, dropping her domino down on the table in disgust and leaning back into her seat. Joe was chuckling wholeheartedly and scooping up the dimes and quarters they had obviously been playing for.

'Why are you holding a casserole dish on your lap?' Harri asked. And then it appeared, as she'd said the words, the realisation dawned on her. 'Oh, God! I am so sorry. I completely forgot about dinner. Iain left… and then I was reading my nana's next letter and then I helped Ruby make some meat pastries for the menu tonight and—'

'Hey,' Mack said. 'It's all good.' He put the pot down on the table. 'If you've eaten already it'll keep until tomorrow. It's nothing fancy. It's sausage and bean. Chorizo mainly, a little paprika, garlic, thyme and a stack of veggies.' And that was way too much of a recipe run-down.

'*I* haven't eaten,' Joe stated enthusiastically. But then he turned to Harri looking concerned. 'Have I?'

'No, Grandpa,' she confirmed, resting a hand over his for a moment until the old guy shifted his away.

Harriet made to stand up. 'I haven't eaten either. I'll go and get some bowls.'

'No,' Joe said, propelling himself upwards, using the chair to keep himself steady. 'I'll get them. You dunno what ones your nana would want us to use.'

Before anyone could say anything further Joe was heading across the wood floor towards the kitchen.

Mack rested his hands on top of the lid of the pot. 'I hope he remembers cutlery. I mean, I have eaten it with my fingers before, but never with company.'

Harri smiled. 'It's a bar and restaurant. There are knives and forks everywhere.'

'You are absolutely right and I am a dumbass.' And what he really wanted to know was where Iain was at.

Harri smiled at him. 'Did you drop a pot to Wendy before you came here?'

'Good one,' he answered with a nod. 'So, will we need a bowl for Iain?' Wow. Despite her joke about Wendy it was a little blunt of him. He'd better rephrase...

'No,' Harri said before he had a chance to speak. 'He... went back to England.'

O-K. That wasn't what he had thought she was going to say. He had him pegged at heading down to American Golf or JCPenney or something.

'There was a problem with one of our properties and—'

'One of your properties? Shit, how many you got?'

'Currently six,' Harri answered. 'But one of them is about to go on the market.' She paused for a second before carrying on. 'That's what I do... what I do with Iain. We buy places, modernise them and sell them on.'

'You didn't buy your shop?' he said before really thinking it through.

'I... well...'

She was looking a little flustered and he almost wished he hadn't made the comment. But he was distracted from saying anything further because Joe was back, banging some bowls and spoons on the table.

'I had a thought,' Joe announced, his eyes bright. 'While I was in the kitchen and Ruby was singing along to Dean Martin.'

'A Christmas karaoke contest?' Mack suggested. 'I'd be in for that.'

Joe shook his head. 'No… ice skating.'

'Ice skating?' Harri queried. 'What does that have to do with Ruby singing old songs?'

'Well,' Joe began, his eyes now carrying a far-off look. 'When your nana and I were younger we used to love to ice skate in the wintertime. Your nana was quite the mover on the rink.' Joe chuckled. 'I was more the kind to shuffle a bit and smile a lot more.' He took a breath, and Mack followed the old man's gaze. It had gone to the full-length windows showing the sea rolling in and out, the palms blowing a little in the breeze and a few flakes of white in the air. Mack looked to Harri. She was solidly focused on her grandpa, waiting for him to say something else.

'You wanna go?' Mack blurted out. 'We could go, after the hotpot… if you want.'

What was he saying? He couldn't ice skate. OK, that was a partial lie. He could ice skate *before* losing part of his leg. And he had ice skated once since, but it hadn't exactly been the best success. But, how bad could it be… with an ill-fitting leg that was going to give him sores if he didn't get it changed soon. He was a crazy person.

But Joe's eyes were already brightening and the old man was nodding and chuckling until he said a loud: 'Yes, sir!'

Harri wasn't looking quite as delighted about the idea so Mack took the lid off the crockpot and started to serve.

'Sausage?' he asked with a grin, offering her a bowl.

Thirty-Five

Buckskill Winter Club, East Hampton

It was snowing. Not a full-on deluge that might have the potential to block roads or fell trees, but there had been enough light flakes in the air to make it a necessity to have the wipers of her grandpa's truck on during the ride here. Not that Harriet had been driving. Joe had decided it was far safer for an amputee to get behind the wheel instead. The three of them had been in the cab together, Harriet pressed up to Mack as Joe sang songs from his youth and wiggled his legs about like he was ready for a dancefloor not an ice rink. This was the grandpa she had known when she was small. There was vigour about him now and enthusiasm. Maybe she hadn't been sure about Mack suggesting this trip to the ice rink when he had blurted it out at the bar but perhaps he had latched onto something Harriet maybe should have. *Good days and bad days*. This was a good day and there was a chance to make the most of it. She was learning you had to lap those moments up and hold onto them.

'You OK?'

It was Mack alongside her as they walked from the car park to the entrance. The ground was speckled with snowflakes that were never going to settle but the white crystals marking the branches of the surrounding trees were giving the area a whole festive vibe that met well with the Christmas songs being played over the sound system. Currently Bing Crosby was singing about a winter wonderland.

She nodded at Mack. 'Yes.'

'Listen,' he said quietly. 'I didn't mean to... I dunno, drop this suggestion in and make this happen. Joe just seemed like he kinda needed it.'

Harriet watched her grandpa forging ahead of them, looking so eager to get in and onto the ice. If Mack hadn't been there tonight would she have suggested going skating when Joe said he'd been thinking about it? Or would she had smiled, listened to his stories but not acted? Looking at her grandpa now, the idea was definitely having a good effect on his mood. She only hoped he would be able to get out on the ice and the whole trip wouldn't end up being a disappointment. She really needed to talk to Dr Ambrose about Joe's all-round health, see if he had any concerns about his absentmindedness. She hoped it was just grief but, as she hadn't been around lately, she needed to get advice from the people who had.

'I think he does need this,' Harriet replied. 'And I think maybe it needed someone else to tell me that he needed something like this.'

'OK then,' Mack said with a smile. 'Let's go catch up with

him.' He offered her his arm and she wrapped hers around it without thinking too much. This was her grandpa's night.

OK, Mack had got the skate on over his prothesis. And that was about the time he realised exactly why it had been so long since he'd last dared to get on the ice. It wasn't a simple case of lacing it up and getting on out there. It was about remembering where his centre was and changing that to match the activity. He'd got it down with running, but it always surprised him how each new pursuit had to be thought through to make it even halfway work. Ice skating was perfect for helping get used to balance, but it took practice, so it wasn't so great when you hadn't engaged in it for a long time and you didn't have a real ankle.

He blew out a breath, taking his eyes off the skates and looking out at the rink from his position sitting on a chair behind the fence that surrounded the ice. There were a good number of people here tonight, of all abilities. Some were tentatively skirting the edge under the glow of the fairy lights entwined around the wire perimeter and the trees, others were shooting off into the centre and performing neat tricks and spins around the wooden planters containing real firs lit up in gold. And Harri and Joe were there, holding onto the edge, then taking their first sweeps forward, hands clasped together.

Mack looked at his leg. 'I know you and I don't fit together quite right, buddy. But I really need you to pull this off for me tonight.' And he was talking to it like it might speak back. He hated that he did that. It was a suggestion his counsellor had made a few sessions in and he had laughed so hard about the idea of talking to a shape of mixed materials connected to his skin. You wouldn't talk to a real part of your body, so why would you talk to an impersonating limb? Allegedly, the therapist had said, it helped with acceptance of his situation, bringing a personal realness to it. Mack remembered being unable to stop chuckling about the concept, and thinking that this crazy nugget of positive thinking was going to be thrown into the spam box of his mind the second he was out of the consulting room. Yet here he was, starting the conversation...

'OK,' he said to himself more than his leg. 'Let's go.'

'Oof! I'm sorry, Joanna,' Joe said, laughing hard as they both scrabbled to grab a hold of the edge of the rink, gloved fingers clawing at wood.

'That's OK,' she answered with a giggle. This was challenging because she only remembered doing it before puberty. She had suggested it to Iain once and he had looked at her like hell was expecting a delivery from Eskimos. But it was invigorating! She couldn't quite call it cardiovascular exercise as such – seeing that her and her grandpa had spent more time grabbing on to each other and the barrier than they had making circuits – but it was certainly getting her heart fluttering and her mind working as it tried to help her make the moves that wouldn't send her toppling onto her arse.

'This takes me back,' Joe said, inhaling deep. 'Skating around here with your nana, wondering how many times I could get away with pretending I was slipping and get her closer to me.'

'Grandpa!' Harriet said in mock shock.

He laughed, the light whiskers on his chin quivering with the motion. 'She always knew how sweet I was on her, right from the beginning. And she played it so cool I didn't think I stood a chance. She had a whole lot of would-be suitors.' He took a step away from the barrier, skinny legs wobbling a little before he found his balance again. Harriet followed his lead, remembering to keep her weight forwards and not lean back.

'Well, what did you do to win her over?' she asked, pushing off with her left foot and keeping a hand on the fabric of her grandpa's winter coat.

'I made her food,' Joe answered, wobbling forward another few steps and just about missing a collision with an enthusiastic boy carrying a hockey stick, tinsel wrapped around the end.

'What?' Harriet exclaimed. 'Nana was always the cook. You were the barbecue king.'

'Not at the very beginning. I had to impress her so I did the one thing I knew would do that. Try and wow her in the kitchen.' Joe winked as Harriet came up alongside him. 'A bit like Mack is doing with you.'

'Oh, Grandpa, no. You've got the wrong end of the stick there. Mack was just being kind and the food was for you as much as for me.' She opened her mouth again to say she had Iain but her grandpa beat her to the punch.

'You believe that? Ha! Come on, Joanna.' He slid forward more confidently and Harriet had to push herself further than she was currently comfortable with to keep up with him.

She swallowed. She didn't want to continue this

conversation. Iain, her *boyfriend* Iain, was somewhere over the Atlantic swooping home to solve a crisis. *Their* crisis. And she and Iain had a whole future mapped out, more properties to reap the benefits from, money to invest, fake cacti to buy...

'Well, what did you cook for Nana that won you her heart?' Harriet asked, diverting back to the topic she wanted to know more about.

Joe touched his nose with his finger and surprisingly didn't flail with the effort. Harriet was still finding she needed to keep her arms outstretched to stay upright. And why was this dish now a secret?

'Hey.'

Harriet wobbled at the sound of Mack's voice so close and then he was moving past her, looking a little bit like he was fighting a battle to stay on his blades too.

'I can't stop,' he called as he slid past Joe too. 'I'm rolling with it and hoping things'll work out!'

Harriet watched him sliding on, arms rolling a little then coming back to some kind of equilibrium, then back to being stuck out like fake fir tree branches that hadn't been slotted into the right sections. She hadn't really thought about the mechanics of him being on the ice. When he'd made the suggestion that they go, she hadn't considered anything except making her grandpa happy and ensuring she grabbed everything they needed to keep him warm. But perhaps she should have mused a little deeper. Mack was missing the bottom of his leg. And here she was worrying about her *own* balance!

'Catch up with him!' Joe ordered. 'Before he does himself an injury!'

Catch up with him? Harriet was having an issue making sure *her* blades didn't knock together, as well as keeping an eye on her grandpa and watching out for all these more experienced skaters who kept on whizzing past her like they were part of a speed-skating team.

Then all at once she saw Mack really reeling, arms windmilling, blades stabbing at the ice as he tried to maintain control. She was going to have to do something. With a quick look to her grandpa, who was thankfully now stopped at the side of the ice, holding onto the barrier, she launched herself forward and hoped this wasn't an even bigger mistake in the making.

Thirty-Six

She hadn't seen the conga line of skaters approaching from behind until it was too late. Now it was Mack reacting to Joe's wailing, willing his legs to hold up as he hurried towards Harriet's still form, lying unmoving on the ice.

She had to be OK, right? It was just a bump. She was winded.

He had no idea how to properly stop himself or how to get down to her without looking like a very awkward camel but who cared about how things looked when she needed him? He reached her, bending and sliding until he was sat on his ass next to her, everything jarring with the action. Her eyes were open but she looked a little in shock.

'Hey, Cookson, stop playing for sympathy.' He put a hand to her hat and then his gloved fingers found her blonde hair underneath.

She groaned a little but began to move, then talk. 'Did I save you from killing yourself?'

He grinned. 'Oh, OK, I see you. Playing the hero.' He

smiled. 'You do know this is the second time you've fallen at my feet since you arrived in Montauk.'

She was starting to sit up now but still appeared a little disorientated. 'Where's my grandpa?'

'He's good,' Mack told her, assisting her rise from the ground. 'But he will have my ass if I take you back over there in more than one piece. How many legs am I holding up?' He lifted his good leg and waved it a little.

'That's not even funny,' Harriet responded, scowling.

'See, you're good. Humour and humerus intact. Come on, let's get you up.' And then he thought about that sentence. He was on the floor, with skates on his feet and this ice – despite his gloves – was far too cold for any kind of handstand exit. He might even have to ask *her* for help. No, he was not even going to consider that.

Harri was up on her knees now, making good progress at getting herself off the ground. He had to do this on his own. Without her watching.

Harriet dusted herself off and put a hand to the back of her head. It felt a tiny bit tender, but her woollen hat had sucked up most of the force. She turned around and Mack was back on his feet. How had he managed that?

'Everything OK over here?' It was her grandpa and he had definitely found his feet, or should that be skates. There was no hint of tremor in any of his limbs. 'You OK, Joanna? That was quite a tumble.'

'We're good,' Harriet said, nodding. She looked to Mack. 'You're OK, right?'

He nodded. 'Yup.'

'Oh, this is one of your nana's favourites,' Joe said as

Doris Day's version of 'I'll Be Home for Christmas' started to play over the sound system.

'Shall we skate to it then?' Harriet asked him.

'If you think you can keep up with me,' Joe said, chuckling, eyes bright.

'Think waltz tempo, not quickstep,' Harriet answered. 'You coming, Mack?'

'I'll be right behind you. I just need a second.'

He was smiling at her, but the mood wasn't quite matched in his eyes and Harriet caught a contraction in the muscle in his jaw.

'Let's do a couple of laps around,' she said to Joe. 'And then we'll get some hot chocolates.'

There was no point asking Mack if he was OK or if he needed help, because she knew he would deny anything was wrong and refuse all aid. It was best to simply leave the scene but keep an eye.

Mack's prosthetic leg was partially out of its socket and it was taking all his strength to keep upright on these blades and not cry out for the pain. The best way he could describe it was it felt like his whole body was balancing on the head of a pin. One wrong move and it was going to slip off completely and then, apart from the certainty of a fall, he would have the indignity of crawling off the ice in front of everyone. In front of Harri. No, he was going to get to the edge of the rink and get it fixed whatever the cost.

He bit his lip in anger and frustration. Yeah, this evening was for Joe, but he would be lying if he said he hadn't thought about spending time with Harri. He had got out here on the ice, he had the balance down, so why was the universe fucking with him this way?

He garnered his energy and took as much weight as he could off the half-in-half-out joint as he slid forward. Right now, the gap in the boards and his way out felt about as far away as Kabul.

Thirty-Seven

The clubhouse was cosy, with a roaring fire and the Christmas music continuing to keep everyone in the festive spirit as they warmed up from the close-to-freezing temperatures outside. Harriet brought a tray of steaming mugs full of hot chocolate over to the table her grandpa and Mack were seated at where they seemed to be taking it in turns to stoke the flames with a metal poker, Joe leaning in far too close for her liking.

'Festive hot chocolates,' Harriet announced as she placed the tray down. 'Chocolate, gingerbread, cinnamon, extra cream and marshmallows.'

'Whoa,' Mack announced, looking at the drinks. 'Diabetes called. They want the star of their advisory posters back.'

'It looks delicious,' Joe said, curling his fingers around the handle of the mug and steadying the bottom with his other hand as he brought it closer.

Harriet wondered whether she should have thought a bit harder about buying a very sugared treat for her grandpa when she needed to speak to Dr Ambrose about his health and make sure everything was as it should be.

'Hey, back in the room,' Mack said, clicking his fingers as he passed Harriet her mug of chocolate. 'I was kidding about it being a potential heart attack wrapped in porcelain, really.'

'So funny!' Harriet joked back. She stuck a finger in the cream and planted a dollop on Mack's nose.

'Rudolph Barker,' Joe said suddenly, gaze going across the room. 'I haven't seen him since high school.'

As Mack reached for a serviette to wipe the cream from his nose, Joe was getting to his feet, leaving the table and taking his hot chocolate with him. Harriet watched her grandpa approach a white-haired man at the counter dressed in a heavy coat and holding the hand of a little girl. The next thing they were engaged in a bro-hug amid exclamations of surprise at meeting each other. She turned back to her drink and Mack stuck a straw into her mug before she could take a taste. She smiled and put her lips to the paper regardless.

'Ugh, man, that paper is gonna disintegrate,' Mack said. As soon as she removed her mouth from the end he took it out again and threw it in the flames. 'You win.'

She smiled, the delicious flavour of the velvety cocoa and warming spicy cinnamon with the candy kick of the marshmallows was a delight to her tongue. 'This was a great idea. Thank you.'

'I didn't do anything. Joe was the one who talked about skating. Waltzing your grandma around the ice back in the day.' He put his arms out and mimicked a ballroom performance while whistling 'Deck the Halls'.

'I know,' Harriet said, smiling with amusement. 'But you made it happen. And, look at him over there, he's having the best time.' She snuck another look at her grandpa, now using his hands in conversation like he always used to. *The fish was this big* – always exaggerated. *Your nana thinks customers look at the length of our curtain poles* – a flap of both arms like an irritated penguin and accompanied by an eye roll. *Score!* – a full-on body roll ending with hands to the heavens when the New York Rangers hit the net in hockey.

'How about you?' Mack asked softly. 'Are you having a good time?'

She nodded. 'What about you?' she countered.

'All good,' Mack answered, drinking his chocolate.

'I was worried you might have, I don't know, injured yourself coming to my rescue.'

She held her breath. She wanted him to open up to her. Even just a tiny bit.

Mack knew Harri was opening the door and he had a decision to make, here by the fire that changed the colour of her eyes a little and picked out the glow on her cheeks. Who was he really hiding from? From her? Or from himself? The trouble was, he had spent so long shutting down he didn't even know if he had it in him to lay his truth on her. The counsellors had tried to ease it out of him with one technique or another but none of them had ever got down to the roots. Because he had let them carry on assuming he was another soldier who'd lost a limb who needed permission to be angry about that before concluding that it was better to be in this shape than not be here at all. Perhaps, for now, it was all he could offer Harri too.

'Yeah, I had a problem with my leg.' He followed the statement up with a shrug of nervous nonchalance – if that was a thing.

'What happened?' Harri asked so quietly he could still hear the crackle of the logs in the grate.

'This leg, being not the one I usually wear, well... things can get a little tricky.' And he had explained exactly nothing. But was she ever going to be ready to hear about the back and girdle pain, the sores he suffered, the nerves massing at the end of his residual limb and telling his brain he still had a real leg? He shrugged again.

'I knew you were in pain on the ice,' Harri said, as blunt as anything. 'There's this thing you do. I noticed it at the tree decorating contest when you were handing out soup. You smile, but then you go quiet and there's a muscle in your face that sort of twitches.'

Damn, she was good. 'I guess I need to work on my poker face before we play Texas Hold 'Em.' He smiled and took a drink of his hot chocolate. But when he had swallowed the sugary goodness she was still looking at him as if he hadn't said enough. Come on, Mack, give a little...

'The leg... it kinda came out of its socket,' he admitted with a nod. 'A bit. Like some of my weight was in the air supported only by denim.' He patted his jean clad leg. 'Tough ask to get off an ice rink and make good.'

'Mack,' Harriet said, eyes wide. 'Why didn't you ask for help?'

'You know why,' Mack replied.

'Because you're stubborn?'

'Yes, ma'am.' He banged a fist to the left side of his chest.

'Because you're arrogant?'

'I mightn't go that far.'

'Is this because I said I didn't want to hear what you had to say?'

'No,' he said straight off. 'It's just... I don't want you to see me weak. Like ever.'

There. That was something he'd given and hadn't expected to. And suddenly, Perry Como was getting very loud up in here. He took another sip of his drink to buy some time.

'And exactly what kind of macho bullshit is that?' Harri blurted out.

She'd said it with such force and conviction he didn't know if she might punch him right then. But he couldn't help it. He started to laugh. Hard. And it felt good. So good. It was like Harri calling him out had released a high-pressure valve inside him and parts of the old him were leaking out.

'Honestly,' Harri said, shaking her head. 'You can take the boy out of the army but...'

'OK, Cookson, enough hating on my machismo or you'll be wearing a marshmallow.'

He picked one out of his mug, made to throw it at her and then popped it into his mouth.

Thirty-Eight

My dearest Joanna,

Never underestimate the value of the community in life. You remember that people here don't have a lot, but what they have they are more than happy to offer? What I'm trying to say, my darling, is... goodness comes in all shapes and sizes. Like for my Christmas charity auction.

I've always taken everything I've been given and found a use for it. I've been thinking of inventive ways to get bids on pumpkins since Ben Hides decided he was going to donate five of the largest varieties you ever did see every year. One year the drama club bid on them and used them as props for their pantomime. Most of the other years I bid on them and made all kinds of pies and soups and even created a cocktail with them. Pie-Eyed Pumpkin was a real hit for a while...

Every year your grandpa always tries to compere the auction. I don't let him anymore. The couple times he did it he told all the inappropriate jokes and, after too many rums, he lost track of the bids. Madame Scarlet is usually my first choice, but she does tend to try to drop advertisements for seances into her spiel and it upsets the priest. It took a whole heap of my chocolate cookies to get him to come back to The Rum Coconut again.

I've actually always thought that your father would make an excellent compere. He's so wonderfully clear when he's speaking on those self-improvement videos on his website. I've even tried some of the breathing techniques myself when your grandpa has done something stupid I've got to fix and made me stress. But, maybe, one day, when you're here for Christmas you might like to present, Joanna. I think you'd be marvellous too.

Now, before the Christmas auction we always have the cocktail making competition. This was Ruby's idea when she first joined The Rum Coconut family and it's been such a success. As has that girl. She will never tell you this, but her parents took off when she was sixteen, leaving her with those boys and she was determined as hell to keep them all out of care. She's been a mother to Rufus and Riley ever since and she works harder than anyone I've ever known. When you visit, Joanna, she'll show you all the sassy madame, but underneath that side of her is a soft simple soul that could do with a hug every now and then...

Harriet had read this latest letter from her nana in bed that morning. Lorna was talking about her dad in every note. Sometimes it was as if there was no rift between them at all, other times it was like her nana had somehow been waiting for a chance to repair things. But no one had taken that first step. Perhaps she should tell her dad that her nana had watched his videos. Maybe there was still a chance for his relationship with Joe to be fixed.

After she had read the letter she had texted Iain to make sure he had made it to England safely. When he didn't reply straightaway she found herself checking the BA website for arrivals. The plane had landed and she guessed he was going to be sleeping for a bit before going to sort out the issues with the property. He could have texted her when he landed though...

Apparently, the Christmas charity auction was one of the jewels in the crown of The Rum Coconut's festive calendar. Harriet was going to have to work hard reminding the community about the event, asking for donations for the auction and making sure it made as much money as possible for charity and filled the bar's till with cash from meals and drinks.

Now down in the restaurant, Harriet passed Rufus and Riley another muffin each then put a finger to her lips in 'sshh'. Ruby had already berated the boys for eating too much of the breakfast buffet even though Harriet said for the amount of work Ruby did – in the kitchen and looking out for Joe – she knew from looking at the accounts that the cook wasn't paid nearly enough. Feeding the boys a good breakfast was the very least The Rum Coconut could do. Harriet watched the boys conceal their treats under their jumpers before racing down the steps from upper restaurant to bar area and heading towards Meryl Cheep in the lobby.

'So, it's the cocktail making event tonight,' Ruby said, sweeping around the diners, clearing plates and topping up cups with coffee.

'My nana said that this is something you started when

you came to work here.' Harriet wasn't going to say that in the closing paragraphs of the letter Lorna had suggested it was wise to hide some of their supplies of rum or there was a chance they'd not have enough for New Year's. But she would speak to her grandpa later about keeping some reserves in his garage.

'Well,' Ruby began. 'I can take the credit for suggesting the idea and getting it off the ground, but Lorna had to embrace it for it to be a success.' She smiled. 'You know what she was like. If she liked something she would want to pin a rosette to it. If she didn't like it, better put that idea out with the trash.'

Harriet grinned. 'She was particular about things. One summer, at The Rum Coconut Summer Food Festival she made Grandpa move a whole wigwam a foot to the left because the aesthetic wasn't quite right.'

'Oh my Jesus,' Ruby said, stopping in her tracks. 'Her homemade ice cream she made for that was the bomb!'

'My favourite was blueberry,' Harriet told her.

'Oh, me too! We should make some!' Ruby said with a nod. 'We could do cocktails with ice cream.'

'Can you do that?' Harriet asked.

'Baby, you can do anything with cocktails.' She smiled. 'So, Joe told me how great ice skating was last night.' Ruby put the plates down and picked up a cloth to wipe some tables.

'Oh, it was,' Harriet answered. Except already she was blushing about it. And there wasn't really anything to blush about. Her grandpa had enjoyed the exercise, he had met an old friend who was going to keep in touch and visit The Rum Coconut sometime and Mack had opened up a little to her. Mack had even convinced Joe to let Harriet drive the Ford back from East Hampton to Montauk with only slight grumpy protest. And when it had come time to say goodnight at the dock that led to *The Warrior*, Harriet's hand had been on the steering wheel and Mack had reached through the window and given it a squeeze. She couldn't deny that her heart had felt the touch too. But it was inappropriate in every which way to feel anything at all. Wasn't it?

'Mack told me, you know, that you know each other,' Ruby said, stopping the cleaning. 'From before.'

'Oh,' Harriet said, that blush spreading faster. She hadn't known that Ruby and Mack were close. What had he said? She was itching to know but also somehow not.

'Cute you wrote each other,' Ruby continued, her stare unabated. 'For so long.'

Harriet nodded. 'Mmm.'

'Wow, you two!' Ruby exclaimed. 'Made from the same bread!'

Harriet had never heard that expression before, but she could kind of guess what Ruby meant. She and Mack – two halves of the same sandwich.

Ruby put her hands on her hips suddenly. 'Do you know what happened to his leg?'

That was an unexpected turn of conversation and the dining clatter suddenly got quiet. 'No,' Harriet answered. Then: 'Do you?'

Ruby shook her head. 'No. He doesn't talk about it.' She put fingers to silver tinsel and tucked a little under a Hawaiian mask to neaten it. 'I asked him once when I was drunk.'

'What did he say?'

'He said he lost it when he was tussling with a crocodile.' Ruby rolled her eyes.

'Typical Mack,' Harriet agreed with a nod.

'So, how's it all gonna play out, do you think?' Ruby asked, back to giving Harriet her full attention again.

'I don't know what you mean.'

'Well, you and Mack rekindling all those feelings you wrapped up in words.'

'We're just friends,' Harriet said quickly. 'And I'm with Iain.'

'O-K,' Ruby replied with a nod that said she was anything but convinced. 'That's Iain who spends his life with his head inside his computer and says he doesn't eat meat but has been raiding the coronation turkey mix I made. The one who's left you and gone back to England. That Iain? Just so we're clear.'

'We are very busy people.'

And *that* was what she had said in her boyfriend's defence? That they were busy people?! She should have been singing Iain's praises and telling Ruby all the great attributes he had, like how he always made her coffee just the way she liked it and how she could always rely on him to be where he said he was going to be. There was a lot to be said for that kind of stable. And had Iain really been raiding the coronation turkey?

'Mmm-huh,' Ruby said, waving her cloth in the air as she picked up the stack of plates and headed toward the kitchen.

'Wait a second,' Harriet said.

Ruby stopped still and Harriet joined her, putting an

arm around her shoulders and squeezing a little. The plates between them was a little awkward.

'What are you doin'?' Ruby exclaimed, shirking away like Harriet might have been about to attack her.

'I was... giving you a hug.' She swallowed. Perhaps she needed to pick a better moment.

'But, the British don't do that!'

Harriet's phone ringing distracted her attention and Ruby left her. It would be Iain, reassuring her he was fine after his flight and telling her good news about the house. But instead the screen said 'Dad'.

Thirty-Nine

The Warrior, Fort Pond

'Do not look at me like that, Mr Mack. I do not know the answers!'

Lester had his hands either side of his face, eyes bulging like Mack had asked him to explain the inner workings of the Hadron Collider. They were out on the deck of the boat, Lester's bicycle once again deconstructed and Scooter yapping at the gulls perched on an icy wooden post. It was cold with a tiny layer of snow on the ground, although the clouds suggested that might be topped up any time soon.

'Come on, man, you must know something. You work there all day. You see what goes on and who goes in and who they're getting up to business with.' He pointed a finger at his friend. 'Is Hamlyn from the dairy still getting it on with Betty from the bookshop?'

'Mr Mack! I told you that in confidence!'

'And I haven't breathed a word,' Mack said. 'Yet.'

'If you tell then—'

'I don't even know why it's a secret. Madame S told me

Betty's been single her entire life and Hamlyn's divorced so...'

'Sometimes people like to keep their private life private,' Lester said, folding his arms across his chest.

'Noted,' Mack said. 'Now, tell me, what's the deal with Iain and is he gonna come back?'

'I am telling you, I do not know! He was there and then he wasn't.'

'Huh! Some snoop you are!' He span the back wheel of the bicycle in frustration.

'Because I am not a snoop,' Lester said. 'I am a barman with a broken bicycle.'

'And I'm an ex-sniper with a busted leg. We all have our cross to bear, Lester. And I don't want to add to your pain by taking this bike hostage until you get me some intel but...'

Mack pulled the bicycle towards the cabin.

'Joe is pleased Iain is gone,' Lester sputtered, putting his hands on the front wheel. 'That is all I have.'

'Is he?' Mack inquired. 'Do you know why?'

'It is not my place to say. I tell you again that I am no snoop.' Lester bent down to fuss Scooter who was back on board, bored with the cawing gulls.

'Come on, Lester, man, give me something,' Mack begged.

Lester clicked his tongue. 'What is it that you want to hear?' the man asked. 'And why do you need to hear it?'

Mack felt his self-confidence plummet like a giant rock tossed overboard and destined for the bottom of the lake. Why did he need to know about Iain? Whether the dude was here or there didn't change the fact that Iain was in a relationship with Harri... Except there was something still between *them*. He knew it. Because he could feel it. Last night when she had dropped him off after the skating they'd had a moment. He'd leaned a little on the door of the old Ford, made a joke about their 'meal' of a hot chocolate and then he had looked into her eyes, *really* looked. And she had gazed back at him. The moonlight was right and Joe was snoozing a little and what Mack had wanted to do was draw her face gently towards his and let Harri decide what happened next. What actually happened next was Joe had given a snore and, the vibe broken, Mack had reached across and squeezed her hand as he said goodnight.

'I dunno,' Mack answered Lester's question. 'I guess... I want to know if... Iain treats her right.' God, he sounded like such a dick now. He meant it, obviously, because currently any guy who tried to half-choke a dog for being a little boisterous was a concern to him. But he also wanted to know if there was any slim, vague, tiny speck of a chance that what he and Harri had together on paper, and what they had planned to have in reality when he'd finished his tour, could be revived. If maybe she still felt something after what he'd put her through or whether she was safely shored up with Iain.

Lester let out the sigh of a prima donna and waggled a finger at Mack. 'I will tell you only this. Mr Joe says that Mr Iain is up to something.'

Mack frowned. 'Well, what does that mean?'

Lester shrugged. 'I do not know. Mr Joe says he does not trust Mr Iain. That is all.'

It was most probably nothing. Joe did have those moments where he got a little blurry round the edges, but, like last night at Buckskill, there were also times when he was as alert as the next person.

'Please, put my bicycle back together,' Lester begged. 'I have a bar to run and I have to help Ruby get ready for the Christmas cocktail party tonight.'

'Not forgotten. I've got my outfit all picked out,' Mack said with a smile.

Scooter let out a bark of concurrence.

Forty

Sag Harbor

Harriet hadn't needed to drive eighteen miles to see if there was anything the bar needed to make the Christmas cocktail night the best success, but after the phone call with her dad she'd been struck with nostalgia. So here she was, at one of her favourite places in the Hamptons. Somewhere that was a little bit of a destination secret compared to its neighbouring towns.

Sag Harbor wasn't the party central that city workers came from New York to visit at weekends, savouring the fresh lobster and champagne bar prices. This town was authentic. Just like the area of Montauk that housed The Rum Coconut. Here there was art and history. It was a throwback to how life used to be around here before everything became about rich lists, mansions and celebrities.

Harriet had stood on the waterfront and breathed deep. It was different being here in December. In the past, when she'd visited it had been all about the summer vibe. Yachts in the harbour, bunting blowing in the breeze, the sunlight dappling the water of the bay. Now it was people wrapped up in thick coats instead of sweltering in cut-offs and vests, drinking steaming coffees instead of sodas, and, as she walked around the town, there were shops with festive window displays and fairy lights encircling every tree on the pavement.

Her dad had started the conversation breezily, talking about the weather in Spain and the freshness of the air and the citrus fruits, barely drawing breath to let her reply, and then he had asked how his dad was. It may have been dropped in like she was supposed to think it was an afterthought, but Harriet wasn't that naïve. It meant something. Her dad cared. Just like her nana had shown she cared in the words of her letters. And it had made her all the sentimental. Whatever was behind their not communicating over the years, maybe it could be moved on from. She had always wondered on the reason behind her dad's need to be a free spirit, to find more joy from an anchorless existence flitting to and from Spain, than he did from family. She mused a little more before she stopped in front of a shop window, small flakes of snow in the breeze catching a little in her hair.

This window display was perfection. Someone had hand-painted bright white glittery snowflakes on the windowpanes – enough to make it super-Christmassy and pretty, but not too much that the wares for sale wouldn't be seen – and there was a small fir tree decorated completely in white and silver, incorporating the most delicate figurines. Set around the tree, the icicle lights framing the space, was everything you might need for a cosy winter. Soft blankets in muted pinks and greys, large woollen cushions Harriet just knew she would sink down into, tea trays painted in chalk-paint carrying beautiful cups and saucers and a matching teapot, cloth-bound novels and vinyl records, a white furry rug…

She swallowed, not wanting to draw her eyes away but somehow thinking she should. This was her shop dream. The one she had written about to Mack. The one he had brought up in conversation. She had wanted to be a curator of beautiful things, the person who wandered far and wide picking out random items that sparked joy in her and that she knew would spark joy in other people. She had wanted a premises of impractical goods. Things you would buy as a gift for someone else or a present to yourself or your home. Not expensive necessarily, but items that somehow had a soul. Pictures that told a story, books that provided an escape, cushions that hugged you no matter how you were feeling. She sighed then. And instead of trying to achieve that, she had turned her back on those plans and made a career out of making houses white and sterile so new owners could put their own stamp on them. Where had that girl gone? The one who had worn her heart on her sleeve, learned to box and danced in the sand around a bonfire at a clambake. Mack rejecting her had hurt her, but perhaps actually she had destroyed herself.

She put fingers to the glass and felt the essence of the homely items seep into her. Iain had helped her find a new focus and put her back together again. Except she was now starting to wonder if some of the pieces had been glued into the wrong position…

Forty-One

The Rum Coconut

'Good… evening… adies and gentle… n,' Joe began.

Harriet gasped and prepared to get down off the bar stool she was sitting on. Her grandpa was standing on the stage that in the summer was used to host steel drum players. Tonight it had tinsel and mistletoe hanging from the ceiling over it and the microphone Joe was speaking into was crackling badly, the sound going in and out. Her grandpa had wanted to host tonight and, remembering her nana's letter about the upcoming charity auction, she had decided to let him take a little charge here and now. Except no one had done a check of the sound system apparently.

A loud whistle filled the lower bar area and all chatter stopped as Ruby bustled on stage carrying a bullhorn. Harriet watched the woman hand the implement to Joe and her grandpa look at it like he couldn't believe his luck. Harriet held her breath and prayed a bit.

'Good evening, ladies and gentlemen,' Joe reattempted. Actually it didn't sound too bad.

'Welcome to the annual Rum Coconut Christmas cocktail making contest. Now, the rules are simple and you know 'em. You pay your entry fee and then you have one hour to come up with the perfect festive drink. Ruby, Lester and my granddaughter, Joanna, will be around with the list of ingredients we have and then we're gonna see those Christmas cocktails come to life.' There was a cheer from the eager participants before Joe continued. 'Ingredient samples are on the table back over there for you to have a small test of your would-be creations but, we've put Meryl Cheep next to them and she will be keeping a very close eye on you all to make sure everything is above board.' There was a groan followed by some laughter.

'And I will be coming round for your food and drink orders,' Joe said. 'Because all this plotting and experimenting and dreaming of having your drink on the menu for the Christmas season is sure to make you hungry and thirsty.' He raised his hands. 'And remember, as well as playing for the honour of raising money for charity and for the accolade of having your cocktail put on the menu, you could be taking home The Rum Coconut's three-tier cheesecake made famous by... my Lorna.' Joe dropped the bullhorn from his mouth and looked a little overcome for a second.

Harriet hurriedly began to clap her grandpa and, as the patrons joined in, he descended from the stage and headed back over to her. He looked very dapper tonight in a blue suit and a tie with tiny candy canes embroidered on it. It appeared he had also put a little gel into his hair. Small steps forward perhaps, but any positive change was good.

'Well done, Grandpa,' she said with a smile.

Joe frowned. 'You're looking at me like I'm not accustomed to public speaking.' The expression changed then, a small smile forming. 'Your nana liked it when I did the auctioneering here.'

'I bet she did,' Harriet agreed. She was not going to be the one to shatter his illusions right now.

'So, are you gonna team up with Mack tonight?' Joe asked as he picked an order pad off the bar top.

'What?' Harriet said.

'Well, you've gotta have a team.' He lowered his mouth to her ear. 'And don't tell anyone I said this, but Mack knows his cocktail flavours.' He hitched his head over to a table of six people by the bi-fold doors, snowflakes speckling the glass, the sky outside dark.

Harriet knew he did. Mack had written her a whole page of one of his letters about the mad combinations of drinks he and his crew had mixed together when they had rare downtime. Perhaps the one that had sounded like it could be part of a crazy cocktail contest to Harriet was *doogh*. It was a traditional Afghan drink of water, yoghurt and mint that the troops had shaken up with whisky and lemonade. Mack had said it tasted great, but she remembered he had also said he had smelled of it for a week afterwards.

Mack was sitting at the back of the room nearest Meryl Cheep and the drink samples. Madame Scarlet was with him, Tina Turner-esque hair tonight, delivering what looked like a plate of loaded nachos. Madame Scarlet was in charge of the kitchen for one night only while Ruby focused on the cocktails and the fundraising bucket that would go round in addition to the competition entrance fee.

'I wouldn't take too long making your mind up,' Joe warned. 'Someone else will snap him up if you wait.'

Harriet was about to protest and say that she had to remain impartial and her job tonight was to aid the entrants with recipe cards and controlled access to the sampling materials, but Joe had already gone, beating one of the casuals to a table, order book poised. At least she now knew that this place was the same kind of eccentric at Christmas as it was at the height of summer. Not that there was any doubt. If it had involved her lovely nana then something special – read 'out there' – was guaranteed.

Her phone buzzed in the pocket of her blue jeans and she pulled it out. It had to be Iain now surely.

Jude: I might have a little mishap with Succulent Number 2 (SN2 I call her). Please do not worry.

Jude: I looked it up on Google and it's totally not fatal no matter how much she has ingested.

Jude: I may have put vodka in a jug waiting to erode some Werther's Originals to make toffee vodka. And Gethin from Matchstick Models Club may have mistaken it for water.

Jude: He did mistake it for water. He watered SN2 for me before I realised. But she's fine really. Look.

Jude: *photo image of mainly her thumb and a slight hint of plant*

★

'It's busy tonight,' Mack said, picking at the nachos Madame Scarlet had delivered that were loaded with crab, shrimp, sour cream, all the cheeses and his special request of a side of spiced guacamole. 'It's good to see.'

'Honey, I've got orders backing up already. I haven't really got time to talk... or drink cold beer.' Madame Scarlet picked up Mack's bottle and took a swig before returning it back to the table.

'Hey!' he protested. 'That was sneaky. And I was thinking of inviting you on my team tonight.'

Madame Scarlet laughed. 'Sweetheart, I'm not gonna have time to do anything but keep the meals coming.' She cleared her throat and raised her eyes, pencilled brows rising up into her hairline. 'But I see someone coming who might want to mix up a thing or two.'

Mack looked away from Madame Scarlet and saw Harri was heading his way. How did she always look so low-key fantastic all the time? His stomach was rolling like a surfer caught in the middle of a wave off of Big Sur. He had to play it down, take it slow and remember she wasn't single. Most importantly, he had to be cool.

'Have fun, my darling,' Madame Scarlet whispered.

Harri's eyes were giving him all the green lights. Except he knew there was a level-crossing stop sign he'd installed himself that needed lifting before he thought about anything else.

'Hello,' Harri said, as Madame Scarlet beat a hasty retreat to the kitchen.

'Hey,' he answered. 'I was saying to Madame Scarlet that it's a great turn-out for the contest tonight.'

'It really is,' Harri agreed. 'I think most of it is Ruby's doing. This night is her baby and I know she really wants her event to bring in the most money for charity and for the bar too.' She smiled. 'I didn't know you were coming.'

'Oh, really? Well,' Mack started. 'I'm pretty much part of the furniture here if I'm honest. The only thing I don't do is work behind the bar, but I have done that in the past and I would do it again if needed.'

'I thought you might be here because you have your eye on the prize. Seeing as how you're a cocktail expert.'

'I hope you're not insinuating that I'm in any way not eligible to compete.'

'I know you're skilled at making drinks out of weird ingredients.' She looked suddenly self-conscious, as if she might have said something out of place. He wanted to tell her that nothing she could say would ever be out of place to him.

'Sorry,' she apologised. 'I was just remembering something you once said in a letter. I don't know if you—'

'Let me stop you right there,' Mack said, interrupting. 'You are talking about The Bagram Bucket challenge and I'm not sure how much the good people of Montauk should hear about that, particularly when they're eating.' He picked up a nacho and put it into his mouth.

'Miss Joanna!'

Mack internally cursed Lester as the barman called across the room. He needed to make the suggestion that she join him before the opportunity passed. He took a breath.

'Listen, I know you're kinda working tonight, but do

you wanna join Team Wyatt and help me make something that's gonna wipe the floor with everyone else?' He grinned. 'Because there's nothing much I love more than Lorna's three-tier cheesecake.'

Say yes. Say yes. He was holding his breath, now suddenly not quite so hungry for the food in front of him.

'I hope it's going to be OK,' Harriet said. 'Ruby and I almost got more cheesecake on ourselves than we did in the trays and do not ask about the tiers. It's literal engineering how we've stacked them up.'

And she hadn't answered the question. He smiled. He wasn't going to ask a second time.

'I'd love to be part of your team,' she told him. 'I just need to hand out some recipe cards and make sure everyone is getting on OK and then I'll come back.'

He couldn't control the width of his smile. 'Sure. Cool.' He nodded.

Had that hit enthusiastic yet keeping it on the downlow? God, why was he even pretending it didn't matter? Of course it mattered. Getting to spend time with her was an absolute gift.

'OK,' Harriet said, putting her hands in the pockets of her jeans. 'I'll be back in a second. Save me some shrimp.'

Mack watched her head back into the thick of the room and he put a hand to his beer bottle. Taking a deep breath, he counselled himself. *OK, Wyatt, don't mess this up.*

Forty-Two

'What is that in your pocket?' Harriet hiss-whispered. 'Really, Harri?' He winked.

'I'm serious!'

'Keep it down,' Mack said, curling his fingers around something he had extracted from his jeans. 'This might be what wins us the cheesecake. It's the only thing that's not out there on the ingredients table.' He unfurled his fingers for a millisecond and then folded them back over again.

'What?' Harriet exclaimed. 'How did you expect me to see that?' She playfully hit his arm but quickly withdrew after contact. Just when she had thought things were feeling easy and relaxed and her jaw was already aching from laughing so much over the good-natured rivalry of cocktail ingredient testing around them, she'd taken it a strike too far. Because every physical contact sent a vibration through her, one she was having an issue with dampening down. Coupling that with the fact she was practically revelling in being around a table with him, talking to him, looking at him... She mentally regrouped and remembered she was a grown-up. She still hadn't heard from Iain. She glanced at the screen of her phone on the table next to their beers. Nothing. Not even another apology message from Jude.

'You expecting a call?' Mack asked, breaking the awkwardness she'd hoped he wasn't sensing.

'No, I, well… it's just…' She took a breath. 'I haven't heard from Iain since he got back to the UK. I checked the flight had landed safely and I've left him some messages but no reply yet.' She shrugged. 'He's probably busy sorting out the problem we have.'

'Or he took a different flight and he's on a beach somewhere sipping from a guava.'

'Iain's not the guava-sipping kind.'

'No?' Mack asked. 'What is his kind?'

'You don't like him.'

'I don't know him.'

'He's been good to me,' Harriet told him. And she meant every word. Iain had been good to her. He had been the shoulder of security she had needed from the moment they met and she could never put a price on that support.

'Then that's all I need to know,' Mack whispered.

Harriet watched him pick up his beer and take a swig.

'So, tell me what secret ingredient is going to win us the cheesecake,' Harriet said, changing the vibe.

Mack put down his beer and leaned his body into the table a little. Then he rolled his fingers out and presented something that looked like a small pebble.

'Nutmeg,' Harriet said. She frowned. 'Who puts nutmeg in a cocktail?'

'I hear doubt in your voice, Harri,' Mack said with a tut. 'Don't you trust me?'

His question gave her all kinds of inner turmoil. There was a time when she would have said she trusted him more than anyone else in her life. But then he'd smashed their trust, broken her heart. She swallowed. Except had that been because of what happened to him? Had the tough guy not wanted to appear weak and simply decided she didn't get a chance to choose? When was the last time she had made her own choices?

'You don't have to answer that,' he said with a half-smile. 'Dumbass question.' He breezed on though. 'It's gonna be invaluable. Because we're making a hot cocktail.'

She must have misheard. 'What?'

'I entered for the first time last year,' Mack admitted. 'But I was just feeling my feet then. My entry didn't quite come out right. I... couldn't set light to the banana.'

Harriet laughed. 'I would like to have seen that.'

'Lorna thought it was funny,' Mack said. 'Gave me points for effort, but I was beaten by a bright purple twist on a daiquiri called Mother of Mary.'

'Was it the priest's team?' Harriet asked.

'How did you know?'

She laughed anew. This was nice. Whatever it was, it was a warm, cosy happy place that was distracting her from the loss of her nana and anything that could be constituted as worrisome. Her concerns for Joe, Iain, Jude's care of her plants, a plot of land ripe for turning into a Sandals... It should have been difficult and emotional but somehow it wasn't. Somehow it was easy and light and a lot of what it had been through their correspondence.

'You think we can train Meryl to do a trick?' Mack asked her.

'Are you joking?' Harriet said. 'No one can train her to even stop talking.'

While everyone was working on their cocktail recipes and she had left Mack talking to the parrot, Harriet took the opportunity to seek out Dr Ambrose. He was in a team with two women she didn't recognise.

'Hello, Dr Ambrose, can I get you anything else to drink?' she offered.

'Oh no thank you, Joanna, I'm grand,' he chortled. 'Listen, I hear you got Joseph out on the ice rink.'

'I did,' Harriet answered. 'That was OK, wasn't it? We looked after him and made sure he didn't do any triple axels or anything.'

'I think it's marvellous you got him out at all. I was a little worried that after Lorna passed his world might start to shrink. I know he loves this place, but it would help if his interests were increased.'

One of the ladies took hold of Harriet's hand and gave it a squeeze. She had white curly hair and kind eyes. 'I'm Mavis Koontz. I styled your nana's hair. Every second Friday.'

'Oh my goodness! Mavis!' Harriet exclaimed. 'She always called you Mavis Waves and I thought for a long time that was your real name.' She was right back to being ten again, her nana putting bobby pins into her own hair and tying plaits with yellow ribbons. Her nana had had so many friends. A full, real community of people around her, caring about her. Maybe it went some way to making up for her dad's absence. 'It's lovely to see you.'

'It's a pleasure to see you back here, Joanna,' Mavis

answered, giving her hand another pump. 'And we're enjoying watching you make that boy over there smile again.'

Boy? Harriet turned around, looking at the room and half-expecting Rufus and Riley to be there. Ruby had installed them in what had become Harriet's room upstairs, with the TV on and a pile of snacks that could have fed the whole of Montauk and probably all Jude's friends from her various societies too. Harriet had been sure they would be OK in the bar with them all, and might enjoy helping with the contest, but Ruby had insisted they would create something that Harriet had envisaged like the rough and tumble of a Boxing Day sale at Next.

'Mackenzie,' Mavis elaborated. 'He's a cute one, there's no doubt about that. But there's always been that air of sadness about him ever since he rolled into town.'

'I'd marry him if he asked,' the other woman who hadn't introduced herself said suddenly. 'I've always loved men with curls like that.'

Harriet was looking at Mack now. He was concentrating, a couple of jars of ingredients on the table, making notes, pen resting on those fleshed out, cute lips... And then all those feelings she used to get from reading his letters and staring at that one photo came rushing over her. She was heating up as if someone had stuck her right next to the log fire and she was melting.

'Dr Ambrose,' she said quickly. 'Could I talk to you for a second? Privately.'

The doctor was out of his chair like she might be ready to collapse there and then, or divulge that she had a life-altering condition she needed extra medication for. She stepped far enough away from the tables so no one could overhear. Between a basket of pine cones and fir fronds and a table housing leaflets about the grand auction night.

'Is everything OK, Joanna?' Dr Ambrose asked, pushing his wire-framed glasses up his nose.

'Yes,' she breathed. 'I think so.' She smiled. 'I hope so.'

'What is it, dear? You look like you have the worries of the world on your shoulders.'

Did she? She supposed she still hadn't really slept properly the whole time she had been in Montauk. There was the time difference still doing its thing and the big hole her nana had left here and Iain wanting to buy real estate and... well... Mack.

'I just...' Harriet began. Her eyes found her grandpa. He was proudly leading a family of four through the main room towards the upper dining area, collecting crayons and drawing mats and popping the Rum Coconut paper pirate hats on the heads of the children. He did look much more like himself now. But she had to ask a professional. 'Is my grandpa going to be alright?'

Dr Ambrose gave a wide smile and put a hand on her shoulder. 'Now, you listen to me,' he began as if he was more than the local figure of authority and maybe on his way to run for senate. 'Joseph is my patient, not yours. As far as his medical needs go, that's my job.'

Harriet went to make reply, but was silenced by this big bear of a man laying another heavy pat on her shoulder.

'Your grandpa is going to be fine,' Dr Ambrose insisted. 'And he's in good health. I would say perfect health for his age, but I know he will never attend one of my diabetic clinics, even if I offered cookies.'

'He needs to cut down on his sugar?' Harriet asked. She was appalled that she had bought him that rich, creamy, sugar-infused hot chocolate now!

'No,' Dr Ambrose said with a shake of his head. 'Only in so far as none of us should be eating cake for breakfast.' He paused for a moment. 'Unless it's your birthday.'

She breathed a short sigh of relief and then remembered what she was really most concerned about. 'And his memory is OK? You know, sometimes he goes a bit distant and talks about the past like it happened yesterday.' She swallowed. 'I don't know if it's just him getting older and the fact I haven't seen him for a while, or whether it's something else.' She meant dementia but there was no way she was going to say it. And you didn't self-diagnose, or diagnose your family members, did you? She'd read somewhere that a firm suggestion to a doctor could sway their own hard-studied-for medical opinion and it might lead to a misdiagnosis of something far more serious…

'Joanna,' Dr Ambrose said in his lowest and most authoritative baritone. 'Your grandpa has lost his soulmate. Someone he was connected to, intimately, in every area of his life for over fifty years. It wasn't expected. It was a huge shock. He needs to process that. Like all of us.' He sighed sadly. 'But for him, it's going to hit harder and deeper and take much longer to adjust. His heart needs to heal and it will take some time for him to get accustomed to new routines and, even then, there will always be a notable absence. Joseph needs to gently learn to acknowledge that, yet somehow separate his everyday from it.' Dr Ambrose sighed and adjusted his glasses again. 'I'm not explaining this very well, am I?'

'No, you are,' Harriet insisted. 'I just wanted to be sure

that there's nothing else going on besides that. Because sadness and grief… it can hide things.'

Dr Ambrose nodded soberly. 'Yes it can. But trust me when I say I have my eyes firmly on your grandpa and I am dropping questions into conversations over apple turnovers that would give me warning bells if they were answered a certain way.'

'OK,' Harriet said, finally letting a relieved breath leave her.

'Not only does your grandpa know who the president currently is. He gave me chapter and verse on his opinions of the old one.'

She smiled, feeling a lot better about things.

'It's good that you're here, Joanna,' Dr Ambrose told her. 'I'm sure having you around is giving Joseph a lift and a purpose.' He grinned. 'If I know Joseph, I expect he was showing off a little to you on the ice the other night.'

'Maybe a little,' she admitted. And then her eyes fell on Mack again. He was right next to Meryl Cheep's cage now, seemingly talking to the bird.

'Was there something else on your mind?' Dr Ambrose queried.

She had called Dr Ambrose over to talk about her grandpa, but this was an opportunity for something else. Should she say what she wanted to say?

'I don't want you to break any patient confidentiality,' she began, watching Mack coax Meryl Cheep onto his hand. 'But could you tell me a little more about… how it might be to lose a leg.' She took a breath. 'You know, the practicalities of it and… the difficulties, I guess.'

'Oh,' Dr Ambrose said, sounding a little surprised by the

question. 'Well, I think the person you should really talk to is... currently trying to get a parrot to hold something with its beak.' They were both watching Meryl and Mack's antics now.

'I realise that,' Harriet answered. 'But I'm worried I'll say the wrong thing and I just thought...'

'You'd ask a doctor,' Dr Ambrose ended for her.

She shrugged. 'Mack keeps things in now,' she said softly. 'He never used to do that before.'

'Well,' Dr Ambrose said. 'They say it only takes one person to make a change.' He patted her shoulder again. 'Mack's a straight-up guy. Ask him whatever it is you want to know.'

As Dr Ambrose headed back to his teammates, Harriet's phone buzzed in the pocket of her jeans. She drew it out and read the message on the screen.

Iain: Water and electric crisis averted. Made an appointment for you to see the land on Navy Road again. Check your schedule. *thumbs up emoji*

Harriet blinked and blinked again, waiting for the bubbles to appear that would tell her he was writing something else or adding a simple kiss. Then... nothing.

Forty-Three

'You nervous?' Mack asked Harriet.

He was partially covered in ingredients, his cream long-sleeved shirt with the light palm tree pattern speckled with all kinds of spices and a green goo he'd managed to get on there when he'd fraternised with a team creating something by hollowing out a pineapple.

Harriet smiled. 'They're not about to announce the winners at the Oscars.'

'Wow,' Mack said. 'I'm more excited than I ever am watching that.'

'Ruby hasn't even told me the criteria for judging,' Harriet admitted.

'Well,' Mack said as they watched Ruby stride the line of cocktail creations now in the centre of the room under a spotlight. 'She notes down colour and presentation first.'

There was every hue imaginable from a dark berry red, through to one that somehow had layers of pink and turquoise and another with squirty cream to make a Santa beard and a piece of red apple to represent his hat. And all eyes were on the judge with the big hair, a no-messing expression and a clipboard.

'Ours doesn't really stand out,' Harriet said.

'What?! Do you know how long it took me to perfect that shade of plum?' He slapped a hand to his chest and pretended she had wounded him.

'I know you drank more than you put into the glass,' she countered.

'Hey, Harri, no one likes a Sober Susan on festive cocktail night.'

'I'm not sober,' she bit back. 'I just haven't soaked up rum like I'm sitting in a hot tub with it.'

He looked at her with the straightest expression he could manage before they both burst into laughter and earned themselves some shushing from the expectant crowd. Mack gasped then, touching her arm. 'Shit, don't get us disqualified. I do really want that cheesecake.'

He watched Harriet straighten her demeanour and get back to watching Ruby. He wet his lips then stood a little closer to her. He could smell her hair. *God, he could smell her hair*. He closed his eyes and let the fragrance do crazy things to him. It was the ocean and the sunlight, it was fall leaves and pumpkins, it was like a memory he'd never even had...

'She's judging ours now,' Harriet said, looking a little over her shoulder at him.

'Right, OK, here comes the magic,' Mack answered, pulling himself together. 'Hey! Ruby!' He strode toward the table with purpose.

'What are you doing?' Ruby asked, staring him down

like she was a member of a parole board and he was getting added time.

'Sorry, Ruby,' Harriet said, following behind him. 'We'd really appreciate it if you could taste our cocktail first because it's a hot cocktail and otherwise it will go cold.'

'Did you hear that folks?' Mack asked, turning around to face the gathered crowd. 'Ours is a *hot* cocktail.'

He loved the fact that everyone made all the astonished wish-we-had-thought-of-that noises right on cue.

'Yours is number six,' Ruby clarified.

'We know,' Harriet said. 'But we just wondered if you could break protocol this once.'

'There's nothing in the rules that states you have to try them in number order,' Mack added. 'Like, you can start wherever you like. *You're* in charge.'

Ruby was looking at him now as she tried to work out how that sentence was a big-up as well as a come-down. She shook her curls and that seemed to spur her into action.

'Fine! I'll taste yours first.' She turned towards the table and was about to pick up the large brandy glass they'd made it in.

'Wait! Stop!' Mack called, rushing forward.

Ruby now looked ferociously mad. 'What's happenin'? You ask me to taste it first! Now you don't want me to pick it up? What the heck am I supposed to do with it? Wipe it on my face like a lotion?'

A few people started to chuckle, but Mack knew they would be laughing on the other side of their faces when they saw what was coming next. He said a silent prayer then put his fingers to his mouth and whistled.

Harriet watched in awe as Meryl Cheep rose like a phoenix from the top of her cage, flapping her way across the room and coming to a halt on Mack's extended arm like she had morphed into a bird of prey. She hadn't really known what Mack was intending for Meryl to do but it certainly hadn't been that.

'Ruby! Ruby!' the parrot said, bobbing its head around.

Mack walked closer to the table and separated their entry from the others. Then he put the nutmeg down on the table.

'What is going on here?' Ruby asked the crowd as much as anyone else. 'This is a cocktail making contest, not a circus.'

Harriet smiled as she watched Meryl get down from Mack's arm and stand in front of the nutmeg. Then the bird lowered her beak to it and began pushing it slowly across the table, stepping on until she had transported it to the base of the glass.

'I don't know what to say,' Ruby said, sounding astonished. 'That bird never does nothing for me.'

Mack produced a grater from somewhere about his person and handed it to Ruby. 'A good few grates of that on top and it's good to go.'

The atmosphere in the room had suddenly changed from festively relaxed to excitedly tense as all the teams and some diners in the restaurant all watched Ruby grating nutmeg over the drink as Mack took hold of Meryl Cheep, letting the bird rest back on his hand.

'Nervous now?' Mack asked Harriet.

'A little bit,' she admitted. Then it suddenly occurred to her there was something she didn't know. 'What's it called?'

'What?'

'Our cocktail,' Harriet said. 'What's the festive name you chose?'

Mack grinned then. 'You'll have to wait and see if we win.'

Harriet watched Ruby take a long slow drink of their cocktail and couldn't tell from her expression what she was feeling about the experience. Harriet had liked it a lot. It was a combination of brandy, white rum, cinnamon, nutmeg, cloves and cream heated up and finished with the extra nutmeg touch on top and a side of dark chocolate. But whether it was enough to win depended on what everyone else had concocted.

Mack nudged her arm. 'Trust me. We've got this in the bag.'

'Jo-anna! Jo-anna!' Meryl chirped.

Forty-Four

They didn't win. Instead they scored third place to the hollowed-out pineapple and a drink named Ring in the Reindeer.

But Harriet didn't care. It had been the best fun, everyone had ordered plenty of drinks and food, Madame Scarlet had managed not to force palm-reading on anyone and the three-tier cheesecake had stayed together long enough to be boxed and given to the winning team to take home. The Rum Coconut had been the lovely, lively, slightly crazy eatery from her youth, and the whole night had been like a hug sent down from her nana. It had been a true tribute to the woman everyone was missing.

Two bowls in her hand, Harriet paused at the back door and watched Mack tending to the fire pit. Yes, there were still flakes of snow in the air, but she was the one who had made this suggestion. To bring drinks out onto her nana's porch to the left of the restaurant's outside decked area, that tiny piece of comfort that housed that swing seat and all the cushions and this half-barrel Mack had filled with kindling, topped with a few logs and set light to. *Was this how things would have been? Would we have ended up here in Montauk together?* She swallowed. She shouldn't allow herself to even think that way. The bar lights were low now, everyone gone home except Lester, who was finishing clearing up, and her grandpa, who had gone to bed. Harriet carried the bowls towards the glowing fire.

'Mack,' she said, getting to him.

He turned around and smiled at the bowl she was offering out. 'What's this? Commiseration pie?'

She smiled. 'It's ice cream. My nana's special blueberry recipe. Ruby and I made some earlier.'

'Ice cream in December,' Mack remarked. 'Well, you always have been a whole host of contradictions.'

'What?!' Harriet exclaimed.

He laughed, throwing the stick he was holding into the flames and taking the bowl from her. 'Come on, you know it.' He sat down on the swing seat. 'Sugar in your coffee. But you try to avoid cake. You hate Bruce Springsteen but you love Journey. You don't like her music but you'd rather kiss Rihanna than Robert Downey Jr – OK, that one maybe I get but, man, the weirdest – you love the smell of coconut but you don't like the taste of it. How is that even possible?'

Harriet froze. They were all things she had told him over the years in their letters. 'You remember,' she whispered as she finally lowered herself into the seat next to him.

He nodded, looking a little like he had revealed a secret he'd been keeping for the longest time. 'Yeah,' he said, voice cracking. 'I remember.'

Harriet let a breath hit the air and it spiralled off into the darkness, merging with the heat from the fire. There was so much between them and she didn't even know where to begin, or if perhaps they would always be in the middle of some kind of an ending. She ploughed on. 'I went to Sag Harbour today.'

'Yeah?'

'I just needed to get out for a bit, you know.' She smiled. 'I love it here but even things you love can sometimes get too much. Everyone saying they're sorry for our loss. Everyone misses Nana so much. Of course I want people to miss her and to have loved her but... I don't know... it's maybe because they all got to spend more time with her than I did.'

'OK, Rihanna, I'm listening.'

'I should have spent more time with her. I don't know why I didn't come over here in three years.' Or maybe she knew exactly why. Perhaps Montauk made her think about the boy she used to know, the boy she'd written letters to on this very swing seat telling him about the birds on the waves and being nipped at by an angry crab. Instead she had stayed with Iain, keeping busy and ignoring everything that made her heart beat a little faster. Living cautiously instead of taking flight. Mack was just looking at her, waiting for whatever she decided came next.

She shook her head. 'So, anyway, I went to Sag Harbour and... I walked through town and I sucked in all the festive... and then I saw it.' She took a sharp breath inward from thinking about the beautiful storefront. She put the bowl of ice cream on the small space on the seat between them and got her phone from her pocket. Swiping to the photos she showed the display to Mack.

'This shop,' she said, letting him look, then swiping to the next photo on the camera roll. 'This is exactly what

I always dreamed of. What I wrote to you about. There were picnic baskets and cosy blankets and bedding with hand-embroidered owls... picture frames and a painting of the lighthouse... mason jars and solar lights in the shape of horseshoes... candles that smelled like cut grass and caramel popcorn.' She had to take a breath before she ran out of air.

'What happened, Harri?' Mack whispered.

'I don't know,' she answered. 'It got away from me somehow.' Then she shook her head. 'No, that's not true. I *let* it get away from me.' She really couldn't blame anyone else. She had chosen to choose practicality over possibility. Iain might have helped to shape the idea of the business but at any time she could have said 'no' and said it wasn't what she wanted. Couldn't she?

'It's never too late,' Mack told her.

She raised her head from looking into her ice cream bowl and took a minute to drink him in. She used to know every centimetre of his face by heart even though she had never touched it. It was the same now... but different. He was furrowing his brow a little and there were tiny creases across his forehead and fine lines at the corners of those eyes. *Those eyes.* It had never only been about the colour, there had always been substance there, even from that one photograph, it had felt like a glimpse inside of him. He had light freckles on his skin she could never have picked up from a Polaroid. They crossed the bridge of his nose and stopped halfway across his cheekbones, where, just below, lay the beginnings of a five o'clock shadow. She was holding her breath as she gazed at the shape of his mouth. It was masculine, but it was also beautiful – like it had been drawn to order. Before she even thought about what she was doing, she had put both the bowls on the floor and she was raising her index finger to his lips and tenderly tracing the line.

Mack didn't move a muscle. *Couldn't* move a muscle. She was touching him and it felt like every part of him had suddenly rushed to the surface and was trying to break out. He closed his eyes. All the memories of her words, the plans they'd talked about, that one video call where they'd both somehow tried to live a whole lifetime in a few minutes, rushing out what they wanted to say with barely room to fit in a breath. Neither of them knew how much things would change so shortly after. But she had never given up on him until her hand was forced. He had shut it down, pushed her away like suddenly she was the enemy. *It's never too late*. If he really meant that then what was he doing sitting here with his eyes closed? Because he didn't want to break the moment. Because he couldn't trust himself not to make a move? She was the love of his life. He had fallen a little deeper as each letter arrived and he had been gone already before he even got to know what she looked like. After that he was completely, utterly, lost.

He opened his eyes and the orange glow from the fire was nothing to the brightness shining in her eyes and the colour splashed across her cheeks. The fact she was even here, was letting him in a little, God, he'd never dreamed it could be possible. He moved his mouth the smallest amount and prayed she wouldn't take her touch away. Her finger was still there, now creating waves over his bottom lip. His heart was thumping out of time. He had two choices now.

He either caught her finger in a kiss or he didn't. The alpha in him was howling like she was the full moon calling him home, the other part of him – the one who knew right from wrong and had respect – was telling him the decision he made now could dictate everything that came next.

He reached up, took her finger and the rest of her hand in his, drawing it down to rest on his knee. He cupped her hand with both of his and held on tight.

'When I was in rehab learning how to walk again,' he began. 'I used to imagine you standing at the end of the room.' He swallowed. 'When I had no energy and nothing left to give I imagined you bawling me out. Telling me "don't be a wuss".' He'd attempted a British accent and he knew it was pretty terrible.

She smiled though and she hadn't claimed back her hand. He used his thumb to caress her fingers, the pad exploring the lengths and the folds in between.

'I could have been there for real,' Harri reminded him.

He shook his head. 'Yeah, don't think I don't think about that every second of every day too.' He sighed. 'I shouldn't have sent your letters back. I shouldn't have got people to lie to you. I should have at least owned my decision. It wasn't that I didn't want to see you. God, I *always* wanted to see you.' He squeezed her hand again. 'Back then I was afraid of you seeing *me*.'

'Mack… I know something happened to you that was more than losing a leg,' she said, squeezing his thumb and holding it tight. She caught his other hand and brought it to her mouth, brushing his knuckles with her lips.

He felt his lips firm up in a tough line the way they

always did when a therapist got a little too deep and grazed the surface of what was really going on. And she had read that. 'Harri.' He breathed out hard.

'I'm still here,' she whispered. 'If you want me to be.'

He swallowed. What did that mean? Because right now that wolfish guy wanted nothing more than to remove the oversized jumper she was wearing. But it really wasn't about the fact that physically she turned him on to the point that it ached so bad. Emotionally he was beaten and bruised. His psyche was so bent out of shape that sometimes reality got blurry. He never wanted to share that with anyone. How could he?

'That's the problem,' he told her, taking his hand from hers. 'I don't know how much of the me you knew is still here.'

And he couldn't give anything else tonight. He got to his feet and put his hands into his hair with an intake of breath. 'I should go.'

Harri nodded, eyes losing their sparkle. That was on him. He had dimmed her shine just like that. How could he not hurt her? He was damned if he did and damned if he didn't.

'Hey,' he said, making her look up. 'You asked earlier what our cocktail was called.'

She didn't say anything, just carried on looking at him like he was ripping her to pieces for about the millionth time.

'Harri Holidays,' he told her. 'You know, kinda like a play on "Happy Holidays".' He sighed. 'Yeah, now I've said that out loud it sounds like a lame-ass name for a cocktail. I'm just gonna go.' He made to leave, but suddenly she was standing, barring the way.

'Be back here at nine-thirty tomorrow morning,' she told him.

It wasn't a question, it was an order. He looked at her quizzically, trying to work out if he had missed something along the way.

'Nine-thirty,' she repeated, placing the flat of her hand on his chest.

If she could feel his heart through his shirt then it would be telling her it hadn't reacted to this much adrenaline in the longest time.

He had to clear his throat before he felt able to speak. 'What do I wear?'

The question made her look puzzled and her fingers moved against the material of his shirt. *Don't let go. Not yet.*

'I mean,' he swallowed. 'If it's a physical thing... I might need a different leg.'

God, that sounded all kinds of wrong. 'By physical I meant, running or something like that.'

She smiled then. 'Dress warm and bring Scooter if you like.'

He nodded. This was his cue to go now. If he stayed and let the warmth of her hand get too familiar it would be even harder to tear himself away.

'Goodnight,' she whispered, finally moving her hand.

'Goodnight.'

Forty-Five

Downtown Montauk

This felt good. The old Ford's steering wheel beneath her hands, the radio playing some festive country music and a guy and his dog riding shotgun. It could have been a scene from a country song itself as they cruised through the town that was jam-packed with holidaymakers every summer but was now much more low-key and homey. She took a quick glance at Mack before focusing again on the road. He'd turned up on the dot of nine-thirty, dressed in jeans, a dark blue cable knit jumper and a brown leather bomber on top. The breakfast sitting was in full swing, Meryl Cheep had tried to eat a customer's scarf as the lady had passed by her cage and Riley and Rufus' lift to school hadn't materialised so Madame Scarlet was back in the kitchen while Ruby rushed off to drop them. Her grandpa had met Mack at the door like he was going to show him to a table until Harriet had appeared, buttoning her coat over leggings and a grey woollen jumper dress. Still trying to get them both to sit down to breakfast, Joe was even less keen to hand over the keys to his truck. In the end Harriet had promised Mack was going to drive to enable them to get out the door.

With a bag of cinnamon-and-custard doughnuts and take-out coffees between Mack's thighs she had driven them around the centre of town, wanting to soak in the memories of her youth and remember what Montauk meant to her. The coffees and the food had come from a tiny pop-up diner that looked like it had been dropped down onto the street from Lapland. It was a small alpine shack decorated in candy canes and lights and all the festive whimsy, with hanging wreaths and buckets of winter blooms for sale too. In the summer Harriet loved the pop-up shops selling ice cold slushies and smoothies and muffins with a cooling ice cream shot of surprise inside. It was all lemon and melon and chilled-out surfers, whereas now it was more about hot spiced tea and everything with cranberries. It seemed that Christmas here was a much more mellow affair, with locals who were usually working every hour in their businesses able to take some well-deserved time off. Although they had driven past Howard's garage and Maggie's florists and both seemed to be busy with customers. She needed to come downtown for a proper visit while she was here. It was just that everywhere here she had previously visited with her nana by her side and the thought of buying a flower arrangement or ingredients for baking something without that special someone to deliberate with didn't hold the same appeal. But, like with her grandpa, she guessed she had to try to find a way through it.

'I have to ask,' Mack said above the radio. 'Why won't your grandpa let you drive the truck?'

Harriet smiled. 'I haven't scared you yet then.'

'You drive too fast,' Mack admitted. 'But I kinda like that.'

She also had her window rolled down as far as was bearable in the temperatures and, every now and then, she would stick her hand out to feel the hit of the cold air whistling through her fingers. She had always done that when her grandpa had been in the driving seat and he had always warned she would lose her fingers if they met a big truck. But that wasn't the reason he didn't trust her with his beloved Ford.

'I broke his lawn mower,' Harriet admitted.

'What?' Mack sputtered, his body movement nearly upturning the cups.

'It could have been worse,' Harriet said. 'He was pushing it at the time. But, honestly, who mows the lawn in the path of a reversing truck.'

'You almost killed Joe,' Mack said, shaking his head. 'I think you should pull over and let me drive.'

'Pass me my coffee before it spills all over your lap.'

'You're not drinking and driving on my watch.'

'Well, what do you think?' Harriet asked, blowing a breath out into the frosty air. She had parked the truck on the side of the road and they'd walked out onto the beach. The surf was furious today, frothing up like it was in a blender, crushing and roaring at the shoreline. She stopped walking at the massive realtor's sign that seemed to have grown in size since her last visit.

Mack was quiet and had been since they had got out of

the truck. As they had walked up and down the sand she had talked about the holiday apartments and how much money it might make after the initial – slightly terrifying – outlay Iain had detailed in an email she'd received overnight, including all the projections displayed in graphs *and* pie charts. She wasn't sure what she thought herself, but seeing all Iain's ideas committed to illustrative outlines made it seem less of a crazy plan she thought he had plucked out of thin air. It made it business-like, strategic and structured. The language of their relationship. The dialect of her last few years.

Scooter jumped up at her then, a piece of driftwood between his jaws. Harriet took it from him and launched it along the sand, watching his little legs pumping up and down as he chased it down. She looked back to his owner, who still hadn't said a word.

'Mack?' she said. 'What do you think?'

'What do I think?' He sighed again. 'Yeah, that's a question.'

'I'd value your opinion,' Harriet said. 'It's a big project. We haven't taken on anything like this before and it's a bit of a risk but—'

'Where did you go, Harri?' Mack asked, looking at her now. 'Between last night when you put your hand on my heart and talked about bedding with owls on, to now speaking like you're gonna create a Trump hotel on the sand?'

She nibbled at her lip and tried to turn his words into something else, something she was able to deal with. Because he was right. Last night she had been the person she used to be. The one who had come out of her parents' divorce relatively unscathed, had maybe small but tailored dreams and expectations, would choose happiness and simplicity over risk and complications. But that person had had to change and adapt, and adaptation and challenge were the only ways to keep your head above water. To dream less and think more. Except being here was making those ideals she had held tight to wobble like a poorly-built house during an earth tremor.

'It has merit, doesn't it?' she asked, a catch in her voice she was struggling to disguise.

'For who?' Mack wanted to know. 'For what? Sure, some of the people round here will be glad of the jobs, but you told me your dream last night. Your store. Yet, this morning, you wanna throw that away for concrete apartments with a communal pool?'

The trouble was Mack saw her in a way Iain never had. Iain had never known the independent, sunny girl who smeared coconut products on her skin but couldn't have it anywhere near her palate. Iain had always led – because she had needed him to – and she had always followed and that basis had worked for all this time. Had she asked Mack here because she knew what he was going to say and she wanted to hear him say it? Or was it because she wanted to see, once he had given his opinion, if she really did have the passion for the project and could debate that with him?

'Ah, I get it,' he said suddenly, relieving Scooter of the wood again and throwing it as far as he could.

'What?' Because she didn't get it herself. Not entirely.

'You want me to make this decision for you.' He was looking at her now and nodding like she had suddenly just been unmasked as the real villain behind every world problem.

'No,' she said, shaking her head.

'No? So, you're fully on board with this? You wanna take this beautiful beachfront and put bricks into the sand and build it up as high as regulations will let you. Look at it, Harri.' He spread his arms wide then, the jacket flaring out a little in the breeze. It made him look a bit like an eagle. She swallowed at the conviction he was showing in protest to her apparent need to tell him this could be what she wanted. *Could be*. But it *was* what Iain wanted.

'If we don't buy it,' she countered. 'Someone else will do exactly the same.'

'Wow,' Mack said, dropping his arms. 'I mean... seriously wow.'

'I don't know what to do!' she admitted, screaming the notion into the air. 'And you're right! I don't know who I am!'

Before Harriet knew it there were tears streaming from her eyes and all the exhaustion and grief and uncertainty decided to come flooding out.

Scooter reached her first, springing up high, trying to lick her face, as she bent in two. She didn't want to pet him. She wanted to drop to the beach and cry all this out. Amid the torrent of salt water from her eyes she sensed Mack was there too now.

'You know who you are,' he told her in no uncertain terms. 'You just need to be brave enough to slice through everyone else's bullshit.'

She sniffed, recovering a little. 'Yeah, like it's that easy.'

'Believe me,' Mack said. 'Everyone else's bullshit gets put into perspective once you've lain in the dust and the dirt and been expected to die.'

She suddenly felt like the most self-indulgent person on the earth. She shook her head and wiped her eyes with the sleeve of her coat. 'Sorry.'

'No!' Mack raged. 'Don't be fucking sorry! I don't wanna hear you apologising for feeling however it is you wanna feel. Ever.'

She held her breath as she watched his anger claw at him. She just wanted to hold him and she wanted nothing more than for him to hold her right back.

'I'm not gonna tell you how to feel, Harri. About anything. I'm not that guy.'

'But?'

'No,' he said. 'There's no buts. That's it.' He shrugged, his demeanour evening out a little. 'So if you brought me down here for me to tell you not to build this complex Iain's made of Lego in his head already, I won't do it.' He sighed. 'But what I will say is… to me, even on paper, you were always the star of your own show.' He picked up Scooter's stick. 'Don't let anyone make you drop back into the chorus line.'

She chewed a little on her bottom lip, thinking about what he'd just said.

'Mack!' she called.

He turned around, Scooter jumping to attention at his feet.

'Let's get out of here before the realtor shows up!'

Forty-Six

Fort Pond

Mack watched Harri put the bottle of beer to her mouth and take a sip. Right now he was imagining her in cut-off jeans and a vest you could see through a little, the heat of the summer on the deck. Instead, it was snowing again and they were both wearing coats and hats. The lake was a hive of activity in the high season, from million-dollar yachts to tiny row boats and each inch of water had to be carefully navigated to avoid collision. Now it was almost like Mack's own watery playground, nothing doing on the excursions at this time of year, the odd winter fishing trip and then only the people that lived here, making the most of being able to turn a full three-sixty without the fear of swimmers or high-end cruisers they really didn't want to be damaging.

'You didn't tell me you were a three-boat family,' Harri said, putting the bottle down and adding a second hand to the fishing rod she was holding.

'I inherited this one.'

'So what, it doesn't count?'

He smiled. They were aboard the smallest boat he owned. It was barely big enough for two people, was a little on the rustic side but it was perfect to take out into the lake for fishing. And that was what Harri had said she wanted to do.

'OK,' he answered. 'I admit it. I have a shipping fleet.'

She laughed then and he indulged in the sound. Maybe it was the alcohol – although it was only her second – maybe it was the fact they had had to run across the sand as someone Harri said was called Denise hollered at them from a silver hatchback. Running wasn't great on this leg, but he had been laughing so hard and Scooter had made his crazy whistling sound trying to beat them back to the truck. Or maybe it was the fact she'd insisted on leaving her phone back on *The Warrior*.

'How long does it take to catch anything?' she asked.

'Man, it's only been an hour. You bored already?'

'No,' she insisted.

'I know you've fished before. You caught a two-pound bass and your grandpa cooked it for you.' He shook his head. 'And I never knew that was Joe.'

'Now you can picture the scene even better,' she replied. 'But, I haven't actually fished since then.'

'Why?'

'It's not something everyone does in the UK like they seem to do here.'

'I've always liked it. But now it's not about the catching the fish. It's more about it being the place where I find my balance,' Mack admitted. Did that sound lame? At least it was honest. 'I dunno,' he carried on. 'It was about the only good thing my dad taught me. We used to head down to Carnegie Lake with a six pack for him and bottles of Coke for me, bread and a big ol' hunk of cheese and there we'd sit, all day, trying to get a bite.' He smiled at the memory. 'Some days we'd not catch a thing.'

'You never told me that before,' Harri said, altering her position a little and making the boat rock.

'I didn't tell you anything much that involved my parents,' he said. 'Even the rare good stuff.'

'Why not?'

'Because they didn't matter,' Mack replied, shrugging. 'They still don't.'

'Do they know…'

The sentence was there hanging but he knew exactly what she was referring to and it irked him a bit that she wasn't straight with it.

'Sorry,' she said. 'I thought something moved my rod then. I was going to say, do your parents know you're an amputee,' she followed up.

He smiled to himself. So she was straight out with it after all. 'Yeah. They know. We don't see each other anymore.'

'Why not?'

'Because they know I don't have a leg.'

'What? And that's the reason?'

No, it was more than that. Way more. But where did you even begin? Sometimes it was better to not rake over old ground. His therapist would disagree, he knew, but that dude literally disagreed with everything that had ever tumbled out of Mack's mouth. Where did you start with feeling like you had never fitted into your own family? He didn't know why he had thought going back as he was now had been a good idea. He'd been lost to them as soon as he was grown enough to not have to follow their rules.

'We're different people, what can I say?' Mack asked with another shrug.

'It's the same with my parents.' Harri sighed. 'Sometimes I wonder how we can be related. My mum is self-absorbed to the point that I'm not sure she would call me if I didn't call her. And my dad…' She sighed again. 'Well, I'm not sure I've ever known what's going on with him.'

'Hey,' Mack said, nudging her arm with his beer bottle. 'They all must have had something about them somewhere. To produce people like us, right?'

'That is a very good point,' Harri answered. 'And I will take it… whoa!' She wobbled up into a standing position and the boat began to waver.

'What's going on?' Mack asked.

'I think I've caught something,' she gasped. 'And it feels big.'

'OK,' Mack said, standing up too and coming closer to her, trying to keep his balance. 'Stay calm.'

'I am calm,' Harri said. 'Why wouldn't I be calm? What's gonna happen? It's not an alligator, is it?'

'That's only a story Madame Scarlet reels out in the summer when the teenagers get a little rowdy on the water.'

'What? She never told *me* that story!'

'Maybe you were a good kid,' Mack suggested.

'First *Santa and the Pirate* and now this! I'm beginning to think my whole life is a lie! I'm panicking, aren't I? I haven't landed a fish since that one bass! What do I do?!'

'Stop screaming at it,' Mack ordered. 'Or you'll scare it and the rest of the fish.'

'The line is getting tight!'

'Hey, listen to me,' Mack said putting his arms around her and fixing his hands to the rod too. 'It's not gonna be Jaws, OK? Because Jaws wasn't real and sharks do not live in lakes.'

'OK,' Harriet said, a shaky breath leaving her mouth.

And now he had his arms around her in the confined space of the small boat. He focused on the task in hand and frowned as he pulled a little on the fishing line. 'Hmm, I thought you said it was pulling at you.'

'I said I'd caught something. The line went tight.' She gasped. 'I didn't get it stuck underneath the boat, did I?'

'I dunno,' Mack said. 'But there's not enough fight happening for it to be living.'

'Well, if it's not a fish,' Harriet began, 'what is it?' *Not living.* 'Oh my God, it's not a body is it?'

'Ease up there, Columbo. It's most likely a shopping cart Rufus or Riley once took for a ride.' He took the rod from her completely. 'I'll try to loosen it. You grab the net,' he directed.

Harriet did as he'd asked, picking up the red handled net that looked only capable of landing a large trout, not a shopping trolley or – heaven forbid – a cadaver.

'I've got it,' Mack said, seeming to now change tack from tugging at the line to gently coercing it towards their vessel. 'Bring the net over here.'

'Over here' was a mere step away but it wasn't easy when an imbalance of weight could send the boat tipping up and into the freezing water. She breathed in and stood next to him, trying to lean forward and lean back, establishing herself with a foot up on the cool box, their bottled beers beginning to sway…

A square trail was made in the water until the object was slowly revealed.

'It's a box,' Harriet huffed with disappointment.

'Grab it in the net before it comes off of the hook,' Mack said. 'It looks old.'

'It's probably not treasure.' She groaned a little as she reached out and snared the container. And, as she drew it back into her, she began to lose her balance. 'Mack! Mack, the boat! I can't stay on my feet!'

She just about managed not to wail like a desperate cartoon character, but in a millisecond her bottom had hit the wood of the boat, Mack was down too and she fell backwards, thumping her head on his leg. The part that wasn't flesh and bone.

'You OK?' Mack asked. She could feel he was shifting his body, trying to make space.

'Yeah,' she answered. She took a breath and was glad that neither of them had ended up in the water. The net was on top of her too, its wet rope exterior dripping all over her. Inside of it was a large wooden box, a little weedy, stained by perhaps years of submergence, but carvings still visible. Were they flowers? Stars?

'What is it?' Mack asked, leaning over her to look at their find.

'I have no idea.'

'Well,' Mack said. 'It looks a little kooky. Let's take it to Madame Scarlet.'

Forty-Seven

Madame Scarlet's Home

Harriet was on the sofa, sandwiched between a life-sized nutcracker soldier and festive cushions piled high like they might be ripe for a princess to sleep on if a pea was nestled under the bottom one. Madame Scarlet was resting her hands in the centre of the now almost dried out box from the river, her eyes closed, humming gently to herself. There had been nothing inside the find except mushed up paper that had turned a sludgy brown colour and resembled mud. It could actually have been mud but when Harriet had dared to test it with her fingers it definitely had paper consistency.

'Are these nuts for eating?' Mack called from where he was leaning against the breakfast bar that led through to the kitchen. 'Or just for display?'

'Sshh,' Madame Scarlet hissed. 'How am I supposed to connect with the spirit of this piece if you won't keep quiet!'

'Sorry,' Mack whispered back. But he picked up the

nutcracker by the side of the bowl and proceeded to crack walnuts.

'It's old,' Madame Scarlet whispered, eyes closed again and head swaying from the right to the left and back again. 'Possibly Jacobean.'

'It might be what now?' Mack asked.

'Sshh!' Harriet said now. She knew that some people in Montauk didn't believe that Madame Scarlet had the powers she claimed she had in order to earn a living reading palms and detecting auras. And Harriet herself didn't know what she felt about all things spiritual, apart from the fact she *wanted* to believe it. Somehow, to think that there was something else was comforting. She liked to think her nana was out there somewhere, looking down and keeping an eye.

'I sense a lot of anger,' Madame Scarlet said. And then the woman started making noises like she was hiding a steam train under the layers of red gauzy clothing. 'Ch-ush. Ch-ush.'

Harriet looked to Mack. He was frowning, mid-chew of a nut. 'Is she speaking Jacobean?' he asked.

'And there's sadness here too,' Madame Scarlet continued, fingers pressing into the wood a little, rocking her body forward.

Harriet didn't need to look to see the movement of Mack's head in her peripheral. Definitely an eye roll. Scooter let out some kind of snort from where he was snoozing at the bottom of the too-big Christmas tree. Cynics!

Then Madame Scarlet snapped open her eyes and said: 'I've no idea who it might belong to.'

'Well,' Harriet began. 'We thought it was a long shot but,

I don't know, it's quite a nice box. Someone must be missing it.' And how had it ended up in the lake?

'Harri, do you wanna put up posters around town? See if we can find its owner?' Mack said with deep sarcasm.

'You can mock, Mackenzie, but you know the town magazine reunited Mrs Willis with the locket her late husband had bought her.' Madame Scarlet put a finger in the air as if an idea had just descended from the ether. 'We can show a picture of it around the clambake tonight.'

Mack nearly choked on the walnut he had in his mouth. Swallowing quickly he cleared his throat. 'The clambake's tonight?'

Madame Scarlet tutted. 'Mackenzie, do you even own a calendar? You do know Christmas Day is the twenty-fifth, yes?'

'Yeah, I know.' And he knew it meant the clambake definitely *was* tonight and he was in trouble. What was he gonna do?

A ring tone penetrated the low tones of Madame Scarlet's festive music and Harri got to her feet, dipping fingers into her jeans for her phone.

'Hello,' she answered. 'Just, give me a second.' She took the phone away from her ear and looked to them as she stepped over Scooter to get to the door of the living area. 'It's my friend, Jude, I'll be back in a sec.' She headed to the front door and stepped out of the house.

'So,' Madame Scarlet said, turning in her seat to look directly at Mack. 'What kind of mess have you got yourself into now?'

'What?' Mack asked, looking down at his top and jacket. 'Did I drop some?'

'Mackenzie, darling, you might think my being able to read people is not a real skill, but I could see by the look on your face the minute I mentioned the clambake that there's something going on with that.'

He sagged, a breath leaving him. 'How do you *know* that?' he grunted. 'I may have... extended an invitation to somebody in the heat of the moment back in... maybe September. And that somebody might have mentioned it again on the Santa Cruise and reminded me how much they were looking forward to it and I clean forgot about it again until now.'

'Wendy Timmons,' Madame Scarlet said with a shake of her head.

'Yeah,' Mack breathed. He didn't know what had happened but Wendy and Matty had been on the dock sometime at the start of fall and Matty had played with Scooter for a while and before he really knew it he was booked to go to the annual clambake with her.

'And that's a problem because...'

Because he wanted to spend every second he had with Harri. Whether it was right or not. Whether his intentions were pure or not. He couldn't deny *that* was what he wanted. That was *all* he wanted. Except he couldn't admit that to Madame Scarlet.

'It's not a problem,' he answered with a firm nod. 'At all.'

'But?'

Madame Scarlet was looking at him now like she was silently somehow able to see every decision he had ever made – good or bad. He really hoped not. Because if she could read thoughts and feelings and 'see' things anything like she claimed, he was in real trouble. 'I never said anything about a but.' That phrasing was bad...

'Oh, Mackenzie,' Madame Scarlet said with a shake of her head. 'I see the way you look at Joanna.'

He couldn't stop the heat hitting his cheeks. He always kept things so tight inside him, but when it came down to Harri he was wide open and apparently transparent. But he didn't say anything. How could he possibly explain?

'You think she's taken,' Madame Scarlet carried on. 'With this Iain.'

He didn't respond, fingers picking at the nut bowl again. What was there to say?

'She's not, by the way,' Madame Scarlet continued. 'I can tell you that right off.'

He looked up. 'Sure looks that way to me.' And hadn't Harri taken him to the potential building lot where Iain obviously wanted to cement their relationship with... cement.

'Mackenzie, a woman is a complex being and I'm not sure how much experience you have in that field but—'

'Whoa!' Mack exclaimed, a Brazil nut clanging against the bowl. 'This conversation is not about to be about my love life.'

'No,' Madame Scarlet answered. 'It's about Joanna's.'

Mack swallowed, holding the nutcracker between his fingers and staring at it like it might shapeshift. He knew he had told Harri that all he needed to know was that Iain had been good to her, but of course there was more to it than that. She deserved *everything*. If he had a chance again he would give her the moon and the stars and catch every damn fish in the lake.

'Iain doesn't move her soul,' Madame Scarlet informed him.

Mack opened his mouth to speak but she shut him down before he could even get out a breath.

'No, I won't let you dismiss it. I have years and years of grass roots experience, believe me. Joanna is not in love with that boy. And, I do not believe that he is in love with her either.'

Mack shook his head. 'You can't know that.' And why *wouldn't* Iain be in love with Harri? Who wouldn't love her? She was sweet and she was self-conscious, yet deep down he knew there was fire in her belly and at the core of it all was this beautiful, pure spirit with a love for life.

'No one can tell her that,' Madame Scarlet said, putting her fingers back to the wooden box. 'It's something she has to conclude for herself.'

'Then why are we even having this awkward conversation?'

'Because you need to be ready,' Madame Scarlet said in a matter-of-fact manner.

'Ready for what?' Mack asked, connecting with her gaze.

'Because you're the one who needs to catch her when she falls this time.'

A sensation rapidly ran through his entire body and Mack couldn't compute whether it was heat or ice but, again, it was as if Madame Scarlet had ripped the lid off *his* soul and was giving it a full investigation with knowledge she shouldn't possess.

The front door opened and he barely had time to fix his expression before Harri was back in the room, cheeks a little pinked.

'You OK?' Mack asked, sensing that something was a little off.

'Yes,' Harri answered. 'Everything's fine. I should head back though. Check in on Grandpa.'

Mack didn't have to be any kind of medium to tell from her body language that everything was far from fine. Who had that phone call really been from?

'Don't forget tonight, honey,' Madame Scarlet said. 'It starts from sundown. Ditch Plains beach, BYOB... and a chair and blankets. The food and music is being provided by Randy's Trailers this year.'

'I don't know,' Harri said. 'I should catch up on some work really. With the funeral arrangements and the tree decorating and the cocktail competition, and the charity auction coming up... well, things have slipped a bit.'

Mack was biting his lip. She was regressing again. Whatever that phone call was, it hadn't been good. Looking at her now, her demeanour was nothing like the same as the girl who had fallen on her ass in the fishing boat, laughing her heart out.

'Oh, honey, you have to come!' Madame Scarlet insisted, getting up out of her seat. 'Christmas ain't Christmas without the Ditch Plains clambake. Your nana loves it and...' She stopped talking as she realised her faux pas. 'I meant—'

'It's OK,' Harri answered. 'I know what you meant.' She gave a weak smile. 'I'll see how things go.'

He should say he would take her. He could drop over to Wendy's, tell her something, anything, and... and then feel like a complete asshole. Whether he'd wanted to or not, somehow he had agreed to it and he didn't want to let Matty down.

'Well,' Harri said, taking a breath, 'I'd better get back and get stuck into some work.'

'I'll walk with you,' Mack said, slipping down off the stool.

'No, it's OK,' Harri answered. 'Thank you for the fishing lesson though.'

'Anytime,' he said as he felt her drifting away from them.

'Bye,' she said to Madame Scarlet. And without anything more, she headed back to the front door and was gone.

Forty-Eight

The Rum Coconut

Harriet chewed the end of the pen in her hand and looked out through the bi-fold doors to the beach and the rumbling sea. It was a rumble rather than a thrash this evening and the sky was beautifully clear, suggesting there wasn't any more snow due but that the temperatures were set to drop overnight. Being here in December was such a sharp contrast to the summer. The beach that was sucking up the cold weather right now was usually filled with loungers, sunbathers on towels under bright umbrellas, others playing volleyball or licking ice creams they'd bought from the summertime shack The Rum Coconut rolled out each June. Now the sand belonged solely to the neighbourhood – walking their dogs, beachcombing, flying kites – harking back to times gone by when this spot hadn't been Vacation Central.

'Jo-anna! Jo-anna!'

She had brought Meryl Cheep over to her table in the hope it would ward everyone off from disturbing her while she worked. When she'd got back from Madame Scarlet's she had trudged up the stairs, smelling of lake water and damp wood from her exertions catching a relic of a box, and taken a shower. Then she had propped her laptop up on one of her nana's crocheted cushion covers and sat on the bed to go through a few costings on one of their houses that needed the flooring replaced. This time she was working to stop her brain going over the conversation she'd had on her mobile outside the cottage. It hadn't been Jude on the phone as she'd told Mack and Madame Scarlet. It had been Iain. And he had been angry.

She sighed, sitting back in her chair. Denise had obviously called him about the missed appointment at the land and he wasn't listening when she tried to tell him that she *had* gone to see it. He'd used words like 'short-sighted' and 'five-year-plan' and her least favourite, 'dynamism'. What did that even mean in reality? What *was* the world's vision of someone who was dynamic?

What made it all worse was the fact that Iain so rarely 'did' angry. He got a little ticked off when he was stuck in traffic. He got mildly irritated when they lost out at an auction, but he never really got angry. It was that stability and evenness of temperament that had helped pull her back from the brink. Ordinarily, if Iain was gung-ho about a particular property, Harriet trusted his judgement and was fully on board from the outset. But, for some reason, she didn't trust this idea of building a hotel complex. She had tried to tell Iain about how stretched they would be financially, but he'd talked about loans against this and that and about how there was always a risk when you were an entrepreneur. And she had let him rant, wondering if perhaps *this* decision wasn't going to be hers to make for much longer. They had never had something where they had stood poles apart before. If they couldn't reach a compromise, what happened then?

'Here you go!'

Ruby banged down a glass of fluorescent coloured liquid in front of her. It had a straw and a cocktail umbrella with reindeers on.

'What's this?' Harriet asked, staring at it.

'Carrot and apple juice,' Ruby informed her. 'You've been sat at your computer for hours. If you don't have something you're gonna go blind.'

She smiled. 'I'm not Rufus or Riley.'

'They can smell healthy stuff from yards away and then they run like the wind.'

Harriet picked up the glass and took a swig. It was good. 'Mmm, it's nice.'

'I know it's nice. I don't make nothing that ain't nice.' Ruby plumped down in the chair opposite and picked up the realtor's information Harriet had been poring over. 'What's all this? You buying a place here?'

She shook her head quickly. 'No.'

'What's a hectare?' Ruby asked, squinting at the words.

Harriet sighed. Perhaps getting it out would stop her from churning it over internally. 'It's a lot.'

Ruby whistled. 'You got this kind of money?' She fanned her face with the documents. 'That's one hefty price tag on there.'

'I know,' Harriet answered. Those figures, even though they were in dollars, were scaring the life out of her. 'And I don't have that kind of money.'

'So what's the deal?' Ruby asked.

Harriet sighed, watching Meryl Cheep use her beak to climb a little nearer to the conversation on her cage. 'Iain wants to buy the land and build some kind of complex for holidays.'

'Is that a joke?' Ruby asked. 'Did he pop a Christmas cracker before he left?'

Harriet shook her head. 'No.'

'Right on this shoreline?' Ruby checked, pointing a finger at the photograph.

'I know.'

'What do you know?' It was Joe, arriving at the table all dressed up in his thick winter coat, hat with sheepskin flaps that went down over his ears, a plaid blanket over his arm.

Harriet made a face at Ruby in the hope she could keep this on the down-low…

'Iain wants to build Bates Motel on the beach!' Ruby announced.

'It's a loose idea,' Harriet insisted, watching the expression on her grandpa's face. 'Iain does that sometimes. He has a thought and it's all systems go and then he loses interest.'

That wasn't at all what Iain did. Iain had a thought, researched it thoroughly, obsessively even, and then he made it happen.

'Where is this?' Joe asked, his gnarled fingers picking up the realtor details. 'Oh, I see, I know exactly where this is.'

Harriet's worry radar was now piqued. She leaned towards her grandpa a little. 'You do?'

Joe scoffed and dropped the details back to the table. 'No one should build anything on there.'

'Agreed,' Ruby stated, folding her arms across her chest.

'It's been natural beachfront as long as I've been alive. Rufus and Riley can run wild there without upsetting people.'

'And there's good reason for that,' Joe continued. 'Back in 1938 a whole village on that site was destroyed by The Great Hurricane.'

The *what*? The Great Hurricane? Harriet knew they could get some pretty impressive storms out here but never a hurricane – was that really a thing? 'I don't…'

'My father told me all about it,' Joe continued. 'That fishing village was completely wiped out from winds that were one hundred and ten miles an hour. Boats were lost too, fishermen never found, even the railroad tracks were under water.'

'So *nothing* can be built there?' Harriet checked.

'I'm not saying nothing can be built there. There's a restaurant on that shore that's been fine for thirty or more years. All I'm saying is, these things happen in a cycle and I wouldn't wanna risk it.'

Could this make Iain think twice? She had already tried to appeal to the business side of his nature when she shared her concerns about the cost. But this was more. There might be difficulty getting insurance, it would no doubt be more expensive, and then what if the worst did happen and the storm came back?

'So, you coming?' Ruby asked Harriet, getting to her feet.

'Coming where?'

'The clambake, Joanna,' Joe said, pulling at the flaps on his hat. 'We're all going.'

'All?' she queried. 'But who's running the bar?'

'We shut tonight,' Joe said. 'Your nana always insisted on it. It's a night for all the community to relax together out at

Ditch Plains.' He grinned. 'Ruby's driving the truck, we're gonna pick up Rufus and Riley. Those kids always want to sit in the flat bed so there's plenty of room for you in the cab.'

'Lester's got my car to pick up Madame Scarlet,' Ruby said. 'It's all arranged.'

And apparently Ruby was allowed to drive the truck. She shouldn't go, should she? She ought to stay here, finish up her work and now tell Iain what her grandpa had said about the land. Maybe then he'd stop being so forthright about it and realise that it was the wrong move on all kinds of levels.

On the other hand though, she did love a clambake and she'd never been to a festive one before...

'Do I have time to change?' she asked, wondering if she had packed anything warm *and* pretty.

'No,' Ruby stated. 'Just go grab another sweater and your coat and hat.'

Forty-Nine

Ditch Plains Beach

'I hate this soda. I can't taste the sugar.'

Matty threw the can to the beach and some of the contents began to soak into the sand. Mack was biting his tongue, wanting to tell him to learn some manners. He was usually such a good kid, but he'd been rude and obnoxious from the minute they got here. And *here* was a spot on beach chairs and a blanket where they could be seen by everyone who was anyone in the Montauk community. Wendy's choice. This was quite obviously meant to be some kind of public date statement, and he had been suckered into it.

'Oh, honey, don't make a mess. I can get you something else. How about an OJ?' Wendy offered, delving hands into a raffia bag that could have held all the food and drink needed for the whole of the Mets team.

'I wanna eat. When can we eat?' Matty demanded.

'Hey, buddy, you gotta learn a little patience there.'

'You ain't saying that to Scooter. He's been eating since he got here.'

Since when had the kid had an answer for everything? And Scooter was chewing on a bone to distract him from the smell coming off of the barbecue. It wasn't just seafood at this clambake, there was all manner of meats, stews and even desserts. It was all being cooked under a big open marquee with fire pits, heaters and flaming torches stuck in the sand to ward off the cold. Mack had spent a lot of time at Ditch Plains when he'd first arrived in Long Island. It was a wild style of beach with rocks that overlooked it and a wide strip of sand. The sea was perfect for surfing and bodyboarding. And that's what he'd done. Starting off lying across the board, despite being pummelled and battered by the ocean, he had taught himself to get up on his hands. It had strained every fibre of his being, he had come down hard time and time again, but eventually he could almost stay on as long as he had when he still had two feet. There were prosthetics now for surfing, like there were for almost every pursuit you could imagine, but, for him, having a cupboard full of legs probably meant all the more available for him to break.

'Why don't you go play with your friends over there?' Wendy suggested to Matty. 'Mack and I want to do some grown-up talking.'

Oh shit. As annoying as Matty was being, he kinda liked having the kid as a chaperone. He got up out of his beach chair. 'I'll go get us some drinks.'

'I have drinks,' Wendy said, waving a beer bottle in the air.

Of course she did. But he was standing up now and it would be a shame to waste the effort...

'I'll take Scooter for a walk.' He clicked his fingers and drew his dog's attention. It only took the merest mention of activity to get Scooter on board, even over and above food.

'He was settled there,' Wendy scoffed and then pouted a little. 'Are you running away from me?'

What was the right answer here? If he said he was it would be the truth – maybe a truth Wendy wouldn't like, but a truth nonetheless. If he said he wasn't, then it could lead to a whole different and probably sexual interpretation from her.

'I'll be back,' he said. Arnold Schwarzenegger eat your heart out.

'Lester, could you pop a top off that Coke for me?' Ruby said, elongating her jeans-clad legs out towards a fire pit they had commandeered to keep Joe warm. Except Ruby had all but set herself on top of it and Joe was bobbing between groups of people settled on the sand. Some of the kids were making sand angels and finding driftwood sticks and shells to decorate the shapes with.

'I have to do the job I do at The Rum Coconut here now for you?' Lester asked with an eye roll of magnificent proportions.

'God! I was asking a friend to do me a solid. I didn't think you'd get all antsy about it.'

Harriet smiled to herself, taking a sip of the bottle of dark ale her grandpa had given her. It was apparently festive homebrew, taken down from a top shelf in the cellar and dusted off. It was spicy and rich in flavour and tasted somewhere between alcoholic mince pie and nutmeg-infused toffee. She already had a little bit of a buzz from the quarter of it she had drunk. She looked at her phone. It was out on her lap and she was hoping Iain would make contact. She had emailed him. After the phone conversation earlier and then what her grandpa had said about the location of the land, she didn't want him to think she hadn't considered the Montauk land proposition fully and from a commercial point of view. There were her own concerns about being cautious and splashing into uncharted territory and there was also now the issue of the land being in a potential storm corridor. Surely, even if Iain didn't agree with her wanting to hold fire for precautionary reasons, he would see that this place wasn't *the* place to throw all their capital. But Harriet had a feeling that no matter how Iain responded, the answer was going to be as much about their relationship as it was about the transaction. How had they ended up like this? When had the personal side of their relationship been sucked into the vortex of their property business? Or maybe they had *never* been separate. Business had brought them together. Maybe that's all there had been, all there still was…

'Joanna! Watch out!'

Her grandpa's warning shout came only a millisecond before a football landed in her lap, knocking her phone off her knee and into the sand.

'Oh no,' she cursed, getting up and plucking her mobile from the beach, shaking off the excess grains of sand and hoping bits hadn't got into any vital components.

'You OK, Miss Joanna?' Lester asked.

'Yes, I'm fine. Just hoping this is going to keep working.'

She continued to brush specks from the screen and shake it a little.

'Is my Coke coming?' Ruby wanted to know.

'Hey there, I apologise for that. My ball skills aren't quite what they used to be.'

Harriet looked up from her phone at the sound of an unfamiliar voice. The owner was six-foot with short dark hair and a smile that could have sold anything. He retrieved the football from the ground.

'You're not hurt, are you?' the man asked.

'No,' Harriet said. 'I'm fine. It's fine.' She smiled.

'Can I get you a drink or something?' he offered. 'They've got rum punch over there?'

'No, honestly, I'm fine.'

'Are you sure?'

She laughed. 'I'm sure.'

'OK. Well, I'm Mike by the way and I'm sitting just over there if you change your mind.' He pointed to a group of guys on blankets taking beer bottles from coolers and watching the scene.

'I will bear that in mind,' she answered.

'Cool,' he said, now looking a little bashful as he backed away holding his ball.

Harriet went back to looking at her phone. Hoping for a notification to signal it was working. Jude had already texted her today though and talked about a pastry workshop she was hosting in the flat, together with more pictures of her succulents no worse off from the effects of vodka…

Mack could feel his fingers tightening around Scooter's lead as he stood a few yards away. Who was that jock talking to Harri? Feeling like he was eighteen years old again and being taught how to prepare to battle with an enemy, he tried to keep a lid on the bitter frustration that was boiling up. He had no right to keep feeling this way – like he had some kind of claim to her – if he wasn't going to be completely honest about how he felt. And what had changed in him since the time he had pushed her away? The ghosts were still there. The guilt was still there unchallenged. How could he be ready to engage with someone else when he still wasn't even fully engaged with himself?

Scooter planted his butt in the sand and began to spin around in his signature move. Yeah, that was kind of how Mack was feeling too.

Fifty

There was a marching band. Only Montauk could have a marching band at a clambake – on the sand, parading up and down with their brass instruments wrapped in tinsel and holly leaves, playing a combination of old-school festive songs from the likes of Nat King Cole, Elvis and Jim Reeves. Madame Scarlet was in her element, hair in bobbed style, taking the hand of any man within twenty feet eligible – or possibly ineligible, judging by the looks on some of the wives' faces – to dance around. Harriet had always admired her absolute zest for life. It was something her nana had had in spades too. It was an unfettered energy from the minute these women woke up in the morning until the last of the household detritus had been tidied away at night. Harriet took a sip of her third beer and watched Madame Scarlet twirling from one partner to the next, shawl flowing out as she moved. It was true abandon and living in the moment…

Surely there had to be a letter about the clambake among the photo album, didn't there? It might not be an event that takes place at The Rum Coconut but if her grandparents enjoyed it as much as everyone said they had – and her grandpa did look like he was enjoying it now – then why wouldn't her nana have written about it?

Harriet looked at her almost empty bottle. She ought to eat something before alcohol really took hold. Yes, she might not be driving, but there were things she needed to do tomorrow to get ready for the charity auction night. She also needed to go through some forms for her grandpa to do with her nana's will and re-registering all the assets into his sole name. It wasn't the kind of thing you could do with a sore head. And then there was Iain. She didn't want to handle *him* with a hangover either. Iain didn't get drunk. She had never even seen him slightly merry. And he was naturally disapproving when she had one too many. He might be the other side of the Atlantic but she would be able to sense the eyebrow raise by the tone of his voice. If he even ever replied...

Slipping her phone back into her pocket she stood up and headed over to the food marquees.

'So...' Wendy said, sliding in close to Mack.

They were standing under the tent, waiting to fill up on the seafood that smelled incredible. There was lobster, soft-shell clams and quahogs (hard clams), mussels and crabs being cooked the traditional way: steaming it over layers of seaweed. It involved adapting big barrels of barbecues with large stones in the base and a whole lot of wet canvas sacks and tarps to cover the food. And there it had steamed for hours, until perfection had been reached. It was only the thought of that sea-sent-heaven reaching his belly that was keeping him here next to Wendy. There were also tables full of sides – slaw, corn, potatoes, salads – and desserts – pumpkin pie, doughnuts and New England Indian puddings. Luckily, Scooter was with Matty now or he'd have been trying to have his fill of all of it.

'So…' she repeated, her body coming in even closer, if that was even possible.

'Does Matty want seafood? Or would he want ribs and burgers?' Mack asked, a plate in each hand.

'When are we gonna go official?'

'What?' He looked at her in shock. This had definitely gone too far now.

'Oh, come on, Mack, we've been on three outings together now and—'

'—Wait, what?' Had someone body-snatched him when he wasn't looking? 'Three outings?'

'The picnic in the summer. The Santa Cruise. And here. Three.'

Wendy had counted those events out on her fingers like they were precious memories. He needed to be straight with her. No beating about the bush.

'Wendy, I like you,' Mack began. 'But—'

'—I like you too,' Wendy whispered. 'I thought I'd made that plain.'

Somehow she had managed to wrap her calf around his – the prosthetic one – he couldn't feel the connection until the back of her knee kept snagging a little at the join. He took a step back. 'Wendy, I was tending the barbecue at the summer picnic, and I was in charge of the boat for the Santa Cruise. They weren't dates.' He took a breath. 'They were just places we ended up together at. With the rest of the town.'

'And tonight? We arrived together! We're sitting together! I told Matty you'd build him a jungle gym!'

As Wendy's voice got louder and louder and the pitch grew more and more piercing, Mack had to take another step away. The smell of the cooking and the smoke in the air was triggering another time, another place. Metal on metal as people served up. The notes of the band music warping a little in and out of tune. All the noise was punching at him, pinching memories he didn't want to relive. He had to make it stop before it took him over. But then came the beat of the drum from the marching band, and he heard it like canon fire…

'Hey, again. No ball this time.'

It was Mike. And Harriet still hadn't eaten. She'd seen Mack with Wendy and her appetite had completely disappeared. Now she was standing watching children toast marshmallows over one of the fire pits while Madame Scarlet showed locals the photo of the box she and Mack had hooked out of the lake earlier. *Mack was on a date.* But then, why shouldn't he be? He was single. She was not. And Iain may be mad at her right now, but they had history together too. They had formed a *business* together. That was as invested as you could get. Except the tinge of beer brain seemed to be convincing her that practicality belonged somewhere other than at the very core of a relationship. Her mind was desperately reaching out for more. Did she *love* Iain? Had she *ever* loved Iain? Had she ever felt about Iain the way she felt about Mack?

'You OK?' Mike asked, putting a hand on her shoulder.

She flinched at the unexpected touch. 'Yes, I'm fine.'

'Hey, leave her alone and back away now.'

Suddenly Mack was right there and Harriet tried desperately to sober up to this situation. She swallowed, observing him. Something was off. This was a look in his eyes she hadn't seen before and she wasn't sure she could describe it. It was fierce and intense and a little vacant…

'Mack,' she said. 'Is everything OK?'

'Listen,' Mike chipped in. 'Maybe we should head over and get some food. He looks a little stoned.'

'What did you say, buddy?' Mack asked.

This wasn't *assertive* coming from him. This was aggressive. And she knew what she had to do. She needed to get Mack out of here, go somewhere quiet, find out what was going on with him.

'Mack, come on, let's go.' She put her hand on his arm and squeezed a little in encouragement. She inhaled. Everything beneath the surface of his skin felt like it was trembling, wriggling, racing to get out, or maybe, instead, fighting to stay in.

'Mack! Where are you going? You're supposed to be here with me!'

It was Wendy, stalking forward on high wedged boots that didn't look sand compatible. She looked sour, like someone had rubbed a lemon all over her face and then made her swallow it whole. And still the marching band played on, children and Madame Scarlet danced, the scent of sugar and cinnamon filled the air…

'I can't… breathe.'

The words had left Mack's lips in a harsh rasp, the colour leaving his face. His expression had altered too now. There was no longer 'fierce' but 'fear' in his beautiful eyes.

'Come on,' Mike said. 'I'm telling you, he's on something.' He reached out to her and it was then Harriet rounded on him, all her senses humming and every instinct not choosing between 'fight' or 'flight' but instead deciding on 'care' and 'protect'.

'I swear to God, if you touch me again I am going to break your nose!' She pointed to Wendy. 'If you want someone to eat crab with, take her!'

Harriet didn't wait for any response but put a firm arm around Mack's shoulders and guided him away.

Fifty-One

Mack was calmer now. More stable and his body wasn't quaking like it was a home for slithering reptiles. He hadn't felt quite that out of control in a while. Months. He took another swig from the bottle of water he was holding and took comfort in being able to breathe, settling into a rhythm he recognised. And there was Harri, adding more pieces of driftwood to the firepit she had gotten a hold of. The carnival atmosphere of the clambake was just far enough away to be a sound drifting on the cold air and, tucked in at the base of the cliff, the only light from the fire, they were virtually invisible to anyone else.

She turned around, checking on him, and this time he had the strength to acknowledge her. He held the water bottle aloft like he was saying cheers to the sky. Although there was really nothing to celebrate. She had just seen him for who he was now. One of the reasons he had ended their relationship.

She covered the few paces back and stood in front of him. He waited to see the pity in her expression. He knew it was coming. Why *wouldn't* it come? He was the crackpot ex-soldier who not only had half a limb missing, but also a psyche that was frayed and still unravelling. Any second now she'd ask him if he was OK...

Instead Harri sat down on the sand next to him and took the water, putting it to her own mouth. When she'd finished drinking she handed it back and he accepted it. What was she waiting for? Surely the desperate sympathy was going to come. That's what happened once that side was seen. It had happened with one of his psychiatrists. It had even unexpectedly happened that last time with his parents, before his anger kicked in and they'd looked so terrified he thought they might call the cops...

As the fire crackled and the orange hue again brought out the colour of Harri's eyes, he couldn't stand it any longer.

'Say it,' he breathed. 'Whatever it is you want to say but you're holding back from. Just say it.'

'Where's Scooter?'

He burst out a laugh. It was a nervous reaction he didn't have control over. It took a second for his brain to catch up. Where *was* Scooter? *Matty. Wendy.* What a fucking mess. He swallowed. 'He's with Matty.'

'OK,' Harri said, nodding.

'What? So that's it? What is this? We don't... I dunno... address what's happened?'

She turned to look at him then. 'You can't address anything unless you're willing to talk about it. You told me you weren't ready to talk about it.'

He *had* said that. He had said it a number of times. And he had meant it. But everything was telling him if he wanted things to change *he* had to make it happen. One of his counsellors told him that real acceptance and forward motion could only be achieved with honesty. He could hear the dude's voice now. *How can you expect to have equilibrium in any of your relationships going forward if you don't enter into them with complete honesty? Try, Mackenzie, or something is going to snap.*

'The issue is… I don't know what to say,' he told her. 'I've never said it before. Not all of it.'

She nodded. 'OK. Well, that's a start.'

'Is it, Harri?' he asked, his eyes meeting hers.

'Yes,' she replied. 'Of course.'

'OK, well, I'm just gonna come right out and say this right now before I lose my nerve.' He rushed out a breath. 'I hate that you're with Iain. I hate it.'

'I hate that you're with Wendy,' she countered.

'I'm not with Wendy.'

'Well, I'm not with Iain.'

What? What had she just said? He needed that clarified. 'What?'

He watched her put her fingers to her temples, and then she held her head in her hands as she let out a sigh. 'I'm not with Iain the way I should be. Because if I was then I wouldn't be spending every minute thinking about you.'

Every minute. He didn't dare to breathe as the atmosphere thickened.

'You're always there, Mack. No matter what I do, no matter how I try to distract myself. You never went away. Not really.' She sighed. 'I might have told myself it was over and I was done, but you don't still dream about someone, dream about *being* with someone, if they're out of your system, do you?' She kept on looking at him. 'You don't re-read the letters they wrote you and smile at the love inside them unless you still feel something.'

'Harri…'

'I want to know what happened to you, Mack. You brush it off and you make jokes and you deny it's an issue but—'

'Yeah,' Mack said. 'But there's no denying my issues after tonight, right? You saw that other side of me spilling out right there on the sand.'

'Mack,' Harri said. 'That wasn't another side of you. That was pain and… trauma… and needing the world to stop turning for a second so you could decompress.'

He nodded. 'Yeah.'

'You can feel not ready right now. That's OK,' Harri told him, turning her body a little towards him. 'But you have to trust that I might be able to help you if you give me *something*.' She reached for his hand. 'Just *something*.'

As much as he wanted to carry on looking into her eyes, he closed his and let the demons that plagued him jog a little on his mind. He *wanted* to unburden himself. How good might it feel to let some of it go? Except he had always held it back in therapy because it felt self-indulgent and he felt unworthy of the release. He needed to suffer. He *wanted* to suffer. What right did he have to escape the feeling of this darkness, when he was one of the lucky ones?

But then she linked their hands, pressing her palm against his, knotting up their fingers so he almost couldn't tell what was his and what was hers. And some of the words were there, a trickle of a sensation on his lips…

'I killed Sanders,' he whispered.

Fifty-Two

Mack swallowed. Pharrell Sanders had been his wingman. And while Mack had focused on nailing the bad guys or destroying the enemy's vital equipment through the barrel of his rifle, Sanders was his spotter and the one he trusted most of all the guys in his unit. The one who made him laugh when things got tough. The one who had led the singing on that one video call with Harri, shaking his khaki-covered ass at the laptop, fooling around making kissing noises to wind Mack up. A tank of a guy with skin the colour of molasses and the biggest smile. And he should still be here.

'I… made a mistake' Mack said. 'And… it cost him his life.'

He had lost focus. He had got slack. He felt his breathing catch all over again. He didn't want to zone out and throw himself back there. He focused on the warmth of Harri's hand in his. That bond they'd shared for so long, knowing each other's hearts better than anyone else. He could trust her. He had always been able to trust her. Why had he forgotten that? Why had he thrown it away?

'They called me The Assassin and Sanders, he was Ghost. Did I tell you that before?' Why couldn't he remember? Were all his memories from that time now a little blurred around the edges?

She shook her head. 'You never told me details of what you did,' she said. 'You told me how tired you always were. What you'd eaten. Who got letters from home and what goodies they'd been sent. You didn't tell me much about... the actual conflict.'

'You remember I was a sniper.'

She nodded.

'Well, Sanders and I, we were... golden,' Mack continued. 'Some kind of dream team, The Assassin and Ghost... protected like you might protect the president.' He swallowed. 'We would set up what we called our work room, high above everyone else, in a burned-out building, or camouflaged halfway up a mountain, and there we'd be, on our bellies, completely still, for hours, like a pair of deadly rattlesnakes, looking, acknowledging, being ready.' He took a shaky breath. 'But that day... we got made. By a kid.' He paused again. 'A kid I'd met weeks before. A kid I'd tossed a ball for.'

He didn't even realised he was crying until the tears plopped onto the beach and melted into the sand. Still Harri held his hand.

'There was no time for talking him down. I had maybe half a second to acknowledge that in his eyes. But... Sanders, he just moved. The kid was running into the room and Sanders... he didn't hesitate.' His shoulders rolled forward now, racking with emotion, as the awful horror came back to him and he tried to keep some kind of control in this letting go. *Keep breathing. Just keep breathing.*

'The kid was wearing a vest,' Mack sobbed. 'Packed with explosives. And Sanders, he took him down and smothered the kid's body with his own, just before the kid took his finger off the dead man's switch.'

He felt Harri squeeze his hand tight as his heart broke all over again for the loss of his best friend. It wasn't fair. It wasn't right. Sanders had left a wife and a one-year-old son.

'How do I live with that?' Mack questioned as much of the universe as of Harri. 'How do I get up every single day and keep living with that?' He sobbed. 'Sanders gave his life for me. And it was my fault the kid knew we were there. Because I thought he was just a kid and not the enemy.' He gritted his teeth. 'My fucking bad.'

'Oh, Mack, come here,' she breathed, gathering him into her arms.

'Why didn't I move first? Did I even think about it? Would I have done the same thing? Would I have given my life for Sanders? That's why I didn't wanna see you, Harri. That's why I wanted you to forget about me. Because when I look at myself in the mirror, even now, I'm not certain who I am anymore.' He took a breath. 'I want to be the guy you wrote, the one you fell in love with once… but I really don't know if he's still around.'

'He is,' she answered straightaway, cupping his face with her hands. 'He's right here with me now.'

She was looking at him so intently, almost as if she was wanting him to absorb all the hope and strength and love via osmosis. God, he wished that would work. He wanted to move on, but how did you eradicate the memory of something so disturbing when you were still sitting with the scars?

'You deserve so much more,' Mack whispered, blinking away more tears.

'Yes,' Harri answered with a nod, her eyes tearing up too. 'Yes, I do.'

She traced a finger down his cheek, following the line of one of his tears and even through all his procedures and treatments and counselling sessions he had never felt this vulnerable.

'Will you come to the lighthouse with me?' she asked him softly.

He frowned, not sure he had heard her right. 'What?'

'I… haven't been to the lighthouse since I got back here and I'm asking if you… would come with me.'

She didn't need to vocalise the suggestion any further. She had told him in her letters how she felt about the Montauk Point Light. She'd climb the spiral stairs to the very top and look out at the view of Block Island Sound and the Atlantic Ocean beyond and feel more at home than she did in the UK. *I feel this place in my heart, Mack. Is that crazy?*

There was the deepest of sentiment wrapped around every one of the words she'd just said and he knew this was as close to her asking him on a date as she was able to give right now. This was re-opening the door, having seen the flashback monster that could sometimes ravage his good sense, and asking if he wanted to try stepping through it and move a little closer to coming back to her. But, how could he? In the real world, a world where he was still messed up, how could he take hold of her heart knowing he might crush it all over again?

She was still holding his hand and he brought hers to his lips, dropping a kiss on the skin.

'I'm sorry, Harri,' he whispered. 'I want to. With everything I have. But... I can't.'

Fifty-Three

The Rum Coconut

'Is that a real parrot?'

Jude got her face really close to the screen as if that would give her her answer. Meryl Cheep gave a squawk and pecked at her cuttlefish. Sipping her coffee, Harriet watched her grandpa putting a couple of logs on the fire. He was growing in confidence as every day passed by, taking things gently but coming out of his grief-stricken shell little by little. Like the Queen and the late Duke of Edinburgh, Joe and Lorna had been together for the longest time. It was going to take some adjustment to simply be just Joe.

'Yes, it is a real parrot. Her name's Meryl Cheep.'

'I like the name Meryl. It reminds me of an actress. I can't think of her name.'

Harriet cut to the chase. 'So, how was Iain when he came round?'

'Weird,' Jude said. 'I said weird in my text.'

Yeah, she *had* said 'weird' and that was weird in itself. Iain didn't do 'weird'. Iain did sensible and measured. Up until now with his land aspirations. It was three days since she'd sent that email on the night of the clambake and he hadn't answered it. He *had* sent her half-a-dozen emails though, all property business related, and not one text message. It was almost as if he had completely cauterised their personal and professional lives and was no longer engaging in the former. She knew she had to do something.

It was also three days since Mack had started to pull back some of his layers... and then right away retreated again. He'd left her by the fire pit at Ditch Plains, tears rolling down her face, contemplating why life was beating her up again. Wasn't it bad enough she'd lost her nana? And why would Fate/God/Whoever put Mack right slap back in her present day if it wasn't going to mean something? Or maybe this was some kind of challenge to her resolve? Did her relationship with Iain need the ultimate test? Or perhaps this wasn't about her at all. Perhaps this situation was meant for Mack's inner evaluation alone. Except all she wanted to do now was be there for him, no matter what form that took. They might have the deepest, most undeniable connection, but did it have to be all or nothing? But, saying that, seventy-two hours with no contact and, without him, it felt like she was the one who had lost a limb. As Meryl nudged her hand with her beak, Harriet tried to clear her thoughts and focus back on this conversation with her best friend.

'Jude, what did Iain do exactly?' Harriet asked. She watched her grandpa again. He was moving chairs around now, brushing against the branches of the Christmas trees by the fire.

'At first I didn't know whether to let him in or not. I

mean, he's never come round before when you haven't been here,' Jude said. 'Like I said… weird.'

'But you did let him in and what did he do?'

'He went into your bedroom.'

'O-K.' Not that unusual. He did have a spare shirt there and a deodorant spray. Maybe he was collecting those things. That would tell a story…

'And then he left,' Jude said.

'Just like that? Without saying anything?'

'With a box.'

His stuff? 'What kind of box?'

'An old looking one,' Jude said. 'Kind of shabby chic. I liked it actually.'

Harriet held her breath. She didn't need to ask any more questions to know it was *the* box. The cream box decorated with lace she had found in a gorgeous little shop in the arcade at Westbourne. She'd bought it when she was sad, to make herself happy. It was from back when she had had time to browse, admire the menagerie of beautiful homey items she thought she one day might make a living out of.

'OK,' she finally answered.

'It's sex toys, isn't it?' Jude surmised as Harriet's fingers worked to lower the volume button as quickly as she could. 'Whatever he says to you about them you should let him know that we have a right to pleasure and if he isn't down with that then—'

'It's not that,' Harriet said.

'Weed then?'

'No,' Harriet said, suppressing a laugh. She was now actually starting to worry that all these things were what *Jude* had hidden under *her* bed, along with the plastic moulds for elaborate baking creations, art supplies and joss sticks.

'What's going on with you two? And when are you coming back?' Jude asked. 'I only ask because I'm thinking of asking Professor Goldman over on Christmas Day. He lost his wife last year and you know I have a soft spot for men with silver hair who are a little bit needy.'

Harriet swallowed, looking at her grandpa. When *was* she going back to the UK? She had to go back, didn't she? She had a successful business, an apartment, Jude, and what about Iain? She had tightly wound her life into the sanctuary of a mould he'd made for them both. He'd been her security for so long... Except there was Mack. What was she going to do about him? Was there anything *to* do? Because you couldn't help someone, you couldn't *love* someone, if they didn't want to accept it.

'I don't know,' she admitted.

'Sorry, that was the answer to *which* question?'

'Both,' she answered with a heavy sigh. 'Listen, Jude, invite Professor Goldman for Christmas. If I'm back I can... do something else. Don't miss out on my account.'

'Oh, it's not my first trip around the pottery wheel with him,' Jude admitted, refastening one of her dungaree straps. 'But it was good enough for one more chuck, if you know what I mean.'

Harriet didn't know *exactly* what she meant and she was really rather grateful.

'Are you OK?' Jude asked, softer and more serious again. 'Do you want me to see if I can tune into your aura? Banish bad energy?'

'No,' Harriet answered. 'But... thanks.'

'Well, if Iain pops round again being weird, what do you want me to do?'

'I...' Harriet began. Then she stopped for a second and took a deep breath. 'Actually, Jude, I don't think he'll be coming back at all.'

Fifty-Four

Downtown Montauk

'OK, what's going on?' Ruby asked, taking her lips away from her take-out coffee. 'You've never taken me out for coffee before and I know I'm not your type so you're not angling after anything more than conversation, so...'

'Can't a guy invite a friend out for coffee and conversation without a whole lot of suspicion?' Mack answered, taking a breath of the freezing air.

'Round here?' Ruby said. 'You're the talk of the town after you went all crazy on the sand at the clambake. Maybe I should be wearing body armour.'

Yeah, that hit him in all the right places but that was Ruby. Blunt and honest to a fault and that was one of the reasons why he wanted her here with him now. Because he needed a second opinion. Because he wanted someone to either tell him he was crazy or tell him that he might be on to something. He didn't know what side he was falling down on yet but he'd had three days of looking at his phone, wanting there to be something, knowing there wouldn't be and realising that the reason it wasn't lighting up was all his own fault. He had given in to everything that still tremored through him and he had let it take control. Worse than that, he had let it make decisions for him. Was he ever going to find his way back to the person he'd been before? Or even simply find a medium place where he was calm and not governed by the guilt he wore right the way through him.

'Is Wendy still pissed at me?' he asked.

'Oh yeah, Wendy's still pissed at you,' Ruby said. 'And she's telling *everyone* she's still pissed at you. But I wouldn't worry about that. She's taking the heat out of whatever really went on.'

He nodded, pulling Scooter to heel as the dog tried to get a little friendly with a passing poodle. 'OK, I get it. The town thinks I'm even more of a freak show.'

'Just so you know, I don't,' Ruby said with a sniff, taking another slurp of coffee, cream sticking to her top lip. 'I get it. Well, not all of it, obviously. But I've dated veterans.'

He nodded. 'We fight for our country, be the best, then all turn into screw-ups, right?'

'Actually, one guy from Atlanta wasn't all bad. But I'm not sure he ever saw active service,' Ruby mused. 'No tattoos.'

Mack smiled a little before he stopped walking, making Scooter sit on the frosty sidewalk. The dog's attention was soon on a flashing reindeer hanging from a streetlight. He barked.

'So, what do you think?' He splayed out his arms like he was revealing a mystery prize in a game show.

'Er, what exactly am I looking at?' Ruby asked, head turning left and right then up and down.

'This store!'

'It's empty.'

'I know it's empty, but what do you see?' Mack asked, people passing them by carrying shopping bags and take-outs, wrapped up against the cold. Decorators were adding more festive trinkets to an already full-on flurry hanging from every building and swaying overhead.

'Peeling paintwork and dust you could write your Christmas list to Santa in,' Ruby said, putting her face to the grubby windowpane.

'Granted, all that,' Mack agreed with a nod. 'And there's been cockroaches in there too.'

'You've been inside?' Ruby asked, looking back at him. 'Why?'

Because he didn't know what to do with himself. Because Lester's bicycle hadn't needed a repair. Because he'd cleaned the boat. Because Scooter was finding four walks a day overkill. Because he didn't want to admit that he still wasn't as recovered as he should be?

He took a breath. 'Because I'm thinking about taking out the lease on it.' He looked down at his feet, both legs shaking a little. This was dumb. Harri had given him the biggest opportunity, an invitation straight from her heart and he had turned his back on it.

'OK, what's going on?' Ruby wanted to know, eyeing him in the way she always did when there was no doubt she was going to get to the truth of the matter.

'Storage,' Mack blurted out. 'You know, things are a little crowded on the boat sometimes and—'

'So, you rent a locker. You don't lease space with a big ol' storefront.' She narrowed her eyes. 'You asked me here to tell me what's really going on. So tell me.'

He shook his head. This almost felt as confronting as the first and only group therapy he'd taken part in when he was still on crutches. That group may have been a circle of amputees exactly like him in the physical sense, but they didn't know him, they were strangers – he wasn't going to burden them with the things that kept him awake at night. But Ruby, she was a friend. Younger than him, but with a wealth of experience when it came to *connections*. And connecting was the problem. So much of him wanted to, but that voice in his head kept on whispering he was never going to be happy because he didn't deserve it.

'How's Harri?' he asked.

'Miserable as crap, as it goes,' Ruby announced, swigging her coffee. 'Is that down to you too? Maybe I need to back away now if your mission is to mess with every girl in this town.'

'Ouch,' Mack replied. But he guessed she had a point. And that's what he had done with Harri before. Messed with her. Hurt her so much her spirit withered away and she turned to a guy like Iain. Now he was doing it all over again.

'So what's the deal?' Ruby asked. 'Am I gonna have to lock you two in Joe's garage until you either bust up or make out?'

'I... don't know,' Mack admitted. 'It could go either way.'

'Mack! What am I doing standing outside this store?!'

Now his body began to judder – a bit with the cold, and the rest was down to this idea he'd had.

'I don't know... I guess... in some universe where busting up doesn't happen... I thought I could... rent it... for Harri.'

Ruby didn't say a word. She didn't need to. Her eyes were wide and everything about her expression was telling him she thought it was cracked. Yeah, probably it was. Because, forget the lighthouse, she wouldn't want to see him for a minute after he had left her at Ditch Plains. But he'd had to leave her. He'd shown her what could happen when the memories overtook the present. He got angry and unstable. Who wanted that in their life? Yet there she had been, cooling him down, knowing exactly how to do that. But it really wasn't what he wanted for her. She deserved the life of her dreams. And that's why he was standing here with Ruby. It wasn't about him. It wasn't about them. It was all about Harri.

'I don't follow,' Ruby finally said after all the staring.

'God, it's so stupid! I see that now!' His hands were in his curls and he was thinking this *was* too much and it was on the verge of controlling. It was exactly like Iain wanting that land project and not seeming to care how Harri felt about it.

'I still don't know what it is!' Ruby cried. 'Is she gonna use a storefront as some kind of holiday home?'

He shook his head, leaning against the building and feeling like a dumbass. 'No. She'd use it as a shop. Maybe. I don't know.'

'Here, have my coffee,' Ruby said, pressing her take-out cup on him. 'It looks like you need a double shot.'

He declined and growled a little, making Scooter look up. 'I'm playing it cool. But I'm not cool. I'm scared.'

'About what?'

'Every day that goes by is taking us closer to Christmas and big things happen at Christmas, don't they? Families are generally together, people spend the time at home with the people they care about most and… I don't know… tick fucking tock.'

'So, you know she's gonna go back to England and I'm thinking that you want another shot at making things happen with you two. And I'm guessing you think the perfect solution is to gift her a rundown ex-laundromat with critters living in the woodwork.'

'Yeah,' Mack replied. 'All of that.'

'Want my advice?' Ruby asked, letting Scooter lick some cream off her finger.

'Maybe.'

'Don't try and make decisions for her,' Ruby said bluntly. 'Someone shouldn't have to be given reasons to stay to *make* them stay. Not that I can't see potential in this dusty store on a busy boulevard.'

He nodded. He knew that. Because he knew Harri. Why was he second-guessing himself? And then he remembered something else. 'Madame Scarlet said I should make sure I'm there to catch her when she falls.'

Ruby made a small squeak of a noise. 'I don't disagree,' she answered. 'But she has to be falling first.' She smiled. 'And you don't wanna be the one to push her.'

Fifty-Five

The Rum Coconut

It could never be said that the tiki bar was minimalist and contemporary but with donations for the Christmas charity auction racking up, the whole bar and restaurant was starting to look like a cross between a car boot sale and TK Maxx. There was every item you could imagine and definitely lots you couldn't. Harriet perused the brand-new-but-from-the-Eighties Mickey Mouse telephone still in its original box – she'd looked that up online and hoped it would fetch at least a hundred dollars. It was sitting next to one of Ben Hides's pumpkins. Rufus and Riley had decorated some of the pumpkins with festive attire – tinsel, stick-on sequins and stars held on with probably bubble gum. She hadn't let them go too wild with the helping but found if she kept feeding them sweet but healthy items from the menu they were able to concentrate on not destroying everything for short periods of time.

Alongside the unwanted gifts, there were offers of cleaning for a week, a lesson in flower arranging and

Madame Scarlet was donating a tarot reading and a session with the Ouija board.

She needed this coffee and she had brought today's letter from her grandma down to read while she drank it. There had been a photograph next to it in the album and she looked at it now. It was a little bit wrinkled and scratched but that only added to the atmosphere that rose up from the image. There her nana and grandpa were, standing proudly in front of a stage stacked with goodies exactly like the one she was next to now. Her nana was more laughing than smiling, her trademark bright earrings were red berries and holly leaves and she was wearing a very Vegas-style dress – black with gold embellishments at the collar and sleeves. It was very different from her usual no-nonsense blouse and slacks or pinafore dresses. Joe was in a suit with a matching waistcoat and had a hand at his tie.

The tiki bar looked almost the same – perhaps there were slightly brighter lightbulbs now and new fringing around the top of the bar – but it still looked like the welcoming and warm slice of Polynesia waiting to give you home cooking and holiday cocktails whatever the weather.

Harriet's finger went to the teenager in the photograph. *Her dad*. There was that slightly long hair and skinny frame. He had his arms folded across his chest and a frown on his face. Not so much of the chilled-out yoga master here, more adolescent who was angry at the world. He'd also worn that expression many times before when engaged in marital battle with her mum. But, in that situation, it was the flaws in their relationship, not to mention the total couple incompatibility Harriet had pegged about the same time she had fully mastered using an epilator, that caused the brooding look of despair. She couldn't imagine how growing up at this beautiful tiki bar could have been anything but idyllic, whether your hormones were raging or not.

She took a swig of her coffee and began to read…

My dearest Joanna,

Am I repeating myself in these notes? I'm starting to forget what I've told you and what I haven't, but, once I began writing, I made a promise to myself that I would put the letters in the album and not read them again. They are all straight from the heart, my darling girl and I know if I revisit them I will make changes and perhaps decide not to talk about some things maybe we should have talked about long ago.

So, today I want to pass on some grandmotherly advice. I want you to promise me that you will always bear in mind in life that people make mistakes. We all make mistakes. I have made my fair share – some I've made amends for, others I regret not doing more about.

I've never believed in good eggs and bad eggs, only eggs that have maybe had less keeping warm, or eggs that were kept warm but somehow fell out of the nest too soon. Sometimes the nest, which should still be there if the egg wants to seek shelter in it again, gets too rigid to hold the egg properly, twigs have gotten misshapen over the years, or the nest has just fallen a little apart with every storm. What I'm trying to tell you is, I know from experience what it is like to lose hope and I have been guilty of giving up too easily. But I want you to go through life stronger than me, being certain that every situation can be made better if you wish it so, Joanna. Please do not spend your life with regrets like I have. Always follow your heart even if that path is paved with challenge.

Nana xx

Harriet's eyes were damp. This was the deepest missive her nana had written to her. This wasn't about cocktail making or dressing trees for Christmas or making sure her grandpa didn't spend too long on a microphone in public, this was something else. Regrets and mistakes and eggs? And it all hit extra hard because of the situation she found herself in with Mack. Regrets. Yes, she definitely had them. Should she have given up? Should she have believed the word of someone else? She put a hand to her chest now as the moment burned. But when the letters stopped and she made enquiries, she'd been told that he was dead. *That* was the ending she was supposed to swallow. Except she still hadn't wanted to believe it. And eventually, after the devastating shock and all the tears, something had still felt off. She needed full details and answers. How had it happened? Where had it happened? Had he been alone? It was all too vague for this tough, bright, vibrant man to be gone without fanfare. And then the letter from Jackson Tate with the truth, or so she thought. Mack was alive but he simply didn't want to write to her anymore. He had reconnected with his childhood sweetheart from back in Pittsburgh. For some reason that had almost hurt her more than the idea that he had died. Because that news kicked away the whole underpinning of their relationship. It had made her feel as if she hadn't ever really known him. She'd been left questioning if he had just used her to pass time until his tour was over. All the time she was sharing her deepest feelings and he was giving back, had she meant nothing to him? Was anything he told her the truth? But what could she have done after that? She couldn't exactly get on the first plane to Afghanistan and confront him. She had had to accept that whatever had happened he didn't want to communicate with her and he was too much of a coward to tell her in person. Except here they were now and she knew the real reason he had called time. He'd lost a leg and his best friend was dead. She took a breath. It was unimaginable the toll that would take. How could Mack have been in any kind of place to make decisions about anything. He might have pushed her away but ultimately she had let go. But what happened if between the pushing away and the letting go, you later found yourselves in the same place at the same time with the same feelings? And what if you felt all that but you had entangled yourself with other things? Made commitments to other people?

She wiped at her eyes and set her focus back on the photograph again, studying it closer. What was that in the background? She brought the image closer still and homed in on a shape on the stage amid all the other paraphernalia. Was that…? Could it be…? The box she and Mack had dragged out of the lake?

Fifty-Six

'I should be helping,' Joe grumbled, his eyes going to the door of the bar where one of the other staff was greeting customers and showing them to tables. Meryl Cheep was in fine form, fluffing up her feathers and mouthing cheeky repartee.

Harriet smiled at her grandpa. Always wanting to be busy, exactly how he used to be. She couldn't be more glad, because sometimes when people properly slowed down they gave up. Some people worked all their lives and then when it came to retirement they withered with the change in their routine and the boredom of the everyday. And that was people who still had a partner in their lives... Her grandpa was doing well.

It was evening now and she had invited her grandpa to dine in the restaurant with her instead of him eating something quick on the kitchen countertop or on his lap in the lounge upstairs. Ruby had put together all of his favourites – fried chicken with Lorna's special recipe coating Harriet *did* know the recipe for, spiced green beans and cabbage, mashed potatoes and shrimp and grits. It was a feast, but so far Joe was doing little more than pick at it.

'Grandpa, you don't need to work every night,' Harriet told him, spooning herself a portion of potatoes.

'It ain't work,' he scoffed. 'It's hospitality.' He sat up a little straighter in his chair. 'It's welcoming friends into our place and sharing it with them.'

'I know,' Harriet said. And that was why, after all these years, the tiki bar was still somehow surviving. In a rapidly changing world where everything was made to improve, move on and diversify, The Rum Coconut was a throwback that the people of Montauk had never let go of. It was heartening that the values and old-fashioned embrace it gave everyone who came through the door still remained. Obviously in the summer months this place was full to the beams with vacationers loving the retro tropical vibe, but it was good to know that in the off-season it was still well-supported by the neighbourhood.

'It's not the same without my girl though,' Joe admitted sadly.

His girl. Her nana. Lorna was still very much wound around everything that went on here, from the food to the décor and all the festive events that were carrying on in her honour. It was like her spirit was still here, overseeing, rooting them along.

Joe took a long, slow breath that seemed to take all his energy, then he spoke again. 'But, I know she ain't coming back. And I know I have to live with that.' He looked up at Harriet then. 'And, I'm learning, that maybe I *can* live with that. With a bit of getting used to… and maybe some card games with Ambrose.'

343

Harriet smiled as her eyes welled with tears. 'That's good to hear, Grandpa.'

'I don't like it,' Joe continued, finally picking up a fork and digging it into the green beans. 'But if there's one thing your nana would have wanted, it would be for things here to stay exactly how she left them.'

Harriet swallowed and thought about her nana's latest letter. She wasn't now convinced Lorna wanted *everything* to stay exactly the same. She'd been talking about regrets. Did Joe know what these were? Could this be about her dad and the space between them? Perhaps she shouldn't address anything while her grandpa was in an upbeat state of mind. She took a piece of fried chicken with her fingers and put it down on the plate, licking the spices off her skin and relishing the taste.

'Grandpa,' she began. She bent in her chair and picked the wooden box up off the floor. She had collected it from Madame Scarlet earlier that day.

'Yep?' he replied, eating at last, eyes on the prize that was grits and fresh shrimp.

'Do you recognise this?' She slid the box onto the table, thankful that it no longer smelt of pond water.

'What?' Joe asked, mouth full of beans. He lifted his head from his plate and that's when his expression changed completely. It wasn't like he had seen a ghost. It was like he *was* the ghost. There was no doubt he knew this box.

'Where… where did you find it?' Joe asked, the words sounding unnatural and stilted.

'Mack and I pulled it out of the lake,' Harriet told him. 'I thought I'd caught a monster of a fish and then this bobbed up.'

Joe put his hands out, fingers creeping over the wooden exterior engraved with swirls of what you could see now were definitely vines. Harriet couldn't fail to notice that his entire body was shaking.

'This…' he started. 'This… can't be.'

His voice had a tremble to it now and he caressed the wood a little more before he lifted the lid.

'There's nothing in it,' Harriet stated. 'All that was in it was some mushed up papers. It looked like it had been down there some time so I suppose whatever it was got soggy.'

'He told me,' Joe mumbled. 'He said they had thrown it in the water.' He took a rattly breath. 'And I didn't believe him.'

'Grandpa, is it *your* box? This morning, I saw it in a photo, of an old auction night, you and Nana smiling underneath the Christmas lights and…'

'I made it and he helped me… and then he took it,' Joe continued to ramble on. 'We thought he'd taken it.'

'Who helped you, Grandpa? And who took it?' Harriet asked.

'Your father,' Joe breathed, his eyes tearing up. 'Joe Junior. We thought he took it and all the money that was inside.'

Harriet swallowed, eyes alive as her gaze travelled back to the old hand-carved box. Her dad had made this with her grandpa, working together to create something that had obviously been beautiful until the elements had got to it. 'There was money inside?'

'Everything we'd collected that year from the charity events. All the donations waiting to go to the Army and Navy Union. Thousands of dollars.' Joe picked the box up, turning it over as if hoping to discover it now had a hidden compartment that was still containing the riches.

'Dad took it?' Harriet gasped. Her mind went back to the photo and her nana's last letter, churning everything over at rapid pace.

'He swore he didn't. And I called him a liar,' Joe carried on, his demeanour hitting agitated as he wriggled a little in his seat. 'I told him to leave and never come back. And that's what he did. He went to England. I mean, that's all I needed to know, right? I mean, how would he afford to get to England if he hadn't stolen the money?'

'Grandpa,' Harriet whispered. 'Is this what happened all those years ago to cause the tension between you?' It couldn't be, could it? That something that had happened when her dad was what... maybe sixteen... involving this box she had found out of nowhere... was the answer to the strains that had been within the family all this time?

'He did take the money, didn't he?' Joe asked, eyes filled with sorrow. 'He took the money and he threw the box in the lake. It has to be that, don't it?'

'I don't know, Grandpa,' Harriet whispered, reaching out to clasp his hand in hers.

'Cos if it ain't that then... I broke Lorna's heart and I sent him away and... he did nothing wrong.'

Harriet gave his hand a squeeze as he fought the battle not to cry and seemed to be on a hiding to nothing. She was going to have to speak to her dad as soon as she could, to try to get to the bottom of this.

Suddenly a whole cacophony of squawking started up from Meryl Cheep and Harriet turned a little in her seat to see what the commotion was all about. And what she saw made her jaw almost hit the floor.

Fifty-Seven

The Warrior, Fort Pond

'What's this?' Mack asked.

Madame Scarlet's beaming face, complete with flowing red hair that could have been in a commercial if it was actually real, appeared from behind a small fir tree in a pot that she was holding as she stood on the deck of his boat. He had to admit, the tree was decorated tastefully in comparison to her boudoir-meets-Moulin-Rouge style in her decoration at the cottage.

'This is Christmas,' Madame Scarlet answered. 'Coming onto *The Warrior*.'

'Oh no,' Mack said shaking his head as Scooter, who had bolted up the steps from the living area, brushed past him and jumped up at their guest. 'You know Christmas never comes onto *The Warrior*.'

'I know it never used to,' Madame Scarlet mused. 'But I feel that things might be changing around here, no?'

'You've lost me,' Mack said, self-consciously folding his arms across his chest.

'Really?' Madame Scarlet asked, eyes heading upwards into her wig line. 'You know that I know everyone around here.'

'Yeah,' Mack replied, taking Scooter by his collar and firmly suggesting he go inside. 'And it's always scared me, so cut to the chase.'

'I know you saw the old laundromat downtown with a view to renting it.'

'Oh, man!' Mack said, hand slapping to his forehead. 'Ruby told you?'

'Ruby knows?' Madame Scarlet exclaimed, sounding a little put out.

'Who told you?' Mack asked.

'I can't tell you that. Now, grab hold of this tree and take it down, cos I got more to come, honey.'

'What? More? No,' Mack protested. But even as he said the words he didn't know why he was bothering to fight this. Whatever she had was going to be on his boat within minutes, whether he wanted it or not. He took the tree from her hands and retreated into his space.

A little over five minutes later and he was the owner of five trugs of festive regalia that Madame Scarlet had already started putting up around the place, much to Scooter's delight. His dog was chasing around pine cones with ribbons like they were miniature footballs, then had to be released when he got his head wedged between the banquette seating and the table. The boat was rocking every time Madame Scarlet moved from one end of the area to the other and all the portholes were now ringed with tinsel. His safe haven had turned into an alpine chalet.

'There!' Madame Scarlet announced finally, looking way too proud of herself.

'It looks like Macy's,' Mack told her.

Madame Scarlet frowned then. 'Oh no, that wasn't the look I was aiming for. The magazine said "log cabin Christmas". Maybe when we put the rug down and—'

'The what now? You bought me a rug?' What was going on?

'I'm just making this boat less of a waterborne man cave and more a...'

She'd dried up. Madame Scarlet never dried up. He watched her dip her hands into one of the wooden baskets and pull out something else, popping it right in the centre of the table.

'A scented candle?!' Mack exclaimed. 'Am I starting a talk show from here or something? Replacing Ellen?'

'It's a very masculine fragrance. Pine and bergamot. A little splash of bay leaf.' She blew out a breath. 'Phew, I'm getting a little warm in here.'

She did look a bit flushed as she flapped her long-sleeved red dress away from her skin. It was warm inside the cabin because it was freezing outside. He tended to get the heaters going full bore during the evening and then turn them off overnight. 'Sit down,' he told her. 'Can I get you something to drink?'

'I thought you'd never ask,' Madame Scarlet said, chuckling. 'I'll have whatever you're drinking.' She plumped down onto the banquette and motioned with her elbow to his glass on the table. Damn, it was the good whisky and somehow she knew it. Unless...

He got the cheaper version down from one of the cupboards, grabbed a glass and unscrewed the cap.

'Mackenzie, I wasn't born yesterday,' Madame Scarlet said. 'That's not what you're drinking.'

Maybe the woman *was* psychic after all. He turned around to give her a grin and saw then she had taken a sip from his own tumbler. Not spiritually intuitive but smart nonetheless.

He poured the good stuff and brought it over to the table, sitting opposite her, his ass catching the edge of an ornamental toy soldier holding a handful of wrapped gifts. It toppled to the floor.

'If you want Joanna to stay you're gonna have to ask her.'

He practically inhaled the whisky and the alcohol scorched his throat. 'Wow. Cut right to the chase.'

'Well,' Madame Scarlet continued, her voice a little shaky. 'I've been told there isn't long.'

'What?' Mack asked. 'You've been told? What does that mean?' Was Harri really going to leave before Christmas was over? Did Madame Scarlet know when? And how could he ask her anything when he told her he couldn't take her to the lighthouse?

'Mackenzie, I know you don't believe in my area of expertise but you not believing in it doesn't make it any less real to me.'

'OK, so you want me to believe that some "being" told you she's leaving soon?'

Madame Scarlet smiled at his apathy the way she always did. 'I also know you've known her a lot longer than the short time she's been in Montauk this time.'

'You've definitely been talking to Ruby now,' Mack said,

curling his fingers around the glass as Scooter, bored with nuzzling at the décor, jumped up and sat down beside him, curling himself up. Ruby was the only one he had told about his relationship with Harri via the letters.

'No,' Madame Scarlet breathed. 'I've been communicating with Lorna.'

'Whoa! No, hold up a second… don't start with me like that.'

'Listen, honey, before you get your jockey shorts all twisted up, she hasn't contacted me from beyond just yet. She left me a letter. And in that letter she talked a lot about Joanna and her worries for that girl's future.' She let out a sigh. 'She told me about a soldier Joanna used to write to years ago. When she came here for those long hot summers Lorna said those letters from the frontline made her smile like nothing else. Even topped the pleasure she got outta Lorna's blueberry ice cream.'

Mack couldn't stop the corners of his own mouth twitching. *God, those letters.* They had been a lifeline when he'd been on tour and he had used them to hold him up all through his recovery, even now he re-read them to remind himself of the guy he'd been. The lucky guy who had once had the love of this incredible woman. He hated that he had lied to her. No, worse than that, he had got other people to lie. He hated that he was still too scared to let her in…

'If Lorna knew then she didn't say, but it *was* you, wasn't it?' Madame Scarlet asked. 'You were the one Joanna wrote to.'

He nodded. God, it wasn't like he was Batman peeling off his mask to be revealed as Bruce Wayne. It wasn't a secret. It simply just didn't fit with the current arrangement of things. Harri knowing he wasn't as complete as the guy she had known and her being with someone else... He took a breath. 'Yeah, I was the one.'

Madame Scarlet shook her head. 'No past tense, Mackenzie. You *are* the one.'

'I don't know,' he said, looking into his whisky glass, swirling the amber liquid around in its base. 'I keep messing things up. There are moments I think I've got this, you know, I can be the man I was to her. Then I think about how I've changed and how desperately I want to go back and... I just don't know.'

'You *do* know,' Madame Scarlet said seriously. 'Because you know *her*.'

'I know I hurt her,' Mack replied. 'I know I broke her apart. And when she got put back together again the outside was tougher and the inside was different. It wasn't made up of that sweet, brave, inquisitive, fierce girl I left behind, it was half-empty and unfulfilled. Because she's been trekking a path someone else has carved out for her and she's been doing that because following her heart devastated her. And that's on me.'

'So, that's it?' Madame Scarlet asked.

He shook his head and shrugged. 'One minute I'm still pushing her away, the next I'm telling myself that maybe I can make it up to her. And, I'm not even talking about being her guy again, I'm talking about maybe helping her find her way to who she really wants to be. Even...' He took a breath. 'Even if that's without me.'

Did he mean that? Yeah, he really did. As much as he loved her – and boy, did he love her – nothing would make him happier than to know she was following her heart again, whatever form that took.

'And that journey could start with these Christmas decorations and the baskets of other things I've put in your bedroom.'

'What?' Mack asked, wondering how she had managed to get into his bedroom without his noticing. He didn't remember making his bed...

'I think you're right, honey. I think the first step on the road begins with Joanna making her own choices.' Madame Scarlet smiled. 'But, as with every form of decision-making, you have to be properly presented with *all* the options.'

Was he really an option? Because he had told her 'no' only a few days ago and the last thing he wanted to do was mess with her head. Could he ever make up for what he did? Could he ever truly have her trust again? But that night on the porch swing, when she had touched his lips, played over and over in his dreams. That was the kind of close they had always talked about. That was real.

'Every one of us struggles, Mackenzie,' Madame Scarlet told him. 'But the winners in life are those who don't quit.'

He mused on her message, his hand on Scooter's belly, feeling the warm solid heartbeat under his fingers. That was wisdom right there.

'Now,' Madame Scarlet said, all business. 'Pour us both some more of the good stuff and gimme your hand.'

'What?' he asked.

'I'm gonna read your palm.'

Fifty-Eight

The Rum Coconut

'You want a double, Miss Joanna?' Lester asked, holding the glass beneath the Jack Daniels optic.

'Damn right she wants a double!' Ruby interjected. 'What a crazy question. Gimme one too.'

Harriet let out a breath she hadn't fully been aware she was holding and let her fingers smooth over the comforting solidity of the bar top as she stood there, back to the room, knowing she was going to have to turn back around sooner or later. One of the tiki masks Rufus and Riley had covered in glitter paint was gurning at her like a warning.

'Iain's here,' she whispered.

'Yeah,' Ruby replied.

'Iain's here. Back in Montauk.' And he hadn't told her he was coming. He'd just ignored all her texts and emails, got back on a plane and was here. It was spontaneous. It was so... not like Iain. And worst of all, she didn't know what to do with it. Because she knew he'd found the box of letters.

'I'm guessing he didn't tell you he was coming,' Ruby surmised.

She shook her head and accepted the glass Lester was holding out, downing the contents in one. It burned her throat and made her cough. Ruby put a hand to her back and rubbed a little.

'Listen, I'll keep Joe in the kitchen with me a while,' Ruby said. 'I'd better get back there because I left him in charge of the fish soup and you know how heavy-handed he can get with the seasoning sometimes.'

'Go,' Harriet said. 'Honestly, I'll be fine.' And Ruby knew nothing about the depth of situation, did she? Although people round here really did seem to have extra sensory skills. Maybe it was because they looked a little harder and took time to care a little more.

Harriet picked up the coffee Lester had made for Iain and took a deep breath. Whatever Iain had to say, he had crossed an ocean to say it and she couldn't put it off any longer.

She headed back across the room to the table for two by the bi-fold doors overlooking the beach and the ocean. The frothing surf and the sand was just visible in the dark, lit a little by the fairy lights and solar lamps surrounding the awning and marking the pathway to the parking.

'Americano,' she said softly. 'Black. Not too strong. How you like it.' She put the cup and saucer on the table in front of Iain and slid down into the seat opposite.

She couldn't read his expression at all. It reminded her of a newsreader at the opening beats of a report, the kind of deadpan that could be about to deliver an uplifting piece about a beached whale being rescued or a frightening revelation that would rock the entire world. She didn't know how to start. Maybe *he* would…

And then Iain moved. He transferred his backpack from the floor to his knees, unzipping it and pulling out his laptop. Then he proceeded to open up the computer and switch it on. Neither of them said anything, just sat there as the start-up noises woke the machine until Iain was able to press keys to make it really come alive. Harriet couldn't bear it any longer.

'Iain—'

'No,' he cut her off. 'Not yet.' He looked directly at her then, although his fingers were still grazing the trackpad.

'Iain,' she tried again. 'I want to say something.'

'Why?' Iain asked.

His voice didn't sound like that *Free Willy* article was coming next…

'Why do you want to say something?' Iain carried on. 'When you have no idea what *I'm* going to say?'

'I know what you're going to say,' Harriet responded. 'I spoke to Jude.'

'Oh, you spoke to Jude,' Iain parroted. 'Well, you must know everything in that case… how to sculpt soap and… eat direct out of saucepans and… I don't know, how to hide a whole different personality underneath your bed maybe?'

Harriet swallowed. She knew then that Iain had not only found the letters, he had also *read* the letters. 'I can explain,' she began.

'I don't need you to explain anything,' Iain responded. 'When this laptop decides to wake the fuck up. *I* am going to be doing the explaining.'

Iain using the F word was another anomaly to this situation. He so rarely swore harder than a 'bloody hell' and a fist shake towards increasing traffic. She sat still, watching his irritation wrinkling his usually cool surface. He hadn't even acknowledged the coffee.

A few more taps on the keyboard and he turned the screen towards her. There in big black type were the words 'Resolution #1'.

Harriet blinked hard. Was this a PowerPoint presentation? 'Iain, I don't understand.'

'Resolution #1,' he began. 'This one involves me buying you out of the company. I've had a couple of valuations done, I'm sure you will want to have your own done, but either way it's not something I will be able to do in one payment. I've suggested a lump sum now with three further instalments over the next three years. I've outlined this on slides two and three.'

'Iain,' Harriet said. 'I… don't know what to say.' Was this really happening? This was a business pitch.

'Resolution #2. This isn't my preferred exit route and I don't think it will be yours either because, from what I've gathered, your dream is running some whimsical shop full of fluffy cushions and artwork of seascapes and not being a leading entrepreneur of a property portfolio. But, if you so wished, I would be amenable to *you* buying *me* out of the company. The same terms would apply. An initial payment followed by payments over the next three years.'

'Iain, stop, please, can't we talk properly? I feel like I'm in a boardroom,' Harriet said. 'I know you must feel—'

'—Disappointed,' Iain snapped. 'That's how I feel. Disappointed.'

'OK,' Harriet said with a nod. 'Well, when we met I did say that—'

'—You were in love with someone else? Because I remember you telling me very little,' Iain carried on. 'I remember thinking that I had finally met someone who was like me and... I felt a deep sense of... satisfaction in that.'

She didn't know what else to say so she stayed silent.

'Harriet... Joanna... *Harri*... whatever your name is.' Iain gasped. 'I spent our time together thinking we were in tune with each other, with the same goals and long-term aspirations and now... now I feel like I put a down payment on a property and that there was hidden damp and undetected subsidence.' He sighed. 'I... didn't mean that to sound quite how it came out, but that's the crux of this issue. That's what I'm talking about.' He took a long slow breath, as if he was desperately trying to find his way through this conversation in a way he was familiar with. 'I do level and even, Harriet. You know that. I do concise and measured. I don't do spontaneous or passionate and I definitely could not write two A4 sides of paper listing all the ways I might want to explore your body with my tongue.'

Harriet closed her eyes then as her cheeks ignited. He had read the most intimate exchanges between her and Mack. She was somewhere between livid that Iain had invaded her personal space and private things, yet somehow also guilt-ridden. She knew the content. How must that have felt for Iain to read?

'And,' Iain began again, sighing. 'I can only presume from the context of the letters, that back in 2013 and 2014 and 2015 you were no doubt also able to tell Lance Corporal

Mackenzie Wyatt vivid literary detail of exactly what you wanted to do to him.'

'Iain,' Harriet begged. She attempted to reach across the table to soften this blow somehow, but the laptop was in the way and Iain was holding his hands in clenched fists.

'It's him, isn't it?' Iain said, sounding defeated. 'The guy who's been here. The one with the out-of-control dog. The one you were on the motorbike with.' He shook his head. 'I don't even know why I'm asking. It may not have been written all over your face, but it was written all over his. I just didn't immediately translate the body language. That's another skill I don't possess in case you didn't pick that up in our time together.'

'Iain,' Harriet tried again. 'It isn't like you think.' Except she knew that was a lie. It was exactly like Iain thought and so much more. Mack might have told her he couldn't move on, but it didn't alter the way she felt about him. And you couldn't continue in a relationship with someone when you were still so emotional connected to someone else. It wasn't fair on Iain and it wasn't fair on her either. This wasn't about choosing one person or another, it was about doing what was right.

'Harriet, this isn't a conversation to apportion blame,' Iain said, sitting a little straighter in his chair. 'If that was all I needed I would have responded to your email and not paid an extortionate amount of money to get a flight back here.'

'Well,' Harriet said. 'I know I *am* to blame. And you deserve an explanation.'

'Honestly,' Iain breathed. 'I am exhausted. I don't know if I even have the energy.'

He did look so worn down and that was on her too. She had quietly, not meaning to, travelled their relationship with her shoes untied. She hadn't ever been fully laced in, confident enough to buckle up or be ready to climb their couple's peak. It had all been half-hearted, she could see that now. She had clung to Iain's predictability and let his routine become part of her. But she hadn't loved it. Because she had always longed for something else. And not just some*one* else. More so the person she had been when she'd been writing to Mack. The girl who had a dream and all the passion and enthusiasm to achieve it. The one who'd had her heart broken, but the one who seemed to have chosen to let her whole self get lost along the way.

'Iain,' she breathed, tears pricking her eyes as she took him in anew. 'It's not an exaggeration when I say you saved me.' She sighed. 'When we met I was at rock bottom and I was doubting absolutely everything about my life and... myself. And you were this white knight who arrived with your ideas and your strategies and the kindest of hearts and I fell for all of that.' She steepled her hands together. 'You never asked anything of me and I was grateful because my heart *was* so scarred. I needed something different, something uncomplicated, something that would help me build a solid foundation to move forward from.'

She looked across the table at him, dressed in a smart white shirt and a pair of his black jeans, leather shoes on his feet. Perhaps if they had both started out with more honesty things might have turned out differently.

'And I thought a solid foundation was still what you wanted. I mean, seriously, Harriet, I'm thirty now. Aren't we a bit old for complicated?'

She swallowed. Iain didn't understand because Iain *couldn't* understand. He liked closed windows and a chain on the door. He didn't, somehow *couldn't*, get the appeal of salty sea breezes and swinging on a porch seat like you were still fifteen...

'I—'

'Listen,' Iain interrupted. 'I know that I am sorely lacking in the romance department, OK? I freely admit that. And, maybe because it holds such little personal appeal, I came up a little short in that area, thinking, obviously foolishly, that you were not the type of girl to be aroused by jeans with holes in them or a T-shirt a few sizes too small or an engine on two wheels with a very uncomfortable seating zone.'

'Iain—'

'Let me get this out, Harriet. Before it all turns into a sorry take on a Shakespearean play.'

'OK,' she whispered, sitting back in her chair.

Iain's hands were shaking a little as he turned the laptop slightly, tilting the screen. 'There is a Resolution #3.'

There was? Harriet looked at the next side as Iain tapped the trackpad.

We stay together

After everything Iain had said, after reading those letters from Mack and discovering that who she had been the last few years wasn't who she was at her core.

'My mother once said that when she got together with my father she was more in love with his pig farm than she was with him.' Iain smiled. 'And she's always boasting that they've been together almost as long as *Coronation Street* has been airing.'

Moaning at each other about lost Tupperware and boiled eggs…

'Iain, I don't think that's going to work,' Harriet told him. 'Not now. It would be like going back to a life together we both know isn't quite how it should be.'

'I don't think I can change,' Iain admitted, sitting forward a little and putting his hands on the table.

'You don't need to change, Iain,' Harriet said softly.

'Will you think about it?' Iain asked, the tiniest bit of emotion quirking at his cheek. He inched his fingers nearer, awkwardly, as if he wanted to hold her hands but didn't know the etiquette.

Harriet bridged the gap and took his hands in hers, squeezing tight. 'Iain,' she breathed, looking into his eyes and drinking in everything that had made her care so much for him. 'I will think about the proposals,' she whispered. 'But not Resolution 3.'

She held his gaze, as well as his hands, and watched for some acknowledgement of what she was saying. This was going to have to be the end of the road for their personal relationship.

'OK,' he answered in a solemn tone.

Harriet smiled at him.

'OK,' he repeated, adding a nod, a change to his demeanour that almost signalled relief. He moved his shoulders up and down the way he used to after a tense auction battle he had either won or was happy to concede when it came down to it.

'Shall I make up the spare bed?' Harriet offered.

'Oh, no,' Iain said, closing the lid on the laptop and putting his fingers back into his rucksack. 'I've... booked a suite at the Beachcomber's resort.'

Of course he had. Because that was the man she'd shared part of her life with. Always far more comfortable being formal than relaxed. 'It's very nice there,' she told him.

He handed her some sheafs of paper, all properly bound up into booklets. Contracts.

'I wasn't looking for your personal things in your bedroom,' Iain said sincerely. 'I was actually looking for my missing dongle.' He gave a wan smile. 'But, I guess, for whatever reason, this now is... meant to be.'

'What are these, Iain?' Harriet asked, leafing through the paperwork.

'Contracts,' Iain answered. 'Resolution 1 and Resolution 2. Brief outlines that can be negotiated on, obviously.'

Harriet nodded. As with everything with Iain, it was swift, organised and had a fool proof hard copy.

'I'm here for three days,' Iain said. 'Just call me when you've made up your mind.'

And then he dipped down, his torso bending underneath the table a little. Rising up, he put the box containing all of Mack's words to her on the table and pushed it forward with the very tips of his fingers.

The letters. Right here between them. Where they perhaps always had been.

Fifty-Nine

The Warrior

'Did you know, there is a bicycle in the Christmas auction,' Lester announced with a wide grin.

Mack couldn't believe they were here again. Him with his hands covered in oil on the deck of his boat, Lester's bicycle in pieces around them. It was morning and Mack had been up and at 'em early, taking a run with Scooter, collecting bacon bagels for his breakfast and composing possibly the sixty-third text message to Harri he already knew he wasn't going to send. He wanted to try and reconnect with her, maybe cook her dinner or take her someplace but, despite what Madame Scarlet had said to him, and the heap of bullshit about his love line in the palm reading, he was too scared to make a move. Like the mist over the freezing water here on the lake, he was holding on, but waiting for that ray of sunshine that was going to lift the temperature a little and help things disperse. But was the perfect situation going to present itself? Or should he be brave and try to make it happen?

'Man, honestly, do you want me to buy you another bike?' he asked Lester.

Lester frowned, folding his arms across his chest. 'You have offered this many times before. And I tell you, I do not accept charity.'

'It wouldn't be for you, dude. It would be so I don't have to keep getting my hands dirty.'

Lester sniffed. 'I have asked too much. I will take it to the garage.' He put his hands on the wheel and looked like he was about to drag the vehicle off the deck.

'Hey,' Mack said. 'Hey, leave it, bro. I was kidding. I can patch it up, no problem.' He carried on adjusting the pedal mechanism. 'You gonna bid on the bike on the night?'

'Well, I will be working but, I have a plan.'

'Yeah?'

'*You* can bid for me!'

Mack frowned. 'Oh, come on, Lester. I am the absolute worst at stuff like that.' He stood up straight. 'Don't you remember last year? I ended up bidding on three Christmas Day dinners and attending all three on the same day. I was close to twenty pounds heavier for a week afterward.'

'But this is one thing to bid on.'

'For you,' Mack said. 'What if there's stuff I wanna bid on? You know how crazy it gets. There's wailing and paddle pinching and that's just from Meryl Cheep.'

'Are you going to the parade tonight?'

The festive parade. It was a huge deal to the town, everyone went and it really was the sign that Christmas was right about the corner. But, this year, with Harri here, it felt all the more poignant and he still didn't know what to do about that. Could this be his 'in'? To take a chance? To do things better this time? To earn her forgiveness?

'I don't know,' Mack answered, sighing.

'What?! You *have* to come,' Lester said. 'Miss Joanna will be there. I do not know about Mr Iain but…'

Mack's heart missed a beat and for a second he wondered if it was going to pound on or give up. Then, finally, it kicked back in, thrumming hard and fast. 'What?'

'Mr Iain is here,' Lester said. 'He came last night.'

'I… didn't think he'd be coming back.' And now he was here, what did that mean? Had he turned up to push forward on the land and hotel idea? Had Harri decided to go for that after all because he had said he couldn't think about a future? Because there was no going back from the hurt he'd caused her? Was she going to settle for the kind of solid and secure he could never offer her? He didn't want to believe it but maybe this was what he deserved. He gritted his teeth a little, trying to maintain calm as inwardly things tightened up. It had always been a risk to open up about what had happened in Afghanistan. But he should have trusted in her, in *them*. He had waited too long…

'He does not stay at The Rum Coconut,' Lester told him. 'That is all I know, so do not ask me anything else.'

'They on good terms? Does Harri seem, you know, OK with it?'

'I just make the drinks,' Lester answered, raising his hands.

He couldn't stand it a second longer. Now was the time to act. If it wasn't too late. He threw Lester the wrench.

'Listen, stay here for just a minute and watch Scooter for me. I'll be back.'

As best as he was able with his current prothesis, he leaped off the boat and began an awkward jog up the dock.

Sixty

Fort Pond Bay

'It doesn't look a bit different,' Ralph gasped as Harriet turned her phone screen around to capture the scene.

The beach was empty except for a few gulls pecking at the crisp, crunchy-under-foot sand and shingle, the water relatively calm. She was hoping the conversation would be calm too and perhaps it would mark a chance to move forward. She had messaged her dad about the box discovered in the lake. There had been a pregnant pause in communication, bubbles had appeared on the message stream and then stopped, appeared again until, finally, some words.

Let's catch up tomorrow

And here they were.

Harriet smiled in response to him. Montauk still resisted change in a way the other areas of the Hamptons hadn't. There weren't so many millionaire mansions or Airbnb's only the wealthy could afford here. It was still the simple place at heart it had always been, a slightly weathered near neighbour to the high-end towns around it. And it was that easy-going vibe that had always hit Harriet deep in her soul. It was still hard to imagine her dad growing up here when he never ever talked about it. Why had they never talked about it, comparing notes on the best place to grab breakfast or discussing theories about the Montauk Monster? When had she decided she had been shut down enough and should stop trying?

She turned the screen back around, settling her jean-clad bottom into a space she had hollowed out a little for comfort. Her dad was in the Spanish sunshine, hair as loose as the decorative shirt he was wearing. Somehow he suited that backdrop of green hills and white sugar-cube houses.

'So...' she began.

Ralph let out a breath. 'I don't even know where to begin, Harriet.'

'Well,' she started. 'Why don't you tell me why Grandpa would have got so upset about that box.'

Ralph shook his head a little, like he was gathering strength to carry on with the conversation. And then finally he said something.

'That box,' he began. 'Is the main reason I haven't properly communicated with your nana and grandpa since I was sixteen years old.'

Harriet swallowed. 'An old wooden box caused that.'

'Yes,' Ralph said. 'I know it sounds a little dramatic, but it wasn't *just* the box. It was what it stood for. And it was my father's low opinion of me... and it was your nana's choice to always side with him and... it was also my stubbornness and anger to resolve the situation on my terms and... run away.'

'Was that why you never stayed here with me?' Harriet said. 'Why, when I was little, Mum always brought me over until I was old enough to fly alone?'

Ralph looked a little uncomfortable, adjusting his sitting position a little and dropping his eyes from the camera. 'I know they were nothing but the best grandparents to you. And you can't imagine them any other way but supportive and loving. And I want you to carry on feeling that way. Because this has no reflection on your relationship with them.'

'Dad,' Harriet breathed, her hair blowing in the wind. 'Tell me what happened with the box.'

'It was so long ago,' Ralph said, sighing. 'I don't know if it's worth rehashing it all again. Especially now... Mum's gone.'

Harriet could see there was emotion in her father's face. There *was* love there. It might have got all wrinkled up and twisted along the way, but it was definitely there. Just like it had still been there for her nana. All that talk of Ralph in those letters, retelling the good memories that sounded so dear to her.

'Dad, please. I've never questioned it as hard as I've wanted to before. But I'm asking now.'

Another deep breath later and Ralph continued.

'That box... it was full of cash your nana and grandpa had collected through their Christmas events, for the army veterans' charity. One night, these guys came into the bar and... they took it.'

Harriet frowned. It was awful to have money stolen, and

charity money too, but was that it? How did that equate to a divided family? 'I don't understand.'

Ralph sighed. 'I was awake. It was maybe one in the morning and I was in the bar, not having locked the door yet. I was... smoking weed and... they took me by surprise and they made off with the box before I even knew what was going on.'

'I still don't understand. How is that your fault?'

'Harriet, did you miss the bit about not having locked the door and smoking weed?'

'No, but it could have happened to anyone, and what if the men had got violent with you if you challenged them? Surely that would have been far worse than losing the money.'

'That money. Those veterans and the bloody army were everything to him,' Ralph stated. 'I remember the look in his eyes when I told him I wasn't ever going to enlist. I had to hear all the "my father's father's father's father were all military men" speech I'd heard a hundred times over,' he said with a shake of his head. 'God forbid anyone following their own path and having their own dreams. Me and my father, we are polar opposites, Harriet. We have nothing in common and he always, *always* looked at me like I was a disappointment. So, I lived up to that.' He sighed. 'I mucked around in school. I got drunk – a lot – and... I went joyriding in a car.' He shrugged. 'Nothing I was ever going to do was going to be enough for my parents so, I rose to the challenge.'

For a moment Harriet couldn't compute. Her father acting out like that was one thing, but this portrayal of her grandpa was at odds with the man she knew. Joe had been nothing but kind and loving and attentive. Although, she did know how stubborn Joe could be once his mind was set on something. But to be estranged from your son for so long over things that had happened so many years ago…

'That night, it was the culmination of everything, the final straw,' Ralph told her, picking up a glass of water and taking a sip. 'I had chased those guys for over a mile, barefoot, because I knew how much that money meant to my parents and to the bloody charity. And as I closed in on them at the lake, I watched them take handfuls of the money out, filling their pockets, and then they threw what was left and that damn box into the water.'

'Well, did they catch them?' Harriet asked.

What sounded like an involuntary laugh passed her dad's lips and he shook his head. 'My parents didn't even call the police.'

'What?' Harriet asked. 'Well, why not?'

'Because they didn't believe my story,' Ralph stated. He gave a heavy sigh then. 'I was the bad guy, remember? They looked at me. They looked at the weed and the unlocked door and they made the assumption they had been making my whole adolescent life. They believed *I* had taken the money, *stolen* from charity… because I was a little out of whack with their ideals and I played up to that, embarrassed them. And that meant I was a bad egg.'

Bad egg. Harriet's mind went to Nana Lorna's letter. This was absolutely what she'd been talking about. Her relationship with Ralph. Mistakes and regrets. All those years wasted.

'I admit I pushed them with my behaviour but I'm not a

thief, Harriet. But that's exactly what my mother and father have thought of me all these years.'

Harriet looked at the screen, taking in her father afresh. She had never seen him look as emotional as he did now. He had always been the one to keep his feelings in check while Marnie took care of the outbursts. She suddenly felt sad that there was this whole other story she never knew about her father. That perhaps she had never really known him at all. How must it have been to leave home at sixteen, and under such a cloud?

'I think Nana knew the truth,' Harriet breathed. 'I get the impression that letting you go was her biggest regret.'

'I did love her,' Ralph said. 'How could I not? She was my mum.' He smiled. 'And I heard about all the fun things she did with you. That was all I ever wanted. For them to see *you*, to know *you*, and to maybe notice that I had done something right with my life. I had helped to make this incredible person who they adored.'

It wasn't the wind that was making Harriet's eyes smart this time. And it was time this sadness was addressed.

'Dad,' Harriet said. 'Come to Montauk. Come and see Grandpa. When he saw the box... the look on his face... he was so shocked. Give him a chance to put things right.'

'I don't know,' Ralph said, his voice shaking a little. 'It's been so long.'

'No,' Harriet stated. 'What it's been is *too* long.' She held the phone a little closer to her face. 'Please, Dad, just say you'll think about it. For me.'

She could see Ralph was conflicted, all the differing emotions were written right there on his expression. His skin spoke of warm days and healthy living but the lines and pits said there had been many challenges. Maybe she couldn't fix it. Maybe it was too long broken.

'I will think about it,' Ralph said all of a sudden. 'For you.'

Sixty-One

The Rum Coconut

'You want another coffee?' Ruby asked Mack, throwing a tea towel over her shoulder as she moved along the bar. 'I don't know where Lester's at. He should have been here thirty minutes ago.'

'Oh, shoot, I said I'd be right back,' Mack exclaimed. 'I left him on *The Warrior* with his bike in pieces.'

Ruby smiled. 'Well, he's got two legs, ain't he?' She gasped. 'No joke meant by the way. So, I'm guessing, you've got other things on your mind than spokes and wheels, right?'

He had been transparent AF running in here like maybe the church was on fire, grease on his fingers and a little on his T-shirt too. Even Meryl Cheep had shouted her alarm for all the customers to hear. He sighed, toying with the empty coffee cup. 'Lester said Iain's here.'

'Yup,' Ruby answered. 'Blew in here last night. Sat at a table right over there and got out his computer.'

'O-K,' Mack said. What did that mean? He didn't think 'computer' was a dick euphemism.

'He's staying at the Beachcomber for a few days, that's all I know.'

Mack growled with irritation. 'What's happened around here? It used to be that if I didn't shave for a couple days it was headline news in the *Montauk Sun*. Now no one seems to know anything about anyone else's business.'

'Well,' Ruby said, rubbing down the brass taps with her cloth. 'I might not know about Iain, but I know something's going on with Joe and that box you and Harriet fished outta the lake.'

'Yeah?'

'Yeah and she went off early and didn't say where she was going... hold up.' Ruby stopped talking. 'Here she is.'

Mack's throat suddenly turned dry, and he began to wish he'd asked for a second coffee. Was this the best timing? It was so fucking self-indulgent and maybe even petulant when it came to jumping in quick because Iain was around. This had to be more grown up than that. But one look at her, dressed in jeans, boots and a cream-coloured jumper underneath her coat and all his emotions dive-bombed to his groin. He internally cursed himself for being an animal.

And then he watched the way she acknowledged he was there. She stopped walking for a second, until she realised she had stopped walking and she began to toy with the strap of her purse. Then her feet began sliding forward a little but the tempo was down, as if she wasn't sure whether to continue or retreat. This was where they were at. He had done this when he had run away at the clambake. And he'd done the same thing years before when he'd got that tool, Jackson Tate to lie for him. What had he been thinking? It had been an insult to their relationship that he hadn't had to guts to face her. He should have given her that. He should have put her first, not himself. Except he knew one of the reasons he hadn't done that was because he knew once she had broken through his walls and seen him for who the explosion had left him as, it would have been too easy to let her stay. And then he would have broken them completely. Because he had spent months on the bottle, months tearing up everyone around him and making them hate him as much as he hated himself. Much better to end the relationship when he only had the very best of memories. It would be so easy to let his inner turmoil talk him out of this again right now, but he hadn't come over here to back up.

'Hey,' he greeted, trying to keep it casual.

'Hey,' she answered, finally moving closer. 'Are you here for breakfast?'

'Just coffee,' he said, holding the empty mug aloft.

'I will leave you guys to it,' Ruby said, turning around and heading back towards the kitchen.

His mind was mush, all competent thoughts leaving on a jet plane now he was with her again. What came next?

'I guess you've been busy... what with the auction coming up,' he started. She didn't immediately respond so on he ploughed. 'Have you been drowning in hand-knitted sweaters made to order by Mavis or pumpkins big enough to sink every boat destined for here next summer?'

'Both of those,' she said with a small smile.

'Gotta love a Rum Coconut auction night.'

God, this was hard. He took a breath. It was now or

never. Did he mention he knew Iain was back or not? Was Iain being here even relevant to his asking? If he didn't say something right now she would likely leave and be across the room with the prize pile before he'd finished stumbling over his words.

'Listen, I wanted to say, that what I said at the clambake—'

'You don't have to say anything,' Harri interrupted.

'I want to,' Mack said quickly. 'Because what I ended up saying that night… it wasn't what I wanted to say.'

'No?'

She wasn't making this easy for him, but why should she? She was so entitled to be done with his shit for good. But the thought that he was all out of chances was killing him. He had to try. If he stopped trying to replace the bad with the good then where did that leave him except in a spiral right back to darkness.

'When you said, about the lighthouse,' he began again. 'What I should have said was that… I want to… but that… I'm a work in progress right now. Still trying to get there, you know. And I don't just mean with my buddy here.' He tapped his prothesis.

'I understand,' she answered.

He shook his head. 'No. No, you don't. Because most days I don't understand either.'

'OK.'

She was listening. This was good. She wasn't walking away.

'I still go to therapy,' he told her. 'I still hate every single session but… I still show up.' And his insides were churning just thinking about it. The sofa that made him itch, the beard his counsellor had started to grow that looked God awful, the total dread that ran through him every time he pulled up on the motorbike in the parking lot... 'And I'm gonna keep on showing up. Keep on keeping on.'

He didn't know he had shed a tear until he found he had to wipe it away with the back of his hand. He took a breath and then he said exactly what was on his mind.

'So, are you... gonna go to the parade tonight?'

'I read a letter from my nana this morning, telling me all about the parade,' Harri finally spoke. 'She said there are festive-themed floats and a yule log decorating contest. Then Rufus and Riley told me about the awesome toffee apples, the cinnamon candy floss and the bobbing for doughnuts.'

'There is all that and more,' Mack agreed, nodding.

'They were serious about bobbing for doughnuts?' she asked, looking surprised.

'Yes they were.'

'Wow, I have never done that before.'

'So... are you going?' he asked before he chickened out. 'I mean, would you... like to come with me?' His breath caught in his throat as he realised what he'd said. 'Come to the parade with me.'

'Well,' Harri began. 'My grandpa is going to his friend Rudolph's place for an early dinner and then they're going to the parade together, so I'm free from around five.'

Was that a yes? It didn't sound like it was a 'no'. Maybe they could work the details out later...

'Cool,' Mack said, nodding like he was cool and not combusting on the inside. 'Want me to pick you up?'

'On the bike?' she queried.

'It's all I've got apart from the boats.'

She laughed then and the sound filled him up. Perhaps there was a way through this.

'It sounds good,' she said. Then she took a breath and pointed towards the upper restaurant area. 'I'd better help with breakfast.'

'Sure,' Mack said, nodding again.

'I'll see you tonight.'

'Five o'clock.'

He waited for Harri to disappear from the room and then he let the biggest smile take hold. There was no way he was going to let her down this time.

Sixty-Two

Downtown Montauk

I always feel the festive parade is a little like the penultimate Advent calendar door. You open it on up and you get that warmth, that glow inside that really makes you feel Christmas. It's somehow suddenly not just in the air or hanging around like the baubles and the berry-red wreaths. It's coming from inside you. It always makes me want to smile wider and dress up in my best sweaters and most sparkly earrings and cook pies with the densest fillings and... be kinder to people. I like to take a little longer asking if people are doing OK. Christmas to me highlights everything I love about the world and gives it a golden glimmer. Maybe that's why it comes before a new year. It's a celebration of the months that have gone before... because we all have something to celebrate at the end of the year, even if it's simply getting through it. I think new beginnings shouldn't wait until January. Let's start them in December. It's when people are at their best...

Harriet closed her eyes and breathed in deep. The sky was starting to darken to a blue-ish black, the air was cold and there were snowflakes dancing in it, bigger sized ones than she had seen the whole time she had been here so far. But it wasn't snow she could smell, it was a combination of every festive fragrance you could imagine. Pumpkin pie, cinnamon rolls, minty candy canes, spruce and the coals of a hot metal barrel roasting chestnuts. She could *feel* Christmas... exactly like her nana had said in her letter.

And here she was with Mack. That realisation, that she was here with him, walking side by side down the main street, through the Montauk community, saying a hello to Betty and Hamlyn, admiring the Santa paintings the school children were selling for charity, it made her feel rich beyond anything. He'd really opened up to her this morning. He hadn't needed to paint her a detailed picture of that war zone that had destroyed him internally and externally for her to feel what it had been like for him. She knew he had always avoided giving her that harsh reality in his letters and was still somehow trying to shield her from it now. However, being sheltered was how she had spent her time with Iain and look how that had turned out. What she needed was to face things head on from now on, no matter how hard, no matter how ugly. And maybe that started with her feelings...

'So, what are we gonna eat?' Mack asked her.

'You're not going to make me choose, are you?' Harriet said, wide-eyed. 'I'd envisaged having maybe a bit of everything. It is my first Christmas parade, after all.'

Mack laughed. 'OK, why not? Starting with roasted nuts?'

She was blushing before she even knew it. Everything had an underlying passion when it came to Mack. It always had.

'I've never had roasted chestnuts before,' Harriet admitted.

'You've gotta be kidding me!' Mack exclaimed. He ordered two servings and they stood by the barrel, the heat warming their cheeks.

She shook her head. 'They don't have them a lot in the UK and I'm more a German sausage kind of a girl at festive markets.'

'Uh huh,' Mack said, grinning. 'Sausage more than nuts. Got it.'

She laughed. 'Stop it!'

'You started it!'

She went to doff his shoulder with her fist and he blocked her, capturing her hand in his and drawing her closer. His strength held her in that position where there was nowhere to look but straight into those green eyes.

'You're really outta practice,' Mack whispered.

'I know,' Harriet breathed. And she wasn't talking about self-defence now…

'Chestnuts are served!' the vendor announced.

'Perfect timing,' Mack said with a smile as he seemed to let her go rather reluctantly.

Harriet accepted the bag and dipped her fingers in. 'Wow, still hot.'

Mack grinned. 'Yes, I am.'

'Idiot,' she countered, nudging him as they started to walk.

'Yeah, that too,' he agreed.

Harriet swallowed. 'Listen, Mack, there's something you should know.'

'If the band play "Grandma Got Run Over By a Reindeer" we have to leave? You know, I would be cool with that. I hate that song.'

'No,' Harriet said. 'It's the fact that… Iain's here right now.' She reclarified. 'Not here as in at the parade, although I guess he might be. No, it's not his thing at all. He would hate it.' She sighed. 'I meant, Iain's here in Montauk.'

He'd tried to hide it but Harriet could see the slight rise in Mack's shoulder line that suggested he felt some degree of uncertainty about it.

'I'm guessing he got the problem fixed with your houses back at home,' Mack said.

'He did,' Harriet agreed. 'But it isn't about that.'

'No?'

'No.'

Why was she making such a meal of this? This situation was difficult, but she couldn't pretend it wasn't happening. Everything she thought was controlled and managed in her life had been up-ended. And *she* had up-ended it. Because she could no longer deny her heart. And whether she had a future with Mack or not, this was the right decision. Separating from Iain. Leaving what had been her safe harbour and being content that she was strong enough to steer her own course now.

'Iain and I… we aren't together anymore.' She let that settle in the snowy air. It felt weird to say it out loud, but it also felt right.

'OK,' Mack said with a firm nod like she might have informed him of army orders.

'He's staying here for a couple of days because I'm deciding what to do about our business.'

'OK,' Mack said again.

'So, I just wanted to tell you that there's that, and there's a bit of family drama with my dad and my grandpa I wasn't aware of until now, plus the auction night and I really think Ben Hides might be getting a little forgetful because he's brought me twelve giant pumpkins now and I'm running out of garage room to store them in before the big night.'

'I would offer you *The Warrior Princess* but I have a feeling the weight of them would most likely sink her.'

Mack had wanted to say more. He had wanted to *do* more too. She had told him she and Iain were done. He wanted to whoop for joy then take her in his arms and have that first kiss they still hadn't got to have yet. But Madame Scarlet and his damn palm-reading was getting into his head. He was caught between wanting to put himself out there as an option and the cards suggesting patience. How did you hit that in-between?

'Anyway, I just wanted to tell you... about Iain. About what was me and Iain but... isn't.'

He couldn't just say 'OK' now. It would seem like he didn't care and boy, did he care.

'Harri,' he whispered. 'Are you OK?'

'Yes,' she said, doing that kind of nodding people did when they wanted you to really believe something they didn't believe themselves.

'Listen, you don't have to be brave with me, you know that right?' Mack said softly.

'I know,' she answered with yet another nod.

'So, you know, you don't have to pretend it's nothing when it's definitely something.'

'Yes.'

There were tears in her eyes and as much as he regretted making that happen here, on their evening together, when everyone around them was on a full-on Christmas crusade to fill themselves with festive food and shop until they ran out of hands to carry the bags, he couldn't let her not acknowledge what had happened. One of the first steps towards newness was apparently making peace with the past. He'd read that too soon in his recovery and torn the book to pieces. But it didn't mean it couldn't be true. He was finding that things he thought were bullshit back then might have held a note of truth if he'd looked or listened a little longer.

'Hey,' he said, putting an arm around her shoulders and gently coaxing her toward him. *Little by little*. 'You've got this. You know you do. But, it's OK to take a minute.'

She nodded, getting a tissue out of her pocket and wiping at her nose. 'Thank you.'

'You're welcome.'

A cell phone ringing interjected and Harriet dug into her other coat pocket for it.

'It's my flatmate, Jude,' she told him. 'I asked her to call me and it's past ten p.m. there so…'

'Sure, answer it,' Mack said. 'The nuts will keep warm.'

Argh! He cringed at himself and watched her check the road before crossing the tree-lined street.

Sixty-Three

'OK, I guess I should have seen that coming after you told me about the letters in the box but... I did not see that coming,' Jude said. 'You and Iain. Iain being all non-risk adverse and buying another plane ticket so he could dump you...'

'It wasn't quite like that,' Harriet said. 'No one really dumped anyone.' Dumping suggested there was some anger and passion involved and neither she or Iain had seemed to feel that way about anything other than their business.

'So, what are you going to do?'

'I don't know quite yet,' Harriet said, looking across the road at Mack and the festivities going on around him. There were jugglers and Father Christmases collecting for charity, majorettes and cheerleaders getting into formation behind the marching band and children laughing and smiling with sugar-coated faces that could only have come from doughnut-bobbing.

'Well, don't let Iain call the shots. You've spent every

waking minute on that business. You love it. It literally *is* you.'

Like having Iain in her life, the business *had* been her saviour, something she had control over, something that wouldn't break her heart. But now was the time to test the waters on that issue. If you didn't love something enough how could you *really* commit to it? It was like setting out for a walk in the snow with a light coat and hoping for the best. The next steps Harriet took she wanted to lead with her own instincts and follow her inner intuition.

'It's not me,' she told Jude. 'And I don't think it ever was.'

'Where are you?' Jude asked. 'It's ever so noisy. Let me see.'

'This is downtown Montauk,' Harriet told her, switching the screen around and showing Jude all the visuals.

'Wow,' Jude exclaimed. 'Is there a diner on the corner that does loaded bagels? You know, where all the cops go?'

Harriet smiled to herself. Still thinking New York was the entire country...

'OK, who's the guy across the street in the leather bomber jacket? You know, like hotness personified!'

Harriet moved the screen back around, feeling her whole body blush. 'Er... that's Mack.'

'Soldier Boy!' Jude blasted as Harriet desperately turned the volume down. 'I know you dribbled in your sleep over him, but I didn't realise he was *that* hot.'

'Sshh,' Harriet urged. 'If you shout that loudly he might be able to hear you over the marching band!'

'So, is he here with you? Or, just hanging out waiting to wash his jeans in the laundromat?'

'He's… with me,' Harriet admitted. 'But, you know, baby steps.'

'What the hell is stopping you? You've been dumped and… look at him!' Jude yelled. 'Plus, it's not like you're jumping on the first guy who walked into the tiki bar. You already know him. You already have history together.'

And there was so much Jude didn't know. Like the fact that the pain Mack carried around inside was more of a burden to him than his prothesis. And then there was the prothesis itself.

'Not physical history though.' It was out in the air and down the line before Harriet had thought it through. Their love story had played out in words on paper. They had been bursting to explore in person back then, but now time had passed by. She watched Mack saying hello to a couple with a baby in a stroller. *Was* she overwhelmed about the idea of the physical aspect? Had she built them up into this picture of sexual perfection they might never be together? She hated to think that her hesitance in thinking about it was because Mack was missing part of a limb. She swallowed. It really didn't matter to her. She loved the whole shape of him – inside and out. But, after everything he had gone through, would it be a worry for him?

'Lubrication is key,' Jude announced.

'What?' Harriet gasped.

'My mum swears by a glass of port. Do they have port readily available on the streets of New York? I'm not sure I've ever seen it consumed in *Sex and the City*.'

She breathed a sigh of relief that Jude was talking about a little alcoholic courage not… anything else. She watched

Mack again, picking up a soft toy the child in the buggy had dropped, dusting it off a little, then handing it back. She almost sensed her ovaries let out a groan...

'Not that I'm suggesting you get plastered,' Jude continued. 'Though, thinking about it, did my mum really say a *glass* of port... or a bottle? She was talking about sex with my dad, after all.'

Harriet watched her friend shudder.

'I don't know why I started this conversation,' Jude finished.

Harriet was facing the other way now, taking in the storefronts, most of them lit up for the season. Some of them were open, serving coffees and sweet baked goods to parade goers, others were just open to take advantage of selling potential gifts to those not prepared for Christmas Day yet. Harriet hadn't yet bought a single gift.

Smiling into the screen at Jude, she strolled along the street a little. 'Ha, there's a laundromat here.' Harriet stopped at this storefront, under the slightly jaded-looking hanging sign that stated 'self-service' and 'open 24 hours'. It didn't look open now or like its doors had been flung wide for quite some time. She stopped at the window and gasped as her eyes started to take everything in.

'Jude, I've got to go,' Harriet said, fingers hovering over the button to end the connection.

'OK, well, remember what I said. You run your world. Base your decision-making on nothing other than that. And, protection as well as lubrication. No glove, no love!'

Harriet cut her off quickly and slipped her phone back into the pocket of her coat again so she could concentrate on the shop window. Unlike the rusty sign and the peeling paint on the brickwork, the glass of the window was spectacularly clean, sparkling even. It was a large frontage, framed by tiny hanging frosted lightbulbs and the scene being depicted was a combination of seaside and cosy – almost a maritime Christmas. There was a rowboat taking up most of the space, roughly chalk-painted, its oars wrapped in ivy vines with holly leaves and berries interspersed between them, and inside the boat was everything you might need for a winter picnic. A seashell embossed Thermos sat on one of the seats, together with proper cups and saucers decorated with tiny robins, alongside thick woollen blankets in muted blues and neutral hues. A wooden picnic basket was open, displaying a dining set complete with silver wine goblets and a decanter in the shape of a large-mouthed fish. There was driftwood made into a tepee of a stack to represent a campfire and next to it were beautifully decorated snack boxes and three cloth-bound Jane Austen novels. A Christmas tree made out of rattan stars twinkled from the bow of the boat, underneath which sat a collection of clear and coloured globes covered in thick rope netting, some glowing with flame-free candles, others holding tiny plants. It was her window display of dreams and, as she looked past the decoration to the main area that once contained washers and driers, she could see the amount of floor space, the aged beams on the ceiling, the *potential*. It was then her imagination began to leap like someone had popped it on a pogo stick.

'You OK over here?'

Harriet jumped at the sound of Mack's voice. 'Sorry I was so long, Jude was, well, Jude… and then I got caught up looking at this.' She breathed long and slow, but unable to calm the shiver inside her.

Mack looked into the window and did a double take. What had happened between him showing Ruby the grubby bug-infested property and now? It was like an entirely different storefront. It was clean and it looked kind of like the interior of *The Warrior* now. Actually, he was sure he recognised the rug and a couple of the hanging rattan heart shapes…

'Someone hauled a boat in there,' he said, because he couldn't think of anything else to say right now.

'Isn't it… wonderful?'

What was wonderful was how Harri sounded right now. Absolutely one hundred per cent happy and smiling with every part of her. He watched her pointing at the scene.

'Aren't those lights so cosy-looking? And the teacups! They're the kind of cup that you think you should keep for best but just the sight of them brightens up your day so you use them all the time.'

'I'm not sure that boat would float with all that weight in it, as well as people. And that's before you think about all those lobster rolls you'd wanna pack in that picnic basket,' he joked.

She caught his shoulder with a playful punch he hadn't anticipated and he laughed. 'Better, Cookson.'

'This is the kind of shop I wanted,' Harri breathed, facing the glass again as snowflakes began to gather on the window frame.

'I remember,' he answered. 'You said you wanted to sell things that had the ability to change someone's day.' He put two fingers to the bridge of his nose and pinched, thinking. 'You said "sometimes when people think they need a holiday, what they actually just need is a soft blanket and a scented candle".'

'You do remember,' she whispered.

'Harri, I told you, I remember everything.' He reached for her hand then, connecting their fingers. 'And I've built shelves out of old tea chests and railway sleepers a thousand times in my mind. Imagined you filling them with... I dunno, vintage teddy bears or... Kilner jars full of sweets and... photo frames and lots of things made out of wicker.' He smiled. 'All the things people don't need, but things they should have because it's gonna make them happy.'

Harri sighed as she gazed at him. The look written there melted his heart. It was almost like the years they had been apart were shrinking to nothing. There was no distance between them anymore. They were both here in this moment together. And he was standing as still as he was able, holding his breath as Harri leaned a little closer. This was what he wanted, more than anything and just maybe, he could finally accept it...

As the snowflakes continued to fall around them and the marching band began to play, Harri's fingers tugged on his jacket as she moved her body even nearer. He wasn't so still now, in fact he was shaking, but he was damned if he was going to blow it this time. Her lips met his and it was light and sweet on the surface, but all the head-rushing, heart-bursting, libido-hitting underneath. This was their first kiss. The first kiss he had thought about for so long. And it was exactly how he had imagined. It was hot and it was deep and the way her mouth moved against his was weaving inside him, marking his soul.

He palmed her cheek, drawing his lips away, scared to outstay his welcome. 'Harri,' he breathed.

Her eyes were shiny, bright with tears as she looked back at him. 'Did you… feel it like I did?' she whispered.

Mack nodded as he put his other hand to her hair. 'Yeah,' he breathed. 'It was… like we had done this before.' He sighed, running a finger through her hair. 'Like we were remembering.'

'Yes!' she exclaimed. 'Yes!'

He closed his eyes as she threw her arms around him and he held her close, never wanting to let her go again.

Sixty-Four

Harvest on Fort Pond, 11 S Emery Street, Montauk

Harriet was late and she knew that would annoy Iain. And she really didn't want to annoy Iain. She checked her hair with her mobile phone. It looked like she had been riding in a green Ford with the windows down, letting the snow and wind whip everything up like a tornado. And that's exactly what she *had* been doing. The auction night was a day away and there was still a lot of donations coming in and businesses to collect things from. Plus, Madame Scarlet had arranged for a choir from one of the local schools to sing carols as well as a steel band to provide festive tiki-style entertainment on the night too. There was talk of a dress rehearsal Harriet really didn't think was necessary. She was beginning to think it had the potential to turn into something like an Olympics opening ceremony if she didn't say no once in a while.

She took a breath and looked into the restaurant. It was lovely here in the summer and now in the winter it had the addition of a tall lean Christmas tree bearing bright golden baubles and big red bows. She immediately saw Iain, sitting at one of the tables by the window with a view of the lake. She took a second to look at him. *Really* look at him and reminisce. The neatness of him. His hair cut not too long, not too short, and his angular frame. He wasn't cute or sexy, but he was all-round handsome in the most unimposing of ways. He pulled up the sleeve of his smart navy blue jumper to check his watch. OK, it was time she joined him.

Harriet smiled as she watched Iain dig into his chicken Milanese. She had ordered the salmon, butternut squash and spinach risotto and it was amazing.

'What are you finding amusing?' Iain asked her. He looked down at his jumper. 'Have I spilled sauce? I don't want to have spilled sauce as I have another meeting after this.'

Another meeting. Yes, she had to remember that's what their relationship was now. Simply business. And, to be honest, it might still be a new arrangement, but it had perhaps been slowly happening longer than they realised.

'You haven't spilled anything,' Harriet told him. 'It's just you're eating chicken.'

'And?' Iain asked, frowning.

'Well, you know you don't *have* to be a vegetarian. No one is going to judge you for liking meat. And I know that we should cut down and everything but—'

'Harriet,' Iain interrupted. 'What are you talking about? I'm not vegetarian.'

She almost choked on her mouthful of lemon *beurre blanc*. 'What?'

'I might like vegetarian food, but you know I'm not a vegetarian. We ate meat together.'

'Well, I know that you sometimes ate it but…'

'But what?'

'I guess I thought when you ate it you were… I don't know… breaking the rules.'

Iain laughed then. 'Oh, Harriet, it would be really funny if it wasn't slightly tragic. And you know I would never break the rules of anything.' He wiped his mouth with his napkin and sobered his tone a little. 'Maybe I was a little harsh… about the letters. Perhaps, in all honesty, I didn't let you know me either.'

'Well, maybe it wasn't what was important at the time.'

'I think not knowing someone you're in a relationship with is fundamental to the workings of that relationship if you're planning on it lasting…' Iain let his words drift to a natural conclusion. 'Ah.'

Harriet took a sip of her cranberry juice before replying. 'Maybe we shouldn't dwell on what we both did wrong and think about everything we did right.' She smiled. 'Like the business.'

'We made excellent partners there,' he said. 'And a lot of money.'

Harriet smiled. She couldn't deny either of those things. But as important as those matters were at the time, when her head was taking control of her heart, the ethos of making more, investing more and growing the company, didn't appeal the way it should if she was going to continue at its core. She had made her mind up and she was ready to tell Iain her decision. It was time to start making a life, not a living.

'Iain, I'd like you to buy me out of the business.'

The expression on his face told her everything. This was completely the right choice. Iain hadn't been able to keep the joyful look out of his eyes. Harriet wasn't sure she had ever seen him wearing such a combination of relieved, happy and fulfilled.

'Wow… I didn't know you were going to say that,' he answered, putting down his knife and fork and clenching hold of a napkin. 'I mean, I hoped you might but… well… are you sure?'

Harriet smiled and nodded. 'Yes. I'm sure. It's… not where my passion lies.' She hesitated, wondering if she should be completely honest. At this stage what was there to lose? 'I don't think it ever was.'

Iain let out a light sigh. 'I hope that I didn't… push you in any way over anything. If you didn't feel the same way I did about growing the portfolio and felt you couldn't say then—'

'No, Iain,' Harriet insisted. 'You were… so good for me in every way. And I don't know where I would be if I hadn't met you when I did.' She smiled. 'I would be poorer. In every sense of the word.'

'Thank you,' Iain said softly.

'For what?'

'For being kinder than you should be.'

'Oh, Iain, that's not true.'

'No, it is,' he insisted. 'I shouldn't have assumed you were as emotionally defunct as I am. I should have asked the right questions.'

Harriet took a deep breath. 'I don't think I would have given you truthful answers.'

He nodded, then extended his hand out across the table,

fingertips grazing over the arrangement of candle, holly and tinsel. 'Friends?'

She didn't hesitate to take his hand in hers and hold it tight as she shook. 'Friends.'

He smiled, letting go and returning his hands to his knife and fork. 'I guess we let our lawyers handle the details from now on.'

'Agreed,' Harriet said. 'But, Iain, I do have one request.'

'Go on.'

She took a deep breath. 'I know it's going to be your company and your decision from now on, but... please don't buy the land on Navy Road.' She swallowed. She had no right to ask really. But the thought of a hotel complex there had never sat right with her and what her grandpa had said about the storm all those years ago... she didn't want Iain to plough everything he'd gained into a project that had such a degree of risk.

He chewed his food slowly, but Harriet could tell he was musing on it. He may have had the best poker face during their house negotiations, but she did know him as well as she'd been able to.

'My plans there may have changed already,' he answered. 'A friend of a friend suggested I take a look at Bulgaria.'

'Oh,' Harriet said. 'OK.'

'I don't know,' Iain said, sounding uncertain. 'Perhaps you were right about it being a step too far out of our comfort zone.' He cleared his throat. '*My* comfort zone.'

'Well, sometimes it's good to reach for the stars,' Harriet told him. Was that what she was going to do, now she was free to follow her dreams? The thought both thrilled and terrified her.

'Oh, Harriet,' Iain said, wiping his mouth with a napkin, laughing. 'Next you'll be telling me to follow my intuition.'

And here they were, all their differences finally laid bare. Harriet smiled and looked through the window and out over the lake. The water was still, the pontoon had a dusting of snow and there was nothing but clear skies ahead.

Sixty-Five

The Rum Coconut

My dearest Joanna,

Well, the very last Rum Coconut Christmas event for the community is my grand Christmas auction. I told you about the pumpkins from Ben Hides, didn't I? There are always too many, do your best. And did I tell you not to let Joe compere? If I didn't tell you before then I am telling you now. The event will be six hours long if you let your grandpa take charge.

Listen to me, I'm talking as if one day you might be here running these events in my place. Well, I'm not getting any younger and it would be foolish of me to not impart this information before the Lord calls me up to the gates. But, I'm not so old and stupid that I don't realise that time moves on. Take my letters as simply a guide of what I have found works but, please, make the night your own, Joanna.

The night is all about raising as much money for charity as possible but it's also about having fun. If

*you're not having fun, what's the point in anything? I
try to keep that in mind more now I'm older than I ever
was able to in the past. They say that youth is wasted
on the young, but I'm inclined to disagree. I think the
trouble is that youth is taken for granted no matter how
old you are. Young people don't appreciate the chance to
be carefree. Older people plain resent being older. Young
people want to live their lives at five hundred miles an
hour and their parents want them to slow down only
because they want to keep them safe. But sometimes by
trying to keep them safe they crush their spirit and that's
when resentment sets in and 'fun' is forgotten about.
Have lots of fun, Joanna, with everything. Never forget
that today is the only time that's guaranteed…*

'Ladies, gentlemen, sailors and scholars,' Madame
Scarlet talked into the microphone. 'Mr Santa Claus
himself and everyone in between! A huge welcome to The
Rum Coconut for the annual Christmas auction night!'

There was whooping and hollering and a packed-out bar
room and restaurant that Harriet had never seen the like of,
not even at the height of summer. Luckily, Ruby had called
in extra staff, and waiters and waitresses were buzzing
around the tables delivering festive treats Montauk style.
From fish fritters with a cranberry dip to turkey and bean
pie and mashed potatoes, it was all being taken to excited
patrons with paddles at the ready, eager to make their bids
on the grand selection of prizes with all the money going to
the veterans' fund.

Iain had left Montauk that morning. He'd sent her a text
before his flight and said that he would put things in motion

with his solicitor, but it would likely be after Christmas before anything happened. She'd messaged back and wished him a safe landing. It was messages between two people, no longer together, who finally understood each other a little better.

She looked at the plate of food for Table Ten on the tray in her hands. Spiced fries, hot fried chicken *and* turkey pie and a side of lobster sliders with two Harri Holidays cocktails. Whoever had ordered this was her soulmate. She sought Table Ten out and smiled at its occupant. She so should have known. She picked up her pace.

'Your food, sir,' Harriet said, placing everything down in front of Mack.

'Hey,' he greeted. 'No wisecracks about anything I ordered because the waitress who served me looked at me like I really should be a family of four.'

Harriet smiled. 'Absolutely no judgement here. They are all excellent choices.'

'Great,' Mack answered. 'So sit down because half of it is for you.'

'Oh, Mack, I can't sit down. Look at this place! I mean, it's like the whole of the Hamptons turned up tonight.' Harriet took another look around the buzzing bar, the steel band beginning to play a rendition of 'Mary's Boy Child'.

'You've gotta eat,' Mack said. He held out a piece of fried chicken to her, encouraging her to take a bite.

'One bite,' she said, sinking her teeth into it.

'And drink some of your very own cocktail,' Mack encouraged, passing her the glass cup.

'You know we shouldn't even be serving this cocktail,'

Harriet said, taking a quick sip. 'We didn't win the competition.'

'Hey,' Mack said. 'That may be true but, you know, Ruby always listens to the special requests of the bar's most valued customers.' He handed her a fork. 'Turkey pie, go, eat some.'

'Where's Scooter tonight?' Harriet asked, putting some pastry and succulent meat into her mouth. It was so delicious!

'Rufus and Riley have him. And before you say anything, yes I have considered the fact that he might end up in the lake and run in here all wet later on, but if no one gives those kids any responsibility how are they ever gonna learn? And they can't be bad at it forever, right?'

'They're good kids,' Harriet told him, spooning in some more pie. 'They just have a lot of energy to burn off.'

'Yeah, I mean, I would play soccer with them or something but the last time I did that my leg ended up in the back of the goal as well as the ball.' He smiled. 'They got pissed when I said it counted double.'

'That's nice,' Harriet answered, putting the plate back on the table and her eyes going back to the room where Madame Scarlet was rearranging the prize collection she had spent hours getting exactly right with the order of the auction.

'Hey, come in Cookson, I'm right here,' Mack said, clicking his fingers in front of her face.

'Sorry,' Harriet said, taking a deep breath. 'What did you say?'

'What's going on?' Mack asked. 'What's on your mind?'

She shook her head. 'Nothing.'

'O-K,' Mack said. 'Now remember you're talking to the guy who knows you best. Sit down a second.'

'I haven't—'

'Take a second, Harri. For me.'

She dropped into the chair next to him and realised exactly how exhausted she was feeling. She hadn't stopped since she'd been back in Montauk. Emotionally and physically, she was all out of gas.

'I want tonight to go so well,' Harriet breathed. 'I want to make this night as successful as all my nana's other auction nights.'

'Live up to Lorna?' Mack asked, raising his eyebrow.

'I know. I can never truly emulate her but... in the letters she left me there's all this detailed talk about the good times here at the bar, but there's also an air of sadness to the life lessons. And she never shared those feelings with me when she was alive.' She sighed. 'I want to do something about that somehow. Make sure my grandpa is OK, look after the people that looked after Nana, keep The Rum Coconut thriving.'

'Harri, look around you, you're already making a difference here.' He took hold of her hand. 'You think this night would be buzzing like it is if it wasn't for you making sure Lorna's traditions carried on exactly as they have been over the years?'

'Make no mistake,' Harriet said, picking up a fry and putting it in her mouth. 'Ruby runs this place and I suspect she's been running it a long time alongside Nana.'

'She's a hard worker,' Mack said.

'I'm thinking of asking her to move in here with the boys.'

'Yeah?'

'Well, there's plenty of rooms in the apartment upstairs and I know her landlord is putting her rent up and she's worried about it. I thought the accommodation could come as part of her job when I get Grandpa to give her official manager status.'

'Wow,' Mack said. 'You've been making plans.'

She nodded. 'I have.'

Mack's stomach was rolling now and the thought of food was suddenly unappealing. She was making plans. He had to remind himself that this was a good thing, wherever it led her. More than anything he wanted her to be happy. But even after their kiss in the snow last night, sharing roasted chestnuts, turkey and stuffing wraps, cranberry Slush Puppies that nearly froze them to death, and a slab of New York cheesecake that he was sure had made him gain ten pounds, they were still very much tiptoeing, reaching out into the dark, rediscovering what it felt like to be together.

'I'm selling my share of the property business to Iain,' she told him. 'Gosh, saying that out loud sounds so strange.'

'A good strange?' Mack asked.

She nodded. 'Definitely a good strange. But it's still going to take some getting used to.'

He swallowed, adrenaline flooding his belly. There were so many questions he wanted to ask her right now but they all felt leading. And then he was talking. 'So you're gonna be rich?'

Dumbass.

She laughed. 'Not really. I mean, Iain can't afford to buy me out all in one go so it's going to be a process over a couple of years, but I hope I'm going to have enough to start a new project.'

'Yeah?' *The shop. Let it be the shop.* As much as he hated the fact he'd now discovered that Madame Scarlet, Lester and Ruby had dragged that old rowboat into the window of the laundromat and decorated it in a perfect replica of all things kitsch, cosy and Christmas, if it paid off then he would be forever in their debt.

'I think,' Harri began. 'That—'

'Joanna! Joanna!'

In a rush of coloured feathers and squawking, Meryl Cheep landed on her shoulder, making her jump to her feet.

'Gosh!' Harri exclaimed. 'What are you doing out of your cage?' She took the bird down off her shoulder and held her on her hand. She looked at Mack. 'I'd better make sure she's secure before she starts picking food from people's plates.'

'Sure,' Mack said, nodding as she turned away. It was her decision. Not his. Maybe if he kept repeating that a couple dozen times it'd start sinking in. But there was one thing he could do. He could let Harri know that he was all in if she still wanted him to be. He took a breath. 'Listen, Harri.'

She turned around, taking a step back to the table.

He wet his lips, words keen to dry up on his tongue. But he wasn't going to give in to the anxiety. This was way too important.

'So, there's this lighthouse around here…' He met her gaze and held on to his nerves.

'Yes,' Harri said, Meryl Cheep flapping her wings a little.

'OK, so… the thing is… I would really like the chance to visit there with you,' he told her. 'If, you know, the invitation is still open.'

He felt a little bit sick and like he was an overcharged device fizzing with excess energy. He was putting himself out there for more than one kiss for the holidays, for as long as she could give him, for a second chance.

The next thing he knew she was putting her mouth up close to his ear and whispering: 'How about tomorrow?'

Sixty-Six

'Sold! For fifty-three dollars and eighty-five cents! Well done, Flossy, you are the owner of no less than six pumpkins, generously donated by Ben Hides. Thank you, Ben!' Madame Scarlet led the clapping as Flossy excitedly waved her paddle in the air and no doubt planned a whole heap of recipes. There were three other lots of pumpkins to be bid on throughout the night but Harriet had split them up a bit.

She pulled the next item forward to the centre of the stage. It was the bicycle.

Suddenly Madame Scarlet thrust the microphone at Harriet as the choir started a rendition of 'Away in a Manger' with the steel band joining in and making it a Caribbean-flavoured remix.

'Here you go, darling, it's your turn.'

'What?' Harriet exclaimed. 'My turn? I... didn't know we were doing turns. When was that discussed?'

'At the dress rehearsal you said we didn't need,' Madame

Scarlet said, with a wink. 'Betcha wish you'd been there now.'

'I don't really do public speaking,' Harriet whispered, looking out at the crowd enjoying the music. She took a deep breath. She didn't really know she *couldn't* do it though. Auctions were her thing after all, except usually Iain was the one doing the actual bidding after she had done the research. But hadn't one of her nana's letters made this very suggestion?

'Just talk clear, clarify if it adds drama and keep it on point,' Madame Scarlet advised. 'Think Oprah and that interview with Harry and Meghan.'

'OK,' Harriet said, taking a deep breath and picking up the clipboard containing all the information on the lots.

'It is the bicycle next,' Lester stated, plumping down in the chair next to Mack.

'I thought you were working all night and someone else was bidding for you,' Mack said, taking a swig of his beer.

'It was too tense,' Lester stated, wringing his hands together. 'Carl and Milo are managing.' He rolled his eyes. 'Will this song ever end?' He started to tap his fingers on the table.

'Hey,' Mack said. 'The first rule about winning an auction is you've gotta play it cool, man.'

'I cannot do that,' Lester said, knees jostling the air, fingers looking for something else to mess about with. He picked up a fork but before he could tap it on the table, Mack snatched it from his hands. 'Hey!'

'Listen, that bike up there is not the only bike in Montauk, right?'

'But it is likely the only bicycle that I can afford. If the bids do not go too high.'

'I'm just saying,' Mack began. 'That sometimes we narrow our thinking. And if you do that then you might miss another opportunity. Something might come along that's a whole world of better. Something you didn't ever think would be possible.' He knew he wasn't just talking about the auction and this two-wheeled dream of Lester's, he was thinking about Harri and the lighthouse. It meant she really was giving him another chance. Giving *them* another chance.

'I want the bike,' Lester said bluntly.

'I know, but hear me out. You think that this bike right here is your only chance to get one. But, if someone else wins this bike, what are you gonna do then?'

'I will cry.'

'No, buddy,' Mack said. 'You're gonna take it like a man and you're gonna be ready to seize the next chance when it comes along.'

'Next year? At the next auction when I have more money?'

'Bud, think positive, that's all I'm saying.' God! Listen to him! *Positive thinking*. He had all but thought that was the work of the Devil up until now. Sure, he had a long way to go, he knew that. But, for once, he was regaining a little control and letting in the good stuff instead of bolting the door and festering with the bad.

'How are you boys doing?' It was Joe, with a collection bucket he was in charge of. He had already swooped by once, but he rattled the bucket again. No one minded. Tonight everyone gave whatever they could for charity.

'Man, the veterans are gonna have more out of me tonight than I gave them in my career,' Mack moaned, pulling his wallet out of the back pocket of his jeans. He dropped a ten-dollar note in the bucket. 'That's from us both.'

'Thanking you kindly,' Joe said, smiling. 'Beautiful bicycle up there, isn't it?'

'It is my bicycle,' Lester stated, a possessive look in his eyes.

Joe chuckled and then Mack watched the expression on the old man's face rapidly change. He didn't look good, skin losing its colour, lips trembling, a visible unbalance in his stance. It was almost like he'd been that morning when Mack had got him out of the freezing water.

'Joe, are you OK?' Mack asked, standing up.

'I... it can't... how...'

Now he wasn't making sense either. Mack looked to the stage, not knowing if he should flag down Harri. She was head down in her notes as the steel band and the choir hit their final chord and the patrons applauded hard.

'Mr Joe,' Lester began. 'How many fingers am I holding up?' He waved a hand of four in the air in front of Joe's face.

Joe clutched for the back of the chair and Mack took hold of him, bearing his weight for a second while he reassessed. Was this a stroke?

'Joe, man, talk to me. What's going on here? You need some water?'

'No,' Joe croaked. 'I need... a whisky.' The old man inhaled as if he was trying to regain his equilibrium, still gripping the chair but a little hue of pink back in his cheeks.

'He is OK,' Lester said with a big grin. 'Now we can focus on my bicycle again.'

Mack wasn't as convinced. 'Joe, buddy, I'll get you a whisky but you've gotta tell me what's got you shook up.'

Joe slowly raised his hand in the air and pointed along the bar in the direction of the door. 'There,' he whispered. 'Him.'

Mack followed the line, looking for anything out of place, just like he had when he'd led on his belly in charge of his rifle. He saw the guy straightaway, sticking out like the sorest of thumbs. A dude in baggy pants and a long leather jacket, hair down to his shoulders, skin the kind of embedded tan you got from living somewhere hot. But who was he?

'You want this guy to leave?' Mack asked. 'I'll make him leave.'

'No,' Joe whispered. 'That's… Joe Junior.' He wet his lips and spoke again. 'Ralph.' There were tears in the old man's eyes now. 'That's my boy.'

Sixty-Seven

'The next lot is this fantastic hybrid bike kindly donated by Howard from AJC Motors. Thank you so much, Howard. Now, I should inform you that we have just had a telephone bid for this bicycle and—' Harriet began.

'What?!'

It was Lester, out of his seat, arms flying up in the air in exasperation. She bit her lip before continuing. 'So, I must start the bidding at three hundred and fifty dollars.'

'This is not fair!' Lester exclaimed. 'Bids on the telephone are not allowed. This has never happened before!'

Harriet had to keep her cool and keep it moving. 'So, do I have any advance on three hundred and fifty dollars?'

She could see Lester was grinding his teeth a little and then: 'Three hundred and fifty-one dollars!' he shouted.

Harriet held her breath. She hadn't been expecting that. Still, she knew what to do. 'OK, that's a bid of three hundred and fifty-one dollars. Any advance on that?'

She looked out into the crowds, checking for paddles or hands raised or anything that would signify a bid. And then she saw something she hadn't ever thought she'd see. Standing by the fireplace, next to one of the Christmas trees, was her dad. Wearing harem pants and a long leather coat, he was talking to her grandpa, both of them seeming oblivious to the auction going on. She continued to watch. Joe was taking a turn to talk now, his shoulders shaking a little, his head stooped.

'Three hundred and fifty-two dollars!' came a shout.

Was her grandpa crying? She knocked the microphone against her hand and it made a boom. 'Sorry,' she apologised, eyes still on the activity by the fireplace. *Her dad was here*. He was *talking* to her grandpa. It was momentous.

'Harri!' Mack called. 'I made a bid!'

'Sorry, what?' Harriet asked. Where was Madame Scarlet? She needed to get off this stage and help. She had asked her dad to come. She should make sure that this didn't turn into an argument. Ensure this was their chance to address the past and try to move on after all these years. After Lorna…

'I bid three hundred and fifty-three dollars!' Lester yelled, holding his paddle aloft. 'Me! Lester Peabody!'

'Three hundred fifty-four! Stop bidding, Lester!'

Were they talking nice or was it cross words? From here Harriet couldn't tell. Suddenly, someone was taking the microphone out of her hand. Mack was there. What was he doing?

'Get down off this stage,' Mack ordered her. 'Go be with your family.'

'I…' Harriet began. She really was dumbstruck at this whole situation and frankly floundering.

'Go see your pop,' Mack said. 'I got the auction.'

'Well, the bicycle—' Harriet started.

'I told you,' Mack said. 'I've got this. Go!'

'Ladies and gentlemen, sailors, airmen, *all* the veterans.' Mack waited for a whoop that was not long coming before carrying. 'Our whole Rum Coconut, Montauk family, let's get ready to dig deep in our pockets for all the other fantastic items on offer here. Because, you all know, we're not auctioning this bicycle.'

He stared directly at Lester who looked about ready to blow a gasket despite the pep talk he'd tried to give him.

'What?! This is injustice!' Lester called out.

'Hold the cavalry there, buddy,' Mack told him. 'We are not auctioning the bicycle because... it's already been sold.'

'What?!' Lester exclaimed. 'No... I...'

Even from this distance Mack could see there was more than frustration in his expression, there were actual tears in his eyes. As much as he wanted to drag this out as long as possible, he wasn't going to.

'Lester, this bike has been bought by the community for three hundred and fifty dollars... and apparently an extra four dollars from me, all going to the veterans' charity,' Mack spoke into the microphone. 'And the community is donating this bike to you.'

A look of complete confusion came over Lester's face and he put the flat of his palm to his chest and mouthed the word 'me'.

'Before you say anything,' Mack carried on. 'This is money for the charity and not charity for you. This is a gift, from everyone you've served here at The Rum Coconut, all the neighbours you've swept leaves for and cleared drives of ice for and dogs you walked – including Scooter. It's the very least we can do to make sure you get to all these jobs on time without pieces breaking or springs popping off.' He paused before carrying on. 'You're a good guy, Lester Peabody and we want you to know it. Happy Holidays from all of us! Now come get your bike!'

It was then the cheer went up and Lester, tears full-on streaming down his cheeks, slowly, stumbling a little, made his way up to the stage. He threw his arms around Mack and held on tight.

'Oh, man, don't you make me cry,' Mack breathed, needing to swallow down the emotion.

'No one has done anything for me like this,' Lester said softly. 'Most of the time because I will not let them but this is... the best gift ever.' He let Mack go and took ownership of the microphone. 'Thank you everybody! Thank you so very much!'

The patrons got to their feet, clapping and stamping, whistling their appreciation as the steel band joined in with some well-timed beats and Lester carefully and proudly wheeled the bicycle off the stage. Then Mack's gaze found Harri. She was clapping along with everyone else, before placing one arm around Joe, the other around her dad. She smiled at him and it warmed him to his core. Things *were* changing and he was ready to ring it all in.

'OK, the next lot we're all bidding on is a year's hairdressing appointments with Mavis! I might wanna bid on this myself. Who wants to start me off with a bid of... fifty dollars?'

Sixty-Eight

The auction had been a massive success. Ruby had put the takings into the safe, but a rough initial count suggested they had made over five thousand dollars for the charity on this one event alone. Just as importantly, The Rum Coconut had had a fantastic night on the food and drink with Ruby declaring it 'record-breaking' since she had worked there. It was all music to Harriet's ears, as was the fact her dad had flown here from Spain and was currently sitting by the fire with Joe, talking like nothing had passed between them. Yes, the big issue in the room had yet to be addressed and the camaraderie was more 'polite conversation with someone you hadn't seen in a while' than 'prodigal son returns' but you had to start somewhere, didn't you? And as she had finished helping Ruby, Lester and the other staff clear up as much as she could, she was now hoping a couple of Harri Holidays hot cocktails were going to set the tone for a real beginning towards reconciliation. She joined them at the table, setting a drink down in front of each of them.

'This doesn't look very organic, Harriet,' Ralph said. 'What is it?'

'It's a cocktail. I helped to create it. It's nice. Try it,' she encouraged.

Joe was already smacking his lips around the cup and slurping it up. 'Organic,' he said with a chuckle. 'I remember you drinking moonshine when you were fourteen and you weren't worried about no organic then.'

'Well, some people learn from their past mistakes,' Ralph said a little stiffly.

'How *was* your flight, Dad?' Harriet interrupted. Perhaps they did need her to chaperone at the beginning. 'Any delays?'

'No, it was very smooth.'

'No flights any earlier?' Joe asked gruffly. 'To come to your mother's funeral?'

Perhaps it wasn't a good idea to fuel her grandpa with any more alcohol if he was going to go down this path. 'Grandpa,' she said warningly. 'Dad has come a long way to be here and he's here because I told him about the box in the lake and I asked him to come so you can talk about that.'

She had poked the bear now. There was no turning back. Except now neither of them were saying *anything*. They were both as stubborn as each other. Yes, they might have very different ideals but there were definite similarities too.

'Come on,' Harriet coaxed. 'This has all been going on for a lifetime and I for one am appalled that neither of you had an honest conversation about it in all these years.'

A heavy sigh left her dad then and he picked up the non-organic drink and took a sip. 'It wasn't that I didn't try.'

'When did you try?' Joe snapped back, immediately on the offensive.

'Dad,' Ralph began. 'So many times.' He let another breath go. 'The day I proposed to Marnie. I dialled the number in full and then I couldn't hit that button to connect the call.' He swallowed. 'When I got my first position as a relaxation technician. At first I wanted to tell you because I knew you would hate the job title, but then I wanted to tell you because I wanted you to know I had made the right choice in not joining the army.'

'Your hair was too long to ever join the army,' Joe muttered.

Ralph looked at Harriet then. 'When Harriet was born I wanted to be the one to call and tell you, but I knew Mom would cry and I'd be opening myself up to a place I swore I would never go back to. Spiritually.'

'Mumbo jumbo,' Joe said, reaching for his drink.

'You don't have to believe in the same things to respect someone's opinion,' Ralph countered defensively. 'When did you ever try to call me?'

Joe said nothing and Harriet's hopes began to fade a little. Had too much time passed? Was this revelation only going to open old wounds all over again? Was it better for everyone if things remained as they had been? She couldn't believe that was going to be to anyone's benefit. This was *family*. This was about years of misunderstanding and missed opportunities. Exactly like her and Mack.

'You didn't name her Joanna,' Joe whispered.

'I know,' Ralph said, a little breathy.

'And you changed *your* name. You did that to hurt me. To break another family tradition.'

Ralph nodded. 'I did. And maybe you think that was petty but, Dad, you believed I was a thief. I know I did some things I'm not proud of, but I would never steal from you.' He sighed. 'I got on a plane and travelled to the other side of the world when I was barely eighteen. I lived in a hostel. I had to lie to get my first job. I didn't get to college until I was twenty-two and I studied while I worked three jobs to pay for the shittiest flat you could ever imagine. I knew no one. I was a geeky-looking kid with an American accent and, to start with, no paperwork. It was rough. It almost broke me.' He stopped talking for a moment and gathered himself. 'But what got me through was self-belief. Because that was all I had. *Knowing* I could be a good person. *Believing* I could be even better. And I got it, Dad, I got it all. I had a wife I loved and I still have the most amazing daughter who is the best thing in my life even though I don't show that enough perhaps. And finally, I'm doing the job I was meant to do. Cleansing people. Taking their inner worries and deep-rooted anxiety and throwing it out like trash. Making them feel better, soothing them, restoring them… giving them a second chance.'

Tears were falling from Harriet's eyes now because there was so much she hadn't known about her dad's start in life. Yes she knew he had come to England when he was young and had humble beginnings, but he had always told the story as if one day he had decided to pack a bag and stow himself away to travel to London where the streets were paved with gold in the manner of Dick Whittington. It had been sold as exciting and adventurous, not completely unplanned and terrifying. She couldn't imagine how scary it must have been to arrive in a new country with nothing and nobody, to escape your family.

'I gave you a second chance,' Ralph carried on. 'When I let you be a part of Harriet's life. That was my choice. And I made that choice for two reasons. The first was because I still loved you and Mom, and I didn't want you to have another reason to hate me.' He sighed. 'The second was, well, maybe I couldn't make you like who you thought I had grown to be, but I hoped that you would see that someone who was no good couldn't possibly have made this incredible girl. I wanted you to be proud of at least that.'

'Dad,' Harriet sobbed, her heart breaking.

'Sorry, sweetheart,' Ralph said, reaching for her hand and giving it a squeeze. 'But you were right to encourage me to come.' He looked to Joe then. ' Yes, I missed Mom's funeral, but not because I didn't want to come. I didn't come out of respect for you. That day deserved to be all about Mom and everything she did for the people she loved in this place. And Harriet said it was exactly that.' He sighed. 'If I had been there, the focus would have been on you and me slugging it out with words at the wake.'

Still her grandpa was silent, but Harriet could see he had got a toothpick and was sucking on the end like he might wish it was a cigarette, eyes on the dying embers in the fire. She didn't know what to say.

'Dad,' Ralph began again. 'Like I said to you on that night. I didn't take that money. Those guys came in here and stole it and I did everything I could to try and get it back but—'

'Sshh,' Joe said, like Ralph might still be in short trousers.

'I let you down.' He sniffed. 'I let you down and I let Lorna down. All the rest of her life without her son because of me.' Joe looked away from the fire and rested his gaze on Ralph. 'I should have jumped a little sooner off that dock.'

Harriet gasped. 'No, Grandpa.' She swallowed. 'You didn't jump. You fell. You said... I mean—'

'She was standing there,' Joe continued, eyes now finding the mid-distance. 'Like my very own lady of the lake. Wearing all white... with these earrings that looked like golden harps gifted from the Lord himself... and she was beckoning me to her.' He started to sob. 'I was so cold and so lonely and I just wanted to be with her again even though... I don't deserve to be.' He sniffed. 'But then I realised, she wasn't calling me to her, she was waving me goodbye... and when I went under the water... it was her who was lifting me up to the surface.'

Harriet went to move, to go to him, to comfort him. But Ralph put a gentle hand on her arm, stopping her. She settled back in her chair, her heart aching for this whole situation.

It was Ralph who got to his feet, swapping to sit in the chair right next to Joe. Harriet watched as Ralph simply leaned in, swaddling his father with a full embrace and rocking him a little like a child.

'Dad, everything is going to be alright,' Ralph whispered in that calming tone he had used so many times to ease Harriet's woes when she was younger. A grazed knee, her rabbit dying, losing at sports day... Just hearing him talk that way to her grandpa was making her believe there was a chance for the two of them to get back on track and lay all the ghosts to rest.

'I'm so sorry, son,' Joe whispered. 'I should have believed you. I should have listened.'

'You're listening now, aren't you?' Ralph asked, squeezing his shoulder and meeting Harriet's tear-filled gaze.

'Yes,' Joe said, voice still trembling.

'And so am I,' Ralph told him.

Harriet didn't wait a second more. She barrelled into them both, joining the hug and crying heavily over all that time wasted, the toll it had taken on them both and the loss of her nana who had tried to hold everything together and keep things normal for her.

'I love you both,' Harriet told them, squeezing hard. 'So much.'

Sixty-Nine

Montauk Point Lighthouse

... I have no idea why you always loved the lighthouse so much, but the first time we took you there you were five years old, and you marched up all those steps like you owned the joint. I remember saying to your grandpa, if lighthouses were like castles and had a royal family, then you would be the queen. You liked to eat your lunch sitting down cross-legged right at the top outside, even if there was a crowd waiting to come out and see the view. And you'd refuse to eat it anywhere else even if it started to rain. I think you knew the history of it from aged seven and could recite all the facts – it's one hundred and eleven feet tall, Nana. Nana, did you know a woman called Giorgina Reid saved the lighthouse from erosion? The lighthouse didn't ever seem to be just a landmark or a sandwich spot to you. In some way it spoke to your soul, maybe in a similar way to how The Rum Coconut spoke to me the second it came up for sale. It was in my DNA somehow. I can't explain it. It

was like it was already part of me and I was already part of it. I only ever felt that same way once before and that was when I met your grandpa. I don't think 'for better or worse' simply means people's actions in life or the situations they may find themselves in. I think it means acceptance of who the whole of a person is. Because the reason we fall in love with someone at first might be for the wonderful qualities we admire about them. But the reason we stay, the reason we keep on loving them, is more to do with acknowledging their imperfections and loving that person because of them. Not in spite of. Because of. You're not looking for perfect in life, Joanna. You're looking for perfectly imperfect...

'I don't wanna complain, but are we gonna get out of this truck?' Mack asked, taking a breath before she kissed him again.

'Just give me a minute,' Harriet breathed, pressing her lips to his. 'Let me pretend I'm twenty a little bit longer.'

'Is that what we're doing?' Mack asked, fingers under the neckline of her jumper, tracing her collarbone.

She palmed his cheek. 'It's what we would have been doing if things had worked out differently.' She smiled. 'I don't want to re-hash it, goodness knows I have enough re-hashing going on with my dad and my grandpa but...'

Mack put his hands up. 'You know I own that. It's my fault that you became a property tycoon when you could have been living the life of luxury on a boat with a guy with one fully-working leg and a mutt who rubs his butt on the ground any chance he gets.'

Harriet laughed. 'You totally saved me.' She whipped

open the door of the truck and barrelled out, slamming it behind her.

'Hey!'

The wind whipped her hair around her face, trying to take her hat too. She always temporarily forgot how fierce it was out here. Well, it really wasn't called the end of world for nothing. She breathed in deep, silently contemplating how these past couple of weeks had changed her everything. Losing her nana had felt like an ending, but that wasn't how she was feeling now. Now her heart and mind were telling her that she might be standing at the end of the world, but that this period was also a life junction she needed to stop and take notice of. She'd already called Jude and told her to firm things up with the professor. Harriet wasn't coming back to the UK for Christmas Day. The big event was a few days away and she wasn't nearly ready to leave. But she needed to decide if her future was here or still back in the UK. Her dad and grandpa were on the road to being reunited, she had made a decision about Iain and the property business... her world was opening up again. And there was Mack. The gorgeous, strong, passionate Soldier Boy she had never ever let go of. Her heart should be full to bursting, it should be a non-decision. Except there was still a niggle in the corner of her mind. Was she really worthy of this? Was she what Mack needed? Mack was giving off all the signals that he was never going to stop trying to fight the battles in his mind, that he was ready to accept her help and work towards a future together, but how could she be sure having her in his corner was going to be enough this time, if the going got tough? She loved him more than anything but perhaps a slower, more cautious approach to their relationship would be better. They'd not done dating the usual way, there had always been that distance. Maybe they needed to ease off the gas – because as old as their relationship was, really it was also brand-new. So should she instead be planning her next *visit* in her head and not even be thinking about staying permanently right off the bat?

Mack arrived at her side and kissed her lips again. He was sporting a little beard growth on his jaw and it suited him. Harriet also liked the way it scratched her cheeks a bit. She cupped his face in her hands and just looked. He was so hot and so real and she knew his heart because he had poured it out to her time and time again in all those letters. He *was* the same man. Yes, life might have bent him out of shape a little, but life could do that. Life was like facing a selection of wind forces, she'd decided. Some days there was a gentle breeze to ease you along, other days a full-on tornado. You never knew quite what you were going to get or for how long. But instead of being scared by that, you could choose to be excited by it. It was up to you to decide the shape you ended up in. And, however long it took, she wanted them to fit together again.

'What are you thinking?' Mack asked her as she joined the zip on his leather jacket together and pulled it up.

'Guess.'

'You're thinking what prize you want when you beat the poor amputee up the one hundred odd steps to the top of the tower.'

She smiled. 'Actually there's one hundred and thirty-seven steps and sometimes I like to do that part twice.'

'Wow, OK.'

She stopped smiling. This was really selfish. She hadn't

thought about the steps at all! Of course they were going to be a problem for him. 'Mack, the steps... we don't have to—'

'Damn straight we have to,' he ordered, rubbing his hands up and down her arms as if to stave off the cold. 'I can do stairs,' he answered. 'I may have to take a rest stop halfway but if all else fails I will take off my leg and I will walk the rest of the way on my hands.'

'You can do that?' Harriet asked.

'It's kinda my party trick,' Mack answered, grinning in that super-cute sexy way he always did. 'In the summer, dressed only in shorts, I could sell tickets.'

Harriet thumped him in the abs and he laughed.

'Damn, Cookson, something tells me you're wanting to get back into self-defence.'

'Something tells me I'm going to need my guard up against all these girls checking out my guy when the summer comes.'

'Your guy,' he said, a smile riding his lips.

'Well,' she answered. 'If you don't want the title then—'

'No, I want it,' Mack said quickly. 'I really *really* want it.'

She smiled. It was possibly all that she had ever wanted to hear. So much had happened that had kept them apart, but now everything was only up to them.

'So,' Harriet said, weaving her fingers into his hair. 'What prize do I get when I get to the top of the stairs?'

'Maybe something *I'd* like to do twice?' Mack asked with a wink.

'That sounds like more of a treat for you,' she answered.

'Well,' he said closing the mere couple of centimetres between their bodies. 'If I remember how to do it right it could be pretty awesome for the both of us.'

She captured his mouth with hers and his thoughts headed south. He wanted nothing more than to hold her in his arms, naked, skin on skin, for the very first time, taking time to get to know one another the way they had talked about in their letters and for a moment on that one video call when they'd finally got a couple minutes' peace from the chaos that had been the camp in Helmand Province. But while he may still talk a good game, he wasn't actually sure he had the walk to back it up. Sure, he knew that everything still worked, but the mechanics of it were a lot different to the emotions of it. And the kind of sex he'd had here in Montauk had involved vacationers who were high on rum and Coke and most of them either couldn't remember his name in the morning or had never asked in the first place. He'd been happy with that. It was what it was. But this was Harri. The last thing in the world he wanted was to disappoint her.

'Stop,' she breathed, pulling away. 'Or I'll want to get you back in the truck.'

'Yay, no stairs! I win!' he joked.

She squeezed his hand. 'Come on, let me show you my castle.'

Seventy

Montauk Point Lighthouse had landmark status and from the large two-storey oblong keeper's dwelling sitting just west of it, to the brown and white striped tower, there wasn't anything about it that Harriet didn't adore. Her nana was right, the place was somehow wound inside her, written through her bones, a beacon reminding her of all those summers spent with her grandparents soaking in Montauk and the beautiful times they'd given her.

Harriet put her hands to the wall that surrounded the narrow spiral staircase that meant the final stages of ascent were coming. The brown and white paint was flaking like it always had been, and there was a rope to hold on to if you needed it. When Harriet was younger she had always refused the rope no matter how many times her nana and grandpa insisted she would be safer using it. She looked back to Mack. He wasn't far behind. She descended a couple of steps back to the previous level and put her face right up to one of the porthole windows that overlooked the ocean. It might be winter but the water was still a vivid blue today, the sunshine having won the battle with the snow clouds for now.

'You're making me feel like an invalid, Harri. Get on up the stairs,' Mack ordered as he made it onto the landing.

She turned and faced him. 'Not without you. We're going to do it together.'

'Why suddenly do I feel I'm on a school visit?' he questioned.

'A teacher fantasy you've never quite been able to shake?' Harriet teased.

'Miss Bradley was fierce,' he said.

'Come on,' she urged, heading back to the stairs. 'You first.'

'So you can make sure I don't fall?' Mack asked.

'No,' Harriet replied. 'So I can check out your arse all the way up.'

As they began to ascend, she watched the way he approached each stair. Having to use his good leg first each time and then bring up the prosthetic to join it. It was the only occasion since they'd been together here that she had really noticed him struggle a little.

'Keep your eyes on my ass, Harri. Don't look at the dumb leg.'

'I wasn't.' She swallowed. How did he know?

'Stairs are not my friend, OK?' he called behind him. 'I manage the couple on the boat, I use elevators in department stores. I never considered lighthouses in my future.'

'Never?' she asked, laughing.

'Maybe a couple times,' he replied, still going upwards. 'There's a girl I know likes them like other people like watching re-runs of *Friends*.'

'Don't make it sound weird,' she begged.

'It is kinda weird.'

'What can I say?' She paused, then added: 'I'm perfectly imperfect.'

They made it to the top and straightaway Harriet pushed open the door to the outside, walking out onto the balcony and bracing herself against the metal barrier made up of diamond shapes. And there it was, the green land below, the sea both sides of Long Island, stretching out to almost infinity. It was like coming home.

She felt Mack behind her before he made contact, wrapping his arms around her and pulling her in tight. He rested his chin on her shoulder and whispered into her ear.

'As good as you remember?'

She shook her head. 'Better.' She leaned into him. 'Because I think sometimes I used to come up here looking for clarity. And... I think I have that now.'

'You do?' he asked.

Mack held her tight as he tried to stop his mind racing away with itself. He needed to be mindful in this moment, not chase the future. Practice that patience. Let Harri be the centre of everything.

'When I saw that shop window,' Harri began. 'You know, the old laundromat. It was like someone had not only handed me all the pieces but put them all together for me.'

'Yeah?'

'Yeah,' she breathed. 'That place, it would have been just perfect for maybe starting that shop I always thought about. But, I suppose someone has beaten me to it.'

'Wait... what?' He separated himself from her, moved up alongside.

'You don't go dragging a boat into a shop window and making it that beautiful for Christmas unless you've got grand plans to launch something in the new year.'

He was biting his tongue. Could he tell her? That he had looked at the store with her in mind? That he'd had a change of heart because he hadn't wanted to try to force her hand...

'So, I suppose I'll have to look at something else. I mean, maybe here isn't right yet. Maybe I need to look at something in Bournemouth first. Maybe I should find my feet with something smaller because—'

'Stop,' Mack ordered. 'Stop talking now.' He put his hands to his curls and let out a frustrated groan.

'What's the matter?' she asked. 'Did I say something wrong?'

'The laundromat,' Mack said. 'No one else has it. It's still available for rent.'

'Well,' Harri said, still looking at him confused. 'How do you know that?'

He let go of a breath. 'Because I might have... because I *did*... go view it myself.'

'You're thinking of renting a shop?'

He could lie to make this conversation easier. He could say what he'd said to Ruby, that there was no storage on the boat and he needed somewhere close and in the window display he could advertise his summer tourist trips and fishing expeditions. But he was her guy. Only the truth was right.

'I... looked at it for you... maybe... just an idea I had.' He was talking like the words were all foreign to him and they were getting caught up on his tongue. 'And then I quickly realised it was absolutely not my decision to make, not even my idea to have, so I… that was it.'

She hadn't taken her eyes off him during the whole of all that crazy-ass rambling mess of an explanation. And he had nothing else to say until she said something in reply. He hoped he hadn't blown it. The last thing he wanted her to think was that he wanted to own her like that.

'You put a boat in there? And all those lovely things?' she queried.

'No!' Mack said, fast. 'No, that was nothing to do with me. I mean, I had the idea, I had a look at the place to check the roof was sound and the wood wasn't full of worm but then I realised it was a mistake… I mean not that the idea of the shop is a mistake, because that's not, I think it's a great idea if you think it's a great idea. I just…' He stopped talking and shoved his hands into the pockets of his jacket. 'Madame Scarlet did it,' he said. 'And possibly Ruby… and maybe Lester… and I think the boat belonged to Skeet.'

He winced then, watching Harri shake her head and fold her arms across her chest. He deserved to be in hot water. But at least he'd been honest. That had to count for something.

'Before you say anything,' Mack carried on. 'I want you to know that I am absolutely not one of these guys who gets obsessive and wants to run your world, or someone who's gonna ask you a million questions about who you've been with or where you're at or any of that bullshit stuff, OK?'

'OK,' Harriet said.

'And I know that your home is in the UK, so a business

here might be all kinds of difficult but, you know, these things can be seasonal. Half the places only open in the summer and I know for a fact that summer brings in the real dollar.'

He watched her break into a smile then and relief flooded his gut. He opened his mouth to speak but she clamped a hand over his lips and held fast.

'Before you say anything,' she whispered. 'I want you to know, that even after all that, I couldn't love you more.'

He knew his eyes were giving him away and he didn't care. She was telling him she loved him. Speaking it instead of writing it at the end of one of her letters way back when.

'Now, I'm going to lift my hand up now,' she warned, gently moving her fingers up and away. 'What do you want to say?'

He didn't say anything. Instead he kissed her, slow and deep until she melted right into him with the winter wind.

Seventy-One

The Warrior, Fort Pond

Christmas Day

It was pouring with rain. The kind of rain that could turn a dry track into a raging river in mere seconds. But even though the tumult was hammering on the deck of the boat, in the cabin below, Harriet was nothing but warm and dry and oh-so satisfied. She slowly opened her eyes and looked again at the homey festive décor all around the tiny bedroom. The hanging gingerbread men were almost close enough to lick if she was so inclined, angel decals stuck to the portholes. She knew Mack especially hated those. Carefully and with stealth, she turned her naked body in the bed, pulling the covers with her as she faced the sleeping guy beside her. *Her guy.*

She lightly traced a finger from his shoulder to his midback and then across to the scars on his stomach. It was still quite the ab show, but a portion of his leg wasn't *all* the damage the incident had done. He had faded gashes and burns over a fair bit of his torso and a deeper valley of a mark just above his hip. Last night he had shared with her more of what had happened that day. Lying in wait, watching, everything had been as controlled as it could be until the boy ran in and Mack's whole world had exploded. The only reason he had survived was because his fall from the window had been broken by an awning before he'd ripped through that and smashed into the ground, semi-conscious and bleeding from more or less everywhere. It was slowly slowly with the information, but every step he took in being strong enough to share it only brought them closer. As had their lovemaking...

Harriet wet her lips as she ran her index finger over his thigh now. Last night was the second night she'd spent here and it had been different from the first. That first night they'd both been nervous, both trying to pretend that it didn't mean everything and so much more. It was going to be their first time together. It was something they'd thought about – and written about – for so long and finally it was going to happen. She could tell Mack was self-conscious about his leg. Despite taking all of life's difficulties with the various adaptations he had to make literally in his stride, this was far more about the emotional than the physical. It was almost like taking his prothesis off in front of her was getting more naked than naked. But it hadn't been long before sheer passion had taken over them both and any other thought, worry or fear, disappeared in a flurry of fingers and tongues and their hearts thumping in their chests. But last night, they'd run down into the boat to escape the thunderstorm and in a mix of wet clothes and wet hair and Christmas decorations falling from their various unsecure vantage points, they'd made love on the banquette seating not thinking about anything but coming together. And they had. And she had… again and again.

She drew a circle over his knee joint now then slipped her hand slightly lower until it trailed over his residual limb. It was a miracle he was here. That's all she thought about his wounds. She was simply just so incredibly grateful he was alive.

'I'd rather you were touching something else,' Mack whispered, coming to.

'Does it hurt?' Harriet asked, laying the flat of her fingers on his skin.

'Not when you touch it,' he answered, moving a little in the bed. 'And, actually, sometimes it feels like the whole leg is still there.'

'Really?'

'Yeah, crazy right?'

'You know what else is crazy?' Harriet asked him.

'What?' he asked, moving up the bed and propping himself up on the pillows.

'It's Christmas morning,' she reminded. 'Merry Christmas.'

'Merry Christmas,' he said, leaning forward and putting his lips to hers.

Before she could luxuriate in his kiss any more there was a bark and Scooter landed in the middle of the bed, tongue lolling, short legs jumping up and down, trying to lick the pair of them.

'Scooter! Play nice and put your tongue away,' Mack ordered.

'He's fine, aren't you, boy?' Harriet said, rubbing the

hound's ears and making sure she was covered by the duvet before he tried to lick anything he shouldn't. He was almost as cute as his owner…

'So, Christmas traditions,' Mack began. 'I remember you telling me you start the day with English sausage.' He winked. 'American is better in my opinion.'

She went to punch his shoulder but he caught her hand in his and before she even realised he had somehow tipped her over onto her back, earning a gasp from her and a yap from Scooter.

'Really, Harri?' Mack asked, his hand still in hers as he leaned over her. 'You make it so easy.'

She smiled up at him. 'That's what life should be for us now though, isn't it? Don't we deserve some plain sailing?'

'And plane flying,' Mack remarked. 'I've always liked the idea of Hawaii.'

And there was his in. It was time to ask her the question he had been chewing over since they'd talked about the shop at the top of the lighthouse. They were together but was she thinking of staying? Her life was in England, her place, the mad friend she lived with. She was here for Christmas but then what? He bit the bullet.

'So, planes.'

She blinked at him, looking way too hot and not helping him out with this conversation. Did he need to do this now? Then she smiled and answered: 'Metal things that fly. I know them.'

He smiled too. She knew him. She was more than aware where this was going.

'You know what I'm gonna ask, don't you?' he said.

He looked down at her, her blonde hair flowing out

behind her on the pillow. If someone told him now his whole life was going to be the inside of this boat and Harri, he'd feel like the luckiest man alive. He *was* the luckiest man alive.

She suddenly jumped up and kissed him before making her escape off the bed. 'I'll answer you over turkey,' she said, diving out the door and into the tiny shower room.

Mack looked at Scooter, who was panting a little. 'I know exactly how you feel, buddy.'

Seventy-Two

The Rum Coconut

My dearest Joanna,

What can I tell you about Christmas Day at The Rum Coconut? Well, all I know is that on Christmas Day I like to make sure everyone feels relaxed. Yes, that might mean I'm in the kitchen again like every day, but on this day it's all about loved ones. When your father was little he used to help me make a giant Christmas coconut cake! It had three layers with buttercream and then frosting all over it until it looked something like a snowflake crossed with a snowball. We used to put one small candle in its centre, light it and think about the people in our community we'd lost that year or say a prayer for those who needed help. And then your father would stick his finger in the icing before your grandpa could cut slices.

Christmas Day is about being together, being a family, no matter what form that family takes. Over the years, the people around the table on Christmas Day have

*ranged from those passing through to friends I've held
dear my whole life. I only wish we could one day spend
a Christmas together, Joanna. I know we have had our
wonderful summers and I know how busy you are with
your work but I want you to know that my festive table
might have always been full, but it has definitely felt the
vacant spots where you and your father should have
been. I hope one day we will all be able to celebrate
together and eat that coconut cake. Maybe you could
give the taste another try...*

Some of the tables in the bar area had been moved away
and others had been pushed together to form one long
table with room for everyone to sit around together in front
of the bi-fold windows, giving a perfect snow-speckled
view of the beach and the sea beyond. The lights were low,
the fire was crackling in the grate and Meryl Cheep's cage
was next to the table so she didn't feel left out. Madame
Scarlet had brought over more Christmas decorations that
the tiki bar certainly did not need and now garish paper
lanterns with palm-tree prints hung from strings Ralph
and Mack had been made to attach to the ceiling under the
woman's loud direction.

The turkey had been eaten – with leftovers Scooter
already seemed to think were destined for him – wine,
beer, and Harri Holidays cocktails had been drunk, along
with an alfalfa shake Ralph had mixed up, that no one but
him had fancied trying. Everyone she cared most about in
the world was here, except Jude and Marnie. Harriet had
got a text from Jude earlier saying 'Happy Christmas' then
declaring that 'the student was now the teacher' so she

could only gather that the professor was already making himself comfortable. Marnie was also fine. When Harriet spoke to her she had her friend Cheryl over for lunch and then Cheryl was being shipped off straight after so Marnie could enjoy the Strictly Christmas Special in peace. Harriet hadn't told her mum anything about Iain and the business, or about Mack yet, because she knew Marnie wouldn't want any news tainting an evening with Aljaz Skorjanec. She would call her tomorrow. Tell her about her dad being here and her future plans…

'Can we eat the cake yet?' Rufus yelled.

'Sshh!' Ruby ordered, finger to her lips. 'You know what we have to do with the cake first.'

'Make a wish?' Riley asked.

'Kinda,' Joe said, getting to his feet.

'Are you OK, Grandpa?' Harriet asked him.

'Dad,' Ralph said, standing up too. 'Why don't you let me?'

Joe looked to Ralph and then he smiled. 'Why don't we do it together, son?'

'Then can we eat it?' Rufus shouted.

'Hush, my love, we have to be quiet now,' Madame Scarlet told the boy.

Under the table Mack took hold of Harriet's hand and threaded their fingers together. Having him here with her for Christmas Day, with her dad here too and he and her grandpa reconciling, it was the biggest and best Christmas gift ever. And watching Ralph and Joe now, both holding the long lit match as they set light to that one white candle in the centre of the coconut cake, it felt like somehow her nana was here with them, seeing and knowing, finally having them all home for Christmas.

A hush descended over the table as Lester lowered his head, Dr Ambrose took off his glasses and the twins closed their eyes and put their hands together in prayer. And right at that moment, Harriet had never felt more certain of where her future lay.

'What is this?' Mack asked as she handed him an envelope.

Harriet smiled at him, curling her feet underneath her on the porch swing and pulling the blanket up around her. It was cold, it was still snowing but it was above freezing. Lester had gone to visit his auntie at the nursing home on his bicycle, despite Joe saying he should take the Ford, Joe and Ralph were upstairs in the lounge area bickering happily over what film to settle down with, Madame Scarlet had left to prepare a festive soiree for friends a little later, Dr Ambrose was taking a turn at the church's soup kitchen and Ruby, Rufus and Riley had gone on a walk with the kites Harriet had got the boys for Christmas.

There were candles and an ethanol burner acting as a mini-warmer on the table in front of them, orange flames licking up the glass. Scooter was asleep on top of the cuddly squeaky beaver he'd been gifted.

'Well, what does it look like?' she asked back.

'It looks exactly like one of the letters you used to send me,' Mack said, smiling. 'It's even on airmail paper.'

She laughed. 'I found it where I used to keep it here. I couldn't resist. Open it.'

'I don't know,' Mack said, toying with it a little, the motion rocking the seat.

'What are you worried about?' she asked.

'You wanting to put our relationship back on paper?'

'Our *relationship*,' Harriet teased. 'Aren't *we* grown up!'

'Yeah,' he answered. 'But, even when we were writing about... the awful country music you were into and... how great Steven Seagal movies are, I always kinda thought we were going to go the distance. Like grown-ups.'

'Me too,' she answered. 'Now open the letter!'

She watched him tear the envelope and pull the piece of paper out and her heart gathered pace as he began to read.

Dear Mack,

It's the first letter I've written to you in so long I'm almost lost for words as to how to start. I know, so unlike all the other letters when I used to spill my guts out about everything that mattered to me and everything that didn't. Sometimes I used to wonder what might have happened if Corporal Javier Gonzales had passed that first care package on to another soldier and not you. But now I like to think that Fate has proved we were meant to be together with this second chance. That maybe, even if I'd been writing to someone else, we would have found our way into each other's lives, each other's hearts. I mean, Montauk is a great place, you might have discovered it through a guidebook or the recommendation from the girl who wrote to Jackson Tate and sent him her underwear... What I'm trying to say is, I think there's no doubt that we are each other's destiny. Our stars are aligned, our planets are colliding, our fishing rods are working in perfect tandem, whatever analogy you want to use, Mack, we're meant to be together.

And that's why I'm not going back to England. I'm not just staying for Christmas and New Year's. I'm staying for good. I want to start a new life in Montauk with a store called 'Lorna's' in an old laundromat with a rowboat in the window. That's my dream, Mack, and I'd really love to share it with you and Scooter if you'll both have me.

Always,

Harri xx

Mack was crying and he didn't care that the tears were running down his face harder than the rain he had kissed her in just last night. He palmed his face, then folded the paper back up. It was everything he had hoped for. Everything he thought he had thrown away when he'd been too screwed up to realise what he was doing. They'd found their way back to each other and this time it was for keeps.

'So,' Harriet began. 'Will you and Scooter have me? I mean, I'm planning on staying here at The Rum Coconut for a while – there's an apartment above the laundromat but it's in a lot worse condition than the store so it's going to need some paint and some flooring and maybe some shelves on the wall and...'

'Scooter!' Mack called.

The sleeping dog jumped to attention, shook himself and padded over to them.

'Are you really going to ask him?' Harriet asked.

'Sure,' Mack said, putting a hand on the dog's collar.

'He's a great judge of character and I trust his instincts on this.' He clicked his fingers and made Scooter look up. 'What d'you think, buddy? Are we gonna let a girl join the crew of *The Warrior*?'

It was as Scooter barked some kind of acknowledgement Harriet couldn't peg as a yes or a no, that she noticed the envelope hanging from his collar. It had her name on it. *Harri*. She laughed. 'You wrote me a letter too?'

'Well,' Mack began. 'To be honest, I think my letter-writing days are kinda over. I'm gonna be busy with the boat trips in the spring and I'm thinking there might be making shelves and painting in my future too.' He took the envelope from Scooter's collar and handed it to her. 'It's just a note really.'

Harriet took it from him and gently eased her finger under the seal until it was open. And out fell a packet of Haribos. Immediately she started to laugh again. 'Oh, Mack, the very first sweets I sent to Afghanistan!'

'Open them,' Mack urged. 'They're limited edition.'

'What?' Harriet said, looking confused as she tore at the packet.

Inside were all red and white gummy hearts except for one jelly ring. Before Harriet had a chance to compute what was going on, Mack had taken the ring from the packet and held it out to her.

'I'm not gonna get down on one knee,' he said with a wry smile. 'I'm claiming an exemption for that part.'

'Mack,' Harriet breathed, tears in her eyes.

'And I haven't asked your father yet because, well the dude only just got here and he's kinda got his hands full with the whole family rebalance thing going on, so I'm claiming a temporary exemption for that part too.' He took hold of her hand. 'I know some people might think it's too soon, but some people aren't me, Harri. And I've never been more sure of anything in my entire life.' He took a deep nervous breath. 'Read the letter.'

Harriet looked back at the envelope in her hands and pulled out a small square of paper from inside. There were only two words hand-written on it.

Marry me?

She looked up from the paper, gazing straight into those beautiful green eyes she'd never been able to forget and gave a definite nod.

'Forever,' she told him. 'For better or worse. For always.'

And, as she threw her arms around him, holding on tight, the snow continued to fall and a grandmother looking down began to smile.

Letter From Mandy

It's the end! *sobs*

I hope Harriet and Mack's story got your insides all warm and fuzzy and you're currently longing for a huge turkey dinner and all the trimmings... I know I was when I was writing it!

So, did you fall in love with the seaside setting of the Hamptons for this festive read? It's the first time I've written a beach-set winter romance and I hope it won't be the last. It was so much fun mixing up snow and sand!

But let's focus on the hero... did you fall for Mack as much as Harriet did? I loved creating Mack and really wanted to get his story right, so I hope I wrote his life as a veteran and an amputee as realistically as possible.

And how about the animal stars? Did you enjoy the antics of Meryl Cheep and Scooter?

As always, I hope you enjoyed the book and I would love to hear what you thought. And, if you have a few minutes, I would LOVE you to write a review on Amazon. Your review could encourage a new reader to try their very first Mandy Baggot book. Imagine that!

Don't forget you can sign up to my newsletter on my website with a chance to win every month and follow me on all social media channels – I'm always there!

Website: www.mandybaggot.com
Twitter: @mandybaggot
Facebook: @mandybaggotauthor
Instagram: @mandybaggot
Join The Mandy Baggot Book Club on Facebook!

Happy Holidays everyone and remember, summer is just around the corner...

Mandy xx

Acknowledgements

As always there are so many people to thank!

- Tanera Simons, my fantastic agent, and the whole team at Darley Anderson. You all work so incredibly hard to achieve greatness for my books and I'm so grateful to be part of the Team DA!
- Thorne Ryan – you were thrown in at the deep end with me! Thank you for all your help with this book and for loving Mack as much as I do.
- My Bagg Ladies and my MB Book Club members and each and every reader who buys, borrows and enjoys my books. Thank you for reading, reviewing and supporting the stories! I wouldn't be doing this without you!
- Everyone I talked to about the themes of this book in a bid to get this right! I would love to have got out and visited Montauk in person, but in Covid times it wasn't to be. So also a big thank you to all the people who

post vacation videos on YouTube – you are this author's dream!

- Sue Fortin – you've had my back the whole way through writing this book. Thank you for being such an amazing friend

About the Author

MANDY BAGGOT is an international bestselling
and award-winning romance writer.
The winner of the Innovation in Romantic Fiction
award at the UK's Festival of Romance, her romantic
comedy novel, *One Wish in Manhattan*, was also
shortlisted for the Romantic Novelists' Association
Romantic Comedy Novel of the Year award in 2016.
Mandy's books have so far been translated into German,
Italian, Czech and Hungarian. Mandy loves the Greek
island of Corfu, white wine, country music and handbags.
Also a singer, she has taken part in ITV1's *Who Dares
Sings* and *The X-Factor*. Mandy lives near Salisbury,
Wiltshire, UK with her husband and two daughters.

Hello from Aria

We hope you enjoyed this book! If you did, let us know – we'd love to hear from you.

We are Aria, a dynamic fiction imprint from award-winning publishers Head of Zeus. At heart, we're committed to publishing fantastic commercial fiction – from romance to sagas to historical fiction. Visit us online and discover a community of like-minded fiction fans!

You can find us at:
www.ariafiction.com

🅕 @ariafiction
🅣 @Aria_Fiction
🅘 @ariafiction